CURTAIN CALL

R. LINDSAY CARTER

ROCK AND FLOWER PRESS

First Edition

Cover design by Angelee van Allman

ISBN
Hardcover: 979-8-9897333-0-9

Paperback: 979-8-9897333-1-6

Ebook: 979-8-9859072-9-2

www.rlindsaycarter.com

CONTENTS

CHAPTER I

Midnight. The witching hour. A time when most people are safely tucked into their beds, secure from anything that might cause them harm and oblivious to the dangers their world possessed.

These days, I only wished I was one of those people.

Alas, I was all too aware of those dangers. It was the reason I found myself out in the cold night air instead of in a cozy sleeping spot.

I had a job to do.

I stood at the edge of a plot of land, surveying it using only the light of the gibbous moon. The field with its faded white picket fence once housed the graves of lost loved ones from a nearby town. Now, it was clear only the headstones were left, many of them knocked askew by hasty departures. The ground in front of the headstones looked like it had been chewed up, the dark soil contrasting starkly with the white of the surrounding snow.

Given the many footprints the snowy ground recorded, the dead had decided to move house.

I tucked a strand of hair behind my ear with a heavy sigh that plumed in front of me like a ghost of my weariness. The crisp air held the cloying smell of rotting flesh, making my nose twitch. I dared not breathe through my mouth, however, imagining that the heaviness of the stench would manifest into a taste, one I had no desire to experience. I spared a glance down at my constant companion, Grimm, who stationed his shaggy body next to mine, his focus on the scene before him. If the smell was intense to me in my human form, I could only imagine how pungent it was to him.

He felt my gaze and returned it, his yellow eyes one of the only discernible features among his pitch-black fur. That, and the tiny patch of white on his chest, the only memento of his near-death experience from the previous fall. He cocked his head.

"I don't think they're very far away," I murmured. "How fast can the undead walk, anyway?"

Grimm turned back to survey the cemetery.

I sighed again, feeling the weight of my task settle upon me. Grimm and I had a good history of hunting down and capturing bad guys of all sorts: werewolves, vampires, elementals, and even plain old mundane criminals.

But dead people? Until earlier in the night, that was a new one for us.

A low moan reached my ears, emanating from just past the row of skeletal trees that marked the far edge of the graveyard. Grimm's ears perked forward, the points becoming unpricked by the intensity of his focus. He growled.

An intense rush of impatience coursed through me. Grimm was making his intentions well known.

"Right," I said, bolstering myself. "Let's do this."

Back in the day, when I was simply a bounty hunter, the only weapon I ever carried was an enchanted knife, Hail Mary, and her replacement, Hail Mary II. Both knives had been lost to separate skirmishes, but it made no difference. Neither would suffice for my current battle.

I was not a bounty hunter anymore. I instead fought to save the world.

And I had been forced to upgrade my armament to keep up with the times.

As Grimm and I stalked determinedly forward, I withdrew my new weapon, a short sword embedded with a silver lacework to repel werewolves and imbued with enchantments for speed, accuracy, and—most importantly—a charm that made it impossible for the wielder to hurt herself upon the blade.

In skirmishes that required bloodshed, it protected me better than my knives ever did, like a fully extended claw. I named it Talon.

Talon and I were still getting used to each other. I'd acquired it two weeks ago after a particularly nasty incident with a werewolf, so I'd only had a crash course in learning to use it. Hence why the anti-injury enchantment was vital to my safety, as I had the unfortunate tendency to put parts of my body in the wrong spot.

Luckily for me, tasks like taking down the undead were excellent on-the-job training.

I stepped softly in my fur-lined, leather boots, but the crisp snow underfoot still crunched as it broke, ruining my sneakiness. Grimm did not fare any better as he padded by my side. It had been a couple of days since our last bout of snow, and the layer of white was iced over.

It didn't matter. They knew I was here.

I reached the copse of trees and ventured to the road beyond them before pausing. A breeze rustled my hair and brought a fresh wave of corruption into my nostrils. Grimm scented the air as well, pointing his nose to the left. I silently agreed with him, and began walking the road in that direction.

Somewhere above us, a crow cawed mournfully.

Another moan filtered from the trees in front of me and to my left. I stopped, focusing on the sound. And then, with a rustling of brush, it appeared on the road before me.

It used to be a man before death had claimed him. He must have been fairly fresh in the grave before his jaunt out of it to still have working vocal cords, but his skin tone was too green and his body too bloated from putrefaction to pass as a living man. He moaned louder at the sight of me and straggled forward.

I raised Talon, ready to take down the revenant before me, but Grimm barked a warning, and I turned in time to see a second undead creature lunging at me from behind.

The corpse went in for a tackle, but I ducked, making it miss and stumble at my feet. Before it could gain its footing, I sliced downward, removing its head with a single sweep. The body instantly fell limp.

That was the key to ending revenants, I'd discovered earlier. I could hack off limbs all day, but until the head was removed or the brain was damaged, these creatures would just keep fighting.

Grimm charged at another revenant to our right as three more crawled out from the trees. None of the others groaned or made any vocalizations besides the first, so I assumed they were older corpses, more decayed.

I'd had worse odds before.

While Grimm battled his own undead, I charged these three, lining them up and swinging Talon once, twice, three times. Three heads rolled and three bodies fell, unmoored from the magic that had reanimated them.

That left Groany. He was faster, another sign of his superior condition. His lips stretched and formed a macabre smile upon his decayed face as he watched me, the revenant magic sparkling within his empty sockets.

"Come on, then," I called out, poised. "What are you waiting for?"

His mouth opened, a hoarse scream of rage emerging as he lurched into a shuffling run.

I waited until he was in range before swinging Talon. The creature blocked my strike with his arm and bent his head to the side, only losing his hand and his ear in the process. Before I could react accordingly, he barreled into me, knocking me backward into the churned and dirty snow on the road.

The impact stunned me, and I dropped my sword. I fought to get a breath as his body landed on me, his face just inches from mine as he gnashed his stained teeth. I used my left hand to hold him back while I frantically searched the area with my right, hoping to land my fingers on the hilt of Talon.

The revenant hissed and managed to get his only hand up and between us, slowly snaking his fingers closer to my neck. A revenant's strength was one its greatest weapons, and if he managed to grasp my throat he'd easily be able to choke the life out of me.

It was time to stop messing around.

I made one last desperate lunge to my right, finally feeling the freezing metal of my sword. I grabbed it unseen, hefting it upright just as the creature placed his rotting fingers around my neck.

I hacked downward at the base of his neck, feeling the decaying flesh split where the sword landed. The dead man screamed in anger, but the wound was not enough to kill him.

I let him go and he fell forward, our noses nearly touching in a parody of intimacy. I gagged at the lack of clean air and held my breath. It was time to finish this. With my free hand, I grasped the blade and with all of my strength I pulled my sword toward me.

The enchantment upon the blade sliced through bone and tendons as if they were butter. With a satisfying plop, Talon severed the revenant's head, and then bounced off of my own throat with the force of my pull.

The corpse above me immediately went limp as the head rolled off to the side. I pushed it off of me and sat up, grimacing as I picked severed green fingers off of my neck. Talon must have also sliced through his other hand that had been about to choke me.

I glanced over at Grimm, who had finally detached the head of the revenant he had attacked. His method was much messier than mine, considering he had to use his teeth to get the job done. The large black dog lifted his lips in a snarl of distaste, stuck out his tongue, and shook his head, likely hoping to dislodge the taste of rotting flesh from his mouth.

"That good, huh?" I asked him with dark humor. "Looks like I'm ahead, though. Get it? *A head.*"

Grimm only stared at me, with no tail wag in sight.

I was about to rebuke my partner for his lack of levity when a distant scream froze me in place. Grimm perked his ears toward the sound and bounded off down the road with a chuff. I got to my feet slower than that, but ran after him.

The road ended at a small cabin, which had a glow of light coming from a window and a wide-open door. I reached the front yard just as Grimm's figure disappeared inside the cabin with a ferocious bark. Another scream of fright emitted from the interior.

I dashed in, only a few seconds slower than my companion. He had trapped another revenant in the corner of the room next to the door, growling and snapping at the creature as it tried to move past him.

Movement in my periphery caught my attention, and I whipped Talon around to face the other possible threat. But this turned out to be a living person, as evidenced by the flush of life in his cheeks, albeit with a nervous pallor that removed some of the rosiness. The bald-headed man shook and ducked his head as he cowered away from my sword. I dropped my weapon back to my side immediately.

He must have been the screamer.

I shifted my attention back to the revenant. "Grimm, move aside," I commanded.

Grimm backed up, allowing me room to position myself in front of the undead woman. Her gray skin was tattered, her teeth bared, and her hair, once the beautiful silver of old age, now hung in clumps around her hideous face. The magical light in her eye sockets shone menacingly.

"Sorry, Granny," I said to her as I lifted Talon. "It's time to rest in peace again."

With a swift slice, my sword did its job, and the revenant's head rolled away from its body, the latter falling in a limp heap upon detachment.

I sighed heavily, sheathing Talon for hopefully the last time tonight. Grimm sniffed the air in the cabin, scenting for more monsters, and then he shook his body, a sure sign that the danger had finally passed.

I turned around to seek out the other living person among us. He crouched behind a table, only his shiny pate and eyes sticking up from his hiding spot. After a moment, he stood, his knees shaky.

"Is it dead?" he asked, his voice quavering.

I nodded. "We took them all out. Sorry to barge in on you, Mr. ..."

"Father," he corrected, his voice becoming sturdy. "Father Quillman, at your service."

"Oh. My mistake." Christianity was just one of the many religions of our world. It had its followers here and there, as evidenced by this small parish, but I was not as familiar with its ways. "Father, I take it you are the caretaker of that graveyard out there."

He nodded dolefully before jerking his head in the direction of the beheaded revenant. "This is my parish, and those are lost members of my flock. I recognized her. She was Dinah Latch, a lovely woman and devoted grandmother, who passed away just five months ago. How could she come back, and why did she want to kill me?" His quaver came back in full force.

"My condolences. That was no longer Dinah, only her shell reanimated with a terrible attitude. She was turned into a revenant by a powerful spell. Don't take it personally, Father; revenants have a vendetta against anything with a pulse. I'm only thankful I heard your scream and could help you out."

"My God sent you to save me; you are an angel."

I shook my head bashfully. "Oh no, nothing of the sort. I just happened to be passing by on my way home when I was attacked by one of them. It alerted me to the fact that there was a graveyard nearby, and I thought I'd investigate. Your parish wasn't the only one affected by the revenants, Father."

In fact, I had been called out to a much bigger cemetery earlier in the evening. All told, I had destroyed twenty of the creatures there, many of them too decomposed to do much damage, but still a possible menace to the area.

Annie Coddle sure had done a number this time.

Father Quillman tutted at my cavalier words, however. "Nonsense. You were meant to be here. You were meant to save me."

"Your scream is what saved you. Grimm and I wouldn't have come this far, otherwise."

"There, you see?" The priest smiled affectionately. "The Lord moves in mysterious ways. My act of fright brought you to me. It was preordained."

"Very well." I was too tired to argue with a religious man. "Happy to assist."

"Young lady, I am in your debt."

I waved a hand to dismiss such claims. "No, no. Not necessary."

He shook his head. "Oh, but I find it is. You have saved my life. I owe you a favor."

I heaved an exhausted sigh. "Fine. Why don't you help me rebury the dead?"

He shook his head in a scolding manner. "That is my duty, and I won't have you helping me. Those are my lambs out there. That is not the favor. I do not expect you to ask it in this instance, either. When your favor manifests, you'll know. Have faith."

I nodded with a wry smile. I could simply claim that a favor never manifested. "Very well, then."

He tilted his head in a sanguine nod, pleased to have won the debate. Then his forehead wrinkled into a frown. "But, child, do you need rest? I would happily lend my bed to you and to your ... ahem ... dog? If you need a place to sleep for the remainder of the night."

I glanced at Grimm. He had stayed in the corner near the body this entire time, his best effort at appearing small and unobtrusive. I'd give him an A for effort, even though his presence was still very much conspicuous.

I smiled politely at the priest. "Thank you, Father, but my horse is near your graveyard, and we were on our way home anyway. It's only another half hour to ride."

"Are you quite sure? I'll be busy with the bodies for the rest of the night, I garner."

"Quite sure. But thank you."

He nodded, grabbing his coat. "Very well. I'd be keen to at least walk you out to your horse, however."

"By all means. I'll show you where the other revenants lay as well."

Our gruesome midnight stroll took us back down the road, to

where the bulk of the bodies lay, and through the graveyard to the main road, upon which a stray revenant had ambushed me, alerting me to the bigger problem at this site. Father Quillman tutted and murmured the name of each deceased member of his flock, recognizing them despite their withered appearances. He claimed that two were missing, but I assured him that we had taken care of them all. Perhaps those two never left the confines of their graves.

He did a double take when I brought him to my horse, Humbert. He apparently wasn't expecting a giant gray Percheron as my mount, given my petite frame.

Until recent events, Humbert had solely been a draft horse, pulling my wagon with aplomb, despite his advancing age. But a werewolf attack last October had weakened him, and pulling the wagon full time was becoming too much for the old horse. Nevertheless, Humbert was not one to enjoy retirement, so we decided to change up our system. For short trips such as this, I was lightweight enough that he didn't mind me on his back, and this way we moved a little faster than before. Longer trips still required the wagon, but they were fewer in number, and this gave Humbert a chance to rest before more grueling excursions.

"How in the heavens do you mount him?" the priest asked when confronted by Humbert's presence.

I grinned. "I have my ways."

He shook his head, dumbfounded. "Well, then, I will let you get back on your journey. You are heaven-sent, saving my life. Remember my debt, young lady. Call on me anytime, day or night."

"I will, Father."

He looked chagrined. "Forgive my manners. I never asked your name."

I smiled as I grabbed Humbert's reins. "Cressida Curtain. At your service."

CHAPTER 2

I waited until the priest had gone back across his graveyard, well out of sight. The truth was, Humbert was much too tall for me to even get a foot in the stirrup to hoist myself up. I may have been limber, but even I had my limits.

Instead, I led him over to the wooden fence that lined the road. I could have climbed it and been able to awkwardly mount my enormous steed using this structure, but I had found a much better system, thanks to my special magic ability.

Most women aren't able to change shapes. Most women aren't born as cats, either. It was as simple as willing myself to revert to my natural cat form. My body shimmered, an in-between ethereal state, before emerging in my smaller stature within the blink of an eye.

Through my cat eyes, the world was a much bigger place. My stature should have been a hindrance to taking my seat upon Humbert's back, except for one important distinction: my jumping skills.

I gracefully leapt to the top of the fence post in one swift move. From here, the saddle was simply a quick jump up. As soon as I landed upon the saddle and faced the proper way, I transformed again, my now-long legs stretching to the sides of the big horse. I made sure to be careful of Humbert's right flank; the werewolf attack had left him with four large scars upon that side, and they were still sensitive to the touch.

Having regained my reins, I clucked my tongue. "Let's go, Humbert."

He came to life below me, instantly rolling into a trot that jarred me and threatened to unseat me until I found his rhythm. This was a different form of locomotion than riding in a wagon; it had taken me many sessions before I was used to the jolting pace and learned to move my own body with it to lessen the impact.

Yet another change in my life.

Humbert moved much faster without the old wooden wagon to pull. Grimm kept up at a trot of his own, happy to be on the road again and heading home after another grueling day of fixing the problems that now beset our world.

It was another job well done. But I was so very tired.

The sudden changes in my life could all be attributed to one thing: Annie Coddle. She was an ancient menace, one that I alone was keeping at bay, thanks to my family's legacy. It all started with my ancestor Glivver, who happened to be Annie's familiar. When Annie was poised to take over the world five hundred years ago, Glivver threw a wrench in her plans by banishing her to a prison dimension, one that absorbed magic, locking it away, and preventing Annie from regaining any of her once-abundant stores.

For five hundred years, my familial line protected this world. And for five hundred years, unbeknownst to us, Annie plotted and schemed and strove to make her comeback.

The fruition of her plans just happened to coincide with my turn on the legacy. Lucky me.

Annie still was not back in this world, but about three months ago, she managed to get her foot in the door when her son Gregory Elkins built a giant magical generator and opened a crack in the gate between worlds. It was enough to allow our magic to trickle into the prison world, which Annie eagerly utilized.

Through a communication crystal, she had warned me, those months ago, that she would stop at nothing to come back. *I'm going to make your life so miserable that you'll have to let me into this world. You'll either be dead, or wish you were!*

She was definitely holding up her end of the bargain. It started with a snowstorm, followed by a giant water construct that flooded parts of Dogwood at the end of October.

November saw a plague of soot sprites, tiny winged artificial beings conjured from dust that coated some of the Oracune Region's towns and cities in a thick layer of the stuff, which caused a wide assortment of breathing issues.

In December, she hit a coastal city with a dancing spell. The poor inhabitants could not stop dancing for days on end, some close to death from exhaustion by the time we were able to undo the magic. This spell was a favorite of hers, and she used it again in January in a different area, along with a fresh bout of winter weather, causing the ground to be covered in a layer of snow for the entire month and into February. While other parts of Vinland would not have batted an eye over this, here in the temperate region of the Serenic Coast we typically experienced snow for perhaps a total of two weeks broken up over the entire winter, making the constant snowfall a very big deal, indeed.

There were other, smaller attacks that Annie snuck in here and there, sprinkling them about the Oracune Region. For many of these magical attacks, I was useless to stop them, but on the occasions she utilized creatures—werewolves, golems, and now revenants—I was in my element.

Most citizens did not know what was happening. Many had never heard of Annie Coddle, or they believed her to be just a myth. We certainly could not fill them in on the reason for why their corner of the world suddenly found itself plagued by numerous mishaps. Some people we talked to believed it to be the end of the world.

Annie was hellbent on destroying me, one way or another. She must not have known where I lived, however, because none of the attacks happened in Knobby Hill, the small town closest to my home. This latest revenant spell had been the closest yet.

The rest of my return journey was thankfully uneventful. Within half an hour, Humbert's cumbersome trot carried us into the yard of Fleurette's cottage, and my home.

Despite the lateness of the hour, a light was still on, illuminating the picture window at the front of the cottage. I could see two heads sitting side by side on the loveseat in front of the window.

I slid off of Humbert's back and led him to the tiny new stable to the side of the house. It was big enough for a stall for my horse employee, and a place to add or remove his tack out of the rain. I used it now for just that purpose, quickly stripping off the saddle, blankets, and reins, giving him a quick brush, and tucking him in for the night with some extra oats and hay. I'd clean everything properly after I'd had some rest myself.

With Humbert taken care of, I strode to the cottage and softly opened the door, letting Grimm enter before me. He wagged his tail in the direction of the sofa, a sure sign that part of his pack waited there.

I entered and shut the door softly. A small gray mouse perched on the loveseat, reaching out toward me with his tiny front paws.

I extended my hand as I shut the door behind me, allowing him to scamper up my arm. "Hey, Lucky."

Fleurette and Kokoro sat together on the loveseat, waiting for me to fully enter, both of their heads turned to me with twin looks of worry.

I shook my head as Lucky nestled into the hair at my shoulder. "I'm in one piece."

Fleurette stood. "What took so long?"

I leveled her with a tired stare. "They were revenants, all right. Annie's spell hit the freshest of the bodies, about twenty of them in one cemetery. And then I happened across another graveyard with another seven. And a priest who nearly died due to their efforts."

"Is everything taken care of?" Fleurette asked. Not waiting for me to answer, she added, "Are you okay?"

I nodded. "I'm fine. One of the fresher ones pinned me down, but Talon did the proper work. At least they were all fairly dry. No juices on me. And yes, I do believe I got them all."

Fleurette nodded, relieved. "I'll send a GOG out that way first thing in the morning to seal the area with a nulling spell, just to be sure. Speaking of, GOGS has requested our presence."

"*Our* presence?" I repeated. Fleurette was a member of the secret society tasked with keeping my kind safe, but I was not a member, being the object of their current protection. As a matter of fact, I was the only cat ever to learn of GOGS' existence. I had never been invited to attend one of their super-secret meetings before.

She affirmed with a nod. "The council specifically mentioned you and me. At ten in the morning tomorrow."

"Why?"

Fleurette splayed out her hands. "I don't know. I guess we'll find out. Maybe they found some information about Brothers."

Hollis Brothers was the last living attorney of the law firm Babcock, Brothers, and Hoterson, which was a legal shell for Elkins' nefarious doings. Thomas Babcock and Nic Hoterson had met their ends in the explosion of the generator building last October. I had neither met nor knew anything about Brothers, but I worried that he was just as rotten as the other two had been. Nic had told me that Brothers was on an extended medical leave, but our concern was that he'd come back eventually looking for revenge. We had GOGS on the lookout for him, but so far they had not turned up anything.

Hollis Brothers was not the only concern that we had GOGS investigating, though. Gregory Elkins had erected multiple towers across the Oracune Region. These mechanical contraptions acted to steal the free energy from a given area and use it to strengthen Annie's magic. They caused blackouts any time Annie pulled magic through the opening in the gateway.

Our hope was that if we destroyed all of the towers, Annie's magic use would diminish. The problem lay in the fact that we knew neither how many towers were out there, nor where they were located. We had asked GOGS to aid in our search for them. So far, they had destroyed two: the first one in the mountain range near the Oracune coast—the one I had stumbled upon while traveling with Nic—and the second south of us, a lucky find. As far as I knew, the members of GOGS were still on the hunt for more, as well as the location of the gateway itself.

This weighed on my mind. "What if it's about the towers?"

Fleurette shrugged her shoulders and stifled a yawn. "Could be, although they haven't asked for your presence for the last tower they found. Anyway, Annie should be quiet for a while, since she just blew her magic stores on that revenant spell. It will be the perfect opportunity for a meeting."

I blinked once in an exaggerated manner. "Well, okay then. I guess I'd better get some rest, seeing how it's ..." I checked my pocket watch. "1:15 in the morning. You two didn't have to wait up for me, you know."

Fleurette glanced at Kokoro.

The other woman stood as well, smiling serenely. "It was not a bother, Cressida. We wished to see you safely home."

I smiled at Kokoro. She was a relative newcomer to our strange little family. She came from Tyonoshima, broken and battered from her deceased husband, delivered to us by a special fox, a kitsune. She and Fleurette had an instant attraction, and now she lived in Knobby Hill with her cousin Gavin. More often than not, though, she was here with Fleurette, including sleepovers recently. The two women claimed they were taking things slow, but I predicted that Kokoro would be a full-time member of this household before much longer.

"Thanks, Kokoro. That's awfully sweet of you. Anything else happen while I was gone?"

The two women exchanged glances. Fleurette spoke first. "The crystal made noise again."

I glanced over at the side table behind the chairs, where a single clear crystal rested within a shallow wooden box. It was the one memento from Gregory Elkins that we saw fit to keep: a shard from Annie's original magic-storing crystal, which Elkins used to communicate with his mother. Fleurette had found a way to cut transmissions from Annie since, but on three separate occasions the witch still managed to break through for just a couple of seconds.

It scared the daylights out of me when it happened once at three in the morning. Poor Grimm nearly got a claw in his eye when I flung myself out of his neck crook in a half-asleep attempt to flee.

I'd since gotten used to the occasional disruption.

"What did she say this time?" I asked.

"Nothing. She only growled like she was frustrated," Fleurette replied with a shrug.

"Poor thing. I hope she *is* frustrated. Anyway, at least I won't be interrupted later tonight. Get some sleep. I'll see you in the morning."

It was my not-so-subtle nudge to get them to leave the room. I was tired, and my body suffered from more than exhaustion. As long as I stayed a human I didn't age, but the longer I kept this form, the more uncomfortable I became. I had gathered a good amount of tolerance when I was a fulltime bounty hunter, but the hiatus I took for six months severely lowered the amount of time I could tolerate. And right about now, I was at my limit.

My friends took the hint graciously—they themselves must surely have been exhausted as well. Within moments, they vacated the room for Fleurette's cozy bed, and Grimm and I were left to our own devices.

I shimmered down instantly, reveling in the relief that came with the change. Grimm approached me, his massive black body towering over me. But his presence was not menacing in any way, despite our size difference. It was a comfort.

He snaked his tongue out and licked the back of my head tenderly. I purred and rose onto my back legs to reach his jaw, rubbing against it with the utmost affection.

Grimm was the love of my life, after all.

I jumped onto the love seat, still purring. Grimm joined me after a moment, the seat dipping with his weight as he carefully turned a circle to settle himself perfectly upon the cushions, avoiding sitting on me.

Once he settled, I picked my way carefully over his legs, settling myself into the crook made by his front leg and neck. It was the perfect size and shape for my petite frame.

I normally groomed myself before sleep, but after a few lazy licks I gave up, too sleepy to continue. I'd simply wake up later and do a more thorough job.

"You were magnificent out there, Cress," Grimm praised me softly. His admiration spread through my chest, a viable warmth made possible by the soulbond we shared. I sent my love back through the bond.

"Not too bad yourself, big guy. I wasn't expecting you to chew through the necks of corpses tonight."

"Don't remind me. They tasted horrible. What did Fleurette tell you? I felt a touch of your apprehension when she spoke."

"We get to meet the GOGS council tomorrow morning. No clue why. This is unprecedented."

Grimm made a small sound in his throat. "Interesting. Best get a few hours of sleep in, then."

"Yes," I agreed, licking his ear where it rested by my head. "We'd better."

Morning came soon enough, along with a rather flustered Fleurette.

"Kokoro, have you seen my brush?" she yelled from the bathroom.

Kokoro, sitting in the wingback chair, smiled knowingly and yelled back, "It was on your nightstand, remember?" She took a sip of her tea.

"Oh yeah." Fleurette's muffled voice changed locations, traveling to her bedroom.

From the kitchen came the sounds of eggs frying and bacon sizzling. The resulting aroma wafted into my nostrils as I washed my face with a wetted paw on the loveseat. Next to me, Grimm's stomach rumbled.

It was Saturday, which meant that Fleurette's wards, Wren and Fal, were home all day, instead of school. They loved making a big breakfast on Saturdays, relishing the strange family dynamic we'd all found ourselves in. Even with Fleurette rushing about to prepare for this meeting with the secret society, they were loath to skip this particular ritual.

I appreciated their work. While Fleurette busied herself, I transformed and took the time to enter the kitchen and sneak a piece of bacon for myself while I waited.

Normally, the household was awake and active no later than eight in the morning on the weekend. But because of the late night we'd had, Fleurette and Kokoro had slept in until past nine. Fleurette was typically as calm as a placid lake, but the short amount of time to get ready had scoured away her normally tranquil demeanor.

"Have you seen Rupert?" Fleurette asked me as she emerged from the hallway, frantically brushing her hair into a fluffy cloud.

Rupert was a crow, one that had been special to Fleurette since before I met her. I never could understand how or why their connection happened, but they could easily cross the natural language barrier between species. Previously, Rupert was Fleurette's little shadow, either hanging around inside the cottage or at the very least waiting in the trees on the property. But now Rupert was a changed bird. He had been captured last October along with Fleurette and Gavin, and imprisoned within a birdcage in Fleurette's mother's room. We discovered him the same night we had burned down the generator building to stop Annie from fully opening the gate. His stint in the cage had not seemed to physically hurt him, but for reasons unknown to us, he never bounced back to his usual self, instead keeping his distance and only coming around for brief visits.

It worried Fleurette.

I shook my head ruefully. "Sorry, no. When was the last time you saw him?"

She pondered for a moment. "He joined me and Fal in Marquat, to dispel the dancing. He hung out on my shoulder the entire time we healed the people, and then flew off as soon as we started to go home." Marquat was the second small town that Annie had targeted with the dancing spell. I hadn't bothered to travel there, knowing I'd be of no use to anyone. "He was so sad, so lost, but wouldn't tell me why ..." She trailed off, her own sadness coloring her words.

Kokoro stood and put her arms around my friend. "Perhaps it is jealousy that keeps him away. It is my fault for taking all of your time."

Fleurette smiled and planted a tender kiss on Kokoro's cheek. "No, it has nothing to do with you. Rupert is happy that I am happy. I believe he's still traumatized from being captured by the ACF in October. He hasn't been the same since. Something's eating at him, but he won't let me get close enough to figure out what."

She gave Kokoro one last affectionate squeeze before releasing her and looking my way. "Ready to go?"

I nodded. It was ten 'til the hour, and I had no idea where exactly we were going, or how we'd get there. Fleurette sometimes disappeared for GOGS meetings, but until now I never questioned where she went. Surely somewhere close by, given the lack of travel time.

She smoothed out her gray sweater and flowing mauve skirt. She wore leggings underneath with winter boots to help with the cold, and she now donned a coat over her sweater. It was hardly ever this cold in the Oracune Region, especially for months on end. I, too, had been forced to modify my usual attire, switching out my supple leather boots for fur-lined ones, and substituting a thicker shirt under my dove-gray vest for my typical linen one. I also put on a coat, something I hardly had to do in the past. My blood ran hotter than a real human's.

I snapped out a quick nod of my head. "Ready when you are."

Wren popped out of the kitchen to see us off, eating one of the last pieces of bacon. "Have fun!"

I rolled my eyes. "I'm not so sure about that," I responded, although a small flutter of nervous energy rolled through my midsection. I honestly did not know what to expect.

Fleurette pecked Kokoro goodbye on the lips and waved at the kids. And then she shooed me out of the front door, with Grimm keeping pace.

It had snowed again in the early morning hours, blanketing everything in a thin layer of sparkling white. Tiny footprints of birds and rabbits marred the otherwise pristine surface. Fleurette walked resolutely to the left, not bothering to venture to Rabbit Hole Road in front of us.

"Um, Fleurette? Where are we going, exactly?" I asked, confused by the fact that we weren't leaving the property.

Fleurette looked at me over her shoulder, a small grin lifting up the corners of her mouth. "It's a secret. I can't say it out loud, but I *can* show you. This way."

She reached the edge of the clearing, where a stand of young cedar saplings encroached, their thin branches feathered with greenery. Gently, she pushed these aside and continued walking, swallowed by the foliage.

"Are you coming?" she asked from within.

I shrugged and followed suit, pushing my way through the small barrier and finding myself in a small alcove of new forest. Grimm joined me.

The middle of this little pocket held the remains of an old growth snag, a once mighty tree now reduced to nothing more than a fire-licked stump. A smooth stone the width and height of a soup bowl perched upon the middle of the snag. It was of a deep gray mineral, made darker still by the sheen of moisture upon it.

Fleurette walked over to it and touched the top. "I still can't tell you anything of how this works. I've been promise-bound."

I understood. Fleurette had done something similar to me almost a year ago, when she made me promise not to tell her father about the fact that we had located her long-lost mother, Althea. Any time I tried to tell Lyle what I knew, my throat and mouth would gum up and not a word could be spoken.

She gestured for me to come over. "I'm sorry Grimm can't come."

Grimm, understanding enough of Fleurette's words, whined and slumped his ears.

I bent down to stroke his head. "Sorry, love. I'll be back soon enough."

He licked my wrist in understanding, sitting to watch whatever would happen next.

Fleurette held out a hand to me. "Take my hand, please. And whatever you do, don't let go."

I did so, making doubly sure I had a tight grip.

Fleurette closed her eyes and spoke, "For Glivver."

A yanking sensation took over my body. I felt the impression of being flung through a vast space. I closed my eyes and tightened my grip on Fleurette, afraid to lose her in the sensation.

And then, it stopped. I opened my eyes.

We were no longer in the wooded alcove.

CHAPTER 3

Our new location was a dark hallway, one of seemingly solid stone cut at precise angles. It was wide enough to fit my wagon down its length, and long enough for both Humbert and the wagon to fit. A single set of elegant double doors graced the far end of the corridor, but no other outlets existed, including windows of any sort. The wall texture and color mimicked that of the stone bowl Fleurette had touched to get us here, surely no coincidence. Lamps lined the walls, a soft glow to add to the eeriness of the location.

"Wait a moment," I said, rounding on Fleurette, who was completely unfazed by our sudden whereabouts, "did we just teleport? I thought you didn't have that ability."

"I don't," Fleurette replied, nipping my accusation in the bud. "It's not my spell. That spell was set up for me when I joined the society. It's the only way to get to the Council Room. This way."

She turned and strode to the doors, flinging them open like she owned the place. I matched her energy, despite feeling like my heart would flutter out of my chest.

This new room was more cavernous, its circular dimensions large enough to fit at least fifty people comfortably. Three tiered rows of chairs made a half-circle facing us at the back of the room. The area we had just walked into was open, clearly a stage for the seated audience.

Half of the seats were currently occupied. And the two of us were the only standing members.

I scanned the faces, recognizing a scant few. There was the society's attorney, Lawrence, who had advocated for the guardianship of the Ramberts under Fleurette's care. There was Melokuhle Ndou, the man who had helped us escape from Addelboro Correctional Facility and who had adopted my feline friend Mitzi after the death of my great-grandmother. He gave me a smile when our eyes met, his teeth contrasting brilliantly with the rich shade of his skin. There was the father of Maurice, the man who once taught Wren about her special magical ability but had met an untimely end at the machinations of the ACF. His name escaped me. Others I recognized from over the years but did not know.

I thought it was proper for us to sit as well, considering there were more chairs available at the ends of the seating crescent, but one man stood as soon as the doors shut behind us and fixed us with an irritated stare.

"Fleurette Williams!" he called out in a booming voice filled with remonstration.

Fleurette turned to look at him, her body posture suggesting boredom. "Yes, Head Grossman?"

Head Grossman—whatever that title meant—narrowed his eyes upon my friend. "You have been summoned to the council today for an official complaint."

Fleurette's face morphed from confusion into anger. "A complaint," she repeated. "About what?"

Head Grossman smirked. I got the feeling that these two might have had some past history and did not see eye to eye. "The confidentiality of GOGS has been breached. By you. On numerous occasions."

Fleurette raised her chin. "I beg to differ. Who are my accusers?"

"Yourself, for one. You confessed to the council that you told one Cressida Curtain."

To hear my name come from this odious man's lips jolted me. "So what?" I blurted out.

Head Grossman's eyes turned to me. They twinkled with the type of malice that people of power sometimes acquired. "Miss Curtain," he said, rearranging his face into a more pleasant mien while giving me a bow of the head, "it is an honor to have you here."

"If it's such an honor, why are we being treated like misbehaving children? And who in Freya's furs are you, anyway?"

He gave another bow, but this one seemed pained. "Apologies. I am Dale Grossman, Head Councilmember for the GOGS. And as much as I am delighted by your presence, it is through grievous violations of society code that you are here in the first place."

"You invited me!" I shouted, my face heating as my own temper ignited.

"True, but only because our hands were forced. The fact of the matter is that you should not even know of our existence in the first place."

"Of all the pointless ..." I murmured under my breath. I straightened. "So, you'd like to punish my friend here because once upon a time she decided to come clean with me when we were neck-deep in trouble? You do realize that she only told me the truth because Annie was making her first bid to eliminate me, don't you?"

The Head cleared his throat. "She also told the two minors currently living with her."

Fleurette spoke up, a snarl in her voice. "They will be GOGs by birthright! And their parents were no longer around to initiate them."

Grossman tilted his head. "It was not your place to do so." He glanced over at two empty chairs on the bottom tier. "May the Ramberts be at peace," he said, as if reading from a script. He turned back to us. "The children should have been brought here immediately once their position was known."

Lawrence cleared his throat to interrupt the tirade. "With all due respect, Head Grossman, it would not have played out well that way. Falcon Rambert was still wanted for burglary. Without Miss Willams' intervention, she would not have had any authority to help him."

Grossman frowned and looked ruffled at the attorney's words, I noted with a small dash of glee. "Yes, well," he continued, trying to hold onto his narrative, "there's still the matter of both Roger Curtain and Belinda Curtain. They seemed to know about us already when we placed them in hiding. And, more recently, one Kokoro Inaba. Plus, another outsider, just recently."

"Of course I told my parents about this society. They should know who their allies are," I shot back, but Grossman ignored me, instead focusing on what Fleurette was saying.

"I did not tell Kokoro anything about GOGS!" Fleurette protested. "She already knew about them from the kitsune."

"According to you. You have no proof of how exactly things went down."

"It's true," I stated, stepping toward the man I now had zero respect for. "Is my word any good?"

Grossman shuffled in place. "Of course, Miss Curtain. Although you must admit, your relationship with Miss Wiliams *does* impact your word slightly."

"What does that mean?" I was already insulted, no matter how he meant it, but some clarification would be beneficial.

"It means that you and your guardian have gotten too close. You may be covering for her."

I pinched the bridge of my nose. "Is that a crime? Befriending my guardian?"

The councilmember looked away for a moment, searching for words. "Well, no. It's unheard of, to say the least. Guardians are there to protect, not befriend."

"Did it ever cross your mind that Fleurette is better able to protect me if she's a solid part of my life? Not some creeper watching me from the bushes? Maybe if other guardians had befriended my ancestors, I wouldn't have lost some to the enemy at a young age!"

Beside me, Fleurette put a hand up to her mouth, covering a smile.

Grossman's face flushed at my statement. "Your foremothers were perfectly safe while we protected them! It was only after they passed on the legacy that a couple of them disappeared."

"Yes, because why? They were no longer worthy of protection? They had passed on the burden, so their lives didn't matter anymore?" I growled.

A few members murmured in their seats. Grossman backpedaled. "Well, no—I mean—"

I interrupted him. "Is that to be my fate as well? Thrown aside as soon as I produce a daughter? Well, Mr. Grossman, I can tell you it's not in my cards. You know why? Because I have a friend—no, a family member—who loves me and will never see me get hurt on her watch."

At that, his eyes turned steely again. "Is that so? Tell me, Miss Curtain. Last spring, did we or did we not tell your guardian that you were to stay hidden and not do anything to put yourself in jeopardy?"

I frowned. "Yes, you effectively grounded me. What of it?"

"Why is it that your friend—I'm sorry, your *family member*—allows you to take on dangerous missions, such as revenant cleanup? Aren't you at risk of getting hurt? Dying, even?"

My brain sputtered. "It's my choice. Not Fleurette's."

"Miss Curtain, we as a council feel it is in your best interest to stay put, not travel, and not engage in risky behaviors, such as fighting monsters."

I unsheathed Talon at my hip, just enough to allow the silver to twinkle in the light. "Then why did you give me the sword?"

Grossman scowled and looked over at Melokuhle, who stoically kept his eyes on me. "Some things have occurred without full council support."

Ah. Some dissidence among the GOGs, then.

"Well, I like it, so I'm keeping it. And here's something that I think you all should hear. You may be a society designed to protect me, but you. Do. Not. Get. To. Tell. Me. What. To. Do. Did I say that clear enough for everyone to hear?"

Grossman cleared his throat. "Miss Curtain—"

"No," I said with a chop of my hand. "I allowed you to boss me around for six months. Where did that get me? Almost killed. And Annie got her foot in the door anyway. It solved nothing. So, no more. This is my life. I will do what I can to protect this world. You can play your games from the shadows, but I am my own agent. I take orders from no one. In fact, it makes much more sense that *you* take orders from *me*. But now I'm curious. By a show of hands, how many of you agree with Mr. Grossman here?"

Four other people raised their hands tentatively.

I barked out a laugh. "Five? Out of ..." I quickly counted. "Twenty-three. And that makes his word law, does it?"

A woman with steely hair tied back in a severe bun put her hand down, her mouth pinched as if she'd been sucking on lemons. "We in agreement are members of the council. Our word holds more weight."

I tutted. "And that makes it right? Something tells me that GOGS has bigger issues than an obvious fall in membership. I think the majority here would agree with me."

More than a few members shuffled uneasily in their seats.

"Now, you mentioned one last infraction Fleurette apparently committed. Care to explain that one, Grossman?" I commented.

The man pointed to a small, mousy woman toward the back. She rose unsteadily at his insistence. "Miss Willoby was contacted yesterday by a woman named Abigail Zamani. She had full knowledge of the inner workings of this society."

Fleurette frowned and shook her head. "I've never heard of her."

"No? I find that hard to believe, given your track record." He mused for a moment before adding, "She claims to be a seer."

I rubbed a hand down my face. "Oh for Freya's sake. If she's a seer, isn't it possible that she *saw* you all in a vision?"

Grossman twitched. "I suppose so ..."

"That's it. We're done here." I'd had enough of this farce. I grabbed Fleurette's hand to move away from the ridiculous council. "Do *not* accuse my friend of 'crimes' you have no proof she committed. Do not stop me from playing the role I was given on this earth. Help me all you want; I don't care. But if you stand in my way, fur will fly."

With that announcement, I stalked out of the room, opening the doors with enough force to bang them against the walls. They shut behind us with an equally forceful click, leaving us in solitude.

"Gaia's garters, Fleurette," I breathed. "I had a different idea of what the council was like before all of that."

She let out a nervous chuckle. "It's gone downhill ever since Grossman took over. I mentioned that we may have to go rogue, remember? Well, I think you summed it up perfectly to them.

Shall we?"

"Get me out of here," I agreed with enthusiasm.

Before we could, however, the doors opened one last time, admitting the mousy woman into the hallway. From behind her came the dull cacophony of the room at large, each voice debating the outcome of the meeting.

"Fleurette!" the woman called out, waving at us. "One moment, please!"

Fleurette smiled politely as the woman shut the doors, sealing off the noise. "Hello, Dora."

Dora returned the smile. She was apparently still in Fleurette's good graces. "I wanted to make sure you received the message before you left."

"What message?" Fleurette asked.

"From Madame Zamani. I've heard of her, you know. They say she's the real deal."

"The seer? The one who contacted you?" I asked, pushing forward.

Dora was the same height as me, and she now looked levelly at me with a measure of admiration. "Miss Curtain, I never thought I'd get to meet you! Dora Willoby. A pleasure to make your acquaintance."

"Dora serves as the society's secretary, of sorts," Fleurette explained. "She has the ability to read messages in her mind between members. And occasionally she picks up on other messages directed toward the society."

Dora nodded, her face flushing at Fleurette's words. "I wrote down the message for you. Abigail was able to volley messages to me back and forth for a time, and she made it clear that this was for you only. I—I'm sorry I told Grossman. I thought it was important that he knew we had been contacted by an outsider. It's protocol, you see. I didn't expect him to accuse you of violating the secrecy, however."

Fleurette shook her head. "I understand. I think he's had it out for me ever since I became Cressida's guardian. He didn't like that someone as young and lowly as me got the prestige of guardianship." She turned to me. "Membership is low, but not everyone was present for that discussion. You'll notice that my father wasn't invited. Grossman was hoping to make an example of me, minus some of my biggest supporters."

"I think it backfired," Dora confided in low tones. "He's not very popular, and this stunt ruffled some feathers, mine included. Do what you need to do, Fleurette. Most of us know what's at stake otherwise."

"Thank you, Dora. I appreciate the sentiment. Listen, while I'm here, have you learned anything more about Brothers?"

Dora shook her head with a bite of her lip. "I'll personally take over the task, though. I'll let you know if I find anything out."

"Especially his whereabouts," I added.

She nodded. "I'll make it a priority. It's for the safety of the legacy bearer, after all. I won't tell Grossman, either. He's downgraded the importance of finding the towers." She ruefully shook her head.

Fleurette flattened her lips. "I was afraid of that. Have any more been found?"

Dora brightened. "Yes, actually. One in the northern section of the region. After the last werewolf attack over there, we were able to pinpoint the area based on the power outages. GOGS ran into a bit of a scuffle with some remaining ACF members, but we were able to neutralize them. We believe that may have been the last of the towers, minus the one that is personally powering the gateway."

That was a small silver lining within all of this. I whistled in appreciation. "How can you be sure? Annie's attacks seem to be increasing in frequency, even with fewer towers."

Dora looked troubled. "Well, Grossman has all but called off the search. We surmise, based on some calculations, that as more magic flows through the opening into Annie's world, the gate opens further, if only fractionally. So the towers are less necessary."

"A rather nasty feedback loop," Fleurette surmised thoughtfully. "Thanks for the information, Dora. I doubt Grossman would have wanted you to give it to me."

Dora sighed. "Frankly, I'm beginning to care less about what he wants. Oh, don't forget this." She handed my friend a folded piece of paper, the apparent message. She looked embarrassed. "I didn't show it to Grossman; I only told him we'd been contacted. This message seemed too personal."

Fleurette glanced at it without opening it. "Do you think it's safe?"

Dora shrugged. "As safe as anything else in our crazy world these days. I need to go back in there before I'm missed. Best of luck to you two."

Once she reentered the council chamber, Fleurette opened the paper. She held it low so that we could both read it.

Greetings, GOGS.

I am seeking the guardian of the cat that walks as a woman, and the cat herself. I believe their names are Flower (or an alternative) and the initials CC. Time is of the essence, as my sight has begun to show me things that are not happy futures. You can find me in the place where a girl once pretended to be a monster. The cat will know.

Best,

Abigail Zamani—Grand Seer

I sucked in a breath. I did indeed know where this Zamani lady was located.

On the outskirts of the dying town of Chargrove, in an old, abandoned school that was said to be haunted.

CHAPTER 4

If time were truly of the essence as the seer suggested, there was only one mode of transportation that would get us to Chargrove's abandoned school in an accelerated manner: Wren.

Wren's magical ability was called projectionism, and it was a rare talent indeed. Her great-grandmother had also been a projectionist, but in today's world we assumed Wren to be one of a kind. It allowed her to create illusions upon her environment, herself, or others, but even more amazing was the fact that Wren could project herself to other places, effectively transporting her body to anywhere she desired. Better yet, she could take others with her.

The only downside was that it took an incredible amount of energy to perform this feat. She would need to rest for a number of hours before bringing us back home.

Fleurette and I were in agreement—it was best to ask Wren right away, and, provided she was willing, leave the same day. It was still morning, after all. Plenty of time to get up to new mischief.

Wren lit up with enthusiasm as soon as the words left Fleurette's mouth. Magical travel was one of her favorite things to do with her powers, probably because she had been forbidden from doing it on her own. The toll it enacted did not seem to bother her overly, either. It was a resounding yes from the young teen.

Fal, of course, refused to allow her to travel without him. He took the role of protective big brother almost a hair too far. It chafed Wren, but she also allowed it most of the time, especially when it came to adventures such as this.

In the end, Wren transported five of us—herself, Fal, Fleurette, Grimm, and me—right after lunch. She knew exactly where to go; it was the location in which I first made her acquaintance. The school had served as a shelter for Fal and Wren after they had been orphaned and become penniless in a string of bad luck we later determined was caused by Annie and her gang of malcontents.

It was not the best of memories for them. Still, they knew what we were getting into.

Wren's magic dumped us right in front of the dilapidated front steps of the school with such abruptness that it left us wheeling for a few seconds. Once my stomach settled, I looked around. It had been one and a half years since I last set eyes on the location, and nothing about the crumbling structure had changed. The only discernible difference was the amount of snow that covered the school and grounds in an untouched blanket of white.

Actually, not quite untouched. My eyes fixated on a small indent in the snow that ran from the road and up the steps. Fresh snow had added a thin layer to the furrow created by trudging feet, hiding it from glancing eyes. Someone was inside, or at least had been here recently.

After transporting five individuals, I was impressed that Wren was still standing. But the exhaustion apparently kicked in, as I watched the girl crumple, her strength finally giving out. Fal, close at hand, caught her before she could hit the ground and he scooped her up in his strong arms, hoisting her like a groom carrying his bride.

"We'll need to get her a bed to rest in," Fleurette said and began to mount the concrete steps to lead the way. She halted in her ascent with a gasp when one of the aging double doors at the top of the stairs opened, displaying a young woman peeking from behind.

"Hello?" the newcomer asked tentatively.

She seemed to be Fal's age, and small and lean, as gangly as a fawn. Her dark hair, similar in color to Wren's, was cropped into a bob that framed her face. Her eyes were round and large, the color of the ocean in wintertime: a light gray, almost with a hint of yellow. They were all but hidden behind large, round glasses.

I scrambled up two steps to be even with Fleurette, a show of solidarity. This person did not appear to be a threat in any way, but I knew from experience that looks could be deceiving. "Um, hi," I called out, raising my hand in an awkward greeting. "We are here to—"

She stopped looking at me and instead stared into the distance, unseeing. Then, her eyes refocused and she smiled at me. "Welcome, Miss Curtain. Will you and your friends please come this way?"

I stole a shocked glance at Fleurette. She raised her eyebrows, and then merely shrugged her shoulders. Behind me, Fal only stared at the young woman with an expression of awe. I sacrificed a second to look at Grimm, who gave his tail a tentative wag as he met my eyes with his sunflower stare. I turned back to the newcomer. "Um, okay then."

She ushered us up the stairs, staying at the door until we had all entered. Then, she took one last look around before shutting it firmly behind her.

"If you will follow me, please," she said pleasantly, if not with a hint of shyness.

"Are you Abigail Zamani?" I asked.

She shook her head, the motion causing her thick hair to bounce from side to side. "I am not, but I will take you to her."

Fal cleared his throat, hoisting up Wren in his arms. "I don't mean to be a bother, but—"

She seemed to know what he was about to ask. "Not at all. You may use one of the dormitory beds to lay your sister upon. If you don't mind, it would be best to stay with her. This meeting is only for Miss Curtain and her friend."

"And Grimm," I added, brooking no argument.

The young woman inclined her head in agreement. "Yes. Of course."

She led us up the grand staircase, a path I traveled once before in a mad dash to reach Wren before another bounty hunter could. The memory brought with it a wave of nostalgia, a yearning for what I once had. Finding the Ramberts was the last piece of normalcy I'd had in my life, back when I was simply a bounty hunter doing my job, with no thought for my legacy, no curse, no Annie.

I shook the feeling off. Now was not the time for sentimentality.

Fal surged ahead of us, knowing the way to the room he once slept in while hiding out.

The rest of us stopped short of the dormitories, instead being led to the old teacher's lounge, another place I had been acquainted with. The young woman opened the door with a smile, beckoning us to enter.

The room had barely changed since I last saw it. The same two dusty couches, where I had once sat with Fal to discuss his future, had been moved to sit perpendicular to each other. It was dark in the room, with a musty undertone, due to one of the windows being broken and allowing moisture in over the years. Now it was boarded up, explaining the lack of natural light in the room. The lounge itself was not unpleasant to be in, though, considering there was an everlasting flame in the corner giving out enough comforting heat to take the edge off the chill.

Two more people waited within, sitting side by side on the old couch facing us.

One was a man, his broad body clothed in a black shirt and baggy gray pants. His hair was dark but graying, cropped close. He wore a small skull cap upon his head.

The other was a woman, her long hair like dark caramel mixed with strands of pure white. She wore a loose-fitting dress that covered her to her ankles and a shawl over her shoulders. A large pair of dark glasses perched upon her nose and blocked the view of her eyes.

She smiled as we entered and rose to her feet, holding her hands out wide for us in welcome. The man smiled but stayed seated.

"Welcome, guests," she said, reaching to take my hand. "I am joyous that you took me up on my offer. I am Abigail Zamani."

Her voice had a rasp to it, but was pleasant enough. I felt no animosity from her.

"Hello," I replied haltingly as she moved from me to Fleurette, who allowed her hand to be clasped in greeting as well.

"Miss Zamani, we don't really know why we're here. It would be nice to be enlightened."

She scoffed. "I haven't been a 'miss' in a very long time. That's my husband, Haris, over there," she said, pointing to the man on the couch, "and you've met my daughter, Sufia. But you may call me Abigail. Or Madame Zamani, if you are prone to theatrics. I certainly am, with the right people, but that's not you, is it?"

I grinned despite the peculiarity we found ourselves in. "I suppose not."

The entire time she had spoken, I got the feeling she was not looking directly at me. I wondered if her dark glasses made it difficult for her to see anything. Yet, she'd had no trouble finding our hands.

"Now that you are here in front of me, I see I was a little off with your names. Fleurette, correct?" She addressed my friend.

"Yes, that's right."

"And Cressida, if I may boldly call you by your first name. And I did say just the two of you, but I now see how important this handsome fellow is to you, so of course he is more than welcome," she continued, smiling in Grimm's direction. "Please, come in and have a seat. I'd offer you a beverage, but this place is not well-stocked." She chuckled at her own joke.

Haris stood, motioning for one of us to take his place, and walked over to his wife to take her hand and guide her back to her seat.

I frowned as I sat in the warmed seat vacated by Haris. "I hope I don't offend you, Abigail, but is there a reason for your glasses? How can you see anything with them on?"

She let out a small laugh of pure joy. "Oh, my dear. It would not make a speck of difference whether I wear them or not. You see—" She removed them to reveal her eyes. They were wide, the irises a blue so light that they were nearly colorless against the whites of her sclera. Her pupils contrasted that much more sharply with the sea glass color of her irises. They also did not both point in the exact same direction, nor did they appear to focus on anything.

Abigail was blind.

She put the glasses back on, covering her unusual eyes. "The glasses are more for your comfort than mine."

"If it's all the same to you, you can keep them off," I suggested politely.

She removed them again, placing them perfectly into Haris' outstretched hand. "Thank you, my love."

"If you can't see, how did you just greet us by the door? And hand him your glasses?" I asked, even more intrigued.

She smiled again, displaying a crooked front tooth. It gave her a girlish look. "I may be blind, child, but I can still see. Using my sight."

I blinked in confusion. "Sight is generally how people see, yes."

She shook her head, grinning at my bewilderment. "I don't see using my eyes. I see in here." She pointed to her forehead.

Fleurette butted in, catching on quicker than me, as usual. "You are a seer. You receive images in your mind."

Abigail nodded. "Yes. When I was young, my eyes worked. But as my magical sight began to manifest, my physical sight began to decline. Within ten years, I was completely blind. And yet, I know that you, Cressida, have two black streaks in your white-blonde hair. And I know that you, Fleurette, are wearing a gray sweater with a skirt patterned of mauve with stylized flowers. You see, I receive visions in my head of the present, interspersed with the past and the future as well. It makes up a mosaic of the world around me, and sometimes beyond. I am not at all bereft of my sight because of my gift; in fact, my sight is more enhanced than yours."

"The past, present, and future all together?" I asked, scrunching up my nose. "Sounds confusing."

"It can be, at times. Most of my future visions are not so far ahead though. It's the reason I knew your names before you said them. Because in one of the futures, you *did* say them. Luckily, this is just what my brain is used to, so I'm able to process things as they come, usually." She frowned. "Of course, sometimes I catch visions that are bigger than day to day. Which is why I'm here."

She shuffled in her seat, smoothing out her dress. "I make a living as a seer, traveling the country with my family. I'm quite popular, you know. I usually stick to the East Coast of Vinland, though. But last October, I became plagued with visions that had nothing to do with that area."

October. When Annie got her foot in the door. I gulped.

Abigail continued. "I saw snowstorms, plagues, fires, any and all forms of destructive energy trying to destroy this country. And in the middle of everything, I saw you, Cressida."

"Me?" I squeaked.

She affirmed with a nod. "I've seen your death countless times in countless ways. I've seen you triumph too. But I've also seen our world plunged into darkness more times than not. It scared me enough to travel all the way over here. And as I did, my visions of the future became bigger, more real, more terrifying. In some, even with you winning, it was too late."

"So, we're doomed?" I asked quietly, my heart sinking like a lead weight.

Abigail pursed her lips. "No, my dear. Even now, I catch glimmers of hope. More so, now that I've met you. And that's important. It means we may be on a good path."

"How can we continue upon this path?" Fleurette asked, her gentle voice filling me with hope.

Abigail mused. "There are so many outcomes for our future. I would like to offer a service to help lock it in."

"What can you do?" I asked, leaning forward.

She took a deep breath and let it out. "I can give you a prophecy."

CHAPTER 5

T he room was silent for a spell as Abigail's words settled into our minds.

"A prophecy?" Fleurette finally asked. "Are you capable of such a thing?"

Abigail, sightless as she was, turned her head toward my friend with her best impression of a sardonic stare. "There are exactly three seers in this world that are able to create prophecies," she stated flatly. "One is my bedridden mother. The other is a maven who tours about Yuroba. And then there's me. Not to toot my own horn, but I am the most skilled of all three."

Fleurette made a placating gesture with her hand. "No offense was meant, Abigail. It's just that ... prophecies are not to be taken lightly."

"No, they are not," the seer agreed readily. "As a matter of fact, I hardly ever offer them at all."

"Why is that?" I asked.

She turned toward me. "The energy and effort to produce a prophecy is excruciating for me, for one reason. I'm often bed-bound for many days after, recuperating. Oy, the headaches! For that reason alone, I normally charge a pretty penny."

I thought of Wren, passed out with exhaustion after taking us here. It must have been a similarly heavy magic load.

She continued, "For another thing, prophecies can be risky

in and of themselves. As I mentioned, I can see many, many future outcomes, and each one has an equally likely chance of happening, whether it's good or bad. But if I create a prophecy, it locks the future in place. All of the other possibilities vanish."

"I see." I pinched my lips to the side, thinking. My ancestor Glivver had created a prophecy, one that I knew by heart, as had the cats that came before me:

By Glivver's blood the witch is bound,
By Glivver's word the witch must obey,
So long as the daughters of Glivver remain,
So long as the cat that walks as a woman lives,
The witch Annie Coddle can never return.

I said, "I am already involved in a prophecy, one that says my familial line is directly responsible for keeping Annie Coddle away. The way it is written, there seems to be two sides to this. Either the prophecy holds true, and my kind keeps her away, or it fails, and Annie comes back. It's like two sides of a coin. Would that hold true for your prophecy?"

She nodded, ruminating. "That's generally the way it works. Either the prophecy holds, or it utterly fails. I can't tell you what the prophecy will say until the time comes. I won't be able to reveal beforehand whether it will be favorable or not. But at least you'll know the outcome one way or another. And look at it this way. Right now, the way the future holds, you could have a thirty percent chance of succeeding. If I make a prophecy, it would give you a fifty percent chance, which would actually be higher if you follow the prophecy to the letter of the law. Generally speaking, prophecies don't just fail for no good reason."

"Cress?" Fleurette asked softly. "What do you think? This is your decision."

"Oh great, no pressure or anything," I muttered. I turned to Abigail. "You mentioned a cost ..."

She waved a hand at me. "From you, I only expect a favor in exchange. After all, this is for the safety of our world."

"A favor?" I repeated. "What would the favor be?"

She showed off her crooked-tooth smile again. "I don't know yet. That future hasn't come to me."

I sighed, beleaguered by the decision I had to make. "Very well. Let's do it."

Abigail clapped her hands once, startling me. "Let's get on with it, then! Haris, chamudi, let's get the table set up, hm?"

Like I said, I was no stranger to prophecies. After all, my whole existence had arisen from the creation of one. Prophecies were what got me into this mess in the first place.

And now, I was moments away from burdening myself with another. I hoped it would be worth it.

It took some time setting up the room. Fleurette and Haris had moved the couch back to make space for a small table and two chairs on either side. Abigail sat in one of the chairs now. The table held a knife, a bowl, a spoon, a small square of thin paper, and a smattering of dried herbs. I took the empty chair on the other side of the table, eyeing the assortment with a small amount of trepidation.

"This is how it works," Abigail said. "Cressida, you will be the focus of the prophecy. Therefore, I need just a couple of personal items from you."

"Like what?"

"I need a small lock of your hair and at least five drops of your blood."

"Oh." I gazed at my palm, hating the thought of slicing a knife through it.

Abigail laughed, seeing in her mind a picture of me. "Everybody goes for the palm slice. I don't understand it. Go for the forearm. Less nerve endings there."

My eyes bulged out at her. "Do *I* need to be the one to do it?"

"Not at all. Who would you like to slice you?"

I turned in my seat to look at Fleurette behind me. "Can you do the honors?"

Fleurette hunched her shoulders and pinched her lips together at my request, but nodded. "If I must. I'll try to heal it as soon as we collect the blood."

"Fal can do it after this is over. Just be sure to wrap it well." Fleurette was an incredibly talented witch of most trades, but when it came to healing magic, Fal was superior.

She nodded. Haris, who stood by Abigail's side, handed her a clean roll of bandage material with a kind smile on his face.

"You don't talk much, do you?" I asked him.

"I have my moments," he returned, his cadence flavored by an accent.

Abigail nodded. "Haris is not just my husband. He's my record keeper and protector as well. See, when I do a prophecy, I'm in a fugue state. He will record what comes out of me on paper. Otherwise, I won't know a word of what I've said."

"And her?" I asked, jerking my head at her daughter, who stood on the other side.

Sufia spoke for herself. "I'm learning the ropes."

Abigail nodded proudly. "Sufia has inherited my gift, as I did from my mother and my bubbeh. She can still see, but her eye color is fading and her sights are becoming more frequent."

"I'm only seventeen. I still have some time to grow into my

gift," Sufia added, a hint of pride in her words.

"Oh, Fal's seventeen," I interjected, thinking that perhaps I could somehow set them up. After all, Fal once had a crush on me when we first met, but since then he'd not shown any interest in dating.

Abigail made a small noise in her throat. "I'm aware. He's a good kid, from what I've seen. But what you're thinking? I can't see anything, one way or another. Maybe they hook up, maybe they don't."

"Mo-om!" Sufia moaned.

Abigail ignored her daughter's protest. "Well, let's get on with it, shall we? No time like the present. That's a seer's joke. First, the hair. Haris?"

Haris pulled a small pair of scissors out of his pants pocket and leaned over the table. "I do not need much," he assured me.

I leaned forward. "I've never had a haircut before."

"Never?" he murmured as he snipped off a few strands of blonde near the front. "Not much hair for a lifetime of growing."

I sat back as he transferred the hairs to the bowl. "It's been this length my entire life." A perk of being a cat, I supposed: no haircuts necessary.

Abigail nodded her approval at the bowl. "Now, the blood."

I swallowed and rolled up my sleeve, exposing the length of my arm. Fleurette took the knife and grasped my arm from underneath. She paused with the blade close to my skin.

"Ready?" she asked, looking me in the eye.

I nodded, even though my heart rate sped up and all I wanted to do was yank my arm away from her. Instead, I held perfectly still, trying not to tremble.

She made a small cut on the top of my arm, the pain sharp but quickly diffusing into a dull ache. I hissed at the sensation, nevertheless.

"A spoonful ought to do," Abigail informed us as Haris handed the small spoon to Fleurette. She pressed the utensil to my arm and tilted my appendage, allowing the blood to dribble from the wound until the spoon captured at least five drops. Haris carefully took it from her and placed it into the bowl with my hair. Fleurette wasted no time in bandaging my cut, although it had already started to clot.

Haris then dumped the various herbs into the bowl and handed the whole thing to Abigail, who stirred the contents with the bloody spoon, coating both herbs and hair with the viscous scarlet liquid. She said some words over the mixture, her raspy voice low and her unseeing eyes closed.

Having done that, she spooned the contents out onto the paper, forming the clumpy blend into a thin line at one end. I could see bits of my hair sticking out between the dried leaves, with everything spattered by the red of my blood. I was not a squeamish creature by any definition, but the sight made my nose scrunch in revulsion.

Abigail did not seem the least bit repulsed. She deftly rolled the contents up in the paper and twisted the ends shut, sealing the tube closed. Some of my blood leaked through the paper, but it otherwise held together well.

"Ready, love?" she asked Haris.

"Ready, habibti," he replied.

She tucked one end of the paper roll into her mouth. Haris leaned down and moved his hands to the other end, the tips of his two first fingers and thumb coming together. A small flame appeared there, like he was pinching the fire in his fingertips.

"You're an elemental," I breathed, remembering the last one I'd had the misfortune of knowing. Hobbs, one of Elkins' lackeys, had been a horrible human who had tried to fry me with his fire magic. Haris, on the other hand, was so gentle and calm. It assuaged the small fear I'd held for elementals in general. They weren't all monsters, after all.

He nodded absently, and Abigail talked around the paper in her mouth. "He is. Now be still. This is the part where you don't distract either one of us."

"Sorry," I said, chagrined.

Haris lit the tip of the roll on fire as Abigail inhaled. The flame snuffed out almost instantly, but the contents smoked, and Abigail drew the smoke deep into her lungs. She exhaled the foul-smelling plume and gave a racking cough.

"I hate this bit. Worst part of the job. But the herbs loosen my third eye and make it possible for me to prophesize. And your essence must become a part of me to focus my eye. This is the quickest way to get the job done. It will be just a moment. Haris, is your paper ready?"

"Ready."

She steeled herself. "Okay then. One more draw ought to do the trick. Hang tight."

Abigail sucked on the end of her roll deeply, the burning tip glowing red as she did. This time when she exhaled, she bent over and released a deep hack. She threw the stub into the bowl with precision.

It did not look pleasant. I was torn between staying still and getting up to assist her, but both her husband and daughter did not seem perturbed, so I stayed put.

Abigail raised her head, her eyes tearing from coughing. "Give me your hand. Quickly!"

I placed my hand down on hers, and she gripped it fiercely.

"Here it comes," she said, her voice low. Goosebumps rose all over my body.

I glanced at Haris, who had paper and a pen in hand, waiting. I brought my attention back to Abigail and nearly let out a startled shriek.

She stared forward, unseeing as usual, but her face had gone slack, and as I watched, her black pupils faded into the barely blue of her irises. Within seconds, those faded too, until her eyes were nothing but white orbs in her sockets.

It was incredibly creepy, to say the least. I was riveted by them.

She spoke, but her voice was not the kind, raspy voice I expected. This was deeper, booming, otherworldly. She spoke each word slowly, carefully. I listened, enraptured.

"A forest deep, a tree must forge
Time is due when blizzards gorge
A potion first you must provide
And murder dark to turn the tide
The cat is key, the only one
For which the gate can be undone
But by yourself, you'll not succeed
A ring of trust will do the deed
Three camps to claim, split from the whole
Together, they will help your goal
Four strong of heart but magic dry
A searching, seeking, fated eye
Two halves, once whole, but torn apart
A mother's love to brace the heart
Two witches strong with magic green
Ancient powers of fourteen
Brother, sister, birds alike
A yellow-hearted little tyke
Companion true and traitor lost
Skin of fire, Breath of frost
Coney swift and otter sleek
All these allies you must seek
For if you don't collect them all

The witch will win. Our world will fall."

CHAPTER 6

Abigail's words hung in the air like crystals from a chandelier. The only sound was the furious scribbling of Haris as he finished writing what she said.

Abigail's eyes unclouded, the faded blue and pupils reappearing as swiftly as they had vanished. Her face went from flat to animated as the blankness receded. She blinked.

"Has it been said?"

"Yes, habibti," Haris replied. "Well done."

"That rhymed. Why did it rhyme?" I asked.

Sufia snorted. "She's the only one who does that. Ima—Mom—has a flair for the dramatic, even when she's in a fugue."

"Ah. So, she rhymes every time?"

Abigail tiredly raised her shoulders. "What can I say? It's a gift. Haris, be a love and read it back to me before I drop to the floor."

He did so, all of us listening carefully.

Abigail whistled. "That's a doozy if I ever heard one."

"But what does it mean?" I asked.

She shook her head at me. "It's not my job to interpret the crazy stuff that comes out of my mouth. That's on you. Although, I know what my favor is now."

I raised my eyebrows. "And what might that be?"

She motioned behind her, at her daughter. "Sufia. She's a part of this. And after you've done what you need to do, you will accept her into your little club."

"Ima, what?" Sufia exclaimed.

Abigail clutched her head, tsking. "Not so loud, mami. The headaches are starting. Sufi, I see it now. You're important to the success of this endeavor. Or you will be, at any rate. This is your destiny."

Sufia huffed, clearly not liking her future to be laid out so plainly.

Abigail groaned, screwing her eyes shut. "Sufia will join you when the time comes. Not now, though. I'll need her sight to get me through this recovery. I have a feeling it will take me longer to recover this time."

"Is that your sight telling you that?" I asked, my curiosity too great to ignore.

Abigail tsked again. "I've got bupkis for sight right now. That's just my plain intuition talking. I know you have more questions for me, Cressida. But for now, I'm going to bid you a pleasant goodbye while I rest. Feel free to stay here as long as you need; we don't own this place. Haris?"

Fleurette and I stood as Haris came around and plucked Abigail off of her chair as if she weighed nothing. She relaxed in his arms, seemingly succumbing to her exhaustion immediately. Haris pointed his head at the table, where his records lay.

"There is a copy for you to keep," he said as he carried Abigail to the door. Sufia followed behind them, a small sulk present in her heavy footfalls.

"Thank you," I called out to their backsides as they disappeared out of the room.

I glanced at Fleurette, who plucked the page off the table. "It looks like we have some homework to do," she said.

Fal furrowed his brow in confusion, his black hair falling over his eyes as he did. "What does it mean?"

We sat in the room Fal had claimed for Wren, the same small abode she had used the last time they camped here. The afternoon light slowly dimmed as Wren continued to sleep in the dusty bed Fal had laid her upon. Fleurette had just read the prophecy to him.

"Well, a forest deep must be where the gate is located," Fleurette started slowly.

"Most of this region is '*a forest deep*,'" I stated. "It doesn't exactly help us to narrow it down."

She rubbed her chin. "No, but we also know that it is upon sacred land. We'll need the support of the Memory Keepers to help locate the area. Unfortunately, they have not responded yet to the GOGS' appeal. They probably don't wish to answer a summons from an unknown entity."

The Memory Keepers were what was left of the Indigenous population after the mass exodus that took place when settlers came to Vinland a thousand years ago. They were highly respected, with an impressive magical population. Most of them also happened to be highly reclusive and protective of their way of life, keeping the bulk of their traditions away from non-native eyes.

"Okay, so we need a to-do checklist," I surmised. "First item: appeal to the Memory Keepers."

"Create a potion?" Fal suggested. "'*A potion first you must provide.*'"

"A potion of what? For what?" Fleurette shook her head. "I'll need to do some research into this part."

I continued to read the next line. "This one troubles me." I pointed to the line. *And murder dark to turn the tide.* "Who are we supposed to kill?"

"Annie?" Fal proposed.

I pursed my lips. "No, I don't think we can kill her. It would definitely turn the tide, however. I suppose we'll have to be vigilant. I'm sure *somebody* will pop up in our minds. I don't like the fact that anybody needs to be killed for this prophecy to come true, though."

Fleurette chimed in. "I agree. Cress, I know you had to get your hands dirty with the ACF last time, and I also know you didn't enjoy it."

"What can I say? I'm a hunter, not a killer." I ruefully chuckled. "I can't even kill mice these days." Ever since I had rescued Lucky from Addelboro and befriended the little rodent, I had sworn mice off the menu.

"Well, at least this next part is obvious," Fal said, skimming the page. "'*The cat is key, the only one for which the gate can be undone.*' You're a cat, Cress, and you're the only one who can destroy the gate."

"But not by myself," I argued, pointing to the next line.

Fleurette narrowed her eyes on the paper. "You're right. And then it goes on to list a bunch of random things and people."

"And here it says we must seek all of these allies!" I exclaimed, jabbing the line near the end.

"These ... eleven lines are all describing the allies, then," Fleurette said, a touch of excitement in her voice.

I recalled the words the kitsune, Kitty, had given to me when I asked her how to defeat Annie. *Great power must be met with great power.* She had gone on to tell me that I would need strength in numbers. This prophecy, if we were reading it correctly, correlated with what Kitty said.

Fleurette studied the lines. "So many people. Let's see ... that would be ... thirty-three. Give or take. I can't tell if *'skin of fire, breath of frost'* is one or two beings. And same for *'companion true and traitor lost.'"*

"Two for sure on your second point," I said, scanning the writing. "Grimm is my companion true. That one is obvious enough." I stroked my true companion along his silky black head with affection. He in turn leaned his weight into my side, blowing out a contented sigh.

Fleurette hummed in her throat. "I'm sure you're right. And look, this must be Wren and Fal." She pointed to *Brother, sister, birds alike.*

"I'm part of a prophecy?" Fal preened. "Awesome."

Fleurette looked at the young man. "It could be dangerous, Fal. I'm not sure it's a good thing."

"If it means ending Annie's stranglehold for once and for all, it's a good thing," Fal argued, keeping his eyes on the paper. "Oh, look, this is you, Fleurette."

She looked again, murmuring the words written down. "'*Two witches strong with magic green.*' You're right, Fal. Kokoro describes me as green, because of my magic. I might not have put that together without her unique neurodiversity." Kokoro was a mundy, but nevertheless she was gifted. She had a condition called synesthesia, in which different senses became cross-wired with each other. It manifested differently for each synesthete, and in Kokoro's case, she could see the color of other people's magic, among other things. In Kokoro's eyes, I gave off a brilliant whiteness because of my innate magic, and Fleurette was a vibrant green due to her natural affinity for botanical magic.

"But who is the other witch?" I asked. "Fal?"

He shook his head. "I'm a mix of green and blue, according to

Kokoro. My healing magic and plant magic are mixed together. Besides, I'm already listed elsewhere."

"Oh yeah. Hm, I guess we'll be on the lookout for another herbalist, then."

Fleurette pondered this. "Not just an herbalist. Someone like me, with a strong affinity for plant magic. I don't think most herbalists would count."

I tapped my chin. "What if we placed an ad? 'ISO: person with botanical skills needed for important job.' Then, when people show up, we have Kokoro assess each one and then we pick the strongest."

Fleurette narrowed her eyes on me. "It's kind of a stupid idea, but it has merit. Perhaps it's simple enough to work."

"I'm going to ignore the fact that you called my idea stupid," I replied. "If you have a better plan, I'm all ears."

We bantered back and forth, discussing the various lines of the prophecy and trying to figure out who might be on the list. After a while the three of us came to the conclusion that the "four strong of heart but magic dry" must refer to the four mundies in our lives: Kokoro, Fleurette's father Lyle, my father Roger, and Kokoro's cousin Gavin. My mother Belinda had to be the "mother's love to brace the heart." Even with those blanks filled in, there were still a surprising number of allies for which we didn't have a clue.

"A fated eye, two halves, one green witch, fourteen unknowns, whatever a tyke is, a traitor, fire and frost, and ... a coney and an otter. What's a coney?" I asked, summing up the missing pieces.

"A type of fish, I think," Fal replied with a head scratch.

I looked at him dubiously. "I highly doubt a *fish* is going to be an ally."

He shrugged his shoulders. "With this lot? Who knows."

"Well, perhaps the shifters will know," I said.

Fleurette perked up. "Shifters?"

I grinned and pointed. "'*Otter sleek*.' I have a feeling I know who that is."

Fleurette raised her eyebrows with dawning recognition. "But Cress, the shifters are a secretive bunch. Most people don't know where the nearest shifter village lies. I certainly don't have a clue."

Slyly, I responded, "Oh, but I know someone who does."

CHAPTER 7

We left the school that night, Wren having rested enough to perform the arduous magic home. Before we left, I decided to check in on Abigail one last time.

Haris did not want to accommodate my request, stating that Abigail was very tired and should not be disturbed. But Sufia intervened after a moment of blankness. Living in a family of two seers, Haris recognized a vision when he saw one, and allowed me entrance to his wife's resting chamber at Sufia's insistence.

Abigail looked older, shrunken in, and wan upon her makeshift bed in one of the dorm rooms. She was awake, however, and motioned with a hand to come closer.

"I'm sorry if I woke you," I said, tiptoeing to her side.

She fumbled with her hand, searching for mine. The action made me realize that her powers were completely depleted, and she was truly blind while she recovered. No wonder she hated dishing out prophecies. I reached over and purposefully grasped her hand in mine.

"You did no such thing, my girl. I was already awake, fighting through this headache of mine. The worst part is being blind. I'm used to seeing more than a person with working eyeballs, but in this state? Bupkus." She shook her head with a rueful smile, showing her crooked tooth.

"I'm sorry. I wanted to say thank you before we head out. I'm not sure what half of the prophecy means, but there are some good clues to it."

She waved her free hand. "Any time, sweetheart. Well, not any time, because I'm swearing off making prophecies for a very long time. But listen, I'll be sending Sufia your way when the time is right. She's young, but she'll need to find her support person sooner than later, given the increasing frequencies of her visions."

"Do seers always need a support person?" I asked.

"Ehhh. No. But it sure comes in handy, especially in my family line. Someone who you can sink full trust into is very important. But you already know that," she added with a fresh grin. Her face turned reflective again. "I'd be lost without my Haris. My mother saw him coming and wasn't too happy, given the differences in our religion. But she couldn't stop true love, and that's more important than which form of god you pray to. And Sufia? We've always let her make her own decisions. So far, neither Judaism nor Islam has caught her fancy. As far as I'm concerned, she could get with a demon worshiper as long as he's a nice boy who reveres the ground she walks on. But she's gotta find herself, and I'm hoping your new organization will be what she needs to do that."

"What new organization?" I asked, my face scrunching in confusion.

"Um. Right. Too soon. Don't worry about it. Just promise me that you'll look out for my daughter, hm?" Abigail evaded my question, and I allowed her that. It must have been difficult to be living in the present and the future simultaneously.

"I promise."

"That's a good girl. A real mensch, you are. I'm glad we got to meet, after all the visions I had of you. You'll either save us, or doom us all. Good luck with that."

The weight of the world crashed down on my shoulders. I

fought to take a breath after her announcement, but willed my stomach to unclench and my heart to settle into a more comfortable rhythm.

After all, I knew what I was getting myself into. Her words were not news to me. Still, I hated to hear them.

"Thanks," I said drily, but I squeezed her hand with affection before letting it go.

Home again, and, after properly putting a comatose Wren to bed, we collectively decided we'd had enough adventure for one day and called it a night.

Time was a-wasting, though, and so early the next morning, I set out for Lyle's farm with a mission.

Lyle lived just one and a half miles from us on the same road as Fleurette's cottage, about half a mile from the town of Knobby Hill. He worked as the town's veterinarian, with people bringing an assortment of pets and farm animals to him for exams.

He also had graciously opened up his home to my parents, after they had returned from hiding last October. He gifted them a small parcel of land out back and away from prying eyes, to build their own home upon. This was where I was headed.

My parents were eager to have a place to call their own, where no one would suspect that my mom spent much of her time as a cat. But building was slow, no thanks to the unusual weather. As it was, only the foundation had been laid for the snug little cabin they planned.

As I suspected, the break in the weather meant that both parents were hard at work with the beginning stages of framework. Ever since my dad came back into her life, my mother spent much more time as a human. Seeing as how that was her form currently, I also approached them wearing my human body.

As soon as Roger saw me, a large grin broke his lean face. He was a plain-looking man, with dusty blonde hair in a high widow's peak, a long face lined with midlife wrinkles, and faded blue eyes hidden by glasses. But he was incredibly special, not just to my mom as her true love, but to me.

I didn't grow up with a father, as Mom had given birth to me away from civilization. It was only a year ago that he had come into my life rather unexpectedly, after being framed by the ACF in a bid to get their hands upon my mother and me. I also missed out on getting to know him for six long months when he and my mom were in hiding and I went slowly mad staying here doing nothing.

These days may have been fraught with peril, but it sure beat the purgatory of inaction.

Despite these delays in our relationship, my father and I had a bond. I returned his genuine smile with one of my own, happy to see him.

He swept me into a hug, mindless of the grime on his overcoat and the manly sweat smell that permeated through his layers. I was naturally fastidious with my hygiene, but I took no mind of the dirt. I'd just groom it away later.

"Cressida, what have you been up to?" he asked as he released me from the hug. "We stopped by yesterday, but Kokoro told us you'd gone adventuring again."

Mom crowded in as well, her green eyes piercing me with a calculated stare. She and I had a rocky past, especially while I was searching for Roger, but she had softened toward me once I reunited them. The stress of leaving her one love had apparently strained our relationship, seeing as how I was the reason she'd left him in the first place. Now that he was back in her life, she had mellowed.

I smiled at his words. "Adventuring" was putting it mildly. "Oh, just off trying to figure out how to save the world, that's all."

My father chuckled as if I'd told a joke, but Mom knew better. "And have you figured it out yet?"

"Getting there." I pulled out the folded paper that contained the prophecy. "I'm not sure how much you two are going to like this," I stated matter-of-factly. "I had a seer create a prophecy. And as far as we can tell, you both are part of it."

Mom raised her eyebrows as she took the paper from me, holding it so that both she and Dad could read it.

He finished first. "A lot of gobbledygook, isn't it?"

I shrugged. "Yes and no. Abigail said the prophecies were like riddles. It *should* make sense when it's all said and done, but some of it is hard to decipher. Anyway, we need to find these allies. Some of them are obvious, like Fal and Wren, and you and Mom. Others are a little trickier. But the one at the bottom? I think you can help us with that, Dad."

"That right? I'm not sure I'm the adventurous type, honey. What can I possibly help you with?"

I pointed to the line on the paper. "'*Otter sleek.*' You mentioned that your shifter friend took you in. Do you happen to know where we might be able to find her?"

Dawning realization lit up Roger's features. "Ah. Yes, you're right. I may be able to help you after all. But we'll need transportation."

It took some planning, but we were on our way. Besides my father, no one had ever seen a shifter village before, so competition was fierce for attendance. But Dad said that too many people might freak out the wary shifters, so he limited the party to five individuals.

I was a shoo-in, of course, and since I was going, so was Grimm. Dad had to come as well, seeing as how he was the only person who actually knew where he was going. Fleurette asked to come, and I felt her presence was a necessary factor. That left one slot open.

I thought for sure my mother or Kokoro would attend, but both parties begged off. Wren and Fal implored us to take them along, but school was in session, and we did not trust the risks associated with this particular journey. Lyle was too busy with the farm and his practice to get away, although he did lend us his large MC, the one he used to transport livestock when needed.

It looked like it would only be the four of us after all.

The next morning at sunrise, Fleurette, Grimm, and I walked to Lyle's to get an early start. The MC was parked out front, and Lyle's backside took up the double doors at the back. He was talking to someone who was inside.

"The throttle sometimes sticks. Be sure to jiggle it if it does. She's an old beast, but she's reliant with the right touch," he told the person inside.

Fleurette knew how to drive the rig, having been brought up on this farm, so she would be our driver. Lyle must have thought it wise to tell my father how to drive it as well, just in case. Smart thinking.

A voice rang out from the interior. "Don't you worry, Dr. Williams. I'll treat the old girl like she was my own."

That was decidedly *not* Roger's voice.

The driver's door opened, and a man jumped out, smoothing his jacket down as he did.

"What are *you* doing here?" I asked with a bug-eyed stare, a tiny wrinkle working its way between my eyes.

"Well, I'm happy to see you too, Cressida," Gavin St. Cloud declared with his usual overdone charm.

I shook my head, smoothing my face to get rid of the frown. "You just surprised me, that's all."

He smiled, and the action lit up his face. Gavin was a handsome man, I still had to admit. It had been a while since I saw him last; he had been "busy," according to him. I personally thought he had been avoiding me ever since learning I was a cat.

That was fair, though. I had avoided him for six months after kissing him.

"Kokoro asked that I join you folks. Something about a shifter village? She thought my driving skills might come in handy, whatever that means," Gavin explained as he switched his weight from one foot to another.

That made sense. Kokoro was Gavin's cousin, and they rented an apartment together above a bakery in town. The poor space barely got any use, however, as Kokoro spent much of her time at Fleurette's, and Gavin was often away on bounty hunting business. Still, the cousins had grown close over these last few months. Gavin seemed the sort to do anything for his older cousin.

"Happy to have you along. Who's taking the first driving shift?" I asked, eager to depart.

Fleurette volunteered, and she and Roger clambered into the front seats. The back of the MC had a large cargo interior, meant to transport large animals. There happened to be bench seats along the left and right walls, however. Only a small window connected the cab with the cargo, so talk between the four of us would be limited once we were on the road.

The only way into the cargo area was through the double

doors at the back, reminiscent of my wooden wagon. Grimm dutifully jumped in, not waiting for any instructions. Gavin gave a flourish of his arm to let me enter next, which I did with as much grace as I could muster. I took the left-hand seat. Gavin clambered in and sat opposite me.

Lyle took a hold of the doors. "Be safe out there. Make it back in one piece."

"We will," I promised, though such a guarantee could not be made. Every time I ventured out, I was taking my life into my hands.

I wouldn't have it any other way.

Lyle shut the doors with a metallic clang, and then walked to the driver's window, which Fleurette rolled down.

"You be careful out there, honey," he intoned.

Fleurette leaned out and kissed the top of his forehead. "I will, Dad."

And that was that. Fleurette put the vehicle into gear and we drove off, following Roger's directions.

Gavin and I rode in silence for a spell. It was not the cozy mutual silence of two friends, however. The disquiet between us was spurred by sneaky glances. The bubble of social rejection grew bigger and bigger, until it finally popped.

"Have you been avoiding me?" I asked. The question was not one I had thought to voice out loud, but apparently the concept of being cooped up with the guy for hours on end wasn't going to be awkward enough for my brain.

Gavin swiveled his head to me, his eyes narrowed. "No more than you've been avoiding me."

"I haven't." I scoffed, perhaps a bit too forcefully.

"No? We kissed, you saved my life, you nearly died, I helped us get back home, and then poof. You just vanished. No word from you for six months. Sure you weren't avoiding me."

"I was in hiding, remember? And I opened up to you. You know my secret now." Not that it was my intention. My hand had been forced, seeing as how Gavin was pretending to be an ACFer.

"And apologies if I'm trying to reconcile the Cressida I thought I knew with what you actually are. It's taken me a bit of getting used to."

I pointed a finger at him. "So you *were* avoiding me!"

He shook his head, his lips a flat line. "Fine. I needed some time away from you. But what about you? Don't deny that something changed between us when you went into hiding."

I sighed. I *had* actively avoided him, only because I knew he still had feelings for me. Feelings that I couldn't reciprocate, thanks to my family's legacy and Annie's curse that had been placed upon me.

The curse was now gone, but the rules of the legacy sure weren't.

"Do you remember how I said I couldn't love you?" I asked him.

He nodded, a wary gleam in his eyes.

I continued, "I wasn't lying. There are ... rules, I guess, around what I am."

"There are rules to being a cat?" he asked sardonically.

"No, you ass. My ancestor set the groundwork for the working of my entire family line. Only one true love for each of us. Any other romantic relationship is meaningless."

"Ouch. Still, you seemed to be having a good time for at least a little while."

I rolled my eyes. "I did enjoy it." I glanced down at Grimm, who lay on the floor between us, his furry head resting on his front paws. As much as he gave off a nonchalant air, he was watching our conversation very closely, despite not being able to fully follow it. Still, I did not wish to wound him with my words. "It was my first kiss, and I got swept up in the moment. But that all came crashing down when my curse kicked in."

"Your curse?" Gavin frowned and leaned forward. "Why is this the first I'm hearing of it?"

"Because I couldn't trust you yet, dummy!" I closed my eyes, calming down. "Sorry. Annie placed a curse on me, that I would never fall in love with a man. It was to stop my lineage with me, which would allow her back into our world. But I broke it. Back in October. I found my true love."

"Do I want to know?" Gavin asked, rubbing his face with his palm.

"Gavin, you're a part of the inner circle. You are a part of the new prophecy. At least, I think you are. Of course you should know."

Gavin held up his hands. "Woah, back up. Prophecy?"

I added to my mental list that when we got back from this little excursion, I'd invite everyone I thought was a part of the allies list together to tell them about their upcoming role. Filling each of them in separately was getting old.

I explained the prophecy to Gavin. As soon as I had, I added, "I'd like to think we are friends now, Gavin. But I need to clear the air. As I said, I found my true love."

"So, who's the lucky man?" Gavin asked, his tone brittle.

"Well, that's just the thing. The curse held true. He's not a man at all. It's Grimm."

Gavin widened his eyes. "Grimm." He looked down at my partner, who looked back up with a small tail wag. "Grimm?" he repeated, a hint of skepticism creeping into his voice.

"Yes."

He huffed out a laugh. "I lost out to a *dog*?"

Grimm let out a small growl directed at Gavin. The two didn't always get along, but there had been an uneasy truce since last March. Gavin was dangerously close to snuffing it out.

I also bristled. "I am not some prize to be won. And if I were, the winner would still be Grimm. You and I? We aren't a good match. We fight, we push each other's buttons. We work well as friends, not lovers. But Grimm? He's always been there for me. Sure, we have our arguments, but that's mostly my stubborn nature not listening to reason. I can't imagine a life without Grimm by my side. We soulbonded, for Freya's sake. If that's not the definition of love at its truest, I don't know what is."

Gavin studied me. "That's how you saved his life. Back at the generator building."

I nodded. "I can feel him, here, always. It's the same for him." I pointed to my heart.

Gavin huffed a heavy sigh. "What about kids, though? Isn't that a part of your legacy?"

I squirmed. "It's something to work out. Fleurette always says not to give up hope. But yes, it's the one thing that hasn't been figured out yet."

Gavin rubbed his chin. "What if ... Grimm stays your true love, but you have someone on the side?"

I stared flatly at him. "No way. Gavin, I don't work that way. You need to face facts; you and I can never be a thing."

"Fine. But just keep that idea on the back burner. You never know."

"I do know. And there's someone out there for you, I'm sure."

Gavin waved his hand to dismiss my words. "Fine. Let's change the subject. When are you going to come back to bounty hunting?"

The turn from lovelorn anger to something as mundane as work gave me mental whiplash. Still, his words churned a desire in me. "I don't know," I replied with all honesty. "Whenever all this is over?"

Gavin made a noncommittal sound. "I wish you would. It's not the same out there without kicking your butt."

"Kicking *my* butt?" I gasped with a mocking open mouth. "I seem to recall a lot of butt-kicking in the other direction as well."

Gavin grinned, his surliness over our previous argument fully evaporating. "Ah, but now you're in the weeds. You'll have to play some major catch-up if you want to regain your previous title of butt-kicker champion." He turned somber again. "But seriously, I miss you out there. And so do the other hunters."

"Now I know you're joking."

"No, it's true. They were asking me the other day what happened to you."

I frowned. "What did you tell them?"

"Only that you're out saving the world instead." He let a small smile slip at my horrified expression. "Kidding. I just said something came up in your personal life and you were on an extended leave."

I rolled my eyes. "Great. They probably think I'm pregnant."

"With my baby, if you want to follow the rumors."

"St. Cloud, I swear to Freya ..."

Grimm rose at my defensive tone. I placed a hand on his head to assure him all was well. Gavin held out his hands to placate me. "I try to squelch them when I hear them. But there's only so much I can do. I'm the only one of the lot that has ever gotten close to you, so it's natural for assumptions to be made, Cress. The fact remains, they've asked when you're coming back."

"Well, that's weirdly nice to hear." I didn't bother to voice my suspicion that the boys didn't miss me, but rather missed the chance to mess with me. "I wish my life was normal again so I could get back out there."

He quirked an eyebrow. "'Normal' might not be the word I'd

use for your situation."

I sighed as I rubbed Grimm's ear absentmindedly. "No, neither would I."

On the faster roads, the vehicle chugged along at an average speed of fifteen miles per hour, not bad for the age and speed of the old beast. Still, it took us a good seven hours of travel time, the majority of that spent sitting on our bottoms until they grew numb.

Dad directed first Fleurette, and then Gavin, to drive through Dogwood, and then over the Willmaunt River, a route identical to the one I took in October with Nic. From there, we gradually traveled north and then west, skirting the very top of the Oracune Region. I had never been this far north before, but the forests we ventured into looked much the same as the ones nearer to home: dense evergreens that stayed lush even in the horrible weather. Thickets of brush lined the road, crowding it in places in a bid to capture a sliver of the sun the trees tended to hoard. I felt right at home any time I got a glimpse out of the window.

Annie's weather magic must have petered out on the outskirts of the region, because the farther we traveled, the sparser the snow became, until the ground remained the usual brown of a typical Oracune winter. I was glad to see this morsel of normalcy.

At last, Gavin parked the MC where Roger directed him to. We all piled out, eager to be at our destination. I looked around, expecting to be in a town, but we had simply stopped at a pullout on the side of the road in the middle of the forest. All I saw were trees surrounding us, with not a hint of civilization in sight, other than the road.

"Um, Dad," I ventured, "where's the village?"

Roger smirked uncharacteristically. "You didn't think it would be that easy, did you? We have a hike ahead of us, my heart."

I grumbled. "Oh, goodie. Well, let's get this started."

Roger walked resolutely forward, seemingly knowing where he was going. I joined directly behind him, with Grimm at my heels. Fleurette followed next, and Gavin took the rear.

We pushed through the bushes with steadfast determination despite the resistance we received from the vegetation. I had half a mind to tell my father this couldn't possibly be the way, but I held my tongue, curious to see what would happen next. Once we had struggled through the thickest of the brush at the edge of the road, it thinned out, allowing us a more pleasant walking experience. I could now see small pathways interspersed through the undergrowth, deer trails that led here and there. At the first junction, Roger halted and closed his eyes. He moved his head back and forth until he nodded once and paused. He turned his face to the left, and then followed it with his body.

"What are you doing?" I asked, the curiosity too much for me to stay quiet this time.

Dad turned to glance at me. "The village is hidden. Only those spelled with the knowledge can find the way to it."

"Spelled? You've been spelled?" This was news to me.

He nodded. "The people in charge of the village recognized I was no threat to them. If I ever needed sanctuary again, I was welcome back. They performed the ritual to spell me with the knowledge. It's quite an honor, I've been told." He rubbed the back of his neck sheepishly. "Technically, I'm not supposed to bring anyone with me. They might not be happy to see us."

"Oh." That was a wrinkle I didn't expect. "But it's for the good of the world. Maybe they'll make an exception."

He nodded, although he did not seem convinced. "Perhaps."

We hiked through the woods, mostly in silence, for an hour. Dad would stop on occasion to use his forehead as a magical homing beacon to tell him which direction to go.

It was not an unpleasant hike, I reflected. The lack of snow was incredibly refreshing, and the afternoon sun broke through the tree cover on occasion, warming us as we walked.

A loud caw came from the trees, breaking my reverie. I turned around quickly, glancing at Fleurette, who had stopped walking and looked at the canopy with an expression of surprise upon her face. The noise sounded again, this time closer, and Fleurette whispered a word under her breath. "Rupert."

I doubted this was the case, unless he had been tracking my movements ever since we left home. Crows were a dime a dozen in the Oracune Region, and they all sounded the same to my human ears.

I ate my metaphorical words a second later as a black shape emerged from the branches and made a beeline to Fleurette. He landed upon her outstretched arm and sidled up to her shoulder. Fleurette began to stroke his black feathers joyfully. "Rupert! Darling, I've missed you," Fleurette cooed at her corvid companion as he rubbed his face against her hair in a rather catlike manner.

"Where did he come from?" I asked. I kept a second question to myself: why did he follow us here?

I could not understand him while wearing this body, but Fleurette could, somehow. She stared at Rupert, as if decoding his language of chirps and cheeps. These articulations sounded much too high and delicate to rightfully be made with a crow's throat, but I knew from experience that crows had an amazing vocal range.

She shook her head after a couple of seconds. "He's not explaining anything. Just that he missed me and wanted to stay with me for a while. I'll take it."

I nodded and turned back around, ready to continue our hike.

The deeper we walked, the older the trees became, going from a young adult circumference that I could wrap my arms around in a full hug, to trees that were the original bones of the forest, great behemoths that stretched upwards and were a full ecosystem in and of themselves. Many of these ancient evergreens could have hidden our whole party comfortably inside, if they had been hollow. I had a feeling that few people had even laid eyes upon these beauties.

It was a full two hours of hiking before we stopped for a breather. We sat on the bare ground, eager to rest our legs after such an extended walk. It was almost comical; here, I had been complaining about sitting too long while in the MC, and now my legs were getting overworked. I couldn't determine which was worse: a sore butt or tired legs.

I checked my watch; the face showed 3:30. "Did anybody bring anything to eat?" I asked.

Fleurette reached into her pack and extended homemade granola bars to each of us. We sat in silence, chewing and soaking in the break.

I popped the remains of my bar in my mouth and stood. "I need to go tend to some things. I'll be right back."

"What are you going to do?" Gavin asked.

I looked at him. "Use the bathroom, for one thing. I thought I'd get a quick grooming session in as well. I'm all sweaty." Despite the coolness of the day, the exercise had made me perspire more than I enjoyed.

Gavin held up a hand. "Say no more."

I smiled and shimmered. Gavin looked away, my sudden change seeming to discomfort him. It was clear from his words and his actions that Gavin still had not fully welcomed the idea of my dual nature.

I thought back to when I had reunited my parents. My father, as mundy as Gavin was, instantly accepted my mother after he saw her true form. It was a sign that they really had true love. Gavin's reluctance to accept me in my true form was just another indicator that he and I were not meant to be. If only he saw that as well.

Brushing these musings of Gavin aside, I scampered a distance away, relishing the freedom of my feline form and keeping my senses alert. Grimm followed, respecting my privacy as I did my business and covered it. As soon as I was finished, I found a nice patch of moss in the sun and set to work cleaning my fur.

"It's nice out here," Grimm remarked as he lounged by my side, his snout sticking up in the air as he took a deep breath through his nostrils.

"I'm just glad it stopped snowing for once," I remarked as I stretched a back leg out in front of me. "Although, it makes me wonder if Annie's saving up her magic for something else. You never can tell until things go sideways."

"True, but—" Grimm stood up suddenly, his ears pricked forward. "Trouble, Cress."

"Trouble?" I asked, but Grimm was already running back the way we came. Only then did the smell of wild animal fill my nostrils. "Freya's furs."

I changed back into human and grabbed Talon from my side before I sprinted after Grimm, emerging into the small clearing to find my three human companions huddled together, fear shining in each face. Grimm positioned himself in front of them, hackles raised. Beyond him, at the far edge of the clearing, stood two of the biggest wolves I had ever seen.

CHAPTER 8

The wolves crouched with heads low, teeth bared. Grimm copied their position, issuing a deep and menacing growl. I glanced from him to the wolves, noting that they were almost evenly matched in size. I had no doubts about Grimm's fighting ability. After all, he tussled with werewolves larger than himself on a regular basis. But two wolves? I didn't like those odds.

I decided to intervene. Quickly, I shrank down into cat form and darted to Grimm's side. Fleurette made a noise of disapproval, but made no move to stop me.

Now that I was here, however, I wasn't sure what to do. My body had the tendency to act before my brain was ready. How could I diffuse this situation?

"Hey, wolves," I called out, trying to keep my body language friendly.

They ignored me. The one on the left, a brownish gray specimen, kept his eyes on Grimm. "You are trespassing. This is *our* territory."

I tried for friendly conversation again. "Yeah, see, that's why we're here, actually. We are trying to fi—"

The other wolf, a dark smoky color, let out a roar. "Shut up, cat! I'll destroy you!"

His warning was so over the top, I almost couldn't take it seriously. This wolf sounded like a kid play-acting as a wolf.

Grimm did not take his words as flippantly as I did, however. He lifted his lips even higher and lunged slightly at the darker wolf. "Touch her and I'll kill you," he threatened with a deep bark.

Apparently the threat was the last straw for the wolves. They growled and charged forward. I screeched and fled to the side as Grimm raced to meet them in the middle. The clearing erupted in snarls and growls as Grimm battled the two wolves. He bit and fought with fury, but as I had dreaded, two against one was not a fair fight. While he lunged at one with a solid bite to the shoulder, the second came from behind and got a mouthful of black fur from my canine companion's backside.

All the while, I begged for the wolves to listen to us, that this was all a misunderstanding. But my pleas fell on angry, deaf ears.

I felt terrible for fleeing while Grimm took a beating, but my feline body would not help him in this situation, and in fact, I surmised I would only get mauled in the process. Perhaps my human form would be better—after all, I had Talon. But I was loath to cause serious injury to these wolves, and I worried about missing them with my sword and accidentally hitting Grimm. Still, it would be better to *do* something rather than watch my true love be battered like this.

That last line of thought made up my mind. I got ready to shift.

But before I could, another figure emerged at the clearing edges, barely noticeable due to its small, low-to-the-ground profile. An otter.

Without a shred of fear, the otter ran straight into the fight and attached her jaws around the nearest ear of the lighter-colored wolf, the one who had attacked Grimm from behind. He let out a yelp of pain and tried to shake her off, but she clung on fiercely.

"Stop this at once!" she exclaimed angrily as she continued to clamp her teeth upon his ear.

The wolf let out a howl, chagrined, and slunk away from Grimm. The second wolf saw the otter through his haze of anger and backed off as well, despite having the upper hand in the fight. Once the brawl stopped, the otter let go of the first wolf's ear.

"What is wrong with you two?" she hissed at them, moving to fill the space between Grimm and the wolves. She raised herself on her back legs, her head barely reaching the wolves' shoulders. Astoundingly, instead of attacking her, both wolves lowered their heads submissively. "These are not trespassers! They are friends. Can you not feel our magic upon the older man?"

"He must have stolen it," the light gray wolf mumbled.

The otter let out a squeaky growl. "How, you crumb? Can you smell a lick of his own magic upon him? I don't think so. Did you two bumbleheads even think to talk to them in person before attacking?"

Both wolves lowered their heads even more. Their tails began to tuck behind their back legs.

I couldn't believe it. This small otter had completely cowed two vicious wolves.

I immediately liked her.

She snorted at their reaction, taking it as a silent answer. "I didn't think so. That would have required using the brain Loki gifted you. You two have really stepped in it this time."

"Don't tell Dad," one of them begged with a slight tail wag.

"I don't need to. You're going to tell him. Or they will." She motioned her sleek head to the humans behind her.

At that declaration, the wolves lowered themselves all the way to their bellies, fawning in front of the otter. It was as impressive as it was absurd to witness.

Satisfied with the wolves' reaction, the otter turned toward me, pert and friendly as she fell to all fours again. "I apologize.

Do you mind switching bodies, though?"

I blinked, startled. "Um, sure."

I transformed, a bit shaken up by the wolf fight and this unexpected savior. She didn't allow me much time to reflect, however. She stood upon her hind legs again, stretching her body up with her thick tail used for balance. And then she continued to stretch upward, her limbs lengthening, her body growing, her fur disappearing.

Within two seconds, a woman stood before me, stark naked. Slender yet well-muscled, I would have recognized her anywhere, even though the last time I saw her, she had purple streaks in her dark hair.

"Rosa," I said, walking toward her.

She smiled and opened her arms in greeting. I was not a hugger, and embracing naked women was even further down my list of desired activities, but I at least clasped her arms, which she mirrored with mine. "Cressida. It's nice to see you again. I thought I recognized that hair. And Grimm, my favorite pony."

Grimm responded by wagging his tail and limping over to lick her outstretched hand.

Rosa straightened after greeting him. "Roger, I felt you coming. I tried to beat these two idiots here, but their legs are longer than mine. Plus, *they don't listen.*" She snarled this last line in their direction. One of the wolves whimpered. She turned back to my father. "I do apologize for my brothers."

"Brothers?" I repeated.

She nodded. "Half-brothers, technically. Ty and Miles. They let their 'superior' wolfish ways get to their heads sometimes."

Roger cleared his throat, a blush encompassing his features as he kept his eyes trained on the woman's face. "Rosa, it's very nice to see you again. I'm sorry for barging in like this. My daughter needs your help, though." He gestured at me.

"Your daughter?" Rosa turned to look at me again, her eyes sparkling with this new information. "Roger is your father?"

I smiled with a nod. "He didn't know of our relationship until after we rescued you two from Addelboro Correctional Facility. It's why he didn't mention it before."

Rosa grinned. "Small world."

Fleurette stepped forward. "I've heard much about you, Rosa," she said, sticking out her hand. "Cressida mentioned an otter with purple streaks on her head, similar to a taxi driver she met in Dogwood. I'm Fleurette, Cressida's friend and one of the people tasked with protecting her. Although she's decent at protecting herself."

"I can see that," Rosa observed, giving the sword at my side a once-over. "It's nice to meet you."

She looked past Fleurette, at Gavin, who had been completely silent during this entire exchange. Rosa's face broke out into a wide smile, transforming her whole demeanor from tensely polite, to fully radiant.

"You," she breathed. She strode unashamedly over to him, grabbed the lapels of his coat, pulled him forward, and kissed him on the mouth.

Gavin did not pull away, but stood and allowed it to happen with wide eyes. We watched in stunned silence at Rosa's bold greeting. When she finally leaned away, she gave him a cheeky grin. "I never got to thank you for saving my life last year," she told him. "Thank you."

Bemused, I said, "Rosa, this is Gavin, a fellow bounty hunter."

Gavin finally unstoppered his tongue. "A pleasure to meet you officially. Truly."

I rolled my eyes.

Rosa gave him a playful push. "I'm sure you say that to all the naked women who kiss you."

Gavin's eyes twinkled. "Only the beautiful ones."

"Say, Rosa," I said to interrupt this flirtfest, "do we have your permission to enter the shifter village? We need to talk to whoever is in charge. It's kind of important."

She stopped gazing at Gavin and stepped toward me again. "Of course. I was on my way to collect you for that reason. Roger was my responsibility, after all. They already know he is on the way. You all will be a surprise, but easily explainable."

"Excellent," I said, breathing a deep sigh of relief. "Lead the way."

Rosa turned to the wolves, who had gotten back up but still eyed us with a glint of animosity. I had the feeling I'd have to watch out for those two, brothers of a friend or not. Rosa ignored their sullen stares and barked orders. "Miles, Ty, go ahead of us and let Dad and Aunt Endy know we're on our way."

The darker wolf stretched upward, his body rearranging and morphing until a young man stood in the buff. Just like Rosa, he seemed to be unashamed by his lack of clothes. I imagined that when one must change shapes as often as these people did, there was no social taboo over being naked around others. It was simply a way of life.

The young man seemed barely older than Fal, his dark hair chin length and his body well-toned. A smattering of stubble graced his jaw. He had a gash on one cheek that smeared blood liberally upon his face, as well as a bleeding bite on his shoulder and few scratches on his neck and chest, but he paid them no mind. He scowled heavily at Rosa.

"Since when do you get to boss us around, spraint?" He sneered at his sister.

She narrowed her eyes. "Careful, dogbrain. You aren't a prince yet."

He huffed and let out a growl that sounded very wolfish.

"Don't insult me! I'm not a dog. That's a dog," he retorted, pointing at Grimm, who once again stood in an alert position, ready to defend us.

"Yes, and he's twice the animal you are. So get out of here before I allow him to finish you off. Coward," she added with spite.

The shifter looked as if he might attack her for those choice words, but Rosa's dark gaze was steely, and she stood poised with Grimm by her side. He deflated, morphed back into the dark wolf, and slunk back into the woods, with the lighter wolf at his heels.

Rosa breathed a deep sigh. "Sorry about that. That was Ty. My brothers are nice boys, sometimes, but Dad is starting to show his age and there will be a new prince chosen soon. The possibility of power has gone to Ty's head, and he's dragged Miles down with it."

References to princes whooshed over my head, but I simply nodded. I assumed I'd be filled in eventually.

She motioned for us to follow her, turning her back to us to walk into the woods and away from the scene.

I turned to Grimm, eyeing his condition carefully. "Are you okay? Can you walk?"

Grimm let out a chuff and wagged his tail. Despite his assurances, I watched him carefully as he followed Rosa. He had a slight limp, but I was satisfied that he could make the rest of the trip unassisted. We all trailed after the shifter.

Just beyond the edge of the clearing, she stooped and picked up a bundle that had been left on the ground. She shook it out into three separate robes, two of which she allowed to flutter to the ground. Rosa put on the third, finally covering her nakedness.

I'm sure Gavin was sad about that. Every time I glanced at the man he had his eyes fixed upon her with appreciation.

"This way," she said with cheer.

"Should we take those with us?" Fleurette asked, pointing to the robes.

Rosa tossed her hand in negation. "Leave them. I brought them for my pigheaded brothers to wear, but since they made asses of themselves it serves them right if their clothing gets rained on." She continued walking.

We did as she bade and followed. I scampered a bit to catch up with her.

"What happened to the purple?" I asked, pointing at her lustrous, chocolate brown locks.

She picked up a tress and laughed. "Hair dye, magical or not, is not so easy to come by in the middle of the forest. I had to give it up when I rejoined the village, and the color's long since faded. I do miss it, though."

She turned toward me. "Not to pry, but it seems to me that when we last met, you were trying your hardest to pretend to be a mundane human. Now I see you changing forms in front of your group. Are you done pretending?"

I tensed. It had been ingrained into me to deny my true form to others. Rosa had seen me change shape, and she did not act surprised in the slightest. Did she already know my secret?

"How do *you* know what I am?" I asked her carefully.

She shrugged. "Like recognizes like, I suppose. I got the feeling that you were more than you let on to be in Dogwood. And then when you and Mr. Handsome over there—"

"Gavin," I supplied.

"When you and Gavin rescued us, you did your best to hide your form. But when I was in that little cage, I could see out the window in the door. Not much, mind you, but I could see you as a human, and then you tried to wallop that awful elemental, but he stopped you. He stayed in frame, but suddenly he was attacked by a small white cat that screamed like a banshee. And then you popped back as a human. I put two and two together, and my suspicions were confirmed after talking to a couple of the cats you helped escape. They mentioned your smell."

"Hmm." My innate magic had an unusual smell to it that marked me as different from mundane cats.

"It's not the first time my kind has had contact with your kind, either, so you aren't exactly a surprise."

Shocked, I glanced up at her. She smiled knowingly. "How?" I blurted. "When?"

Rosa shrugged. "I'll let Nana tell you about it."

"Who?"

"My grandmother. She can fill you in better than I could, since it was so long ago."

I let that rattle around in my head as our hike stretched out. I truly knew nothing about who my ancestors were, what they did, or where they lived. It was more than possible that at least one of them would have come into contact with shifters.

My stomach soured as I walked. I thought it might be nerves over what Rosa had told me. Usually my anxiety was not enough to assault me with a roiling, clenching nausea, though.

From behind me, Gavin called out, "Um, Miss? Do you think we could stop for a moment? I'm not feeling great."

Our party stopped at his words. I turned to look at him, and sure enough, he looked a little green around the gills. Grimm let out a whine of discomfort as he nuzzled my hand.

Fleurette clutched her midsection with a wince. "I thought I was the only one."

"Food poisoning?" I ventured, the nausea creeping in intensity. We had just consumed her granola bars, after all. I glanced at each of my companions. Only my father seemed unaffected. He frowned in concern.

"Rosa, what's going on?" he asked.

She patted my shoulder. "It's a spell we have placed on the outskirts of the village, for extra protection. I almost forgot about it. Dad gave me some chews to counteract the spell. Here ..." She fumbled into a pocket of her robe while my stomach clenched painfully. After a moment she withdrew her hand with two small objects wrapped in waxed paper. She unwrapped one, exposing a cream-colored cube, which she artfully pulled into two imperfect halves, handing one to me and offering the other to Grimm.

It was slightly gooey in my hand. "What is it?" I asked, trying not to moan with discomfort.

"You chew it and swallow. It will help you feel better, even though you only get a half dose. Sorry, I wasn't expecting such a crowd," Rosa explained as she split the second one and gave the pieces to Fleurette and Gavin.

"Why haven't I been affected?" Dad asked. Knowing him, he felt guilty that he wasn't in queasy pain like the rest of us.

Rosa smiled. "You have already been accepted at the village. This spell only affects outsiders. We added this extra securi-ty measure after I got back from the prison, so you didn't go through with this the first time anyway."

"Ah, that makes sense."

I chewed on the glob. It was sweet and gingery, not unpleasant in the slightest. As I swallowed, my stomach gave one last churn before settling. A low-grade nausea still simmered, but it was better than before.

My companions also recovered, enough so that we could con-tinue to walk without complete pain. Rosa urged us forward again.

"Rosa, that's quite the spell. How did you come up with that, and who performed it?" Fleurette asked, her inquisitive mind always at work.

Rosa turned around, her bare feet still sure on the uneven path as she walked backwards. Her mouth quirked into a wry smile. "Shifter secrets. Sorry."

"Understandable," Fleurette commented.

Within fifteen minutes, my keen ears picked up the sounds of civilization: people talking, goats bleating, children laughing. The barely discernible path opened into a wider walkway, clearly well-used by the packed dirt and visible edges. The path guided us on a slight incline, and the hill blocked our view of anything else.

Rosa turned suddenly when we were halfway up the hill. "Ladies, gentlemen, almost there. Let's go!"

She turned and dashed the rest of the way up the slope. Grimm was delighted to follow her at a swifter pace, and I too found myself eager to crest the hill. Leaving the other three behind, I pumped my legs to chase after the shifter and my companion, and then the three of us stopped at the apex.

The shifter village lay before me at the same elevation. My eye first caught on a large central area surrounded by the most unusual buildings I had ever seen. Each one was of similar architecture, with the wooden plank face and back of the dwelling in the shape of an A, and the roof reaching all the way to the ground. The roof itself was not shingled, but rather lain with sod, and a lovely blanket of green grass grew upon each shelter. I counted four such dwellings on either side of the open communal area, with a much larger one at the far end directly in front of us. More houses filled in the spaces of the humanmade clearing behind these primary dwellings, almost as if afterthoughts. The planks on their faces appeared less weatherworn than their closer brethren, so I assumed they were of newer construction and added as the population expanded.

Benches made of split logs lined the central area and flanked a large fire pit in the center, and a few people sat at these now, peering over at us once they sensed our presence. A group of children ran about one of the houses, screaming with laughter as they tried to tag each other. A wolf lay near one of the green rooftops, lounging its white head against the slope in a patch of sun. A doe nimbly cropped the grass of another roof.

Farther out, past the dwellings, the clearing continued, showing off land that would be served as garden space once the weather cleared, and goat pasture, since I could hear the familiar bleats of the capricious animals coming from a structure that served as a barn.

Fleurette, Roger, and Gavin caught up to us. Rosa turned with a smile. "Welcome to Cedrus." She tugged on my sleeve, bidding me to walk with her into the heart of the village.

CHAPTER 9

Before we got very far into Cedrus, the white wolf tilted its head toward us, stood up slowly, and shifted into an old woman with hair as white as her wolf pelt had been. She picked up the robe she had been lounging upon and deftly wrapped it around her nudity before walking up to us.

Rosa placed a hand on my arm, halting me. She bowed her head a fraction toward the woman. "Nana, may I introduce you?"

Rosa's grandmother locked eyes with me and, other than holding up a hand for silence, ignored her granddaughter. Her gray eyes were keen, and they shrewdly inspected me. I felt a moment of misbehaving kitten nostalgia, but I stoically took her scrutiny. With a nod, she moved on to Fleurette, then Gavin. Finally, she held out her hands to my father, who grasped them with affection.

"Roger, you should not have brought them. But my, it's good to see you again," she said, her admonishment smoothing over with a smile for Dad.

He looked appropriately remorseful but returned her grin. "It's good to see you as well, Astrid. But I would not have brought them unless it was important." He reached out to me, holding onto my hand. "Astrid, this is my daughter, Cressida. And this is her friend and protector Fleurette, and her other friend Gavin, who helped rescue Rosa and me from the prison."

Astrid let out a small cry at that and advanced upon Gavin with open arms. Gavin, suspecting that he was about to be thanked in a similar fashion as Rosa, backed up a step before realizing his actions may be construed as rude. Astrid did indeed grasp him by his arms and pull him in for a kiss, but only on the cheek. "My boy, thank you! Rosa may be a headstrong idiot, but she is of my blood, and her safe return was much celebrated after hearing about her harrowing escape."

"Thanks, Nana," Rosa commented dryly.

Astrid turned back to me. "Cressida, I am in your debt as well. It is wonderful to meet you. All of you. I am Astrid, former prince of Cedrus. Come, come meet the others. You must have an official welcome with the princes."

Astrid hobbled away, toward the center of the village, where more people had congregated. The novelty of guests was too much of an attraction to pass up, apparently.

Rosa raised her eyebrows at me. "That's my nana," she said with a grin. "Don't worry, the rest of the introductions will be easier now that she's accepted you."

We followed the older lady as she moved deeper into the throng of shifters. Each one was now human, and they all wore odd clothing. Robes that wrapped around their bodies, or shapeless tunics that reached down to their ankles. I realized that when one lost their garments when one changed shape, clothing that was easy to take on and off without a lot of bells and whistles made a lot of sense. And it made me that much more appreciative of my interdimensional pocket, which allowed me to change bodies without the loss of my clothing.

Outside of the largest building, a man and a woman stood, waiting. Both looked to be the same age as my parents, mid to late forties if I had to guess. The man, tall and wide at the shoulders, had the darker tone of the people from Atlanuak, the country at Vinland's southern border. His long, white-streaked brown hair was worn in a bun, and his face sported a trimmed beard, also liberally frosted with white. The woman beside him was shorter and broader, but still well-muscled. Her round face was of a slightly lighter complexion, similar to Rosa's, but her hair was fading from a deep black into gray.

The man's more angular face and hair color gave away the fact that this was Rosa's father. I hazarded a guess that the woman was her mother, given the skin tone similarities, as well as a softening of her eyes when she laid them upon the otter shifter.

To the left of the man, I spied Rosa's brothers, now in human form and dressed in tunics that matched their father's garb. They eyed us sullenly as we approached, their faces still showing signs of the fight. Miles, the younger brother, held a towel up to his bleeding ear.

At the woman's side, a young woman and a teenaged boy stood solemnly, waiting for us to close the distance.

Astrid stopped in front of the two imposing figures and opened her arms wide. She swept them toward my party as she turned to address us and the gathering crowd at our back. "I present to you the princes of Cedrus: my son and daughter, Leander Vargas and Endelyn Brock. They have co-led us with great wisdom and determination ever since I stepped down from the role, some fifteen years ago."

My mind stuttered on the term "princes" again. Astrid had called them leaders. One was a woman, though. The term must apply to the leadership position, and did not mean a male heir to the throne as it did in other cultures. Until I learned more about shifters, I'd have to go with that assumption.

Leander bowed his head slowly at us, but kept his face neutral. "Welcome and be as friends until otherwise proven. I do believe you have already met my children, as my eldest walks among you, and my two sons skulk beside me with signs of battle upon their bodies. Let me assure you, it is not our custom to greet newcomers with violence, and I apologize for their behavior." He tossed a steely stare their way, and both boys ducked their heads. If they had been sporting their wolf bodies, their tails would have been tucked. "Rosa, I expect a full report from you in private once our guests have settled so that I can get to the bottom of this."

Rosa sighed. "I'm not their nursemaid. They're old enough to make their own decisions, and they should also be of enough maturity to tell you their story without involving me."

Ty snorted. "You just don't want to be a tattletale."

Rosa bared her teeth at her brother, but Leander whipped his head around to glare at his oldest son with such ferocity that even I wanted to tuck my tail. Ty quieted and stared at the ground again, his bravado failing in the face of his father's ire.

"Old enough or not, maturity has not quite grasped these two yet. You'd be smart to think about that for now, Ty. Now," he turned back to us with a much more pleasant mien, "I could not help but notice the beating these two took. Is anyone in your party injured? Or worse?"

I spoke up. "Sir, this is Grimm, my Lycanhund companion. He was the one to give them their wounds. He has a slight limp and a few bites on his face and back. Nothing serious. No one else was injured."

Leander inspected Grimm with interest. "A Lycanhund? Quite a rare find these days. It's no wonder my pups got a beating. Young lady, we have a healer in our midst. I would like for your Grimm to be seen by him once we are done here."

I nodded. "Thank you, sir."

He guffawed, the smile that went along with it transforming

his face. "Call me Leander. And who might you be?"

"I'm Cressida Curtain, Roger's daughter."

The woman, Endelyn, stepped forward, extending an arm. "I am delighted to meet you. Rosa told me about your part in her rescue last year. And to hear you are Roger's offspring? Well, even better!" She gestured behind her. "These are my children and Rosa's cousins, Linden and Zephyr."

I nodded a quick greeting to them, which they returned in a much more pleasant manner than Leander's sons did.

"You must be tired and perhaps a little sick from your journey here. Where is Jasper?" Leander called out to the crowd.

A small voice came from the back, "H-here, Prince."

Leander smiled beyond our heads and beckoned. "Come with us, Jasper. Please tend to the dog in the hall while we have a discussion with our new friends."

A young man with light gingery hair and a short beard slowly picked his way to the front of the crowd. He was much shorter than many of the individuals, with a slight build. Most of the people refused to move out of their way for him, so he had to skirt around them in order to join us.

He hunched his shoulders to appear even smaller in the presence of his leaders, but Rosa wrapped an arm around his neck in a comforting fashion, and he seemed to melt into her touch.

Leander turned and began walking toward the large dwelling in front of him. Endelyn motioned with a hand for us to follow before she accompanied her brother. Fleurette readily followed, but paused as Rupert launched himself off her shoulder and took to the sky once more. With a morose expression, she watched him disappear into the surrounding old growth before she entered the building.

Ty and Miles began to join them, but Rosa put up a hand to halt their motion.

"Not this time, boys," she told them firmly.

Ty scoffed. "What, the spraint and the coward get to listen in, but future princes don't?"

Jasper flinched at those words. Rosa narrowed her eyes. "You won't be future *anything* unless you begin using that thing between your ears. And I'd rather be otter dung than a piece of shit like you."

Ty's face flushed. He bared his teeth and began a lunge toward her, as Jasper hid behind her. She stood her ground, however, and I rushed to her side, as did Grimm. Ty frowned in confusion and backed up a step.

"Ty!" Leander barked from the hall entrance. "I did not invite you. Take your pack and go on a hunt for dinner."

Ty let out a wolfish whine but backed up further. Both he and Miles began to strip off their tunics. They rolled them into bundles that they flung at a random person in the crowd. In one quick motion, they hunched over until their arms nearly touched the ground, and then their bodies morphed into their wolf forms. The dark one, Ty, let out a small snarl in my direction before throwing his head back and letting out a loud howl. Seconds later, this was answered by several other howls from around the village. Ty and Miles trotted toward the fields, followed by five other wolves that had answered his call.

Rosa squeezed my arm. "Thanks for standing up for me. You didn't have to, though. Jas and I are used to dealing with those numbskulls. Aren't we?" she added, rubbing the top of the man's red hair.

His grin was shy. "I suppose so. It's nice to meet you. I'm Jasper, the village healer." He held out a hand.

I grasped it. "Cressida. Thanks for offering to patch Grimm up. Although, I'm not sure how well it will go, considering that healing magic usually only works on humans."

Jasper's grin gained an edge of confidence. "Normal healers, sure. But have you ever worked with a shifter healer?"

I chuckled. "I suppose not."

By now we had made our way to the entrance of the hall. Rosa stepped in ahead of me, and I urged Jasper to go next.

"Watch for the steps," he said as he slid past me.

I was confused at first, but then realized that the interior began three feet below ground, so there was a short flight of steps leading to the main floor. The hall had no windows, but plenty of light thanks to the many electric lanterns placed on the walls. There was a set of stairs leading up to a second floor as well, although we stayed on this ground floor, taking our seats at a set of wooden chairs that were arranged in a circle around a low table.

Jasper cleared his throat. "May I start my healing?"

I looked down at Grimm, who had remained close to my side throughout this whole event. "Go to him," I told him, searching his sunflower eyes. "He just wants to help."

Grimm made a small chuffing noise and limped over to the healer. Jasper eyed the dog with apprehension, given his massive size.

"He won't eat me, will he?" he asked with a tremor.

I stifled a laugh. "He won't eat you. He's not in the habit of eating people."

Endelyn snorted. "People, no, but I have a feeling he'd find Jasper's other form quite tasty."

Her words did nothing to sway Jasper's nerves. His hand trembled as he took shallow breaths.

I was struck by a duty to quell the nervous man's anxiety. "I promise Grimm won't harm you. My other form is quite small, so I can't imagine you will be much smaller."

Rosa only grinned.

My words seemed to be enough to put Jasper's mind at ease, for he shucked off his robe and began transforming. When he was done, he had shrunk down into a small rabbit with brown fur which glinted with undertones of reddish gold in the light of the lamps.

I suppose I was not expecting that. No wonder he was nervous.

The two animals stood nose to nose before Grimm slowly flopped to his side. Jasper hopped up onto his body and began placing his front paws upon Grimm's wounds. I couldn't see anything, but Grimm let out a sigh, and I could feel a spreading contentment through our bond. It was enough for me to stop worrying about his condition and to let the rabbit do his thing.

A woman with dark blonde hair in a braid down her back came over, bearing a tray with steaming mugs. She set them down on the low table in the center of the chairs. Leander smiled at her, and she paused, reaching out to grasp his outstretched hand.

"Let me introduce you to my mate, my wife, and the mother of my boys, Heloise," Leander said with pride. He turned to her. "You were missed at the greeting, love."

She smiled and nodded at each of us in welcome. "My apologies. I was in the kitchen and did not hear the ruckus."

"Please, stay," Leander insisted, pulling on his wife's arm toward the seat beside him. She let out a girlish laugh and complied.

"Shouldn't Thad be here too?" she asked, looking around.

Endelyn piped up, "He went off this morning to fish. He had no clue anything was happening today." She turned to us. "Thaddeus is my husband," she explained.

Leander made a noise in his throat. "Now that we are here, I'd like to know the reason for our friend Roger bringing you to our village. It is rather unheard of, you know."

I grimaced. "I apologize. I put him up to it. You see … hm, how do I start? I have a secret …"

Fleurette put a hand on my arm, stopping my useless rambling. "Princes, we come to you today to ask for assistance. Five hundred years ago, our world was on the brink of disaster, brought on by one witch with vast powers, Annie Coddle. Have you heard of her?"

Both leaders scrunched their brows. Endelyn cocked her head to the side. "There are stories passed down through the generations, told around campfires or on cold wintry nights. About the dark times, when all Vinlandian shifters lived in fear."

Fleurette tipped her head in acknowledgement. "Although most assume that Annie never existed, her impact left lasting scars upon our collective psyches. But Annie was indeed real, and is in fact still alive. She made herself immortal in a bid to become a ruling god for this world. The only thing that stopped her was her familiar. After the familiar banished Annie, it lost its immortality and became a mortal cat with one bit of magical talent left."

"The ability to change into a woman?" Astrid guessed.

I stared at her. "Yes. How did you know?"

She only winked at me, and then gave her attention back to Fleurette.

My friend continued, "This familiar passed down a legacy to her daughter and to the rest of her line: as long as there is a cat that walks as a woman, Annie Coddle cannot return to our world. Normally, we do everything in our power to keep the identity of this cat safe, but, well, this generation's cat has a penchant for trouble." She smirked at me.

Now that Fleurette had laid the groundwork, I once again took up the narrative. "I am the bearer of that legacy. I'm the cat that walks as a woman. And Annie is very close to making a comeback."

"How?" Leander asked.

I pursed my lips. "Her son managed to open a gateway between worlds. It's not enough to let her back in, but it's enough to allow the magic of this world to trickle into her magically void prison. I'm sure you've noticed the unusual weather since October?"

Endelyn and Leander both nodded, and the former added, "It hardly ever snows here, but it's been more common than not this winter. That was Annie's doing?"

I pulled the prophecy out of my vest pocket. "We've been battling against Annie's tricks for months now, and it's slowly draining us. We sought the help of a powerful seer, and she made this prophecy." I handed the paper to Leander.

He opened it with a blank look and then glanced at me. "What makes you think we can read?"

I blanched. "I-I'm sorry, I didn't think—"

Rosa interrupted me with an eye roll. "Dad! That joke wasn't funny when you did it to Roger either!"

Confused, I turned back to Leander to see his face split into a wide grin, and then he threw his head back and roared with laughter. Clearly, he held a higher opinion of his prank than I or Rosa did.

"I'm sorry. I rarely get the chance to mess with outsiders. Of course we can read." He cleared his throat as his demeanor became more serious and then carefully read the prophecy before passing it to his sister.

Endelyn's eyes widened as she read it. "This is why you are here?"

"We've decoded parts of the prophecy. It was the otter bit that got me thinking about the shifters."

Leander leaned forward. "You think Rosa is the otter that is needed?"

His sudden intensity discomfited me. "Well, yes. I have no

knowledge of other otters."

Rosa yanked the paper from her aunt. She devoured the words, raising her eyebrows as she got to the end. She handed the paper to me.

"'*Coney swift and otter sleek?*' Count us in."

The room erupted with several voices at once.

"Is that wise?" Leander asked.

"Rosa, you need our permission!" Endelyn objected.

The rabbit said nothing, but he stood up on his hind legs while still perched upon Grimm, his long ears sticking straight up and a look of alarm blossoming in his round eyes.

I added to the uproar. "*Us?*"

Rosa stood, holding out her hands for silence. She closed her eyes. "Out of the half-million people who live in Dogwood, Cressida found *me*. She sought *my* help in her search for her father. And I felt a connection with her. I didn't question it at the time, but now I know. We were meant to run into each other. I was put in her path for a purpose. I'll never be a prince. No one will respect an otter shifter, and definitely not an otter shifter whose mother wasn't a shifter. But maybe I was meant for a different destiny."

"But Rosa—" Leander tried to cut in.

"No, Dad. The timing is too perfect. I needed a break from shifter life, and left to find my way in Dogwood. Not three months later, Cressida comes along. I was supposed to be there, not hiding away in the woods."

"Hiding away in the woods is how we shifters have survived as a people!" Endelyn countered with a hint of ire in her voice.

Rosa shook her head. "The world is changing. Not everyone remembers why the war happened. Perhaps this is a sign that we need to start integrating back into regular society."

Her words tickled out a small idea. "'*Three camps to claim, split from the whole,'"* I murmured. Louder, I mused, "What if that's a part of it? Different people living separate from others, needing to seek each other? It clearly mentions uniting them to beat Annie."

Leander and Endelyn exchanged glances. He turned to look at me. "Do you understand what shifters have gone through?"

I shuffled in my chair. "Not exactly. My mother was light on the history lessons. All I know is that there was a war back in the late 19th century. They called it the Shifter War."

Leander scoffed. "A *war*. It was attempted genocide dressed up in a more palatable word. The humans tried their hardest to wipe us off the face of the planet."

"Why?" I asked.

Fleurette spoke up. "Shifters have been blamed for the emergence of werewolves, dearest. They suspect that the shifting ability somehow jumped from shifter wolves to ordinary humans, but it manifested as a disease that warped the shift into something terrifying. People assumed that all shifters naturally carried and spread lycanthropy to the population, and began to shun them or worse. Even before the war, shifters had been driven from most of their original locations."

Leander added, "That is why many shifter populations emigrated to Vinland after the continent was discovered. Too many wolf hunts in the old lands threatened our very lives. For a while, we lived in peace among the Indigenous populations and the human immigrants. Unfortunately, the old and deadly mindset eventually made its way here, resulting in the official war against us. These days, people understand that lycanthropy does not come directly from us, but still, we've become wary of outside interaction."

"I had no idea," I said with a heavy breath. "I can understand your reluctance if that's the case. But then why was Rosa living in Dogwood if it's frowned upon?"

"We have never denied our young the chance to go and explore. Cedrus is not a prison, and Endelyn and I are not jailers. Rosa needed a change of scenery, and as much as it pained me to see her go, she was free to do so."

Rosa did not add any words to clear up why she had left in the first place, but nodded her agreement at her father's speech. After a moment, she added, "I can understand that it's scary to move away from what is considered safe, Dad. But I agree with Cressida. The outside world could use us. Her prophecy needs us."

"There's that 'us' again," I said, rubbing my chin. "Who else are you volunteering?"

Rosa grinned. "My best friend, who happens to be a rabbit. The prophecy mentions both of us in the same breath. It's too much of a coincidence to be anyone else."

I swiveled my head to Jasper, who was timidly placing his paws on Grimm's bad leg. His ears vibrated under the tremors he currently possessed. What need did the prophecy have of a rabbit?

I frowned. "Rosa, there's no mention of a rabbit in the text. What are you talking about?"

Rosa narrowed her eyes at me. "What did you think a coney was? It's an old-world name for rabbit."

Coney swift and otter sleek. "Oh," I simply stated.

CHAPTER 10

I sat on a log bench in front of the communal fire, poring over the words on the page before me. It had only been two days since I received the prophecy, and I'd already read it a hundred times, it seemed. Still, I kept rereading the words until I had nearly memorized them. It was still mostly a muddle, but I was beginning to untangle some of those knots.

After the meeting with the princes—in which an enthusiastic Rosa and a reluctant Jasper agreed to assist us, and Leander and Endelyn continued to hold tight to the village for safety—we had been let free to roam Cedrus and given a promise of lodging for the night. Fleurette had run off with Heloise to chat about herbs and witchy things, and Roger was catching up with various villagers he'd met during his time here last year. Gavin had clung near to me for a time, but ultimately a gaggle of young women had absconded with him, and I did not want to think about what they were possibly doing.

Grimm, of course, sat by my side, enjoying the warmth of the fire. Jasper had done a bang-up job of healing him, I was happy to discover. The bite wounds were closed, and his leg no longer pained him. Jasper had taken an extra step to magic away the slightly sour stomachs we still had as well.

I had transformed into my cat form at the end of the meeting, to double-check Grimm's health. I did so without feeling a morsel of guilt at showing off my abilities in front of people, and in fact felt oddly at ease with shifting so freely in front of these perfect strangers. But in a way, I was one of them. Here, I was among dual-natured folk. For once, I was the normal one, and my human friends were the odd people out.

"How do you feel?" I'd asked Grimm as soon as I was a cat.

He'd stretched and wagged his tail. "Wonderful. Not a scratch on me. That rabbit knows his stuff."

"Good, because he'll be around us more in the near future. He's a part of the prophecy."

Grimm had cocked his head to one side. "You don't say. Well, who else do we need to find?"

I'd flicked my tail in thought. "I'm not sure. I'm starting to have a hard time keeping up."

And that was when I had the idea to borrow a writing implement. So now, I sat with the fire keeping me warm, a pencil in one hand and the paper spread out on my lap. I looked over what I had written:

A forest deep, a tree must forge - trees grow, not forged?
Time is due when blizzards gorge - gorge=eat?
A potion first you must provide
And murder dark to turn the tide - who do we need to kill??
The cat is key, the only one - Me
For which the gate can be undone
But by yourself, you'll not succeed
A ring of trust will do the deed
Three camps to claim, split from the whole - camps=groups?
Shifters? Who else?
Together, they will help your goal
Four strong of heart but magic dry - Lyle, Gavin, Roger, Kokoro
A searching, seeking, fated eye - Sufia??
Two halves, once whole, but torn apart

A mother's love to brace the heart - Mom
Two witches strong with magic green - Fleurette and ?
Ancient powers of fourteen
Brother, sister, birds alike - Fal & Wren
A yellow-hearted little tyke
Companion true and traitor lost - Grimm and ?
Wing of fire, Breath of frost
Coney swift and otter sleek - Jasper, Rosa
All these allies you must seek
For if you don't collect them all
The witch will win. Our world will fall. - And we don't want that!

I sighed. Still so many holes to fill.

Rosa plopped down on the bench next to me. "Hiya. Hanging in there?"

I nodded with a small smile. "I was never good at riddles."

She leaned over my shoulder to read my notes. "Hey, at least you have another line filled out. And I can offer a suggestion."

"What's that?" I asked, perking up.

"We have as close of a relationship as we can get to the nearest town, which happens to be a Memory Keeper town, Tlatskanai. Out of all the non-shifter folks, Memory Keepers are the most understanding and respectful of our ways. We live in harmony with nature, for the most part, and they respect that. Anyway, I'm not sure if you're aware, but most of the Indigenous people left our world when the first settlers arrived a thousand years ago."

"I'm aware. They were incredibly talented magic-wise, and left their land to the settlers to enter a new world all for them-selves. Which is why we call the remaining people Memory Keep-ers—they keep the memories of their people to continue the old ways."

"Yes, exactly. Did you know that they are also referred to as 'Ancient Ones?'"

"Yes, I'd heard that. Wait—" I traced down the lines with my finger. *Ancient powers of fourteen.* "Do you think ...?"

She nodded. "It's pretty likely, don't you think? And they keep themselves fairly separated from the rest of mainstream civilization. Many of them do, at any rate. So perhaps that's another camp you have to bring together with the rest of us."

I grinned as I added these notes. "Rosa, you're a genius!"

She shrugged one shoulder. "I get that sometimes." She studied me. "So, this is the real you. It must be nice to let it all hang out without worrying about your secret."

I chuckled. "You have no idea. Even letting some of the people I know in on it has been freeing. Like Gavin. It was so hard to be around him at times when I was pretending to be something I'm not."

"Yes, Gavin ..." Rosa replied. "Say, you two aren't a thing, are you? Did I accidentally step on some toes when I kissed him? It was not my intent if so."

Grimm, who had been resting his head by my feet, perked up and looked at me, as if eager to hear my reply. I laughed. "No, Gavin and I are not a thing, although he's made it clear he'd like us to be. My kind are 'one and done' in the love department, and Gavin didn't make the cut. He's a great guy, but we work better as just friends."

Rosa smiled. "I should have figured that out when the harem squad made off with him and you didn't bat an eye. That's what I call that friend group. There's six of them between the ages of nineteen and twenty-five, and they're attracted to anything with the proper anatomy."

"And that's not your friend group?" I teased.

She shuddered. "Nothing at all against them, but no. Shifters are known to be a bit … relaxed with sexual freedoms. Once we find our mate, we mate for life, but before that? Exploration is encouraged. In fact, don't be surprised if you get a few propositions tonight."

"They certainly will not be accepted," I said.

"And that's fine. Asking for a romantic encounter is acceptable, and so is being turned down. Our kind has a 'no means no' policy, and no one will be upset over a rejection, so don't worry about it. As for me, I'm a bit pickier than the average shifter. If I'm going to have a fun time, I want it to be with someone who might mean something more. So, no, no harem squad for me. But what about you? If you're not looking for love, does that mean you've already found it?"

I blushed. Feeling the way I felt for Grimm was natural to me. It worked in my mind. But saying it out loud to others was a different story.

"I fell in love with someone who has been with me every step of the way. I am not physically attracted to him, and we are completely incompatible for romance anyway, but I love him for who he is, and what he signifies. It's the type of love that means I couldn't imagine a life without him."

"Sounds amazing. Who is he?"

I ran a hand down Grimm's head between his ears. "It sounds weird, but it's Grimm."

She paused for a moment, watching us. "Cool. Not everyone needs the romance part in a loving relationship."

I sighed. "Well, technically, I do, or I will, at least. I'll need to have a kitten of my own to keep the legacy going. So something needs to change."

Rosa studied us for a moment longer. "I just remembered something I have to take care of. Be back later!" She rushed off toward the hall.

I smiled and continued to stroke Grimm's ear. She may be a wild card, but I was glad Rosa was on my side.

Rosa had been right: as soon as the feast began, I received no less than three different propositions for nighttime accommodations. Each man was incredibly respectful with his invitation, and politely backed off after I said no. There was no harassment, no objection to my rejection, simply acceptance. It was incredibly refreshing.

I was not the only one of my party to experience the shifter's interest. Fleurette had to blatantly tell two men that she did not swing that way, and when she was approached by a young woman, Fleurette explained kindly that she was already in a relationship. Dad seemed to have gone through this once before when Rosa had taken him here the first time, but he still had an older admirer hanging near him.

And then there was Gavin.

He flopped down on the bench beside me, letting out his breath in a whoosh. I had barely seen him since our earlier meeting with the princes, and he looked exhausted.

I picked at the meat on my plate, giving him the side-eye as I stuffed it in my mouth. "Tough day?"

A young woman handed him a plate with a cut of venison and chopped potatoes upon it. He smiled up at her and thanked her. As soon as she stopped hovering, he dropped his shoulders. "It's not every day that a group of women practically abducts you to try to have a six-way."

My eyes popped wide open. "*Try*? You mean you didn't take

them up on it?"

Gavin raised an eyebrow and mashed his lips to the side. "What kind of a cad do you take me for? If you recall, just hours ago I was trying to rekindle something with you."

"And if *you* recall, I outright rejected your attempt. You're a single man, Gavin. Live a little."

"After having their tongues shoved down my throat, I've lived all I can momentarily take. I've decided that I don't enjoy being treated like a piece of meat."

I picked up the largest cut on my plate and jiggled it at him. "Welcome to my world."

He smirked. "On behalf of all men, I apologize." He looked down at his food. "Say, there was a deer in the village earlier. You don't suppose we're eating her now, do you?"

Rosa, who had been coming up from behind us, laughed, causing us to turn quickly in our seats. "We aren't cannibals. I can't tell you who she is, but I can see her on the other side of the fire, enjoying the venison just as much as you are."

"Why can't you tell us who she is?" I asked.

At the same time, Gavin asked, "Deer shifters eat meat?"

Rosa blinked at our simultaneous questions. "Okay, let's see. Cressida, we have a rule around here. We are only allowed to reveal what our own animal is. Most shifters keep that information tight to their chest, outside of friends and family, of course. It is the absolute rudest behavior to out another shifter."

She turned to Gavin, her brilliant smile lighting up her face. "Yes, shifters of all types of animals eat meat. We do sometimes eat food while in animal form, and that would be the diet of said animal, but we are humans first, and humans are omnivores. Also, a deer shifter eating venison is not considered cannibalism. Eating a human would be, however. But we don't make a habit of eating our guests. Unless they're into that sort of thing, that is," she added with a wink directed at him.

Gavin's neck flushed. "Ahem. I see."

I turned back toward the fire, amused. Perhaps this Gavin problem would work itself out sooner than expected.

CHAPTER 11

After an evening of feasting and general merriment, I was ready to call it a night.

Shifters were generally not prone to guests staying in their village, but nevertheless they were gracious hosts, and they went out of their way to accommodate us, lending us the use of the great hall for our sleeping quarters. After all, each and every one of us had turned down offers for bed sharing from various shifters. Even Gavin, which somehow surprised me, given the rakish persona he liked to embody.

I wouldn't pass up the opportunity to give him a good ribbing over it, either. I clutched my hand to my chest in an exaggerated fashion. "I am shocked—shocked! That you did not take up any of those gorgeous women's offers."

Gavin shook his head with a rueful grin. "Maybe the right one didn't ask me. Stop tormenting me and do your cat thing. What's the plan for tomorrow?"

I rubbed my forehead, yawning. "The princes still aren't convinced that Rosa and Jasper should come with us. And Rosa mentioned talking to the Memory Keepers tomorrow, perhaps. Otherwise, we need to figure out the rest of these question marks."

"Well, I hope you have pleasant dreams in the meantime," he said, and pointed to the stairs. "Roger and I will be up here if you need us."

Fleurette came over with a bundle of blankets in her arms. "This is a charming place. I had no idea the shifters would be so friendly."

I pursed my lips. "They don't quite trust us yet. Rosa said that if a shifter trusts you, they'll show you their animal. Other than the meathead brothers and Astrid, I don't know what anyone else shifts into. We aren't part of the family yet, so to speak."

"Patience, dearest. Get some sleep." She began laying out her blankets, making a bed on a thin mattress lent to her, her shadows cast against the wall by the low light of a single lit lantern that hung near the door.

I shimmered, stretching my back and sighing deeply at the comfort my true body brought. Grimm approached and licked my ear, engulfing the side of my head with his tongue. He settled first, and I found my spot against his neck, purring and kneading a bit to settle myself.

"What's it like being around all of these people who can turn into animals?" he asked me.

"It's nice, but they're not the same as me. It's funny; I told Fleurette that I was a shifter when we first met, once I realized that she already knew I was different. Now, having met real shifters, I can see we aren't anything the same, really."

"How so?"

"I keep my clothes, for one thing."

He let out a quiet grunt. "Is that a big difference?"

"Of course." I rubbed my head on his jaw. "The only time I was ever naked in my human form was the first time I shifted. Shifters can't tuck their clothes away when they change forms, so they need to be naked every time. And most humans have hang-ups over that. It'd certainly make it harder for me to blend in, what with the way I switch bodies all the time."

"Hmm. What else?"

I pondered his question. "They don't shimmer, like me. They just ... morph. That by itself is very telling that we are two different things."

"You smell different, too. Like a cat."

His words amused me. "Oh yeah, smart aleck? What am I supposed to smell like?"

Grimm grumbled in his throat. "Like a cat. I'm just saying, these people smell of wilderness and magic, but overall they have a human scent. You smell of cat and magic. It's a big difference."

"Hm. Not one that most people would pick up on."

"Well, I'm not most people, am I?"

I licked his ear as he flopped his head down next to me. "Nope. You're even better."

I awoke in the early morning hours, if my inner clock was to be trusted. It was completely dark in the hall, however. The lamp that had been on all night was now off, and with no windows, it was hard to tell what time it actually was.

A knot of unease gripped my chest, although there did not seem to be any cause for it. Fleurette still slept near us, wrapped in her cocoon of blankets. But Grimm raised his head as soon as I stirred.

"What is it?" he asked, his tone edgy.

"Do you feel it too?"

He licked his lips. "Something isn't right. Is that what you're referring to?"

"Yeah. I can't say for sure, but I'm anxious." I paused, rotating my ears. "Let's get outside."

I shimmered quickly, rushing up the steps to the door. I opened it and surveyed the village. The light of day was still absent except for the barest hint of gray in the sky, congruent with my inner clock. Some of the villagers had stayed out later than us, and a couple of people had opted to sleep outside, either cuddled together under blankets for warmth, or fast asleep as their animal counterparts, as a large black bear, cougar, and coyote illustrated. The dregs of last night's fire still smoldered, helping the outside folk with warmth. All was quiet.

Too quiet.

"The birds," I murmured.

Normally by this hour, the feathered denizens of the forest were roused and ready to start the day with a cheerful cacophony of birdsong. This morning, not a cheep could be heard.

A growing dread settled in my stomach. Something was wrong.

"Grimm, we need to get Fleurette and the others—"

The bear woke with a start and a loud groan, and with a grace that contradicted her size, quickly stood on all fours. The cougar and coyote next to her also startled awake and leapt to their feet. The cougar transformed into a young woman and the coyote into a teen, and they both swiftly donned their tunics. I barely had time to recognize them as Linden and Zephyr, Rosa's cousins, before all hell broke loose.

The ground beneath me shook. I let out a yelp and crouched down, grasping both sides of the doorway. From inside, I heard Fleurette give a startled scream. This cry was echoed through the various dwellings on either side of us by multiple people.

Grimm whined and pressed against my body in an attempt to stabilize himself. I let go of the frame with one hand to wrap my arm around his neck, grasping him tightly.

The homes in front of me swayed as the ground under the

firepit buckled and cracked, a jagged fissure opening and running the length of the communal area. The bear roared and backed away, herding Linden and Zephyr away from the maw in the terrain.

Unfortunately, the couple in human form who had been sleeping close to the fire were not fast enough. As they tried to get out of the blankets, the ground crumbled, and they were both sent screaming into the earth.

"Cressida!" Fleurette yelled from behind me. I turned to see her stumbling on unsteady legs toward the steps. She crawled up them like an uncoordinated baby before collapsing at Grimm's side.

The hall groaned as it shimmied. The ground rumbled, an angry monster come to claim a sacrifice. Fleurette held on to Grimm and the doorframe, her disheveled hair hiding her face.

From somewhere behind the hall, a large boom echoed as something hit the field. The screams of frightened people and neighs and bleats of terror from the penned animals intensified as the shaking continued and more trees fell to the onslaught in the woods.

I could barely hear over the churning of earth, trees falling, and people crying out. And then, the hall shuddered as a deafening crash rent the air. The sound of splintering wood filled my ears, as did a shout of pained alarm from a man upstairs.

"Dad," I breathed. Without thinking, I transformed, slipping past Grimm and Fleurette, and bounded down the small flight of stairs and over to the set that led to the second floor, where Dad and Gavin had slept. My smaller body, while still being tossed about a bit, was much lower to the ground, and I navigated the stairs at a breakneck pace.

I had to stop at the top, however. A tree had landed on the roof and caved a part of it in. I examined the mess before me before gingerly picking my way through broken beams, dirt clods, and tree branches. Finally, I made it to the other side.

The tree had dislodged more of the roof than where it had fallen. Sheets of sod hung down from above, obstructing my view of the rest of the room. A man coughed from beyond the dirt curtain.

I transformed, crouching low to the ground as the floor continued to sway. "Dad! Gavin!"

"Cressida!" Gavin called back, coughing again.

I regained my cat body and crawled along the ground, pushing through the sod to the other side. Gavin was under a table, trying to wipe dirt out of his eyes. The sod must have hit him when it fell through the roof.

I quickly changed back to human and scrambled over to him on my hands and knees, joining him under the table. "Where's Roger?"

Gavin shook his head, wracked by another coughing fit. I looked around, finally seeing my father's prostrate form on the ground, half hidden by a fallen beam from the roof.

"No," I whispered, fearing the worst. Gavin reached out and clung to me, refusing to allow me to leave the relative safety the table provided.

Finally, the swaying stopped, and the groans of the buildings and rumbles of discontented earth ceased. A lamp that had miraculously stayed tethered to the wall blazed with sudden intensity.

Gavin let go of me, and I rushed over to my father. He lay on his back, his eyes closed, with the diagonal beam covering one of his arms. I knelt by his side, feeling for a pulse in his neck.

His heart beat at a steady rate, dissolving the worst of my fears. I placed my palm on his cheek.

"Dad, can you hear me?"

He groaned and moved his head slightly. "Belinda?"

"Close. It's Cress. Are you hurt?"

Roger grimaced at the question. "My arm. I can't move it. And when I try, it feels like knives stabbing into it."

I glanced over. Now that I was closer, I could see that the beam pinned his arm down where it rested against the floor. No wonder it hurt.

I bit my upper lip. "Stay put, and don't try to move. I'm going to get help."

My dad nodded, resting his head weakly against the wooden floor again.

I stood and nearly bumped into Gavin, who had snuck up behind me. "Keep an eye on him. I'm going to run downstairs."

He nodded and took up my vacated position at Roger's side.

I once again shimmered, certain that I would be faster in cat form. I zipped through the obstacle course that was the tree, and raced down the stairs, stopping in front of Fleurette.

"There you are," she told me as I regained my human form in front of her. "You scared me half to death when you darted up there."

"Sorry. Listen, a tree landed on the roof and Dad's been trapped by a fallen beam. We need to get him help."

Leander, who had been entering the hall as I said this, hummed in his throat. "I can help him. Let me round up my sister and a couple of others—"

I shook my head. "The tree is blocking the way. You couldn't fit. We need to remove the tree first to get to them."

"How?" Leander asked, his tone belying how overwhelmed he must have felt.

Fleurette huffed out a breath. "Let me investigate." She marched out of the hall.

I ran out of the hall after her. She skirted to the right and stopped to survey the damage. The tree, an old cedar, had stood on the outskirts of the village, but it was so tall that when it fell, the end of it hit the hall. It was no wonder it forcefully crashed through the roof like it did. Frankly, I was surprised it hadn't pancaked the whole building.

Fleurette rested her fist against the underside of her nose in thought. "I need to see the other end," she finally declared, and strode off towards the edge of the clearing.

Curious about her plans, I followed, looking around at the destruction the earthquake had wrought upon Cedrus. Surprisingly, most of the houses were intact, the wooden A-frame architecture apparently a hardy design when it came to earth-shaking events. Still, the villagers milled about in a daze, some helping their neighbors who were not quite as lucky to avoid injuries.

Fleurette stopped at the base of the old tree. It leaned over at a thirty-degree angle. Half of the roots were yanked out of the ground, lifted high into the air like tentacles. But the other half still clung deep to the earth. Fleurette studied the mess intently.

"Can you do anything about it?" I asked her.

She did not look at me, but kept her eyes on the roots. "I might be able to. It's a big task, though."

She took a deep breath, closing her eyes. Then, with a concentrated determination, she placed her hands on the rough bark of the tree, about five feet away from the root system.

I'd seen Fleurette work her botanical magic on multiple plants over the past couple of years. She could make a dying plant come back to life, and tell a vine which way to go with a simple touch. Now, I witnessed the full power of her magic.

The ground quaked slightly, and I worried about aftershocks, but as soon as I saw the exposed roots shudder and writhe, I realized Fleurette's intention. The uncovered roots contorted and turned downward, seeking soil. A couple of smaller tendrils touched the ground and immediately began to grow and length-en, burrowing down into the dirt and encouraging surrounding roots to follow. Slowly, ever so slowly, the ripped-out roots re-seated themselves, and the giant tree moved a fraction toward a more upright position.

The entire time, Fleurette strained silently, her eyes pinched tightly closed and her forehead beading with sweat. The roots continued to dig down into the soil, strengthening the tree's hold, inching the cedar upright little by little.

Once the tree was fully vertical, Fleurette still poured her mag-ic into it, urging the roots to go ever deeper, anchoring it well. Finally, she severed her contact with the tree, collapsing back and landing on her rear with a heavy breath. She scrutinized the cedar intently.

The tree held.

A collective gasp sounded from behind us, causing me to star-tle and turn. An audience had formed while she worked, unbe-knownst to either of us. Each shifter's face held an expression of awe and wonder at the feat the witch had performed.

Fleurette took no notice, however. "Go and help your dad," she said to me, exhausted, her voice breathy.

An older man stepped forward. "Go," he told me, his eyes on Fleurette. "We'll tend to her."

I ran back into the heart of the village, where Leander, Ende-lyn, Ty, Miles, and Rosa stood, gaping at the now treeless hole in their hall. I tugged on Leander's arm to get his attention.

"I need your strongest villagers to help my dad, now!" I com-manded.

He shook off his astonished mien and turned to his sister. "Endy, run and grab Victor and Jasper. I'll meet you up there."

He bounded into the hall, taking the steps two at a time. I followed after him as quickly as I could, although my short human legs were no match for his powerful strides. Grimm also came along, patiently taking up the rear. Leander stopped at the top of the stairs, surveying the destruction. But other than a few loose branches and the fallen beams and sod, it was much easier to traverse the room.

"He's there, at the far end," I said, pointing to the beam that was trapping my father.

Leander nodded and picked his way through the debris on the floor. I echoed his footsteps, until we both stood near Roger. Gavin stood up, his demeanor shaken.

"How did you move the tree?" he asked with a slight tremor in his voice.

I replied, "Fleurette did it. Dad, how are you?"

Roger let out a grunt. "I've been better. Are you able to get this thing off of my arm?"

"Hang tight, Roger," Leander soothed. "We just need a couple more bodies to lift the beam."

Footsteps pounded up the stairs behind us. "We're here," Endelyn called out. She came into view, followed by a giant of a man who made Jasper look smaller than ever in comparison.

The man—I assumed he was Victor—glanced at me. "Are we doing this as animals, Prince?"

Leander shrugged, his keen eyes assessing the situation. "I will, since my strength is greater. We need you to be on standby, Victor, in case the roof starts to cave in. Hopefully, we won't need your expertise. Endy, I'll position myself under the beam. You lift with your bare arms, and I'll transform to take the weight onto my back. Victor, stand by. You—" he stared at Gavin, clearly trying to remember his name.

"Gavin," I supplied.

"Gavin, be prepared to drag Roger away from the beam. Actually, Cressida, why don't you take his other arm, and Gavin can take his feet. Ready?"

We scrambled into position. I grasped Dad's hand, holding tight. He gave me a squeeze of reassurance. Gavin moved down to his legs, ready to yank them out of harm's way. Leander and Endelyn disrobed. The male leader ducked under the beam, his shoulders directly under the slanting surface. Endelyn crouched at the end that rested on the floor, trapping my father.

She shifted first, her body growing larger, shiny black fur sprouting everywhere. Soon, she was a black bear, the same one I'd seen before the earthquake hit. She placed her front claws on the sides of the massive beam, ready to lift.

I must have misinterpreted what Leander had previously said. She wasn't using her bare arms; she was using her *bear* arms.

As she slowly began to lift the beam off of the floor, Leander also shifted, becoming a massive elk, minus the antlers, as it was the wrong season. His size grew to the point that the beam was pushed up by his tall shoulders. Within seconds, the huge pillar of wood lifted off the ground. Gavin and I pulled my father toward us, away from the shifters.

Gavin let go first and stood, backing up a few steps. Dad began to sit up before wincing in pain. I crouched down to help him as Jasper rushed forward, already shifting into his small rabbit form. He placed his paws on my father, eager to begin the healing.

An electric scream came from Leander, clearly a warning. The beam had slipped down off his shoulders, and his neck was not strong enough to stop its trajectory. With its new positioning, the shaft of wood fully detached from the ceiling and rolled off of Leander's neck. I watched in horror as the massive plank of timber came rushing toward me, Jasper, and my dad.

CHAPTER 12

We would be crushed if the beam hit us. I didn't think; I only acted instinctually.

I gripped Dad's hand tightly. I grabbed onto Jasper's ears with my free hand and I shimmered, taking Dad and Jasper with me.

I held the shimmer, though, refusing to transform or go into my interdimensional pocket. It was surprisingly easy to do this time. My senses came back to me, and I saw everything happening around us. I also sensed alien presences with me, an odd sensation. The first was a bland flavor that was easy to ignore, but the second gave an impression of wild animal energy and a soothing sensation of healing magic.

The beam crashed to the floor as it flipped off Leander's lowered neck, hitting the spot in which we currently shimmered and going through us. It bounced and rolled two feet further, clearing our area.

I let go of the shimmer state, urging my human body and Jasper and Roger's to come back. My control over the situation allowed this to happen, a curious new development that I hadn't had time to explore since Kitty had unlocked my interdimensional pocket for me. We materialized in the same position we had been in before, with the beam a foot away from my back.

All eyes stared at us in shock, but I ignored them. Instead, I let go of Jasper's ears and checked over my dad.

"Sweet Freya, are you okay?" I asked the both of them.

Roger's eyes were wide and his face pale, but a slow smile dawned on his face. "How did you do that?"

I shook my head, at a loss for words momentarily. "I don't know. I just did it."

Jasper transformed back into his human body, crouched on Roger's other side. "What *was* that?"

I let out a chuckle brought on by sheer nerves. "That was my shimmer state. It's my in-between form. The closest form to a true familiar I can get."

Jasper gaped at me. "That—that was *incredible*. And you saved my life too. I wasn't looking forward to being a rabbit pancake."

"Sweetheart, that was amazing. I was here, but ... not." Dad ran his undamaged hand down the side of my head with fatherly love.

For a man who hadn't become a father until the age of forty-two, and then didn't know of his daughter's existence until the age of forty-four, Roger sure had an excellent grasp of fatherhood. I felt seen and loved in that moment.

Still, I worried. "You two are really okay?"

Jasper nodded eagerly. "I feel great. Roger?"

Dad began to nod, but grimaced as he tried to move his right arm, the one that had been pinned. Jasper placed a careful hand on his shoulder. "Roger, your arm is clearly broken. Can you stand? I'd like to get you out of here to a safer place to start your treatment."

Dad grunted at his forearm, which stuck out at an odd angle past the elbow. Without thinking, I placed a hand on his arm above the injury. A cool sensation slithered out of my fingertips and into Dad, who furrowed his brow as he glanced at our connection.

It only lasted the span of a breath before the sensation petered out.

"Cress, what did you just do?" Dad asked me, his voice laced with confusion. "The pain went away for a moment."

I looked at my hand. "I must have borrowed some of Jasper's magic. Jasper, do you feel any different?" My heart rate sped up as I thought through the implications. What if I had stripped Jasper of his healing powers?

The rabbit shifter only shook his head. "I feel fine. But let's get your dad to my house."

Assuaged for the moment, I stood first, and Gavin came forward to assist in helping Dad stand. Once upright, Jasper wrapped an arm around the older man's midsection, slowly guiding him to the stairs.

"We'll be in my house if you need us," he called out to us before navigating the steps. I watched them go with trepidation, still unsure if I had siphoned Jasper's healing powers from him. I supposed I'd hear if that were the case.

Leander cleared his throat. "Cressida, I've never seen anything like that before. If I hadn't already believed that you were special, I would now. You *and* your witch friend. It has been an honor to show you my animal."

I bowed my head, overwhelmed with a rush of gratitude that grabbed my throat and made it difficult to swallow. I willed the influx of burgeoning tears to retreat. "Thank you," I finally choked out.

Endelyn put a hand on my shoulder. "You knew the earthquake was coming, didn't you?"

I looked at her face, ignoring her nakedness from the neck down. "Yes and no. I knew something was wrong. I could sense it. But I couldn't figure out what it was until the shaking started."

I thought back to the earthquake. Had it only been fifteen minutes ago? The darkness of the hall should have tipped me off. But it was the light turning back on as soon as the shaking stopped that finally alerted me to what had actually happened.

"It's my fault," I stated.

Endelyn's brows creased. "What do you mean?"

I swept my arms out, gesturing at the damage to the upstairs hall. "This. My dad's arm. The people who have been injured or … killed." That last word nearly stuck in my throat. I scrunched my eyes closed, the guilt eating a hole into my psyche. "That wasn't a natural earthquake. It was Annie's."

Realization dawned in Gavin's eyes. "The lamp up here. It stayed lit all night, but it was off when the quake awoke us."

I nodded. "And it's lit again now. It turned on the second the shaking stopped." I took a deep breath. "She knows I'm here. She must."

Leander stiffened. "But, according to Fleurette, Annie has targeted towns that aren't anywhere near you before. What makes you think that it's not a coincidence this time?"

"I suppose I don't. It's just a gut feeling." I shook my head in resignation. "I need to talk with Fleurette."

We made our way back outside, where Leander and Endelyn immediately parted ways to aid the villagers. Gavin and I found Fleurette near the new rift that scored straight through the communal area. Her face was streaked with tears as she placed her hands on the ground. Three men and a woman stood behind her, concerned expressions marking each of their faces.

"Fleurette?" I softly called to her.

The woman turned to us. "She's searching for Mavis and Walker."

"Ah." Mavis and Walker must have been the two people who had fallen into the chasm when it first opened. I did not have high hopes for their survival.

Fleurette jerked her head up. She pointed off to the left, within the rift. "There. Hurry!"

The woman and men stripped quickly, turning into wolves. All four of them jumped into the fissure and began to furiously dig where Fleurette directed. Within seconds, one of them let out an excited bark, and the other three crowded around to focus on the spot. I watched as their digging produced a dirt-encrusted raccoon and a weaselly looking animal, both clinging together and seemingly asleep. Or dead.

The wolves became humans again, wasting no time in ferrying the limp animals out of the rift, placing them on the ground next to Fleurette. One of them yelled for Jasper, his voice panicked.

Jasper had been in his dwelling with Roger, but he ran out as soon as he heard his name. He took one look at the two unresponsive animals and shifted, not even bothering to remove his clothes first but simply hopping out of them. He raced to the ailing shifters and placed a paw on each, closing his round dark eyes as he did.

The weasel-like creature—a marten, I realized after a better look—let out a gasp and raised its head. The wolf woman crouched down to keep it still.

"Easy, Mavis," she soothed.

After a couple more gasping breaths, Mavis began breathing normally, and Jasper removed his paw from her to focus on the raccoon—Walker.

"C'mon, Walker," one of the men murmured. By now, a crowd had gathered, and the people muttered among themselves worriedly.

Mavis shifted, expanding in size until she was human again. She placed her hands on the racoon's head, tears running down her dirty cheeks. "It's because of him that I'm still alive," she uttered in a shaky voice. "After we fell in and the ground covered us, Walker told me to shift to my smaller size, to give me more room for an air pocket. He did the same, but he was bigger."

Jasper began pressing into Walker's side with both paws, the most furious rabbit I'd ever seen. Mavis dropped her head, her deep auburn hair hiding her face, but her bare shoulders shook with silent sobs. The wolf woman threw her head back and cried out a haunting song that seemed to blend a beautiful singing voice with the keening qualities of a wolf's howl, weaving them together into a dirge.

Jasper gave the prone body one last thump of his paws.

The raccoon gasped.

The crowd gasped with him.

My heart leaped with hope as the shifter gasped twice more, and then coughed. Jasper kept filling him with healing magic, helping Walker to breathe more efficiently. Finally, Jasper backed off.

If I'd had my concerns about stealing Jasper's magic, this was undeniable proof that I had only borrowed a smidgeon of it. A heavy weight lifted from my soul.

Walker shifted into his human form, and the village cheered. Mavis barely waited for him to be human again before hugging him and giving him a heartfelt kiss, which he returned with aplomb as he cried from the shock and joy of being alive.

Fleurette, meanwhile, had straightened, and she backed up until side by side with me.

"How did you find them?" I asked her, watching this touching reunion with tears threatening to fall.

She wiped her face with her sleeve. "They asked me to help, after seeing me fix the tree. I had no hope, but I used the roots in the ground to search for obstructions. I honestly can't believe it worked. Their shifting ability and quick thinking are the only reason they're still alive."

Her hands shook as she talked. I leaned in and engulfed her

in a reassuring embrace. "First the tree, then saving two shifters. You're amazing, Fleurette."

Rosa walked up to us, having heard my comment. "I think you both are amazing. If Dad and Aunt Endy refuse to help after that, nothing will sway them."

A vibration reverberated against Fleurette's side. I let her go and she fumbled into her skirt pocket, extracting her message mirror. She opened the device and frowned.

"We need to get back home," she remarked.

My heart pounded. "Is it the earthquake?"

Fleurette shook her head. "It's a green witch."

I narrowed my eyes, trying to make sense of her short sentence. "Say what?"

Fleurette looked up from her mirror, a bemused expression warring with the frown. "Kokoro said my advertisement worked. She went into the bakery first thing this morning—that's where we told any applicants to meet us—and there was a woman waiting there."

"You actually placed the ad?" I asked. "You do realize I was joking when I gave that solution."

She grinned wryly. "Yes, but the plan had merit. What other choice was there? Anyway, I'm hesitant to get excited over a single applicant. Kokoro seems to think this one's a shoo-in, but she'd like us to come home as soon as possible."

I raised my eyebrows. "Well, then, we'll need to wrap things up here fast, won't we?"

Leander and Endelyn were understanding of our need to leave quickly. They had their hands full, what with the damage to buildings, the huge rift in the middle of Cedrus, and the various injured villagers. I felt incredibly guilty leaving like this after being the cause of the destruction in the first place, but Endelyn waved my concern away.

"We don't fault you for this. We shifters have been on the tail end of troubles for so long that an earthquake is just a drop in the bucket. And you've already helped us so much. You, Fleurette, saved lives, not to mention the grandmother cedar. We love that tree; it's the reason my ancestor chose this location for his new village. And Cressida, your abilities saved not only yourself and your father, but Jasper too. You both are incredible."

I studied the bear shifter, my heart warm with her praise. "Thank you, Prince. I wish we could do more."

Leander and Endelyn exchanged glances. "Well, we have been talking. We'd like to officially welcome you into the pack."

"What do you mean?" I asked, intrigued.

Leander smiled. "You and your kin—Fleurette and Gavin and Grimm—will be allowed free access to Cedrus, if you agree to be spelled."

Fleurette bowed her head. "I can't speak for everyone, but I accept with a grateful heart. I'd like to come back to help rebuild where I can. Perhaps I can stabilize the sod roofs to help them grow after this destruction."

"Sign me up!" Gavin said with cheer.

I looked at Grimm, who wagged his tail. He didn't fully understand, but he felt the lightness in my heart at the gesture. I gave my attention back to the princes. "It would be an honor."

Endelyn smiled broadly. "Very well. Follow me, please."

She led us to one of the small houses at the outskirts of the village, the facade less faded than some of the others.

At our approach, a woman stepped out of the open doorway, a sleeping toddler attached to her back. Her nonchalant expression suggested she was not surprised to see us.

Leander introduced us to her. "Jenna is not a shifter, but she is a part of Cedrus. She is married to Victor. She also is a talented witch. She is the one who put the wards around our village and came up with the navigating spell. She will perform the spell now, so that you will always be able to find your way back here."

Jenna came to each of us, chanting a spell under her breath as she sprinkled a concoction of herbs onto our scalps. Lastly, she placed a gentle hand upon each of our heads with special words to complete the spell. As she said the words, a warm sensation slid from her palm into the crown of my head.

She stepped back. "It's finished. If you need to find Cedrus, you only need to turn your head from side to side until a feeling of rightness comes over you. Then, follow that direction."

"Thank you," I told her, smiling broadly at the witch.

With the spell in place, it was time to leave. There was just one problem with that plan: my father.

We headed to Jasper's abode to collect him, but Jasper met us at the door. "His arm was severely damaged by the size of the beam. If I weren't here, I'd say the chances would be high he'd need amputation. As it is, he'll be fine, but he needs rest. Walking anywhere for a couple of days is not in his best interest."

Dad called from the interior to corroborate Jasper's words. "I'm sorry, honey. I don't think I can make the trip right now."

Leander, who had followed us over, said, "I will send Jasper and Roger to you when they are ready. As it is, Jasper will be busy for a while, I suspect."

The rabbit shifter nodded wearily.

"And Cressida," Leander continued with his full attention on me, "you have our full support. If the earthquake was an example of what life with Annie Coddle would be like, we want nothing to do with her. The village of Cedrus will stand with you to do what is necessary to keep our world safe."

"Thank you," I said, my throat feeling suspiciously tight again.

"My sons will guide you back to your MC," he continued.

"What about Rosa?" I asked, unsure I liked the idea of her meathead brothers alone with us.

Rosa piped up, "I'm going to the Memory Keepers today. I will make your case for you, and travel with Jasper and Roger after."

I hugged her, happy to have made another true friend. She returned the hug with ferociousness.

"You got this, cat girl," she whispered into my shoulder.

Astrid walked us to the edge of the village, where Ty and Miles waited for us in their wolf bodies. She clucked her tongue. "You sure know how to shake up some old bones, girlie. You know, this isn't the first time my kind has come across your kind. The first time wasn't quite so momentous, though."

I turned to her, intrigued. "Can you tell me more?"

"It was my great-grandfather who knew your ancestor. He was an amazing man, the first prince of this village. Traveled across the country to found Cedrus and keep us safe, as the war died down. He met her while helping the woman who would become his wife, my great-grandmother. The cat ended up marrying her brother, so in a way, you and I are cousins." She chuckled.

There was so much of my own family that had been lost to history. Astrid's story took me back in time, even with so few details. "Was he a shifter? The brother?"

Astrid laughed. "No, a regular human. So was my great-grandmother. Shifters do marry outside their kind sometimes, as Jenna and my son's first mate are evidence of. But shifter genes are hardy, and nearly all babies born from such couples are also shifters."

"I had no idea."

"We tend not to share much about ourselves with outsiders. But back to what I was saying, Grand-grand, as I called him, was still here when I was born. He died when I was ten. A great storyteller. When he died, it was the end of an era." We arrived at the edge of the hill, the natural border of Cedrus. Astrid halted and grasped my hand, her own warm and smooth like a river rock laying in the sun. "This is where I stop. You take care and come back someday in one piece."

"I plan to," I promised.

CHAPTER 13

We made excellent time coming home. The wolf brothers were surprisingly respectful as they guided us back to the MC, and even bid us a kind farewell, morphing into their human bodies to do so. I saw for the first time that perhaps their tough exterior was more of a charade, a foolish bid to become the new leaders.

I sat next to Fleurette as she took her turn driving the first leg. She apparently had a few things to say to me.

"I've been giving it some thought, Cress. The potion we need to provide?"

"Yes?" I responded.

She took a deep breath as she watched the road. "What if it's to strengthen us?"

I chuckled. "What if you're meant to make a potion to turn us into biting ants that crawl up Annie's legs to leave welts on her bottom? Fleurette, I have no clue what we are supposed to be doing here. Your guess is as good as mine."

"First of all, I can't transform us into ants," Fleurette pointed out. "But the transforming bit is an interesting side topic. Rosa had something to say about it yesterday, and I've been diving deep into Mom's research. She mentions a Horten Gelbert often. He apparently did a lot of studying of werewolves. It's given me some ideas."

I widened my eyes at her. "You aren't thinking of messing around with werewolves like your dear mother, are you?"

"Of course not!" Fleurette gripped the wheel tighter. "I only meant that the concept of someone turning into something they're normally not for three days a month has some merit, that's all."

"How is that going to help us close the gate and stop Annie?" I asked, frowning in confusion.

She shook her head. "It's not. Forget I said anything. My idea is only half-baked at the moment. I need to stay home and do more research."

After that, she clammed up about potions and bewildering ideas.

Much later, Gavin dropped us off at the cottage, promising to return the MC to Lyle. We watched him drive away with the lights on to penetrate through the deepening gloom of evening, and then the three of us entered the house.

All seemed to be well and normal; we had seen no signs of damage past the village, so the earthquake truly was centered in the heart of Cedrus. It was too much of a coincidence to be anything but purposeful. But the cottage was in fine shape, and the glow from the everlasting flame warmed us as soon as we entered.

Wren was in a wingback chair, reading. She jumped up as soon as we opened the door, a childlike exuberance lighting her face. "You're back! Kokoro's in the dining room with our guests."

"Guests?" Fleurette repeated the word with confusion. "I was under the impression there was only one woman."

Wren gave a sly smile. "Oh, just go and see! It's too perfect."

Now full of suspense, Fleurette and I walked over to the dining room, leaving Wren in the sitting room where she went back to her reading. Kokoro had been busy in the kitchen, as delightful smells emanated from the oven, making my empty stomach gurgle. Curiosity would have to be assuaged first, however.

Kokoro sat at the table with a steaming mug in her hand, facing our direction. Another woman sat at the table as well, her back to us. I caught sight of golden blonde hair cropped into a pixie cut before the stranger turned in her seat to watch us enter.

Her brown eyes widened upon first glance, and she swiveled more in her seat to better view us. An odd bundle was strapped to her chest.

Kokoro set down her mug, stood, and rushed over to us, hugging Fleurette tightly. "I've missed you," she said into Fleurette's shoulder before straightening. "Let me introduce you."

Kokoro's oddly exuberant mood clashed with the subdued nature of the stranger. Nevertheless, the blonde woman stood up, the bulge on her front prominent.

"Fleurette, Cressida, this is Holly," Kokoro introduced, beaming. "And ..."

Holly's bundle moved. She peeled back a layer of fabric to display a tiny head covered in a fine layer of hair only slightly darker than my own.

"A baby!" I exclaimed.

Holly smiled at the sleeping infant. "This is Katinka. Tinka for short. She's four months old now." She looked back at me, letting the fabric cover up her baby again. "It's nice to meet you. Your last name isn't Curtain, is it?"

I paused my inspection of the baby at these words, the familiar anxiety over my secret strangling me for a second. I straightened and tried not to look too much like a deer in headlights.

Holly nodded, sensing my silence as an affirmative and continued. "I've been traveling around for the last two months after losing my house to the Dogwood flood. You're a bit of a celebrity around here. The last person I stayed with was a nice priest out in Fallon Creek. He told me a lovely young woman with black streaks in her hair saved him from a revenant."

My chest loosened. "Oh, yes. Father Quill …" His full name escaped me.

"Quillman. That's right. Anyway, I happened to be traveling this way and thought I'd stop in Knobby Hill. That's when I saw the ad, and since I was already here, I thought I'd see exactly what the job was."

The woman held herself with bearing, and she did not seem to give out smiles freely. I supposed a traveling lifestyle with a baby would be hard on anyone. Still, I needed to know if she was what we were looking for.

I glanced at Kokoro, who beamed at us. "Ko, is she right for the job?" I had to be careful how I spoke until we got to know Holly better.

Kokoro nodded enthusiastically. "Even better than you hoped! You see, Holly is the green witch."

"Excuse me?" the woman in question interrupted. Clearly, she had not been filled in during our absence.

I turned to Holly. "Kokoro has a gift. She can see the magic within someone and know not only the type, but the strength of the magic. She believes you are incredibly talented in botanical magic. Are you?"

Holly shifted where she stood. She shook off her reluctance and nodded.

"Could we have a demonstration?" Fleurette asked.

Another reluctant nod. Fleurette opened the back door and ushered us out until we all stood near her herb garden, which was fairly barren at the moment, given the winter weather.

Fleurette motioned to the yard in general. "Please, show us what you can do."

"This is the job interview, I take it?" the woman asked. She arched a brow at us, which I could see in the waning light, but may have been missed by Fleurette and Kokoro. "I'm not sure you'll appreciate my talent."

Fleurette produced a glowing will-o-the-wisp in her hand to counteract the deepening gloom. "I'm sure you'll do just fine," Fleurette assured her.

"Okay, then," Holly muttered. She raised her hands until they stretched out in front of her. She focused on the rosemary, the small evergreen having withstood the brunt of the seasonal changes.

I had watched Fleurette's plant magic in action many times: leaves became brighter, stems grew taller, roots moved, and vines shifted. I expected much of the same from Holly.

I was wrong.

The rosemary dulled, and seemed to shrink in on itself. Fleurette let out a gasp as the plant browned and withered, turning into a husk of itself before it completely fell apart and scattered on the ground. This was not the same plant magic that Fleurette had at all.

Holly wasn't finished, however. She closed her eyes and wrapped her hands around each other in the air. The smell of rosemary filled my nostrils as something formed between her hands. A sudden brightness filled the space she worked around, and the white light turned to green as it coalesced into a perfect, smaller, younger rosemary plant, complete with roots. Holly plucked it out of the air and handed it to Fleurette, who gaped at the action.

"What just happened?" I asked.

Holly shrugged her shoulders. "I can draw out the essence of a plant, store it in me, and basically create it from scratch, albeit smaller. I use some of the nutrients while I work my magic. You should plant that," she added to Fleurette.

Fleurette placed the new rosemary where the old one had sat. She worked her own magic to seat the roots and give the plant a boost, making it grow slightly before our eyes. Holly nodded.

"I figured you had plant magic as well. Your place screams 'herbalist,'" she said casually.

A frigid breeze blew through our little party. Fleurette straightened, the rosemary fully planted, and hugged herself. "Let's get back inside. It's much too cold out here to be hanging out."

We trudged back in and made our way to the sitting room. Wren was absent, probably in her room. I took one of the chairs, allowing Fleurette and Kokoro to sit together on the loveseat. Holly sat in the other chair, and Grimm parked himself between us. She removed her baby from the wrap carrier. Katinka was awake now, and looking about with wide, dark blue eyes.

Grimm's fervent interest in the tiny human filtered into me. I hadn't had the chance to be around babies, and they were a bit of an enigma to me. Tinka was cute, all right, but she seemed very fragile. Her round head seemed too big for her neck, and she could only sit up with her mother propping her. Katinka let out a few coos before smashing her fist into her mouth, sucking on it.

"Well, given that demonstration, I'd say you're perfect," Fleurette declared, once we were all settled.

Holly stared at her with the same stony face she'd exhibited since we met. "You're kidding."

Fleurette shook her head. "Not at all. Your botanical magic is ... unique, I'll give you that, but it's botanical all the same. I take it you can't do that to any other living organisms?"

Holly furrowed her brow. "No. Only plants."

"Good." Fleurette turned to Kokoro. "Was there something else?"

Kokoro nodded, her dark eyes beaming. "Holly fills the role of the green witch, but she brings with her another line we have not yet found."

"Another?" I asked. My voice rose as hope again blossomed and filled me with a sense of positivity.

Kokoro nodded. "When I look at Holly, I see a very strong green. No other colors, like Fleurette, just green. But the first time I saw her, I was mistaken. I thought she had a patch of yellow upon her chest."

"Yellow," I repeated, looking over at Holly again.

"Yes, but it is not Holly. It is her daughter." Kokoro motioned toward the drooling Katinka. "'Tyke' is slang for a small child. An infant is the smallest a child can get. And her heart. She glows a bright yellow!"

"*'A yellow-hearted little tyke,'*" I mused aloud. "She's a kharismorph?"

Kokoro shook her head, but then see-sawed her hand. "Not yet. Her color is still deep inside of her. But she will be."

"Excuse me, but what are you saying?" Holly butted in.

I turned to her. "Katinka will have the power to influence the emotions of others. She will be a kharismorph when her magic manifests."

Holly blanched. "She'll be an herbalist like me."

She clearly did not like what I was saying. I could understand that. After all, the only kharismorph I had known was Nic Hoterson, Fleurette's half-brother. We only knew each other for a handful of days, but he had heavily manipulated me during that time, to the point where I had almost artificially loved him.

Grimm had been my saving grace, but he'd nearly died for his efforts.

"Kokoro is very accurate with her gift," I told her as gently as I could.

Holly frowned. "Fine," she practically snapped, indicating that it was not fine, but she was ready to move on. "So, tell me. What's the job?"

CHAPTER 14

All my life, my mother had drilled into me that I had to keep what I was a secret.

This week, I bared myself to a whole village of shifters, no questions asked.

Now, granted, the leaders already had a good idea of what I was. But Holly? She was a perfect stranger. We knew nothing of her background, other than the fact that she was homeless, and she had a baby and strong magic.

I had been burned a couple of months before, trusting a complete stranger.

Still, if she and Katinka truly were a part of the prophecy, we had to tell her *something*.

"We are ... collaborating with some other people on a big project," I began. "It involves creating a solution to end the power outages and disasters our area has faced over the past few months."

Holly looked thoughtful as she leaned back in her chair. She loosened her button-up shirt and began nursing Katinka, who had started to root in hunger. Holly let out a breath as her baby latched.

"A magical team of sorts? I thought that might be the case. But how will my plant magic be useful? And why were you so gleeful over my daughter's potential magic?"

I exchanged a look with Fleurette. She raised her eyebrows and shrugged, handing the responsibility to me. I fished the prophecy out of my pocket, keeping my attention on the folded paper as I spoke my next words carefully. "Honestly, we don't know. We only have this to guide us. Now"—I held it up out of Holly's grasp as she leaned forward to receive it— "you are a perfect stranger to us. How can I trust you with this information?"

Holly sighed again, a look of defeat flitting across her face. "You have a choice. Either believe that I am here to help you and let me in on your weird little job, or don't believe me, in which case, I move on and that's that."

I worried at my upper lip as I stared into the woman's frank eyes. It was a stroke of luck to find a green witch and a child with a yellow heart in one go. Could I really pass up the opportunity?

No. I could not.

I passed her the paper. She unfolded it one-handed and read it over with a deep line tracking through her brow.

She looked up at me and handed the paper back. "This is bigger than putting out some proverbial fires, isn't it?"

My mouth in a tight line, I nodded in agreement.

Fleurette added, "This is about removing the oxygen in order to kill the main blaze, yes. It's a matter of survival, of preventing our world from suffering immense harm. We don't know the full gist, but we do know that you and Katinka are a part of this, one way or another."

Holly didn't seem convinced, her eyes darting first to me and then to Fleurette. "Do you have proof? How do I know you didn't just write this poem yourself?"

I bit the inside of my lip. "It's a prophecy, not a poem." I paused and pondered. Could I expect this stranger to take my word on something so ... so ... big, so crazy as this? No, no I could not. But how could I prove we were telling the truth?

I craned my upper body, peering behind my chair. There was one definitive bit of evidence to present to her. I stood up.

"Cress, are you sure?" Fleurette asked, her voice tight.

I strode the couple of feet over to the side table and plucked the crystal from its place. I studied the ethereal clear shard, weighing my options.

"I'm sure," I said, and opened the line of communication.

The crystal stayed silent as I sat back down. "Aaaannie," I crooned. "Annie? You there?"

Her tinny voice finally filled the confines of the room. "Trollop! Laggard! Just wait until I'm free; I can't wait to wring the life out of your puny, cat-brained skull—"

Well, she certainly did not waste her time insulting me this time. I quickly shut off the line of communication before she could give away my secrets.

I focused on Holly. "Was that enough for you?"

Her eyebrows raised. "That was her? The witch?"

I nodded. "She's trapped in a different dimension, but she's hellbent on coming back here, in case it wasn't obvious. I need to stop her, and I need that prophecy to do it. What do you say?"

Holly clasped the child closer to her, her eyes widening. "Is it safe?"

"Well ..." I grasped at what to say. "We can't promise anything. It might not be safe for everybody, because we honestly don't know how to stop the witch. But I can tell you from personal experience, *not* doing anything will definitely be unsafe."

Holly nodded, her lips in a tight line. "Do I need to make a decision at this moment?"

"Not at all," Fleurette assured her. "If you need time to think about it, please take it. In the meantime, do you have a place to stay?"

The blonde woman shook her head, her eyes downcast.

Kokoro chimed in, "You may stay in my home. It is above the bakery where I found you. I can stay here in the meantime."

Fleurette smiled warmly at her girlfriend and placed a hand over hers. "Thank you, Kokoro. Holly, no matter what you decide to do, I'd like for you to come here tomorrow. I'd be interested in getting to know how your magic works, if that's okay with you. And I have some research matters. I don't suppose you are versed in spellwork or potions?"

"Afraid not. My parents were not keen on letting me explore my talents once my main magic came through. But, now that I have a place to stay, I might as well take you up on your job offer. I'd be happy to assist in any way I can while I'm here."

Fleurette stood to shake her hand. "Welcome aboard."

A handful of days went by in a rather mundane fashion. Nothing catastrophic occurred in the Oracune Region, so I spent the time relaxing, catching up with Grimm and Lucky, and bouncing ideas around with the members of our forming group. This involved speculation about the various undetermined lines in the prophecy, specifically what kind of a potion we should provide, who needed to be murdered, and how exactly we were supposed to close the gate and keep Annie out. There was much disagreement over any topic we chose.

I also decided we needed a name for our growing group, but in true fashion no one could agree on what to call ourselves.

"Anti-Annies!" Wren proclaimed with a twinkle in her hazel eyes.

"The League of Allies," Fleurette added thoughtfully.

"How about Team Gatecrashers?" I added without a hint of

seriousness.

No compromises could seemingly be made, so we gave up, referring to ourselves as the allies, which in my mind was boring and anticlimactic.

Dad returned from the shifter village on the third day—alone, I noted with some dismay. He had been antsy to get back home and insisted on leaving once his arm was mostly healed, but Jasper was still needed in the aftermath of the earthquake. Dad promised that Jasper and Rosa would see us soon.

Fleurette took the time to research potions, poring over the various tomes she owned, including the new ones she had obtained after her mother died. She also made sure to invite Holly over each day to further explore the woman's unique botanical magic.

Holly stayed aloof around us, as if she had spent a lifetime experiencing the worst aspects life had to offer and she was waiting for the other shoe to drop with us. She kept a surface-deep friendliness about her, but anytime we asked personal questions, she'd evade the answers. It made me wary of her. We truly did not know a thing about the woman.

Still, she was helpful. She pointed out that the line about forging a tree sounded like it might pertain to her magic, except for the fact that she'd never tried to recreate anything larger than a blueberry bush. Fleurette grabbed the idea with both hands, as was her wont, and insisted that Holly set her sights on something bigger, starting with a small alder tree growing at the edge of her property.

It backfired horribly, leaving Holly to produce something very untree-like. She refused to try again.

Undaunted, Fleurette began preparations for a strength potion, like she had talked about in the MC.

Overall, the time spent was almost ... normal. It left me on edge, a sure sign that my life had gotten too chaotic as of late. As expected, though, the peace couldn't last.

On the fourth day, we had unexpected visitors.

Fleurette and Holly were out back, near the edge of her property, with Tinka strapped to her mother as usual. Kokoro had taken Humbert to Lyle's farm, where Lyle would pamper the old horse with some treatments to help with his scarring. Both kids were in school. I was keeping my human form more and more since Holly's arrival, not wishing to tip her off to my secret. And I just happened to be passing through the sitting room when the knock sounded on the door. I opened it.

"Are you Cressida Curtain?" the man in front of me asked before I could say anything.

I looked him over. He was a shorter man, middle-aged, with tan skin like Fleurette's, a rounded face, proud nose, and sleek black hair that fell like a sheet to his waist. He wore a long-sleeved tunic made of fur over cotton trousers.

A Memory Keeper.

I nodded, keeping my eyes riveted upon his impressive figure before looking past him to the three other people behind him. Two were men and one was a woman, all dressed similarly.

The front man accepted my nod and spoke again. "I am Towakh, and these are Olillie, Kwolann', and Tukwilla." He gestured at his companions. "We are council members of the Oracune Confederated Tribes."

I gave a reverent head nod to each member. "Please, come in," I said, moving to the side.

They accepted my invitation, shuffling into the sitting room.

Grimm stood in the kitchen entrance, his head cocked. He padded over to stand at my right hand as the council members took their seats at my bidding.

I pulled up a dining room chair and placed it near the front door where I could face both the nearest chair and the loveseat at a perpendicular. "Would anybody like something to drink?"

Tukwilla shook her head, her mouth in a neutral line. "Thank you, but no. We have matters of importance to discuss."

A flare of anxiety shot through my midsection, leaving a wake of nausea. "How can I help you?"

Towakh replied, "The town of Tlatskanai has requested a meeting with the council. One of their shifter neighbors had some interesting things to say involving you."

I gulped. "Yes, Rosa said she'd ask for their help. We weren't sure how to reach you, otherwise."

"You have knowledge of what is happening in our world?" asked one of the other men, a short and husky fellow with hair the same length as mine and a thin mustache.

"If you are referring to the unusual weather and natural disasters, yes."

The last man piped up, "And what about the barring of our own sacred site?"

A flare of hope replaced the anxiety. "I do have knowledge of this as well. A rather slimy lawyer by the name of Babcock used unseemly channels to take the site from you. He's dead, but another lawyer from the firm is still out there somewhere. We haven't found him yet. He may know more about it."

Tukwilla waved my words away. "We don't care about legality. *La Po'te Tamáhnowas* will always belong to us. What Kwolann' means is that we physically have been barred."

"In what way?" I asked, leaning forward.

The woman glanced at the floor in thought. "It is not very

high elevation, yet the snowstorms refuse to move. They fall constantly in a ring around the space. Too cold and too deep to cross. And dead people roam the outskirts, attacking anyone who goes near. It should be a place of worship. Now it is a cursed place."

"Revenants. Dead bodies brought back to animation. I know exactly what is happening there." I had not heard of any other graveyards being robbed of their dead, but perhaps Annie's revenant spell had been farther reaching than we'd originally thought. I paused, considering what to say next. "How much do you know about Annie Coddle?"

All four people closed their eyes, becoming still as statues. I furrowed my brow, perplexed by the action. One by one, they opened their eyes.

"What was that?" I asked.

The one called Kwolann' looked uneasy. I recognized the emotion, given it was exactly how I felt any time I had to decide how much of my secret to give to another. "There is a reason our people became known as the Memory Keepers after the Ancient Ones left. We members of the confederated council are carefully chosen. When we take up the mantle, the memories of the previous council members are given to us. These memories go back to the time when the settlers first arrived."

I blinked, trying to comprehend that new information. "Are you saying that you have first-hand knowledge of a thousand years ago?"

Olillie, the mustached man, nodded. "It is a heavy responsibility. But in this way, we can access our traditions and help our people. The Ancient Ones will never be forgotten as long as we are here."

"That's ... impressive. So just now, you were all accessing your memories?"

Tukwilla spoke up. "Yes. Any memories from before us are stored separately, otherwise the vastness of our knowledge would surely drive us mad. We simply have to bring up the full catalog of memories and then flip through them like pages of a book."

"And what did you find?"

They all exchanged glances. "The one called Annie Coddle was not in the Oracune Region during the last thousand years. We have no knowledge of her other than anecdotal reference from settlers from time to time."

I thought back to the night Holly joined us. If I could prove Annie's existence to her, I could do the same for this group. I stood and walked to the table to collect the crystal.

It was missing.

I was sure I'd put it back after Holly left that night. Where else could it be?

I quelled the rising panic as best I could, putting on an indifferent face for these strangers. I could panic later. "Hm. She became a bit of a myth through the years, so it's no surprise the settlers talked about her from time to time. But Annie was bad news, as I'm sure your Eastern counterparts could tell you. Suffice it to say, she is the reason for everything that has happened these past few months. There is an opening gateway in your sacred spot, and she is trying her hardest to come through it and take over this world."

Kwolann' nodded, as if expecting this. "That corresponds to what the small man said. He also mentioned you, and your importance to this dilemma."

I frowned. "I'm sorry, who now?"

Towakh grunted. "The small man. He came from the ring blizzard, half dead, just two days ago. We nursed him back to health, but he has spoken at length about a witch, a gateway, a prison, and impending doom. He also told us of you, Cressida, and your role as a cat. So, tell us, is there credence to the ramblings of a small yellow man?"

CHAPTER 15

The "small yellow man" happened to be outside with another member of the council. We all trooped back out, walking down Rabbit Hole Road a short distance to where they had been stationed.

I wasn't sure what to expect, in all honesty. I had stayed tight-lipped about the whole cat thing, instead asking to meet with the mystery man and figure out who—or what—he was before spilling my secret to more people.

As it turned out, the Memory Keepers had used their adjectives succinctly when describing the individual in question. As we approached, I discerned one man who was easily recognizable as one of the Indigenous people, and another who was decidedly not. Even from a distance, I could see that he was only two-thirds the size of the other man, and his skin was yellow. Not yellow like a jaundiced complexion, but a bright otherworldly hue reminiscent of goldenrods.

The council members led me straight to him. Up close, his appearance was even stranger. The individual was thin to the point of emaciation, his long neck almost birdlike. His nose was much too large for his gangly face, and his chin receded to nearly nothing. His hair was dark orange and his eyes a deep violet. He squinted at me shiftily under long dark lashes. A smattering of orange stubble graced his weaselly face.

He wore Memory Keeper clothing, much too big for his small frame. I wondered if he had shown up naked.

"Are you she?" he asked me in a voice that was almost feminine in timbre. It also held a manic tone that set me on guard.

I found it an odd sensation to tilt my head down at the man. "I suppose it depends on who 'she' is, and who you are."

He rubbed a hand down his face. From a distance, he had seemed perfectly proportioned in his small stature. Now that I had gotten a better look at him, I saw that his hands and feet were larger than they should be.

"You are the cat, the bane of the witch, yes?"

The more I talked to him, the less I enjoyed it. "Sir, I'd very much like to know how you might be familiar with who I am. I can neither deny nor confirm my identity until you offer more about your own circumstances." I couldn't explain why I was being so cagey, but there was something about this individual that made my metaphorical hackles stand at attention.

He took an exaggerated breath. "But there is no time, no time! My other half is in anguish while I am here!"

"Your other half?" I asked, hoping for clarification.

"She is still with the witch! Growing weaker by the hour, although the magic from this place helps. I can't live without her, though." He mashed his large hands into his eyes, a thin wail of despair escaping him.

I glanced at Olillie, who stood closest to me. "Is he okay?"

He shrugged. "He has said similar things to us. He must have left his beloved behind. It has left him broken, possibly in mind as well as spirit."

"Hey," I said gently, bending slightly to place a hand on his arm. The yellow man stiffened and lowered his hands to look at me. "It's okay. Can you tell me your name?"

He took another deep breath through his oversized nose. "Alfrothooll."

It took me a moment to understand that the syllables that came from his mouth formed his name. "Al-fro ..."

"Thooll. Yes. Alfrothooll. And Artali. But she is not here. Not here!" He began to wail again.

"No, please, listen. Is she with the witch? Annie?" I desperately wished for him to shut up. His keening was grating to my ears.

Alfrothooll sniffled. "Yes, my other half is still in the Crystal Graveyard. We tried to leave together, but the gate wasn't open enough, so we split apart. She begged me to go, as I am the stronger of us. But it hurt so much to leave her! I must get her back!"

He seemed to be winding himself up again. I was desperate to keep that from happening. "Okay, okay. I can help. I need to close the gate, but perhaps your girlfriend—wife—partner can get through before that."

"Close ... the gate? You mustn't! Not without my other half!" Alfrothooll began to take shallow breaths, a sheen of panic in his eyes.

I straightened, trying to get a handle on my frazzled nerves. This odd little man was beginning to wear on me.

"Cressida? What's going on?"

I spun, startled. Wren and Fal were coming up the road, walking home after school. Wren's inquisitive eyes landed first on the Memory Keepers, who fanned out at her approach, and then on Alfrothooll. She widened them further as she took in his unusual appearance.

I was hesitant to involve Wren and Fal in this particular discussion. But Wren was too quick for me. "Hello," she said to everyone, meeting each person's stares with a polite nod.

Alfrothooll craned his thin neck forward, watching her intently. He sniffed the air between them. A smile broke out on his face for the first time, making his thin countenance glow with a childlike wonder.

He turned to me. "Cat, you said you'd help my other half. But then you said you'd close the gate. This would doom her, and me as well. So, which is it?"

I raised my hands up on either side of me, at a loss. "I want to help you. I do. But the gate is the most important part. I must close it, no matter what."

The yellow man's face clouded over at my words. "Then, per-haps the court will help me. They put me in this mess in the first place. I'm sorry. You have a good heart, but I have no choice."

I didn't like his statement, not one bit. "Alfrothooll, what are you about to do?"

He ignored me, turning to Tukwilla. "Thank you for your care and hospitality."

Alarm bloomed upon the woman's face. "Wait, you are still under our—"

The strange individual grabbed Wren's arms. She shrieked, and then stilled, her body going rigid with her head thrown back and eyes closed. Fal cried out and tried to wrest her sister's arms from Alfrothooll's grasp. But the small man held on, a frown creasing his forehead.

I also tried to intervene, but the Memory Keepers crowded around, blocking me from reaching the Ramberts. Before I could get around them, the three intertwined people—Wren, Fal, and the strange yellow man—folded into themselves, and vanished from view.

Fleurette paced the front lawn, where we all stood in a panic.

She and Holly had come running as soon as she heard my yelling for help, quite surprised to find five Memory Keepers keeping me company. Kokoro had also joined us, having left Humbert at Lyle's. The three women had just received a rather garbled version of what had happened, told mostly by me while the strangers looked on.

"Let me get this straight," Fleurette said to the group at large. "This man. He grabbed Wren, Fal grabbed him, and all three disappeared?"

"They used Wren's magic. I'm sure of it," I confirmed. I had seen her take two men away in a similar fashion. The same folding motion was too much of a coincidence.

"But it wasn't her idea?" Fleurette asked, pausing her pacing to look at me.

I shook my head. "She seemed like she was in a trance from the moment he touched her. I think ... he was controlling her somehow."

"Okay." She pinched the bridge of her nose. "What did this man look like?"

"About this high," I recollected, holding my hand out to my chest, "really skinny with a big nose, and yellow."

"Yellow," Fleurette repeated in a deadpan.

"Mm-hm. With orange hair."

She blew out an exasperated breath. "And where did he come from?"

Towakh spoke up, "He came through the snowstorm that surrounds *La Po'te Tamáhnowas*. Our sacred site," he explained.

Fleurette perked up. "Sir, where is this located?"

The Memory Keepers shuffled about. Tukwilla answered with reluctance, "It is our knowledge only, and we do not tend to share with outsiders."

Fleurette nodded grimly. "I understand that. But don't you

see? This is where the gate has been opened. This is where Annie has been stealing our magic, where she intends to come back after she has done away with the last protector of this earth. If we are to stop her, we must do it there. The lives of your people will suffer just as much if she gets her way."

"We will consider this, but it must be discussed amongst the council," Kwolann' declared.

Fleurette bobbed her head slowly in acknowledgement. She turned to me. "I think I know where the man took Wren and Fal."

"Where?"

"Think about it. His very unusual appearance, and the fact that he must have escaped from the gate? Besides Annie, who else can be found in the prison dimension?"

I smacked my head. A vision of a green-skinned girl with sharp teeth sprang into my mind. I had met Dunisha in Annie's world, and she had been a helpful ally until her ill-fated demise. "Fae. Of course. He said something about going to the court for help. Is there such a thing as the Faerie Court?"

"If the lore is to be believed, yes." She took a deep breath, letting it out on a long sigh. "But how can we get to the Fae realm? Wren is the only world walker I know of."

Olillie and Tukwilla exchanged glances. The former straightened and cleared his throat. "We might be able to help with that, but on one condition."

"Name it!" I practically yelled.

"You must come with us and tell us everything about what is happening in our world pertaining to this Annie person and yourself. We Memory Keepers have mostly ignored the world beyond us for a very long time, and it would seem that it has been detrimental in some ways. We need to know the entire story."

I looked over at Fleurette, who raised her eyebrows at me. I heaved a sigh. "You got yourself a deal. But we can't wait very long; Wren and Fal may be in danger."

"No need to worry about that. Our mode of transportation is swift. Shall we?" Towakh said.

"I'm coming too," Fleurette declared. She turned to Kokoro. "Please take care of the house while I'm gone?"

Kokoro embraced her, giving her a soft kiss on the lips. "I will. Holly can stay here as well to keep me company. Be safe."

Grimm nuzzled my hand, lending me support. We said a quick farewell to Kokoro and Holly, and together, along with the five Memory Keepers, walked down Rabbit Hole Road until the cottage was out of sight.

I expected to see a group of horses or MCs waiting for us, but the road was empty. "How are we getting there?" I asked, perplexed.

As if to answer my question, the space to the side of us took on an odd appearance, like mirage waves on a hot day. A rip tore across the air, widening until it was as big as a person. Tukwilla wasted no time and stepped into the anomaly, showing no signs of fear. Olillie followed, and then the nameless man. Kwolann' gestured at it.

"Please, follow us. Do not be afraid." He stepped into the rift.

Shrugging my shoulders, I trudged ahead, Grimm by my side. It definitely wasn't the strangest thing I'd ever done.

CHAPTER 16

I expected to feel something unusual as I walked through the rift in the air: a thickening of the space like molasses, the popping of my ears, or perhaps a distortion of vision. *Anything,* really.

Instead, it felt just like walking from one room to the next. Boring.

Still, I now stood in a large room instead of on Rabbit Hole Road. I walked ahead and turned to see Fleurette step through, followed by Towakh. As soon as he cleared the rift, it closed.

I looked around. I had a very small amount of knowledge about how the Memory Keepers lived. Many resided in towns similar to the style the settlers introduced all those years ago, with some modifications to give them a more unique cultural flair. I also knew that the council members met in a special place, away from any prying eyes. This must be their meeting location.

It was a plank house, based on the size and shape, a traditional building for many of the Oracune tribes. But this was a contemporary version, built impeccably from polished cedar planks, and complete with a stunning round mahogany door and skylights that let in natural light from above, seeing as there were no windows.

It would appear that the whole council was here. Numerous people sat on benches or stood at the back of the room. They all focused their attention on me and Fleurette.

I felt like it was GOGS all over again.

"Welcome, strangers," a timeworn voice said to us. I turned to find the speaker off to our left, an old lady shrunken by age. She smiled kindly, showing impressive teeth for someone as old as she was. Her dark eyes, practically hidden by wrinkles, twinkled nonetheless.

I bowed my head in her direction, and acknowledged the rest of the gathered people as well. Fleurette did the same. "We are honored to be here," she said, ever the diplomat.

"I am Na'ah," the elderly woman said. She gestured for us to sit across from her on a simple wooden bench. The other members also sat, forming a ring.

Towakh broke the silence. "The yellow one was truthful about this one's involvement," he said pointing to me. "But he removed himself, and took two of her family members with him. I have agreed to help her reach their destination if she explains all that has been happening."

The council members, minus the five that had been with us from the start, murmured among themselves. Fleurette gave me one last nod of encouragement.

Despite my clammy hands and pounding heart, I knew spilling my secret to these people was for the best. I told them everything—about Annie and my ancestor Glivver, the legacy, what I was, and my adventures and trials leading up to this point. The room was spellbound until I stopped talking, at which point multiple members began asking me questions all at once.

Na'ah raised her hands and the noise diminished. "What a bunch of noise you make, like clucking chickens! We are better than this, friends. Do not give our guests the wrong impression."

The council quieted, chastised by the grandmotherly figure they obviously respected.

Na'ah fixed her sunken eyes upon me. "Now, we would appreciate some answers to our questions we clearly want to ask, but you seem to be in a hurry. Is that right?"

A breath tumbled out of me. "You could say that."

Fleurette leaned forward with an anxious smile. "It's not that we don't want to further discuss anything, but we do worry for the safety of the two children. As it is, they've already been gone for an hour."

Na'ah nodded in understanding. "Yes, of course. Perhaps when your shoulders have been unburdened we can have a more relaxed conversation."

"I'd like nothing more," I answered honestly.

"Very good." Na'ah stood carefully. "I am happy to live up to my end of the bargain. You are lucky indeed. We do not usually share our magic so freely, and I am only one of a small handful of my people who have the talents of the Ancient Ones."

"You were the one to open the rift?" I asked.

She nodded. "It was once a plentiful magic for our people. But nearly all of the world walkers left this plane for the new home when the settlers came, and now only two or three are born each generation who can harness this rare gift. I am the only one left in all of the Oracune Region. A shame, really. I had hoped to train a young one in the ways before I die, but it is looking like our confederated tribes have not yielded any since I was born. Well, no matter. Where is it that you need to go?"

"The Fae Realm, if you are able," Fleurette answered.

Na'ah's face went slack briefly, then reanimated with a twinkle. "You are twice lucky. If I had not had contact with the yellow man, it would have been very difficult to narrow down the essence. But I can sense it now. One moment."

She positioned her hands as if holding an invisible ball, her wrinkled face concentrating. She threw the nonexistent ball out into the far space, toward the blank wall. As before, the air shimmered before cracking open, the wall disappearing where a rift large enough to travel through formed.

She let out a cackling laugh. "There you are, friends! Go through and be well!"

"Wait!" I called to her. "The prophecy. I think you—the Memory Keepers—are a part of it."

She made a tsking noise. "If we are meant to be a part of your prophecy, then we will be where we need to be when we need to be. Have faith in the Great Spirit. If it's meant to be, it will be."

I knew she meant to be reassuring, but her words were anything but. "Okay, then," I said, trying not to show my disappointment. "Thanks for your help. See you soon, I hope."

We stepped through the rift, which closed as soon as we were clear.

My eyes, attuned to the relative darkness of the plank house, squinted shut at the brightness of our new scene. Once the brilliance stopped paining me enough to open them again, I stared at my surroundings with wonder.

The quality of light held an alien luster, an intensity to it that made the color of our surroundings more saturated than I was accustomed to seeing. The sky above us contained no clouds, only a solid blue sheen verging on violet. In the distance, rolling hills of emerald green beckoned, and beyond them lay a sea of a most perfect turquoise.

The rift had spit us out on a road of cobblestones, where each stone contained what appeared to be precious gems embedded within the surface, which glowed under the strange sun's energy.

In the direction we stood, the road led toward a wooded area. Each tree in this copse showcased leaves of a different color—red, blue, violet, and yellow, as well as the more traditional green.

I turned around, following the road with my eyes to see where it led in the other direction. The road terminated close to where we stood at a closed gate. Walls of shining white marble flanked the barrier and extended on either side. Rounded towers bumped out from the wall close to the gate in near-perfect symmetry to each other. The right-hand tower had a small door in the side, the only discrepancy between the two.

"Cressida, look at this," Fleurette said softly as she stepped off the road. Her eyes had been drawn to a batch of flowers growing along the side.

I walked over to her side to examine them. They reminded me of lilies, except the color of their petals morphed and danced in the sun like soap bubbles. Entranced, I longed to reach my hand out to touch one.

Grimm growled, shaking me from the flowers' allure. There was something not quite right about the plants. I yanked Fleurette back a step, preventing her from stroking the shining petals. She straightened, blinking rapidly at me as if dazed.

I tilted my head toward the compelling flora. "Don't. We shouldn't touch anything while we're here."

She nodded, her forehead creasing into a frown. "You're right. I was so mesmerized by the flowers that I stopped thinking all together. If it's one thing fairy tales have taught me, it's to be wary of anything this place has to offer. We must be on our toes."

"Right you are!" a voice spoke from behind us, making all three of us jump and turn. "Unfortunately, you've already let your guard down."

The speaker was shorter than me by a foot, hunched over but not old. He was humanoid, but he had a snout that was decidedly rat like, and patches of brown fur sprouted here and there from his face and neck. He wore a shirt of steel mail over wool hose. The chainmail formed a hood that covered the top of his head, with slits for his large, oddly shaped ears.

Fleurette and I stared at this newcomer, while Grimm postured in front of me. The rat-man apparently felt no fear toward my partner but brandished a long knife at us.

"Now, then," he said conversationally. "I be the keeper of the gate. And you be trespassing. The course o' action is clear as day in these situations."

Fleurette gathered her wits with her normal alacrity. "Sir, we are not trespassers. We seek an audience with the Queen."

The gatekeeper threw his head back with a chortle, showing off large, long teeth that ended in points. He grew serious again. "A meeting with the Queen? Nay, you must be bleeding blinking balmy to believe she has the time o' day for you lot. It's the dungeon for you."

"I must insist. We seek sanctuary, and we have news from one of her colonies to confer with her." Fleurette held her bearing regally.

The ratty man paused and rubbed his sunken chin. "Sanctuary, eh? It's not done proper around these parts, but you lot aren't from here, yeh? Best I can do is pop you in the waiting cell, and I'll send word to her peoples."

Fleurette was unmoving. "It's quite urgent."

He nodded. "Yeh, yeh. O' course. You come with me easy enough, I'll go myself to announce you. Best I can do. Otherwise, you fight me, I'll lock you up in the deepest pits, and maybe in a thousand years or so I'll remember to announce you."

Fleurette nodded sanguinely. "That's very kind of you, sir. We shall accept your offer. But please, it truly is important that we speak with the court."

"You and that other lot," he mumbled as he hobbled to the solid gate. He muttered something and the gate swung open. "After you," he said with a mocking flourish.

CHAPTER 17

True to his word, the gatekeeper placed us in a holding cell, which resided on the main floor on the other side of the gate. It was relatively clean, with fresh straw on the ground, a bench to sit on, and a high window for airflow and natural light.

I sat next to Fleurette on the bench after a quick perusal of the enclosure. Grimm likewise kicked back, settling his bulk comfortably against my legs. "You know, out of the three prison cells I've been in, this one is by far the nicest," I commented to Fleurette.

She snorted, stretching her legs out. "I swear, Cress. You are a magnet for trouble. Is it the legacy, or is it just your natural inclination?"

"I'd like to blame it on the legacy but seeing as how my mom never got into any trouble, I don't think that theory holds much water."

"I never would have guessed I'd be incarcerated in the Fae Realm before lunch today," Fleurette remarked with a small smile as she peered about our shared space.

"That reminds me. How in Freya's furs did you know what to say to that guy?"

She shrugged. "Travelers to this place have been few and far between over the years, but those select few have left writings behind that spoke of the dos and don'ts of talking with the Fae.

You might want me to be the spokesperson while we're here. No offense, Cress, but sometimes your quick words get you in trouble."

"No offense taken. I'm well aware of my poor impulse skills."

Our conversation halted with the sound of the door beyond our cell opening. All three of us leaned forward, expecting to see the gatekeeper walk in. Instead, I was hit by a shock of surprise.

"Wren!" I exclaimed as she slid through the door, shutting it behind her. She rushed over to the bars, grasping them in her hands.

Fleurette and I sprung out of our seats, joining her at the bars. Fleurette snaked a hand through and ran it down the girl's hair. "Are you okay?" she asked, her voice full of motherly worry.

Wren nodded. "I'm fine. We were captured as soon as we got here, since I apparently dropped us off in the middle of court. The Queen took a liking to me and Fal. He was sent elsewhere, but I've been kept at her side ever since we appeared. She calls me her pet."

"And what of the yellow man?" I asked.

"He was taken to the dungeons until the Queen could calm down. She was very angry to see him."

"Can't say I blame her." I was feeling particularly salty toward Alfrothooll as well. Served him right to be locked up. I hoped it was an older, mustier version of this cell.

"Anyway, some ratty-looking man came and told the Queen that two women and a big black dog were asking for an audience. It didn't take much guesswork to figure out it was you. I told her you were friends and to please let me speak with you. She sent me to tell you to prepare yourselves."

"Oh. Well, that was quicker than I thought," I mused out loud.

"I've got to get back. See you soon," Wren beamed as she

scampered away and out the door. At least she didn't appear to be traumatized by the ordeal.

Fleurette frowned after Wren's disappearance, however. "This isn't good."

"What do you mean?" From what I could tell, we were about to see the Queen and get back home. I was thrilled to speed up this process.

She pursed her lips. "If the Queen has taken a liking to the Ramberts, she may decide to keep them. And if she does, there won't be much we can do to stop her."

My heart sank at her words. "But Wren can leave any time she wants."

"Yes, but Fal can't. And the Queen must know that, which is why she sent him away from his sister immediately."

The door opened again before I could further discuss this hypothetical headache. The gatekeeper poked his head in, jingling keys on a large ring at us.

"Ready to go and see the Queen? I told you I'd keep to my bargain."

Fleurette plastered on a smile. "And we are most grateful to you. Yes, we are ready."

He shuffled over, inserting the key but giving us a narrowed-eye look. "Now then, no funny business. These teeth aren't just pretty. I have a venomous bite that will knock you down quick-like."

I shuddered at the thought of those teeth anywhere on my body. "We wouldn't dream of it," I assured him. Even Grimm gave a whuff of agreement.

The strange man nodded in approval and unlocked the cell door, swinging it wide with a flourish. "This way, if you please," he said, leading us to the same door Wren had used.

I expected the court to be in a great hall, but instead we were taken to an outside arena at what I could only guess was the middle of the castle. A purple carpet ran from the entrance, across the length of the open area, and stopped in front of an enormous crystalline throne, which caught the overhead sun and threw a multitude of rainbows every which way. Wren sat on a stool off to the side of the throne, dwarfed by its scale.

At the edges of the arena on either side of the carpet stood a gaggle of Fae, blocked from the main portion by velvet ropes. I took a moment to take in the bizarre nature of this court; each individual was unique in coloration, size, and even shape. Some looked more human, while others sported the heads or feet of animals, and a select few looked like they were comprised of plant parts.

At our appearance, the Fae nobility tittered and whispered amongst themselves. I nearly smiled at the thought that to them, Fleurette and I were the freakish ones, instead of the other way around. But the amusement of the moment faded as soon as I brought my attention back to the throne ahead of us.

Upon the throne sat a woman. From a distance, all I could discern was her dress, a silver garment that dipped low in the front to show off ample cleavage, hugged her torso like a second skin, and then flowed out at the hips until it was much too long for her legs. The excess fabric pooled to the sides of her bare feet, which could be seen thanks to a shorter section at the front of the gown. Likewise, her shoulders were bare, but the sleeves wrapped her upper arms before the volume expanded and left streamers that trailed to the ground from her wrists.

Her hair was loose, sleek, and midnight blue; it fell like a sheet of spilled ink down to her waist. As I approached, her face became clearer, and despite the utter beauty of her countenance, a chill ran within me upon witnessing it.

Her jet-black irises were much too large for human standards, nearly blotting out the whites of her eyes. She regarded us coolly.

"I hope you understand how foolhardy it was of you to come barging into my kingdom demanding an audience with me," she declared in a haughty voice that filled the arena.

Fleurette bowed deeply, and after a beat I copied her. Grimm dropped his head in reverence as well.

"Our deepest apologies, Your Majesty," Fleurette said as she continued to bow. "But my wards were taken from me unexpectedly. We feared for their safety and traveled here as soon as we could. Had we known they were in your good hands, we would not have been so hasty."

"Hmm, yes, so the girl told me. You may rise." We did so, and she studied us with interest, her perfect midnight brows smoothing out into a more pleasant, if still terrifying, expression. "Speaking of the reason for you being here, let's bring the prisoner out. We might as well unravel this from the beginning with everyone present."

Two guards bowed and departed to do her bidding. The Queen cocked her head to the side. "When I saw *him* again, I was so angry that I threw him in the dungeon without bequeathing him time to explain. I thought I'd torture him a little to appease my ire, but Wren here has done a lovely job of appeasing me."

Wren stood from her stool and curtseyed, despite wearing pants.

"She is a marvel, Your Majesty," Fleurette replied.

The Queen looked beyond our position, her face morphing into an expression of malice. I turned to see the yellow man being bodily escorted by the guards.

"Alfrothooll!" the Queen bellowed. "I am quite certain that I never wanted to see your face again. And not by itself, certainly. Where is your other half?"

Alfrothooll blanched, his yellow skin becoming a more pastel color. "A thousand pardons, Majesty. We found a chance to escape, but we had to split apart to do so. There was a gate, you see, but it was only open a crack. I squeezed through, but the witch came before Artali could leave. And now I am no longer whole." His face crumpled.

The Queen waved her hand pompously. "Yes, yes. Refrain from breaking down before me, because I couldn't care a whit less than I already do about your circumstances. Or did you forget that you were sentenced to die on that plane? And what is this talk of witches?"

"If I may, Your Majesty," I butted in. Her black eyes shot to me and I instantly wished I had kept my mouth shut. Once again, my impulse control had failed me, but there was no taking it back. I swallowed to add moisture to my suddenly dry throat. "I can help explain what Alfrothooll is talking about. You see, a witch of great power was marooned in that dimension some five hundred years ago. She was stripped of her magic, but she has been building it up over the centuries with the help of the Fae prisoners left to die. This last October, she managed to create a gate between her world and mine—with the help of some others—and open it a crack. She's been able to siphon magic from my world, and she plans to destroy me so that she can fully come back and take over as a god."

The Queen leaned forward as she peered at me. "There's been a witch in the prison dimension this whole time?"

"Yes, Your Majesty."

She straightened. "Carpus!" she bellowed.

A spindly, human-looking fellow made his way out of the crowd to our right. He hunched his shoulders and tried to look small. "Y-yes, Your Majesty?"

She leveled him with a stare and a furrowed brow. "Did I, or did I not, task you with thoroughly inspecting the Crystal

Graveyard before we began sending criminals there?"

Huh. The Crystal Graveyard. That had a nice ring to it.

Carpus fidgeted, rubbing his narrow hands together. "Why, yes, you did, Your Benevolence. I turned up no witches when we first set out. Of course, it was a number of years before we implemented the actual program—"

"Enough!" The air around the Queen grew shadowed. The black of her eyes completely swallowed what little white remained, and her neck seemed to elongate ever so slightly, giving her a more menacing appearance than before. Carpus quailed as she loomed over him with a sneer. "Your incompetence has no place in my court. Because of your lack of foresight, a leak has been created. I hereby sentence you to five hundred years in the deepest dungeon. Guards!"

As Carpus was dragged off by the same two guards who had brought Alfrothooll into the arena, my mind spun. This lady was dangerous.

And her attention was fixed back on me. "So, whatever your name is—"

"It's Cressida Curtain, Your Majesty."

"Did I ask for it?" she snarled.

I shook my head, cowed.

"So, *Cressida Curtain*, Alfrothooll the fool escaped through a gate between your world and The Crystal Graveyard, is that what I am hearing? And how exactly do you know all that you know?"

I tried to swallow again. "My ancestor was the witch's familiar, Your Majesty. She was the one who banished the witch, Annie, to the dimension in the first place. And my line has been tasked with making sure she stays there."

The Queen's eyes lost some of their black, and she seemed to shrink slightly into more human proportions. "I see. Well, you certainly haven't done a good job, have you?"

I bristled. "Annie has never tried to come back until it was my turn. Given the fact that all of my ancestors got to live normal lives and I expected the same for me, and also given the fact that I've already stopped her twice before, *and* I have a plan to stop her this time, I think I'm doing a pretty fantastic job. *Your Majesty*," I added with perhaps too much snark in my tone to be respectful.

I expected the Queen to turn scary again at my obvious disrespect. But she merely continued to study me. "You plan to stop a powerful witch from entering your world? How?"

I wriggled my toes in my boots. "Well, I haven't quite figured out how, exactly. But I have a prophecy ..."

"A prophecy. Why am I not surprised?" The Queen breathed deeply through her nose and threw her head back before leveling me with a black stare. "I suppose you should be on your way and fix your little problem, then, hm?"

Fleurette spoke up again. "We would like nothing better, Your Majesty. We can leave just as soon as Fal and Wren join us."

The Queen snorted, a rather unladylike noise for an eternal ruler to make. "I never said I was releasing my new pets. They will stay with me."

The court around us tittered with amusement at her words.

CHAPTER 18

Fleurette and I froze, mulling over what the Queen had just said.

As usual, my mouth moved before my brain could tell it to stop. "What do you mean? You can't keep them; they belong with us!" I took a step closer to her, unbidden.

The Queen fixed her black eyes on me, her perfect brows drawing together. She withdrew a tiny vial, unstoppered it, and threw the contents at me. A light misting of liquid splashed upon my skin. I tried to rub it off.

"What was that?" I asked her.

She sighed. "A sticking potion. You should know not to get too close to an all-powerful queen. It's very dangerous for both of us."

I tried to take a step back, but my feet acted as if they were glued to the carpet. "I can't move!"

"Of course you can't, you silly creature. Not until I allow it." She fixed me with another black-eyed stare. "Now, about the boy and girl. I'm not sure why you think you have a claim over them. They were brought to me, and they are in my demesne. Therefore, their fates rest in my hands. I say they stay."

I looked over at Wren. She sat perfectly still upon her stool, pretending to be a doting pet while the Queen handed down her sentence. I knew a caged animal when I saw one, however.

"But they're *her* wards!" I exclaimed, pointing at Fleurette, who looked like she was two seconds from tackling me to get me to shut up. "Besides, they are part of the prophecy—"

"Ugh, I am so *bored* with your prattle over prophecies," the Queen groaned with an eyeroll. "You'd best remember whose home you've invaded, little one. My kingdom. My realm. My rules."

I growled, baring my teeth as if I were in animal form.

"Cressida," Fleurette murmured at me, trying to rein me in.

Grimm nuzzled my hand. His anxiety filled me, but it only served to feed my frustrated ire.

"The kids are coming with us," I stated slowly.

The Queen leaned forward, a sly smile blooming on her face. "The girl stays by my side until she is an old woman. That will take some time; humans age so slowly when they live in Elphame. The boy? He's a fine colt, and I've been lonely. I'll give him a couple of years to grow some more, and then I'll make him my consort. At least until I tire of him. The bucks never last very long with me."

Rage inflamed my cheeks. "You wouldn't dare."

"No?" She blinked once slowly. "Perhaps you're right, but you are still much too late. You see, he has great magical potential. Rather like your friend here. I'd keep her too, but she's a bit too old for my taste."

Fleurette flinched in my periphery.

"But the one you call Fal? He's perfect. Even if I didn't expect him to be my consort, I plan to work with him, build up his magic. He'll make a fine knight for my army. I've already granted him a boon. And in doing so, he now is my property."

"You foul hag," I seethed.

"Cressida!" Fleurette looked about her, alarmed, expecting to be detained by guards any minute now.

I found I didn't care. This woman before me had gone too far.

And the Queen still did nothing to call on her wardens. Instead, her smile only deepened, showing teeth too sharp to be human. "You have spirit, I'll give you that. Usually when people insult me to my face, they don't live long enough to fully grasp the repercussions." She straightened in her seat. "I tell you what. I'm in the mood for some entertainment. I meant to use the girl for some magical amusement later, but you will do even more nicely. I'd like to strike a bargain with you, Cressida Curtain."

At last, a proverbial bone thrown my way. "Name it."

"I challenge you to a battle. Not with me, of course, but with one of my best champions. Only innate magic will be allowed. No weapons. If you win, I will give you your wards back, with one exception: the boy will train with me for one year of his life, after which he will choose whether he stays here with me or leaves for his home world. That is, if you manage to fix your little witch problem."

I itched to grab Talon from my hip, but I had not been prepared for what the day would bring me, and I'd left it at home. "I will make no bargains on anyone's behalf. Let me speak to Fal first. He deserves a say in this."

The Queen inclined her head with grace. "So be it. Bring the boy to me!" she called out.

A handful of minutes passed in which I awkwardly stood in the center of the purple runner staring at the Queen with a shrewd eye while she pretended I didn't exist, before Fal was brought to my side. Fleurette engulfed him in a squeezing hug, which he gladly returned. I swiveled my upper body awkwardly to inspect him.

"Are you okay?" I asked, looking up into his sweet face.

He nodded, although a glimmer of apprehension hid within his hazel eyes. "What's going on?"

"The Queen wants me to fight for you and Wren. No problem; I can handle that. But she tells me you must complete a year of training here. I wanted you to make that decision."

He turned to his captor. "Is this true?"

The Queen gracefully bowed her head in affirmation. "She speaks the truth."

Fleurette grasped his hand. "You don't have to agree to it. If you don't want to, we'll find another way to get you back home."

The Queen laughed at her words.

Fal scrunched his face into a thoughtful frown. "What happens if I agree, but fail to return?"

She slowly shrugged her pale shoulders. "I already bequeathed you with the promise of enhancing your magical prowess. I meant for lessons to last a lifetime, but a year is the least amount I can offer. If you do not accept my minimum generosity, then I'm afraid the magic of the boon will eventually kill you."

Fleurette gasped as she stepped forward. I growled my frustration and opened my mouth to call her some choice words. But Fal stopped me with a hand on my shoulder.

"I will agree to a year of your tutelage, if Cressida wins our freedom. But I will not come until I am finished with my primary studies. And I reserve the right to come home during the year to visit my family. You didn't specify that the year had to be done in a single session."

"Quite the bargainer, aren't you?" the Queen smiled placatingly at the teen. "Very well. I shall allow you holiday breaks, but I *will* get my full year from you." She turned her black eyes on me again. "Cressida Curtain, do you accept these terms?"

"What happens if I were to lose?"

"If my champion beats you, the boy and girl stay with me, and you would be placed in my dungeon for no less than ten years, because I do not take kindly to being called a hag. Really, I am being incredibly generous."

"Generous?" I repeated.

Her eyes flashed. "I could do away with you here and now, without allowing you a chance at freedom. Yes. I am being generous. My altruism stems from the fact that I am so utterly bored. This will be great entertainment."

I raised my eyebrows and did some quick mental calculations. Our odds of all of us leaving were slim. But I had faith in my fighting skills. I looked around at the crowd on either side of us. The people were strange, some barely humanoid, but they were more or less my size. My confidence grew.

"Alright, Your Majesty." I straightened my spine. "You have a deal."

"Delightful," the Queen drawled. "You might want this." She tossed another vial at me.

I caught it. "What is it?"

"Drink it. It is to unstick you. Unless you'd enjoy the added difficulty of fighting my champion with your feet glued to one spot. Actually, that might be most diverting."

"Nope." I uncorked the tiny bottle and upended it into my mouth. The taste was sour but not unpleasant. Even better, my feet came up when I lifted them.

The murmuring of the crowd swelled, this time with a subtle gaiety. I glanced about me, noticing some of the Fae had eager eyes, leaning over the velvet ropes to get a closer look at the action that was about to take place.

Others hung back, whispering to comrades with worried glances. One woman, seemingly made of ice and snow, leaned against a stone column by herself, casually observing me.

The sudden interest from the audience ratcheted up my stomach butterflies into a frenzy. Was there something they knew that I didn't?

I was an ant in a glass jar, and the Queen was about to drop an unknown element in and shake it up. It was too late to back out now.

The unadulterated smile of satisfaction upon the Queen's face softened her features. "I am delighted with your acceptance. Let us begin."

She swept an arm across her chest, a grand gesture to the arena at large. The ground rumbled, nearly throwing me off balance. The purple carpet under my feet grew, expanding to either side. Fleurette, Fal, and Grimm were pushed farther away from me, along with the rest of the court, until I stood by myself upon a large circle of the violet fabric. A band of gold encircled the carpet, no less than twenty feet in diameter.

Grimm instantly began walking to rejoin me, but he seemingly hit an invisible wall once he tried to step over the gold band. Alarm shot through me; whether it was his through our bond or organically my production, I couldn't tell.

The Queen was also outside of the ring. She smirked. "The rules are simple," she said to me. "You shall battle my champion with whatever magic you possess, but without spellwork or weapons. Defeat comes in the form of death or oblivion. Willfully crossing the golden line will count as disqualification, which will also count as a defeat. Lastly, you may yield at any time. Do you have any questions?"

"Just one. Who am I fighting?"

She gestured with a hand. "He is right behind you."

I startled at her words and turned quickly.

An immense hairy chest filled my view. I craned my head up until an equally hairy, ursine face appeared.

While I froze in terror, the Queen's words infiltrated my ears. "I introduce you, Cressida Curtain, to my champion, Growler."

CHAPTER 19

Growler was at least seven feet tall. His naked body conformed to human standards, minus the copious amounts of shaggy brown hair that coated its surface, and the large size of his hands and feet. His head was an odd mix of a man's and bear's, with a short snout full of pointed teeth, a shiny bear nose, protruding human ears, and oversized human eyes that gave off a hint of instability. These eyes now regarded me with a malicious interest.

I wasn't sure what I had been expecting when the Queen talked of a champion. A Fae knight, perhaps. One of the courtiers. At the worst, a dragon. Not this human-bear hybrid monstrosity.

I snapped out of my fear-induced suspension. "What are you?"

His voice was incredibly deep, and his inhuman mouth garbled any crispness to his words, but he was fully understandable. "Bugbear."

My knowledge of bugbears was dismal. I'd heard of the name, but only in the sense that they were occasionally used to frighten children into being good. Well, given what they looked like, it was an apt tactic.

Still, perhaps a little civility would make this easier for me. "What do you do for a living, Growler?"

He frowned at me, clearly put off by my chatter. "Fight."

I backed up a step as he loomed over me. "Not much of a talker, are you?" My forehead broke out into a sweat.

He growled like a bear. "No."

My armpits itched. I could do this. I had to do this.

Behind me, the Queen called out, "Begin!"

Growler lunged instantly, allowing no hesitation on his part. I let out a small, "Eep!" and scuttled to the side before he could wrap his muscular arms around me. Still, his claws from one hand raked down my arm, ripping the sleeve of my shirt and leaving a decent scratch.

I hissed in pain and clamped a hand onto the offended limb as I danced farther away from the bugbear. I was one second into the match and I had already gotten injured. I needed to get my head in the game, and fast.

Growler recovered from his lunge and turned to face me again. His forehead furrowed as he made eye contact with me.

I may have been small, but I knew I could pack a punch. Perhaps that was the ticket.

Before he could lunge, I ran at him. I meant to sidestep before I was within arm's length and wallop him in the kidney, but Growler must have seen my ploy. He stuck out an oversized foot and tripped me.

The crowd let out a shared, "Ooh!"

The carpet cushioned my fall slightly, but I had the wind knocked out of me. Before I could pick myself back up, hands wrapped around my midsection and pulled me upright.

Growler held me off the ground, his hands large enough to encircle my waist. "Yield," he said in his baritone mouthful-of-marbles voice.

"Are you yielding to me?" I mocked.

He squeezed me just enough to serve as a warning. "No."

I tried to pry his fingers from my body. I may as well have been trying to bend steel with my bare hands.

He said the word again. "Yield."

I squirmed as he applied more pressure to my abdomen. He was beginning to hurt me. "No."

He grunted like a bear and continued squeezing while I thrashed and tried to kick him. I connected once with his belly, but he only held me farther from his body in response.

The bottoms of my ribs were on fire. Much more of this and I'd know the agony of broken ribs.

"Oh, enough of this," I groaned, and then I shimmered.

Truthfully, I did not give much thought to what might happen to the bugbear when I shimmered. Belatedly, I realized that since he connected with me, there was a chance I'd take him into the incorporeal state too. After all, anything I held went into my pocket. But since *he* was holding *me*, well, chances were good that he'd stay as he was.

I got my answer right away.

Growler's hands clunked together in the absence of my body. I held onto my immaterial form for the five seconds I was able to, until he withdrew his arms from my shimmering space with a look of surprise in his eyes.

I let my feline body take over, falling five feet to the ground. I landed daintily on all fours.

My midsection still ached, but I also felt a new sensation, one of vast power. Strength. Invincibility.

So, I thought to myself as I squared off once again, *that's your magic, eh, Growler?*

The crowd gasped at my transformation, but I paid them little mind. I had my sights set on the bugbear. It was time to end this.

I let out a blood-curdling scream and raced toward him. He kept his wits about him enough to swipe at me as I advanced, but my small body easily avoided his clumsy passes. I leaped to the space between his legs and flipped over onto my back. And then I quickly transformed before he could move.

Human again, I punched upward. My fist connected with the exact anatomy I was hoping to hit. The bugbear's magical strength did wonders for my force.

Growler howled and dropped to his knees, his large hands cupping his wounded ... pride. I reverted to feline and hightailed it away from that scene, lest I be crushed by his body weight.

It was a cheap shot, I'd admit. But desperate times call for desperate measures.

And to his credit, Growler's agony seemed much more short-lived than it should have been. He was still on his knees and looking too wide-eyed to be considered normal, but he was beginning to gather himself for a return onslaught.

I let out a scream of pure rage, the sound reverberating through the arena space. Keeping my front limbs stiff with all claws extended, I puffed up my fur to its fullest height, stuck my tail in the air, and advanced on Growler with small sideways hops as I hissed in fury.

I was small, but I was terrifying. I could see it in the bugbear's eyes, which widened and took on a desperate quality. He was still in too much pain to jump to his feet, but he scuttled away from me on his hands and knees.

I was not about to go easy on him, however. With one last scream, I advanced, climbing his shaggy arm like a tree trunk. He bellowed in pain as my claws dug into his flesh, but I wasn't done there. I didn't stop my movement until I had positioned myself on his head like an angry hat, and then I battered his bear snout with my fully extended clawed paws in incredibly quick succession: *bap-bap-bap-bap-bap-bap-bap.*

Growler squealed as my claws dug into the tender flesh of his shiny nose. He managed to grab me in one hand, but I shimmered the moment I felt the squeeze, and punched him in the eye socket as soon as I had my human fists, before turning back into the cat from hell.

He fell onto his back from my punch, and I jumped onto his stomach, ready to inflict more damage upon his tender parts. He curled into a ball on his side, gasping. One long arm reached for the golden circle, intent on touching it, but it was just out of his grasp.

"Yield," Growler panted.

I shimmered again, regaining my larger body. I straddled his side, looming over his head. "Do you yield to me?" I repeated my previous question, this time minus the sarcasm.

He nodded his head quickly. "Yes."

I hopped off his prone body. The bugbear did not move, only cowering and protecting his soft spots.

The golden circle dissipated like an apparition. I glanced over at the Queen, expecting to be met with rage over my victory. But surprisingly, she stood, her hands raised and a bright smile on her perfect face.

"The winner, Cressida Curtain!" she announced cheerfully to the waiting audience.

The arena exploded with cheers and whistles. Again, it was not the response I had been expecting, but I'd be a fool to lament my good fortune. I grinned and waved to the crowds as the purple carpet began to shrink, bringing the court closer together again in the process.

Grimm bounded over and planted his feet on my shoulders, covering my face with his exuberant licks and whining his delight at my safety. His happiness spread through me like a cozy blanket. Fleurette joined him a moment later, hugging me from the back.

"That was the single most terrifying thing I've ever had to

witness," she breathed in my ear. "Don't ever do that again."

I pulled some of her hair off my cheek, where it had stuck to the fresh dog slobber. "Duly noted. I don't plan to do a curtain call, believe me."

Grimm finally backed down, content to rub his face on my side. Fleurette also let go, just as the Queen approached us. We fell into a bow.

"Rise," she drawled. As soon as I straightened, she met my eyes. A subtle change had taken place in them, I realized; the irises had shrunk to a more human size, allowing the whites to have more coverage. And instead of jet black, they now took on a deep violet hue.

She smiled again with genuine warmth. Her teeth were less pointed. "Cressida Curtain, you have surprised me today. That is not something that has happened in a very long time."

"Thank you—I think, Your Majesty," I replied graciously with a quick bob of my head. "Does this mean the kids are free to go with us?"

"I am true to my word. Your wards will stay your wards. I still expect the boy to live up to his end of the bargain, once he is of adult years. But I do not wish you to be hasty in leaving. Will you do me the honor of walking with me, Cressida Curtain?"

"Oh." I glanced at Fleurette, who had an arm around Wren's shoulders and Fal's waist. She nodded. "The honor is all mine, Your Majesty."

CHAPTER 20

How on earth had I gone from relaxing at home to walking side by side with a faerie queen in the span of a few hours? I nearly chuckled out loud at the absurdity.

The Queen strolled next to me, oblivious to my thoughts. She had continued to metamorphose before my eyes since the fight. Her midnight blue hair brightened into a more electric shade, and her now violet eyes continued to lighten. Even her facial features softened, losing some of the harsh edges from before. She also shrunk from an incredible size to closer to Fleurette's height, humanizing her further.

She ambled leisurely through her royal garden, a sprawling area filled with magical flowers, incredible hedge sculptures, fountains, benches, long-legged colorful birds, and enough varying paths to make an outsider lose her bearings altogether too quickly. She seemed to know exactly where to go, so I made sure to stick to her like glue.

She stopped to smell what looked like roses, their perfume much more intense than anything we had in my world, before leveling me with an inscrutable stare. "Cressida Curtain, I did not expect you to change into a cat. What is your magic?"

I took a breath. "If it pleases Your Majesty, you can call me just Cressida—"

"And you may simply call me Queen away from court."

"Thank you. Queen, I am the latest descendant of a witch's familiar. Are you knowledgeable about them?"

The Queen studied me shrewdly. "Indeed, I am. I gather your ancestor was the one and same who banished the witch, the one residing within the Crystal Graveyard?"

I nodded. "I hate to say it, but the prisoners you have sent there over the years have helped Annie gain magic that she otherwise would not possess. I have to ask, is it possible to halt the transfer of prisoners?"

"It is either very brave or very foolish of you to ask such questions of a queen."

Her tone of voice was neutral, but I felt it prudent to placate her. "I'm sorry."

"Having said that," she turned to me with a wry smile, "I was thinking of doing just that. Tell me, Cressida. Have you heard of the terms Seelie and Unseelie?"

"I believe so. Seelie refers to good Fae, and Unseelie is bad, as I understand it."

She puckered her lips together momentarily. "A concise answer, though not exactly accurate. People do believe Seelie and Unseelie are two distinct types of Fae. But the truth is, we can be either. And for the past five hundred years or so, I have been an Unseelie queen."

"How is that possible?" I asked her, intrigued.

The Queen smiled. "'Curiosity killed the cat,' Cressida."

I held up a finger. "'But satisfaction brought it back.'"

She laughed. "Well, then, let me satisfy you. To be Seelie is to see the joy in life. I was the Seelie Queen for a millennium. And then, around six hundred years ago, my latest consort died."

"How terrible!"

She nodded her agreement. "I loved him dearly. And after his passing, I could see no joy in life. I became bored, but not restless.

I was quick to anger. All happiness fled, and much of my court caught my melancholia and turned Unseelie as well. It served as a negative loop, dragging all of us down.

"I began to take out my frustrations on my subjects, which is how The Crystal Graveyard came to pass. At first, I only sent the worst kinds of criminals there. But after a few hundred years, I devolved into delivering petty criminals to their magicless demise. Including that moron Alfrothooll."

"I see," I said slowly. "What was his crime, anyway?"

She shook her head. "When he was whole, they tried to seduce me."

An unbidden image of that weaselly pipsqueak trying to woo this gorgeous specimen before me nearly made me snort. And then, I further analyzed her words. "'They?'"

"Apart, they are Alfrothooll and Artali. Together, they are Manisol."

That made zero sense to me, but I let it slide.

The Queen continued, "No matter their name, they snuck into my bed chambers, using magic they stole from my guards."

The sight of Alfrothooll forcing Wren to transport him made more sense. "I take it their advances were not welcome?"

A dainty laugh escaped the Queen. "Not in the slightest. I've taken lovers here and there since my last consort, but only on my terms. I was not interested in what they had to offer. So, I banished them to The Crystal Graveyard post haste."

I stayed silent, keeping my thoughts to myself.

She noticed. "You don't agree with my sentencing."

"I ... that is ..."

The Queen laughed, the sound musical and cheerful. "I don't either, now that I've had a change of demeanor. You may be certain that I will cease the transfer of any more prisoners. And I will also review all the punishments inflicted. I foresee lighter sentences for many."

"And what about Alfrothooll? What will you do with him?"

She sighed. "I am still quite angry with them. If Artali can be retrieved, they will still need to face punishment. In the meantime, Alfrothooll will stay in your dimension."

"What?" I blurted.

She faced me, her expression cunning. "It will be punishment enough. Plus, perhaps he can help you with your little issue, seeing as how he had an unobstructed view of the goings-on. Then, after you have finished whatever you need to do, you can send them back. I imagine by then Artali will have joined him."

I mulled this over. "Does he have the magic necessary to return to this realm? He stole my friend to accomplish it last time. I'd hate for him to do that again."

The Queen tapped a tapered silver nail on her lips. "No, he does not. Manisol can force magic from people; it is their gift. I suppose I shall have to send a guard with you as well. She can keep an eye on Alfrothooll, and she has the power of dimension hopping, so you needn't rely on your little friend."

I was apprehensive about adding more Fae to my retinue, but I was not about to deny the Queen, no matter how friendly she was now being. "Thank you, Queen."

"Ah, here she is now," the Queen said as our walking took us around a bend. I trained my eyes forward, catching them on the same Fae I had noticed during my fight, the snowy one.

She stood near a fountain, running her fingers through the spray and turning the liquid into shards of ice, which clattered into the basin and shattered musically. The Fae was as tall as the Queen, her skin an icy blue with freckles of a deeper hue smattered over the bridge of her nose and cheeks. She almost sparkled in the sun. She wore her long white hair intricately braided down her back.

"Kyoni," the Queen greeted as we approached.

The Fae gave a respectful bow to her ruler and then clicked her shiny black heels together smartly. "Your Majesty."

The Queen inclined her head slightly. Kyoni relaxed. "I have an assignment for you. Allow me to introduce you to Cressida Curtain."

Kyoni's silver eyes brushed over me like a winter's breeze. She smiled, showing off human-looking teeth. "Quite the performance you put on."

"Thanks." I stuck my hand out. "Nice to meet you."

Kyoni backed up a step and held up a finger. "One moment." She wore a crudely cut white fur vest wrapped about her torso, which she now parted to reach into with one hand. After a couple of seconds of fumbling, she withdrew her hand, revealing something red.

I leaned in to peer closer at the object, but I quickly shrank back when it moved of its own volition. Whatever it was, it was alive.

Kyoni laughed. "No worries, Aodh won't hurt you. Not while I have him."

I paused. "Ee?" I repeated what had sounded like the creature's name.

She nodded at my pronunciation. "Aodh is a salamander. Come take a peek."

Putting trust into a Fae I had just met was perhaps not the wisest decision. Regardless, I cautiously inched closer to peer at the salamander.

The Oracune Region was known for its temperate climate and its penchant for rain. These qualities made it the perfect home for a variety of amphibians, including newts and salamanders. I'd seen more than my fair share of such critters.

Aodh was unlike any salamander I had ever seen, however. He

was bigger, for one thing, measuring the size of a fully grown rat, although skinnier than one. His skin was not smooth, but rather bumpy, with a soft frill down his back. His underside was jet black from lower jaw to tail tip, and the rest of his body was a brilliant red with small spots of electric blue here and there. His eyes reminded me of Grimm's, both in color and—surprisingly—keenness. This little creature was intelligent; that much was evident by the way he regarded me.

"Nice to meet you, Aodh," I told him.

My inspection completed, Kyoni covered the salamander with her other hand, cupping him between her fingers. She closed her eyes, her brows knitting together momentarily.

I leaned toward the Queen. "What is she doing?" I whispered.

"You wanted to shake hands," Kyoni answered, having heard my question. "My grip could give you frostbite, so I'm warming it first."

She opened her eyes and transferred the salamander into her left hand, giving her right a little shake before sticking it out for me. "Pleased to meet you."

I clasped her proffered hand with some small amount of trepidation. Her hand was initially cool, but as I gripped it, a bite of deeper chill saturated my skin. Kyoni jerked her hand back, using it to reestablish Aodh back within the confines of her vest.

"Sorry about that. Aodh comes in handy for warming me up, but it doesn't last long. It was necessary to make that physical contact with you, though."

"Why?" I asked.

The Queen made a small noise in her throat. "Kyoni is the head of my security, and for good reason."

"My magic can assess people's networks: the trustworthiness of their contacts and the strength of their bonds."

"Impressive."

"If she is trusting *you* with this information, it means that you are reliable, Cressida," the Queen said. "And what of her network, Kyoni?"

The Fae dropped her frosted eyes. "Nearly all are dedicated to her, Your Majesty. She has a remarkable crew."

"Nearly all?" I could not help but get caught on that one word.

She looked me in the eyes. "You have a traitor in your midst."

My stomach flipped, a wave of dread cascading over me. I glanced around. "Who?"

Kyoni smirked. "Not in your general vicinity. I meant, in your network. And I don't know who. My magic doesn't differentiate between people unless I can touch them. All I know is I feel a wall of love and support surrounding you, with one missing brick. You'd best sort that out."

"Thank you," I said absentmindedly. A traitor. We needed to get to the bottom of it. Time was running out.

"Kyoni, perhaps you'll get the chance to find the traitor yourself. I am assigning you to guard duty over Alfrothooll until Artali joins him and you can bring them back here."

Kyoni bowed again, a simple acceptance. "I've always wanted to go off-world. Thank you, Queen."

The Queen waved her hand to brush away the gratitude, but her demeanor was pleased.

A thought struck me, something that had niggled in the back of my mind until it had finally wriggled to the forefront. "Kyoni, will you be bringing Aodh with you?"

She nodded. "I never go anywhere without him. Why?"

I breathed a quick breath of relief. "Because I have the feeling you are also a part of my prophecy."

Skin of fire, breath of frost. Who better to fill those spots than a fiery salamander and a Fae of snow and ice?

CHAPTER 21

After a day of surprise visitors, literal kidnapping, a duel that could have spelled death, and the befriending of a faerie queen, the sun set in the Fae realm. The activity had taxed us all, and the Queen graciously offered the five of us lodging for the night, which we accepted lest we diminish her newfound levity.

While much of the Fae castle was open to the elements, a whole wing of guest quarters existed, fully enclosed and chock full of the most luxurious amenities as befit an eternal ruler. Grimm and I were given a spacious room all to ourselves, with the rest of my family close at hand.

The bed was much too big for a cat and a dog to rest on, but it was also the softest surface I had ever had the privilege to experience. I groomed myself in absolute bliss, while Grimm rolled about on the bedding, snuffling and snorting and rubbing his shaggy head with glee on every horizontal surface.

"This beats sleeping on the ground," he proclaimed, as he flopped onto his side with his tail thumping for a few beats.

"It's not every day we get to sleep in a faerie castle."

"It's not every day that you must battle a giant creature either. What *was* that thing?"

I finished grooming my tail, stretched, and sauntered over, my feet sinking into the plush surface with every step. I crushed my forehead into Grimm's jaw before flopping over as well, landing in my favorite concave against his neck, the perfect place to be a little spoon. "A bugbear. Part bear, part … ogre? I'm not entirely sure. He was strong, whatever he was."

He sighed, a contented breath. "I wish I could have helped you, but in the end, you didn't need my help, did you?"

"Did that bother you?"

He paused. I felt nothing through the bond. "No, actually. I knew already that you are strong in your own way, and resourceful. Had you gotten hurt, it might have been a different story, but I had full faith in you."

"I'm certainly glad one of us did. It worked out well in the end. And now we have another camp—Fae—to add to the prophecy. Plus, Kyoni and Aodh. And I even think Alfrothooll has something to do with this as well. There's a piece of his story that I can't quite figure out."

"So, that's it then?" Grimm asked sleepily. "We found all of the allies?"

"It's possible. I wish I knew who the traitor was, and who needs to be murdered, but otherwise I think we have everything figured out."

Grimm breathed out another peaceful lungful. "It's all coming together. I'm so proud of you."

With these last words he fell asleep, and while I was still basking in the pride that had leaked into me, I reserved space for a touch of apprehension. This seemed too easy.

The next morning, we gathered in front of the Queen one last time. She had kept her more cheerful demeanor, and it showed in the lighter colorations of hair and eyes, plus a much less rigid and angular countenance.

"May your quest be fruitful, Cressida Curtain," she said to me.

I smiled. I liked that word, fruitful. "Thank you, Queen."

Her gaze roamed to Alfrothooll, who was nervously avoiding her eyes. "Alfrothooll. I am rescinding your sentence. If you can be Manisol once more, you are welcome back to this kingdom, with a lighter punishment. But only if you promise to behave yourself in the future. In the meantime, obey Kyoni."

He rubbed the back of one hand and then the other in quick succession before knitting his fingers together. "Th-thank you, Your Majesty. You are most wise and gracious."

She narrowed her eyes. "Hmm, yes, we shall see how wise my decision turns out to be. If I ever catch you in my personal chambers again, I will quickly change my mind on the gracious part as well."

The small yellow man dropped his head, mumbling something about understanding. The Queen let it drop.

She turned to Kyoni. "Ready?"

Kyoni gave a curt nod and positioned herself away from us. She spread her hands, palms out, and created a spray of frost from them. The frost swirled with eddies of snow before seemingly sticking to the air in front of her in a round thin sheet of a six-foot diameter. The opacity of the snow turned to clear ice as we watched.

I peered at the ice with narrowed eyes, sure that they were playing tricks on me. I thought at first that the ice had distorted the view behind it, but upon closer inspection, the background within the circle was completely different. To drive the point home, Kyoni stepped through the circle.

It wasn't ice at all. It was a portal.

From the other side, she called out, "Everybody through!"

Alfrothooll stepped through next, with Wren behind him. Fal

began to ready himself to go after her.

"Falcon Rambert, remember your promise," the Queen called out to him before he left. She had a calculating look on her face, with a hint of the old arrogance about her.

I did not like this reminder, especially if she still had more personal sights set on him. Still, I trusted Fal and had faith that he would not allow himself to be taken advantage of in any way when the time came for him to live out a year here.

Fal only swallowed visibly and nodded, and then joined his sister on the other side.

Fleurette motioned for me to go next. I placed a hand on Grimm's head for emotional support and together we stepped through. A bite of freezing cold briefly fell over me, and then I was on the other side, where the air was not as warm as the Fae realm had been, but at least it hadn't snowed again while we were away.

Fleurette joined us and Kyoni dismantled the portal, the surface turning to true ice and dropping to the ground, shattering.

I looked around. We were back on Rabbit Hole Road, on a stretch farther past Fleurette's cottage. The trees, many of them naked of adornment but some with evergreen finery, were less attractive than the colorful trees of Fae, yet they felt like old friends to me. As amazing as Elphame had been, I was happy to be home.

Fleurette also had a smile on her face, but it was cut short as her pocket buzzed eagerly. She lifted her mirror out of it, flipping it open to read the message.

"I don't understand," she said, her brows furrowed with puzzlement. She handed the mirror to me.

It was from Dora Willoby, the GOGS secretary. "I thought GOGS was ignoring you," I commented before reading the message.

"Dora said she'd continue to help us. It looks like she found some answers," Fleurette replied as she tapped a finger against the mirror surface. I read it.

"FINALLY FOUND INFO ON BROTHERS. NOT A MAN AT ALL. HOLLIS IS UNISEX NAME. BROTHERS LEFT BB&H TO GO ON MEDICAL LEAVE ALMOST ONE YEAR AGO. SHE IS STILL AT LARGE."

"*She?*" I exclaimed.

Fleurette's face went pale. "Hollis is a woman's name? You don't suppose ..."

My eyes widened. "Holly."

Fleurette and I stared at each other in complete shock, before we both turned in the direction of the cottage, resolute. If Holly *was* Hollis Brothers, we'd need to address this, and fast.

Everyone else fell in behind us, matching our marching pace. The kids understood what was happening, but the Fae were clueless, simply keeping up with the rest of us. My mind whirled and spun like leaves in the wind.

Holly. Hollis. Holly. Hollis.

Within minutes we came to the last bend in the road before the cottage could be viewed. But I could tell something was amiss, even before then.

Grimm, with his keen nose, detected the smoke first. He whined, and his concern shot through me. I lifted my blunt human nose, sniffing. It was faint, but detectable even to my unrefined senses.

"Fleurette," I cautioned, laying a hand on her arm. She stopped. "Something's wrong. We smell smoke."

Fleurette's eyes widened and she took off running. We all followed at her heels, rounding the bend but stopping short of the property.

Fleurette let out a wail. Tears sprang to my eyes. From behind me, I heard Wren gasp.

The cottage, the lovely little stone-and-wood cottage that Fleurette loved so dearly, was heavily damaged. The left side had been bashed in somehow, leaving a jagged hole that exposed both Fleurette's and Wren's bedrooms to the elements. Smoke still curled lazily from the scorched exposed walls.

Many of the bushes and plants had been torn from the ground and mangled, lying on their sides like fallen soldiers.

All was quiet.

"*Kokoro!*" Fleurette screamed, breaking the eerie silence. When no one responded, Fleurette rushed to the cottage, going in through the front door. I ran after her, as did Grimm. Our sitting room was a mess, chairs overturned and plants torn from pots. It made me sick to my stomach to see.

Panic swirled through me. The interior was deathly still, with not a soul in sight. Where was Kokoro? Where was Lucky?

I dashed to the windowsill behind the sofa, where Lucky's box lay overturned, the downy fluff of his nesting material spilling onto the floor. I crouched down, half expecting to find a tiny corpse, and at the thought a lance of pain shot through my chest.

But there he was, safe and sound, emerging from the back of the sofa where he once chewed a hole. He let out a squeak and waggled his nose at the sight of me.

"Lucky, there you are!" I'd never been happier to see my mouse. Once again, he lived up to his name.

While I comforted my diminutive friend, Fleurette cried out her girlfriend's name a couple more times, but the answer was obvious. There was no sign of Kokoro, Holly/Hollis, or her daughter Katinka.

They were gone.

CHAPTER 22

Normally, I was the one in my little group who tended to be hot-headed. I had a flair for losing my temper that was usually unmatched by any of my family.

But this time, it was Fleurette's wrath that was not to be trifled with.

We'd made our way from the damaged cottage—making sure nothing was actively burning first—to Kokoro's apartment, which was unsurprisingly empty, and finally stopping at Lyle's house. His property had remained unmolested, and in fact he'd had no idea that something had even happened down the road. I filled him in as well as I could, but Fleurette was making it difficult as she paced in his living room spewing heated threats. Lyle, having learned the bulk of the story eventually, tried to console his distraught daughter, but she was much too worked up to allow any such comforts. He eventually gave up and removed himself to finish some work.

That left just me and Fleurette in the sitting room.

"I'll kill her!" she muttered to anyone who would listen. "How dare she—*how dare she*—come to us pretending to be friendly, only to stab us in the back. If I get my hands on her, I'll *destroy* her."

I'd never seen Fleurette so agitated. I knew her motivation; she was worried sick about Kokoro.

I couldn't blame her, either. The timing was awfully coincidental. Holly *had* to be Hollis Brothers. She had posed as someone else to win us over and had evaded our questions to hide her identity. And I couldn't help but wonder if she had taken the communication crystal. Still, something wasn't adding up for me.

"Take a breath, Flo," I tried to soothe. "We don't actually know it was Holly."

"No?" She spun to face me, fire in her eyes. "I left Kokoro with her. I trusted her. But she played us, Cress. Both of us. She's nothing but a lying, scheming *traitor.*"

I pursed my lips. Kyoni had told me there was a traitor in our midst. A traitor was listed in the prophecy. And Holly—Hollis—had repeatedly dodged some of our questions about her past, her circumstances. We hadn't even asked what her last name was. But the obvious answer still felt ... wrong.

"She may seem to be a traitor, but we still need her as the green witch. And Katinka too, remember?" I pointed out to her.

"Oh, so it's just a coincidence that the first time I leave her and Kokoro together, they go missing?" Fleurette scoffed.

"Well, yes."

"You really think she wasn't just biding her time?"

I threw up my hands. "For what reason? To steal your girlfriend? Don't you think if she wanted to cause us harm, she'd take it out on me? On you? What does it get her to take Kokoro?"

Fleurette huffed as I poked holes in her assumptions. "I don't know about you, but stealing away my loved one sure has caused me harm."

The L-word hovered in the air between us.

"You love Kokoro?" I finally asked in a soft voice.

Fleurette pulled her wild hair away from her face in a brutal fashion. "Well, yes! I suppose I do. How would you feel if it were

Grimm that had been snatched?"

I thought back to the time when I thought Grimm had abandoned me, only to find out he had been taken from me. "That did happen. And you're right; it hurt. But it still makes more sense to take one of us when she had ample opportunity to do so. Hell, she stayed at Kokoro's home! Hollis could have taken her any time then as well, and we'd have been none the wiser. Don't you see?"

Fleurette shook her head with her lips pulled down grimly. She began pacing again. "Perhaps this is just her warm-up act of revenge."

I shook my head. Fleurette needed to calm down, clearly, before I could have a rational conversation with her. I left the room.

Kyoni waylaid me the minute I stepped into the kitchen. She and Alfrothooll had calmly followed us into Lyle's house, staying silent and out of the way as Fleurette ranted from the next room over.

"Is your life always this chaotic?" she asked me with a sardonic grin.

I puffed out a ghost of a laugh. "I'd love to say no, but really, the past few months have been bad. I've felt like I'm one mishap away from my ninth life."

"You've had multiple lives?" Her silver eyes widened.

I almost put a hand on her shoulder but remembered at the last moment that touching her was a bad idea. "No, no. It's just a misnomer that cats have nine lives. I only have the one, like everyone else."

"Well ..." she drummed her fingers on her lips. "Not everyone. Phoenixes can die and be reborn multiple times."

"That's ... cool. Hey, listen. Now that you are here and you've met some of my inner circle, can you tell me who betrayed us?"

Kyoni shook her head. "I can tell you it's no one in this house, but other than that? No."

I slumped my shoulders.

The back door opened, revealing my mother and father. They crossed the room to me, Mom pulling me in for a hug. "Gods, Cressida! We just heard what happened. It's terrible! Is Fleurette okay?"

I gave her an extra-tight squeeze, relishing the contact before I let go. "Physically, yes. But she's out of her mind with worry over Kokoro."

Mom glanced at Dad with a concerned expression, probably imagining herself to be in Fleurette's shoes. "Yes, I can imagine."

"But you two are fine? You haven't seen anyone slinking around? No trouble?"

Dad shrugged. He still had a sling around his arm, but he was nearly healed. "It's been normal over here. We didn't even know something was amiss."

Kyoni hummed in her throat. "That's an interesting point."

Beside me, Mom stiffened, apparently not having noticed the newcomers in the kitchen until Kyoni spoke. "Who are you?"

I swiftly made the introductions. "Mom, Dad, this is Kyoni. And that over there is Alfrothooll."

Kyoni gave a slight bow. "Kyoni Kriacardia, daughter of the West Wind, Captain of the Guard and head of security for Her Eternal Majesty of Elphame."

From his corner, Alfrothooll gave my parents a half-hearted wave.

Mom was at a loss of words for a moment, her eyes moving from one Fae to the next, then to me. I felt the need to clarify something. "They know, Mom. It's okay. They're on our side."

She frowned at me, a wrinkling of her brow that vanished as quickly as it appeared. No doubt she was remembering the many times she drilled into me the notion that I protect my lineage's secret at all costs. But she managed to stammer, "It's nice to meet you. I'm Belinda, Cressida's mother."

"And I'm Roger, her father," Dad said with a touch more friendly intonation than my mother had achieved. He made to shake hands, but I gripped his outstretched left arm and pushed it down.

"You don't want to shake hands with her, trust me," I said with a half-smile. I turned to the frost Fae. "You were saying something. About a point?"

Kyoni nodded. "Fleurette's father didn't know anything had happened. Neither did your parents. The traitor either didn't know about the familial connection of this household, or they were selective with the knowledge they shared."

An excellent point. I wracked my brain—had we told Holly about Lyle? I couldn't be certain one way or another.

It didn't matter anyway; the important task at hand was getting Kokoro back. And Holly, if she was innocent. And to do that, I needed a plan.

I whipped out my message mirror and tuned it to Gavin's frequency. "YOU AROUND? NEED TO MEET WITH YOU ASAP AT LYLE'S."

Kyoni had begun to chat with my parents while I was lost in my own machinations. Now she was showing Aodh to them, explaining why he was necessary to her brand of magic. I listened with half an ear, too agitated to fully follow along.

My mirror vibrated. I flipped it open and read Gavin's message. "BE THERE SOON."

I breathed my relief out in one long sigh.

I don't think Gavin was prepared for either the quantity or the unique nature of the people in Lyle's house. Once introductions were given all around, I dragged him off to a secluded bedroom to explain what had happened without Fleurette's ire-colored version getting in the way.

Gavin, who had apparently only been in town since the previous day, was shocked. "When did the attack happen?"

I shook my head subtly. "I don't know. We were gone for less than twenty-four hours. It would seem that whatever happened, happened shortly after we left, which would point to the idea that the perpetrator didn't want us there to interfere."

"Hmm. And this Holly person, you're sure she's Hollis Brothers?"

"I suppose so. The organization that shadows me—GOGS—seems to think so. And Nic did mention Brothers had stepped out months prior due to a medical condition. Well, pregnancy can certainly be categorized as such, can't it? And I did the math. She would have been just a couple of months along in her pregnancy when she went on medical leave."

He rubbed his chin in thought. "Seems pretty cut and clear to me. She ratted you out."

"I disagree."

Gavin cocked his head. "Why? Did she come across as particularly trustworthy?"

"Well, no. I knew she was hiding something, but I assumed it had to do with Katinka's father. Perhaps she'd fled a domestic violence situation. I certainly never would have guessed she was our missing lawyer."

"Does she have a motive to hurt you and Fleurette?" Gavin pressed.

I flattened my lips. "She could blame us for her business partners' deaths, certainly. If they were close, it would be motive enough. And if she has her fingers in the ACF's pie like they did, all the more reason. But why wait until we leave? Wouldn't she want to hurt *us*, not Kokoro?"

"Maybe, maybe not. Perhaps she has ties to Kokoro's husband." Inaba Ebiru was a ruthless businessman who had connections to Gavin's father. He also treated Kokoro horribly during their marriage. Once Kokoro was possessed by Kitty the fox, she killed Ebiru, inciting the wrath of his cronies.

But Kitty had been tasked with destroying all the men who would do Kokoro harm, and she had succeeded, gaining another tail in her bid for returning home. Surely Kitty hadn't missed any.

But then again, Hollis was a *woman*. Perhaps Kitty was being more literal than I would have guessed.

Still, I shook my head. "It doesn't feel right. I can't blame Holly for this mess."

Gavin scrutinized me. "I'd like to gently remind you that your track record for trusting people is a little tarnished."

I scowled. "I trusted you, didn't I?"

He held out a placating hand. "Yes, but you also trusted Nic, who turned out to be using you the whole time."

I heaved a sigh. "If I had known from the get-go that he was a kharismorph, that wouldn't have been the case. And I know for a fact that Holly is not a kharismorph. Although her daughter will be."

There was something about that fact that niggled at the back of my brain. But nothing came of it. I shook it off. "Look, it doesn't matter if Holly or somebody else did it. We need to find Kokoro, and fast. I need your help."

"Of course. She's my only family. I'll do anything to help her."

"I'm glad to hear it. Here's my plan. I'm going to take Grimm to the cottage and let him smell around, see if he can find her scent. In the meantime, I want you to appeal to the bounty hunters."

"The bounty hunters?" Gavin repeated. "Why them?"

I narrowed an eye, trying for a steely expression. "I'm going to need the best trackers in this area. And I have the feeling that we're about to go to war. We'll need an army of our own."

"Aren't you being just a bit melodramatic?"

I huffed out a breath. "I am not. We got rid of a good few ACFers with the whole explosion debacle, but who knows how many more are out there? I refuse to believe they were all there was. If anything, they're cozied up in some corner like a bunch of rats. And I want to sink my teeth into them."

Gavin gave me a wry grin. "That's the cat talking, isn't it?"

"The cat is always talking. So, will you do it?"

He steepled his finger under his nose. "Why me? Why don't you go talk to them yourself?"

I rolled my eyes. "They're less likely to take me seriously."

"Aw, you don't know that for certain."

"Gavin, I'm a walking joke to those ignoramuses and you know it."

"I've already told you; they've actually missed you," Gavin argued.

"Missed making jokes at my expense, you mean."

He shook his head.

I pressed on. "What about the bet you all made about me? You still haven't paid my half, by the way."

Now it was his turn to roll his eyes. "That's because we went on a date under false pretenses, got caught, went on a steamy train ride, nearly died under a lake, and then you disappeared for six months before putting my cousin at risk and then looping me into the full craziness that is your life."

I let a pause hang between us. "That's not exactly how I remember the last year going down."

He laughed, a solid, honest response. "Fine. I'll do it. I suppose life has been more interesting since I opened myself up to the craziness."

"See? I knew I could count on you. And don't forget to pay up."

CHAPTER 23

The acrid smell of old smoke filled my nostrils as I crept about the outside of the damaged cottage. Seeing my chosen home in such a state filled me with a profound sorrow, and rage burned deep in my gut. It had been torn into, damaged, violated. And its wounds could be keenly felt by the people who loved the eclectic little building.

It was enough to almost make me want to stop everything and mourn the life I once had, to tuck myself into a small ball of fluff and forget the world. I was too small, too insignificant to keep going. I was tired of fooling anyone into believing otherwise. My actions only hurt people, as evidenced by my ruined home.

Wallowing in the engulfing despondency, I leaned against a tree stationed near the road. It was a linden tree, if memory served, and in the spring and summer it came to life with vibrant verdancy. Right now, though, it was lifeless, its white bark reminding me of skeletons and death, of an echoing hopelessness in my task.

I glance up at the trunk. No, it wasn't completely white. Small flecks of a brilliant golden orange bedazzled the surface. Lichen. A sign of life.

Even in the prolonged winter weather, there was hope for the future. I couldn't lose sight of that, not when I was so close to fulfilling the prophecy. My self-pity turned to anger, anger at the normal life I could never have, anger at Annie for putting me in this position. And that anger urged me on, whispering the only word that could motivate me in my desperation: *revenge.*

It was time to get to work.

Grimm, ignoring my inner turmoil, walked nearby with his snout to the ground. He scented the perimeter in a very thorough fashion, allowing his nose to lead him and often circling back to a spot that piqued his interest. So far, though, he could not discern any individual scents. I decided to go inside to see if there were any clues we overlooked during our initial hasty inspection.

The interior was dark and cold, a dampness to the air belying its normally dry and cheerful vibe. This was no longer my safe haven. I slunk along the floor, keeping my senses alert for any dangers the cottage might be hiding.

The bedrooms were the worst of it, as a part of the wall was missing, exposing them to the winter elements. But as I crept down the hallway, I noticed that Fleurette's tiny workroom had also taken a good thrashing. It was never a fully tidy space, admittedly, but its current state was a far cry from the usual lively chaos. Fleurette had been working on a strength potion before we left, and, at last examination, the bottles had been lined neatly up on her workstation, resting individually before the next step of the process. Now, every single container had been dumped and smashed on the floor. The contents mingled in a muddy pool, a miasma nearly making me sneeze with its intensity.

So much for providing a potion.

"Cressida, I found something!" Grimm's voice came to me faintly.

A pang of something akin to hope warred with my ever-present fear. I bolted back out through the hole in Wren's bedroom, crossing the yard and skidding to a halt in front of him. "What is it?"

He still sniffed the ground, closer to the road. "Right ... here, there's a faint scent of Kokoro. And over here ..." he paced a couple of steps to the right, "it smells like the baby. Specifically, her diaper smell."

"Was her diaper dropped on the ground?" I asked, intrigued.

"It's possible. She's too little to crawl, but I can see someone dropping a diaper and picking it back up when they leave. Plus, there's the scent of an unknown human."

"Holly?"

He took another whiff. "No, I got a good scent profile of her at our first meeting. This is someone new. The smells all conglomerate over here. And this is where I smell rubber."

"Rubber," I repeated, thinking. "Tires?"

"I think there's a good chance that everyone left in an MC. Judging by the freshness of the scent, they went that way." He pointed his snout in the direction away from town.

I'd traversed Rabbit Hole Road that way, once. It eventually led to Knobby Hill, but it was in major disuse ever since the newer highway had been built.

"This is great," I praised him with elevated spirits. "We'll need to track the scent. Let's get going."

"Now?" Grimm asked. "Don't we want to tell Fleurette first?"

"No. I'm worried you won't be able to track it for long if we continue to wait. The skies look angry right now." Fat gray clouds had been rolling in all afternoon. Rain, or even snow could easily wash away any remaining scent. Grimm had remarkable olfactory capabilities, but even he couldn't track through that much water.

"Good point. Let's go." Grimm stuck his snout back down and began to track.

We made it a good mile into the wooded portion of the road before the scent officially petered out.

"Sorry, love. It's gone," Grimm confessed, his ears drooping.

"Well, we at least know the direction the MC traveled in. It's more than we knew before. Don't worry, Grimm. I'm proud of you."

He wagged his tail, but the motion was subdued.

A caw suddenly filled the air near us. I looked around, recognizing the voice.

"Rupert?" I called out.

A flapping of wings drew my attention to a branch overhanging the road above us by ten feet. Rupert settled himself on the branch, shaking his head briskly but otherwise holding onto an air of melancholy.

"Are you alright?" I asked him.

"Fine, fine," he assured us, but he did not seem fine.

"Did you see what happened to the cottage? To Kokoro?"

He hung his head. "Yes. A shame. It shouldn't have happened."

"*What* happened, Rupert?" I pressed.

"I saw an MC pull up, a large one: four doors, shiny, gray body with yellow trim. It parked outside of the cottage. Two men got out. A fireball came out of nowhere and hit the side of the cottage, destroying the wall. Luckily, it was too wet to catch fire. The two men swarmed in through the hole. I heard screaming. Plants tore from the ground and withered."

That must have been Holly's magic. "And then what?"

He paused, thinking. "One man carried Kokoro out over his shoulder, like she was sleeping. The other held a baby. Another woman followed them out. She dropped a piece of cloth—she had a bunch of stuff in her hands—but the man with the baby picked it up. They all got in the MC and drove off down this road."

I heaved a great breath. Holly went willingly with the men,

from the sounds of it. Could she have been in cahoots with them after all? Then again, perhaps she was only protecting Katinka. I still didn't have enough facts to make an educated decision.

"I'm glad you are safe, Rupert. You should go and see Fleurette; she could use some comfort right now and seeing you would lift her spirits."

Rupert croaked at my words. "No, not now. I think I'll fly around and see if I can't find the MC. I'll be in touch." Without waiting for me to respond, he flew off.

I watched him turn into a black blob against the sky. "That bird is cracked," I muttered to Grimm. "I wish I knew what he was hiding." I flexed a paw. "Come on. Let's go back and tell the group what we found out. Perhaps Gavin's had success in rounding up some bounty hunters."

Success was an understatement.

Lyle's house already held too many people; he'd gone from hosting my mother and father only, to adding myself, Grimm, Fleurette, Wren, Fal, and two Fae. With the house close to bursting as it was, he ordered Gavin to hold the bounty hunters in the barn.

Since Fleurette was resting and I didn't wish to rile her up again with my discoveries, I chose to deal with the bounty hunters first. Grimm, of course, followed along.

I counted heads as I entered the barn, noting that there were now seven hulking men with various scars and battle wounds sitting contentedly on hay bales and chatting amongst themselves. Gavin sat by himself on a bale closer to the entrance, absent-mindedly stroking the feral barn cat Gin, who had an unusually large soft spot for Gavin and Gavin alone.

"Hi Gin," I said as I squeezed in next to her. Being wedged between two people was apparently too much for her aloof sensibilities. She took a small amount of offense at my intrusion and jumped down, skirting around the rest of the humans in her normal skittish way and disappearing into the darkness of the barn.

"Is this everybody?" I asked Gavin. Some of the men had noticed my entrance, but they didn't say anything yet.

Gavin nodded. "A good turnout. Some were off on jobs, but everyone available signed up to come here."

"How did you manage it?"

He smirked. "Two things. I told them I was footing the bill and would pay handsomely for a job well done. I've got the funds so I can afford it." That was an understatement. With the death of his father, Gavin had inherited a fortune.

"What was the second thing?" I asked.

He rubbed his neck. "I might have told them that you had gotten a temporary contract with an independent company that took on more than just petty criminal stuff."

I let out a guffaw. "You didn't."

"Hey, that kind of work is every hunter's dream. To help a fellow hunter in such a job was too much temptation to pass up."

I frowned. "But what do I tell them?"

He tapped my forehead. "I'm not far off with my white lie. Tell them as close to the truth as you can get. You're a pro at lying."

I narrowed my eyes. "Gee, thanks. Ass."

He smirked at me and gestured grandly for me to begin.

I stood up and walked toward the gaggle of men, trying to quell my sudden nerves. I knew this bunch. I had nothing to be nervous about. They'd only hazed me, and ogled me, and made me feel lesser than them over and over again throughout our working history. Nothing I couldn't handle. No big deal.

I cleared my throat.

Allen, a hunter with a visible scar on his face, turned and shouted, "Look who it is! Baby Bounty Hunter herself!"

The barn erupted with whoops and cheers. I knew some of it to be mocking, but surprisingly, I saw true warmth on the faces of most of the men. Perhaps Gavin had been right. Perhaps I *had* been missed.

"Where you been hiding, BB?" one man, Colton, asked over the ruckus.

Another, Mathers, added, "And how did you land such a prestigious job?"

A third nudged Mathers with a wink. "I bet I have some ideas."

I shouldn't have heard that last remark over the commotion, but my ears were more sensitive than a normal human's. My face heated, partly with embarrassment, but mostly with anger at the last speaker. I walked up to him. He didn't notice at first because he was too busy gloating over the epic burn he had just given me. Mathers alerted him of my presence, giving me a "I'm not with him" glance.

I didn't recognize this man. "You. What's your name?"

He leered at me. The two men sitting closest to him scooted farther down their hay bales. "It's Harvey."

"I've never met you. Why is that?"

Harvey wanted to roll his eyes at my directness, I could tell. "I joined the guild this summer. I've certainly heard about you, though." His mouth widened in a lazy grin.

I straightened my spine. "Is that so? Enough so that you feel it is appropriate to insinuate that I sleep my way to the top?"

He looked me up and down slowly. I held my body rigid, the roots of rage deepening my desire for carnage. In an offhanded manner, he answered, "There's not much to you. How else would you be offered such a cushy job? You have to have skills somewhere, and baby, it ain't in the field, I can tell you that much."

The men who knew me better looked incredibly uncomfortable as they further disengaged themselves from this interaction.

I pointed at the barn entrance. "Get out."

"What?" The brains were not strong with this one.

I bent toward him, giving my best impression of a looming force. "Get. Out. This meeting is only for those interested in working under me."

My looming did not threaten him. He glanced at my chest, which was fully hidden by my thick shirt and vest; it was not much to look at even if it wasn't. "I'm more interested in working over you, if you get my drift. Right, guys?"

No one joined in his ribaldry. And with that lewd comment, my patience was up.

I growled and leaped at the man, tackling his chest and pushing him backwards off the hay bale. He let out a sound of surprise before the floor knocked the wind out of his lungs.

Meanwhile, Grimm, who had stayed near Gavin this whole time, raced to my side. As I picked myself off Harvey's lap—gross—Grimm positioned himself at Harvey's head, waiting for my word.

I allowed the lech to pick himself up. He sat, still on the floor, but his open leer had been replaced by an ugly scowl.

"What the hell is wrong with you?" he yelled at me.

I morphed my face back into one of haughtiness, quelling the fury that tried to bubble over. "I've asked you to leave. I will not employ you, nor will Mr. St. Cloud. You continued to objectify me and harass me. So, now you know I'm serious. I'm sure if you've heard of *me*, you've heard of my business partner, Grimm. We are a package deal, after all. And now, if you do not remove yourself, Grimm will bodily remove you, by your head if necessary. So, Harvey, what's it going to be?"

Harvey looked behind his back and flinched away from the hovering Grimm. He swore under his breath and slowly picked himself off the ground. "You crazy bitch," he seethed at me.

I rolled my eyes. "Yes, yes, that's been established. It's too bad you couldn't leave your sexism at home for once and get an amazing job out of the deal. I'm sure the rest of the men here will be more than happy to split up your share as a bonus."

"I don't want to work for you, anyway," he spat as he headed for the open doorway. "And everyone knows you're shtupping Gavin, so I stand by what I said." With his last words spoken, he exited the barn.

My face went from heated to blanched at his words. Gavin had alluded to this little wrinkle earlier in the week but hearing it directly from the source sent me into a poorly contained rage. "Who here says that?" I demanded of the remaining participants.

More than a few of the hunters looked sheepish, refusing to make eye contact with me.

I clenched my fists. "Let it be known that Gavin and I have *never* been an item, nor will we be. We are friends, and nothing more. And anybody who believes otherwise can join Harvey right now."

Gavin walked over and stood by me. I refused to look at him. He spoke to the group. "I stand by everything Cressida has said. We have no designs on each other, but I will gladly work alongside her as a friend. Anyone who wants to be as disrespectful as Harvey has no place on this team."

I gave him a grateful smile before turning my attention back to the six remaining men. They slowly straightened and worked up the courage to meet our eyes, like wilted flowers getting a much-needed watering.

Allen spoke first. "I never believed the rumors. You're too good to muck about with the likes of any of us. I'd like to stay and hear about the job."

The others chorused similar sentiments. Despite not fully trusting this new camaraderie, my heart swelled.

"Glad to hear it," I told them. "Let's break it down, shall we?"

It took an hour to hash out what I expected of the bounty hunters, skirting around the need-to-know details. I explained that two women and a baby were missing and needed to be found right away. I gave a description of the MC and the direction it traveled in. I made it clear that the leftover ACFers would be dangerous, and that brute force was possibly needed to take them down. Gavin ended the meeting by offering a rather hefty sum per person, with a generous stipend paid up front, which every single hunter present took.

After that, I turned them loose.

Once the extra men were gone, I turned to Gavin with sigh. "Is this day over yet?"

He huffed a laugh, the easygoing twinkle present in his dark eyes. "Is this *year* over yet? Cressida, is it just me, or do you attract trouble like flies to dung?"

"I rather resent you likening me to dung, you know. If you're talking about that Harvey fellow, that's just the culmination of my experience as a sole female hunter being boiled down into the epitome of male chauvinism. That trash needed to take itself out."

He laughed affectionately. "Well put, and sorry if I once added to that scene. But I am very glad you never physically attacked me over it.”

“Well ...” I thought back to the time I clawed his wrist in the old school to prevent him from shooting Wren. But Gavin didn't know that had been me. I decided it was best not to mention it now. “*I'm* thankful that you helped set the record straight about *us*. I figured you’d play into it.”

“Me? Never.”

I narrowed my eyes at him. “Mm-hm. There’s something I’m missing here.”

He tried his best to look innocent. “You’re sharp as a tack.”

A thought struck me. “I think we should get in touch with Cedrus. We might need the shifters’ help in this.”

Gavin looked away. “I ... already alerted them.”

“You did? When?”

He grinned a little more toothily than usual. “Before the meeting. I messaged Rosa. She and Jasper are on their way, along with the entire wolf pack. When you said you needed an army, I acted.”

I tried my hardest not to smile. “Since when have you and Rosa been in contact with each other?”

“I returned to the village to help them rebuild. I felt a little guilty about ditching them after the earthquake.”

“Is that so? And it had nothing to do with a good-looking otter shifter, then?”

He blushed. “It’s not like that. But we did exchange our info while I was there.”

“Did you exchange saliva samples as well?”

“Cress!” Gavin looked appalled at my lack of decorum. “I’m not stooping to answer that.”

I looked at Grimm, who did his best to follow our discussion. “That’s a yes.”

“It is not a yes. And don’t bring Grimm into our conversation.

Listen, the fact is, I let Rosa know what was happening on our end. She agreed that the best course of action was to gather some troops, just in case."

I clapped him on the arm. "Good work. I knew your charms would one day work on somebody."

He only saw fit to roll his eyes at me.

CHAPTER 24

At dinner, I filled our group in on everything I had learned since we were last together, as well as the plan I had concocted to find Kokoro, Holly, and Katinka.

Fleurette was quiet, pensive. I did not want to cause her further anguish by rubbing it in that Holly was likely innocent in all of this. But she brought it up herself.

"I still don't know where Hollis Brothers falls into this. She could be the mastermind, or she could be a victim herself. Rupert's eyewitness testimony still does not completely exonerate her, you know," she said slowly. She sighed. "But I'll admit I may be wrong about her. Time will tell, won't it?"

"Gavin and Grimm and I are leaving tomorrow to join the search. I think you should come, too. Busy hands are the enemy of anxiety and all."

She nodded.

Kyoni, sitting at the far end of the table so as not to make anybody too cold, cleared her throat. "I'd like to come as well. I can portal us to where you might think the ACF will have taken them."

"Thank you, Kyoni. That would be faster than taking an MC. Roomier too."

The next morning, I received my first bit of intel from my hired hunters. One of them had found fresh tire marks on the old road leading to Chargrove. He'd followed them through the night, past the dying town and onto the newer highway, where his luck ended. He did mention that the vehicle must have taken a left-hand turn, a clue that at least narrowed down the possibilities a little.

Allen and Mathers, who had teamed up, scouted areas of the highway and had found a soiled cloth diaper by the side of the road a few miles from Chargrove. Another clue to point the way.

This was where we would take up the hunt. We left Lyle, the kids, and—after a stern talking to about not hijacking people—Alfrothooll. The latter had been rather subdued after the Fae realm jaunt, but he promised to be on his best behavior, and knew that his ultimate salvation would lie in working with us to get Artali back.

Plus, Kyoni threatened to freeze him to the ground if he didn't behave himself.

We trudged outside directly after eating a quick breakfast. We knew it was a long shot that we would find them today, but having an active role certainly beat sitting on our thumbs at home.

I was about to give Kyoni the go ahead to open the portal, when I heard a crow cawing in the distance. Fleurette heard it too, and perked up.

"Is it Rupert?" I asked her.

She nodded.

"Hang on a sec, guys," I told the group as Fleurette began walking toward the sound. Grimm and I followed.

Rupert perched high in a tree bordering the property and the road. Fleurette motioned for him to come down, but the crow stubbornly refused.

She frowned. "He knows where they are."

"What?" I exclaimed, my spirits lifting. "I'm going to talk to him."

I transformed. "Rupert! What's going on?"

The crow cocked his head to look at me with one eye, but he made no move to come closer. "I found them. I flew all night, but I found them. They're holed up in an old building in the woods, near the town of Hokumel."

"That's amazing!" I gushed, but Rupert didn't seem too pleased. I eyed him. "What's wrong?"

He shook his head to fluff up his feathers. "Nothing. I mean, I didn't actually see the female humans you are looking for. But it's the same MC I saw at the cottage."

"That's not surprising. But it's better than any other information I've gotten." I laid out a mental map, noting with satisfaction that the quickest way from Chargrove to Hokumel would be a left-hand turn onto the highway. "That's some great work you've done, Rupert. Thanks."

He still did not look pleased. He and I hardly ever saw eye to eye, but he'd normally take praise from me to heart. Instead, he only said, "Not really," before opening his wings and sailing away.

Now that we had a more focused search area, I messaged the hunters to meet us in the town of Hokumel at their earliest convenience. I also messaged Rosa, updating her on where to take the shifter backup, just in case.

Having done all of that, it was time to go.

"Where to?" Kyoni asked, getting ready to do her magic portal trick.

"Hokumel. It's a small town to the west and south of here. Do you need to see it on a map?"

She shook her head. "As long as you know where to go, so do I." The frost Fae wasted no time opening the portal, taking us to a patch of woods.

"Where are we?" I asked.

Kyoni pointed. "We are about a mile away from the town. I figured people would be a little shocked if we portaled into the middle of it."

"Good thinking." I took a moment to get my bearings, not an easy thing to do when one has been dropped off in the woods through a magic portal. "This way, you said?"

Kyoni nodded.

"Um, Kyoni," I heard Fleurette say behind me, "you don't happen to know how to glamour, do you?"

There was a slight pause. "I do not. Why?"

I slowed down my walking, interested to hear this conversation. Fleurette responded, "Well, it's just that Fae are not something people tend to see here. Your kind has mostly been relegated to myths. A woman who looks like she's made of frost might turn one too many heads."

"Good point," I interjected. "It's hard enough for me and Grimm sometimes, let alone this entire entourage. No offense, Kyoni. You're beautiful as you are. Just very … unique."

The Fae smiled. "I understand. I will stick to the woods so as not to arouse any suspicions."

The town of Hokumel was predominantly inhabited by Memory Keepers. I had been to similar towns in the past for random jobs, and the citizens were always friendly and welcoming.

This time, there was an undercurrent of tension surrounding the town.

Also, I noted with a dollop of apprehension, the lights were out in all the buildings. Although it was only morning, I expected the shops to be open.

We split up, Kyoni staying unseen in the woods, Gavin and Fleurette going one way and Grimm and I going another. Our goal was to seek information about the surrounding area, something that us bounty hunters were adept at.

I instantly clicked back into my bounty hunting ways, as rusty as they were after being off the job for nearly a year. The first step was to determine who might hold the most information. Normally, that would be the sheriff of the community. But Gavin had already called dibs on that locale. So, who else was there?

I ended up stopping at the post office and the grocer's store. The clerk at the post office was altogether too grumpy to get much out of, but he had not heard or seen anything unusual. The grocer was out, but his employee told me that there had been some new faces in town since last October. They came into the store on occasion, bought supplies, and left without saying more than a handful of words. He did not know their names, nor how many there were, and he had no clue where they lived.

Still, it was a step in the right direction. It pointed to the fact that the ACF was still around, or at least a small faction of them was.

I wished Rupert were here. He'd be able to show us exactly where they were holed up. This was still a big area to search.

I pondered this as Grimm and I walked down the street after leaving the grocer's. This was a small town, close-knit by the sounds of it. Surely *someone* would have the information needed to ascertain the whereabouts of this faction.

A storefront caught my eye. A boutique, the windows filled with tiny clothes, with bunting going across the window proclaiming, "Welcome, Baby!" in pastel greens and pinks. I thought of Katinka, and that lost diaper.

It was a long shot, but it was also worth a look.

A tinkling bell announced my entrance. The shop smelled of strawberries, lanolin, and cotton. It was filled to the brim with all things baby, from blankets to diapers, teething toys to miniature dishware. The natural light filtering through the front windows was not enough to fully brighten the interior. The lack of lighting lent the shop an eerie quality.

"Morning!" chirped a voice from behind a display of baby clothes. A young woman popped out, her face pale enough to make the freckles that scattered over the bridge of her nose stand out in contrast. Her golden red hair was swept away from her face in a ponytail. "Sorry about the lights; they popped off about an hour ago. Happens all the time these days. Can I help you?"

She did a double take at Grimm before passing her eyes over my body and settling on my stomach.

Her gaze made me want to shield my midsection with my hands, but I refrained. "No, not for me," I said pleasantly. "I'm actually looking for a friend who is supposed to be in the area unexpectedly. She has a baby of about four months old."

"Unexpectedly?" The woman absentmindedly rearranged a display of soft cloth squares. "Most people settle in Keeper towns because they've done their due diligence. Like me."

"I understand. This ... may not have been her idea."

"Oh?" I had her full attention again.

I sighed. "My friend may have gotten involved with some shady people, who are purported to be living near Hokumel. Have you seen anything fishy lately?"

Her guard was up. "And who are you?"

"My name is Cressida Curtain. I am a bounty hunter, and this is my partner, Grimm," I said, placing a hand on Grimm's head. "The woman in question is a friend of mine, and I believe she was taken by force. I'm worried about her welfare, and the welfare of her daughter. Any information you have would be greatly appreciated."

She glanced to the side, seemingly warring with herself. A second later, she made up her mind and turned back to me. "I did have someone unusual stop into my store just yesterday. It was definitely weird."

"Define 'weird,' if you please."

"It was a man, first of all. I'm not saying that men can't shop here; in fact, I love it when fathers take an interest in their baby's welfare. But this guy? He wasn't friendly, first of all. And he gave off, well, menacing vibes. He honestly creeped me out."

Aha. This was the lead I needed. I hoped it would continue to play out and not come up short like at the grocer's. "Go on," I urged.

"He told me that his sister had unexpectedly left her baby girl with him, and he needed supplies to tide her over until his mother could get here and take over raising her. I'd never seen this man before, and I know everyone in this town."

"Did you get him the supplies?"

She nodded. "Well, not everything. Some of the stuff I had to special order because I didn't have it in stock. I asked for an address so that I could deliver the goods when they arrived, but he got cagey with me. Mumbled something about living near Mt. Tamanus and that he'd come back in a couple of days to pick up the rest. But there's no housing out that way."

"Mt. Tamanus?" The name was familiar, but I couldn't place it. "Where is that?"

The woman let out a small laugh, a puff of mirth. She pointed behind her, even though there was more store and a wall in the direction she pointed. "You must not be familiar with this area. Mt. Tamanus is the only mountain you can see from town. It's not very big, but if you see a protrusion in the distance, that's it. It's especially pretty this season, what with all the snow it's been getting."

That caught my interest, but I tried to stay nonchalant. "Thanks. Why wouldn't anyone live near it?"

She shrugged. "It's sacred to the Memory Keepers."

Hope quivered in my chest. "You don't say."

"They are rather protective of the mountain. There *are* some ceremonial buildings and what-not near it, and about fifty years ago, some people built a compound nearby to start an intentional community, but the Memory Keepers didn't approve of a bunch of *settlers* taking over the area like that, so the commune was abandoned some thirty years ago."

The quiver turned into a flutter of optimism. "Thank you for being so forthcoming. Is the building still there?"

She nodded. "Yeah. They built a solid wall around the place, and everything is still intact. But nobody goes out there anymore."

I could guess at a few people who might jump at the chance to take over an abandoned building, but I kept it to myself. "And the man that came into your shop. Did he happen to give his name?"

She shook her head. "That was the last weird thing. I needed a name for the items I was special ordering. He seemed a little dodgy with that question, and told me to put down his mother's name, since she would be the one to raise the baby. Now, I don't know about you, but when I was a little girl and I was being naughty, my mom used to tell me to behave myself or a certain witch would get me. Just a fairy tale, mind you. But I never forgot the name. And I swear to you, this man gave me the same exact name as the witch for his mother."

"What was it?" I asked, even though I knew the answer.

She looked me in the eye, daring me to disbelieve her. "Annie Coddle."

CHAPTER 25

It was easy to piece together the rest from there. Grimm and I met up with Gavin and Fleurette, and as we walked back to where Kyoni waited, I filled them in on what I had learned. It matched up nicely with the small amount of information the sheriff had divulged to them.

"So, Tamanus is the sacred mountain, eh?" Gavin mused out loud. The mountain, small as it was, did loom over the surrounding scenery. It was also hard to see through the gloom of the overcast day, but it seemed especially stormy around the mountain.

"Mm-hm. You think it's our gate site?"

Fleurette made a noise of agreement. "It could be a coincidence, but if there are ACFers about, it's highly unlikely the two things aren't connected. And the fact that there's an abandoned commune nearby? It's too good for them to pass up."

"My thinking exactly." I frowned. "The only thing that doesn't make sense is why Annie wants the baby."

"If Hollis is in cahoots, and, let's face it, the other two lawyers were, she could be *giving* Katinka to Annie, for all we know," Fleurette reasoned.

I shook my head. "Or Holly is innocent, and she's been hiding from the ACF for this very reason. Why leave her practice months before giving birth, otherwise? Just have the kid and pass her off."

Fleurette was silent. "I guess we won't know until we can further assess the situation," she finally spoke, clearly steadfast in her views.

We reached Kyoni, who had passed the time creating detailed, life-size snow sculptures about the small woodland clearing. I spied a mouse, the Queen, and, peeking from behind a tree, a large four-footed animal that looked like a cross between a goat and a horse, with a single spiraling horn upon its forehead.

"Is that ...?" Fleurette asked, her voice drenched with wonder.

Kyoni nodded in affirmation. "A unicorn, yes. That's the smaller, shyer variety that lives in the rainbow woods near the castle. There are some real bruisers that live elsewhere in Elphame." She flicked her wrist, and the sculptures all fell apart into heaps of snow. A collective sound of dismay rose from us three humans, unbidden. Kyoni pretended not to notice.

"So. What have you learned?" she asked us briskly.

Gavin and I took turns filling her in. At the end of our shared information, I added, "I think our next step is to scout out the old compound."

Kyoni agreed with a head nod. "Give me just a moment, please."

She focused before opening her eyes and creating a new portal.

I whistled. "It doesn't even tire you out, does it?"

She cocked her head to the side, quizzical. "Why would it?"

"Whenever Wren transports us to a new location, it wipes her out. I assumed it would be the same for anyone with similar capabilities."

"Ah." Kyoni shrugged, her pale blue face breaking into a beautiful smile. "There's a vast difference between the magic stores of a mortal such as Wren, and that of a Fae. Our very essence is made of magic. It is why we die if we are stripped of it, much like you would die if you lost too much blood. For mortals, you can burn through your magic and become exhausted much more easily, because you have less of it. This portal? It's as draining as running a couple of laps."

She gestured for me to step through, Gavin already having done so as Kyoni talked. Once we were on the other side, she broke the portal, the sheet of ice crashing to the new forest floor with a sound like shattering glass.

Fleurette flinched. "I hope there's no one near to hear that."

Kyoni tsked. "The fort isn't close enough. We have a short walk before we'll get there."

She led the way, her magic guiding her through the hilly forest. Within fifteen minutes, she put a finger to her icy lips. "It's just over that incline," she whispered.

We crept closer, getting down on our bellies to barely crest the hill. Below us, an old cement wall came into our field of vision, encompassing an impressive amount of land. From our vantage point, the wall was angled to give us a view of one side and the front, where a solitary gate stood, complete with two men in unusual obsidian armor flanking the entrance.

I let out a faint curse. "That's the armor Annie's children wore in the prison realm."

Fleurette, stationed next to me, turned her head to look at me. "Are you sure?"

I nodded. "Does it look like anything you've seen in this world?"

"I suppose not."

I thought through the ramifications. "She's still trapped there, but others are able to pass through the gate. It must be slowly opening, but she still can't fit through."

"That, or the magic of your legacy is physically barring her from exiting the gate," Fleurette theorized.

"How do you mean?" I asked.

She heaved a breath. "Think about it. *So long as the cat that walks as a woman lives, the witch Annie Coddle can never return.* What if, by your very presence here, she's unable to step through that gate?"

"I never thought of that before." If that were true, all her other attempts—using the magic of her deceased partner to create a portal, forcing Wren to take her—would have failed with or without my interference. I could have been thwarting her this whole time by just *existing*.

That was a heavy thought.

I blew out a breath. "Well, regardless of how Annie's still trapped, this seems like the place her minions have taken over. Which means this is where we're going to find Kokoro and Holly."

"How can you be certain?" Gavin asked from my other side.

I smirked. "I can't be. Not until I get inside. But call it a hunch."

"You and your hunches," he murmured. "How on earth are you planning on getting in there?"

It was a high wall, too tall for any of us to jump or climb over. But the gate the men guarded had a small window, and I estimated from my vantage point that it would be just big enough for a cat to fit through. I pointed to the front entrance, a plan forming in my mind. "Through there, of course. I might need backup, though. Gavin, let's get in touch with Rosa."

So far, Rosa had been game for anything. But when Kyoni pinpointed her location and opened a portal directly in front of her, I saw hesitation from the otter shifter for the first time. She peered through the portal from her side, her dark eyes wide.

"Are you sure this is safe?" she asked with trepidation.

"Perfectly," I responded. "Here, I'll show you."

I jumped through the portal to join her. "I'm on this side," I said as I jumped back. "I'm on the other side." Jump. "I'm on the shifter side." One last jump. "I'm on the fort side."

"Okay, okay," Rosa said, exasperated amusement etched on her face. "I get it. Here I come." She stepped through, followed by Jasper, who wrung his hands as he glanced at his new surroundings.

"Just you two?" Gavin asked, giving Rosa a beaming smile.

She returned it. "Just us. For now. We were on our way to Hokumel with the whole wolf pack ahead of us when Cressida messaged me. So, tell me, what are we doing here?"

"Gavin had filled you in about Kokoro, right?" I asked.

She nodded.

I continued, "We think she's being kept in the old compound on the other side of this hill. Her, and our guest Holly and her baby."

"Who happens to be the last lawyer of the firm Elkins employed," Fleurette butted in.

"Holly, not the baby," Gavin supplied.

I ignored these contributions. "I'm going in through the front, but I thought it would be good to have some small animal backup. You know, easier to sneak around that way. And Jasper, if our friends are hurt, you would be good to have along as well, if you're willing."

He sighed and closed his eyes but nodded. "I can do that."

Rosa clapped him on the back. "That's the spirit, Jas." She turned to me. "What about the ice queen over there? What's her deal?"

Kyoni chuckled. She had moved away from our group to give the shifters a chance to acclimate. Now, she approached our little party.

"Sorry. It's becoming hard to remember who's met who already," I apologized. "Rosa, Jasper, meet Kyoni, the Fae Queen's head of security. Kyoni is also the one who makes the amazing portals. It's way quicker to travel this way."

"Nice to meet you," Kyoni greeted the shifters. She did not offer to shake their hands, however.

Rosa didn't notice the possible slight. "Likewise. Okay, Cress, show us this compound."

We crept back into position, snaking our way to the crest of the hill. I pointed to the window on the gate.

"How are we going to get to that door?" Rosa whispered.

"Distraction." I moved my finger from the gate to the road leading to the entrance. It stretched out over the cleared terrain before disappearing around a bend. "I'm going to tell Grimm to make some noise over there. Hopefully, the guards will go investigate, and when they are lured over there, Gavin and Fleurette can keep them occupied."

"What if they don't come?" Fleurette asked.

I looked at Kyoni. "Can you make it snow?"

She gave me a look. "Are you seriously asking a frost Fae if she can conjure winter weather? It's what I was created to do."

"Excellent. Why don't you give us a little extra cover, then. That way, even if they don't move very far, it will give the three of us a chance to sneak in there."

"I'm on it." Kyoni closed her eyes and let out a gusty sigh. The air around us cooled immediately. Before long, tiny snowflakes began to fall in the area outside of the commune.

A thrill shot through me. "You guys. Teamwork makes the dream work."

For once, I wasn't completely winging a plan, and it felt … odd. Satisfying, but odd.

I was already in my cat form, having filled Grimm in on the plan. He was keen to play his part, and eager to possibly sink his teeth into some ACFer. He was worried about me, though, which I felt through our bond like a crease in an otherwise perfect piece of paper.

"CC, love, I swear if you take any unnecessary risks—"

I shushed him, rubbing my body against his front legs. "I'll be fine. Since when do I take unnecessary risks?"

He breathed out a beleaguered sigh. "If you are trying to put me at ease, you're going about it the wrong way, as it makes me think of all the ways you've risked yourself in the past."

"Psh. And here I am still, right?"

He licked the top of my head. "If what they say is true, you must be on your ninth life by now."

"Nonsense. If I recall, you're the one who has died already. But enough. Stop with the worry; you'll distract me. Grimm, you go with Gavin and Fleurette and you do your best to distract those guards. I love you. I'll see you soon."

He trotted off toward my two friends, giving me one last glance with his sunflower eyes. "I love you too."

I turned, facing Rosa, who had also transformed. Her cute otter face seemed to be smiling at me.

"What?" I asked.

"You two are cute together. I didn't really see it before, but I see it now."

I rolled my cat eyes as best I could. "Thanks. Shall we?"

"Let's." She bounded over to Jasper in her rolling gait. I followed.

It took a few minutes for Grimm, Gavin and Fleurette to get into position. The whole while, I tried my best not to let my anxiety gnaw at my insides, knowing that Grimm would feel it as well and wonder what was happening with me.

Soon enough, I heard him off in the distance. Grimm's vocalization was a mixture of bark and yelp, with anger mixed into the tone. It sounded nothing doglike, and if I hadn't already known it was a distraction, this noise would have brought me rushing over to see what was wrong.

Perfect.

A second later, Fleurette screamed as if she were dying.

I shivered despite knowing it was all an act. Surely that would get the guards' attention.

And yes, there they went, clutching their obsidian spears as they clanked down the road and out of sight.

Kyoni breathed another heavy sigh, causing the weather to turn even fouler around her. She sprinted downhill, following the two guards. "Good luck," she whispered to me.

I raced to the entrance, with the otter and rabbit at my heels. The gate was solid up close, and now that I was here, I could estimate the circular window—a glorified peephole—to be about eight inches tall at five feet up. It was higher than I had anticipated, but nothing I couldn't handle.

To be thorough, I pushed on the gate, but it did not sway. The hard way it was.

"Hang on a sec," I told my companions.

I bunched up my muscles and sprung, grasping at the cement surface with my claws and thankfully finding enough purchase to keep propelling myself up the door. I gripped the hole with my front claws, dragging my body up and through.

Before I jumped down into the commune, I did a quick survey. The immediate ground on the other side of the door was designed as a courtyard, and beyond that sat small wooden dwellings—dilapidated, but still structurally sound.

A few people milled about past the first line of houses, but no one seemed to be on guard for this side of the entrance. Apparently, they figured two outside guards would be enough.

Suckers.

I jumped down. Making sure one last time that the coast was clear, I shimmered. The door was locked on this side with a simple latch. I undid it, swung the door open enough to allow an otter and a rabbit to lope through, and closed the door again, latching it. Then I retransformed.

"Let's go. I want to check out each of the houses," I told Rosa and Jasper.

There was not much in terms of ground cover to shield us from view, so I performed a mad dash from the gateway to the nearest dwelling. I bent down, placing my nose on the threshold, and breathed deeply.

"What are you doing?" Rosa asked, the two shifters following me closely.

"I'm scenting for Kokoro. I've been around her enough to have her scent signature in my brain. I can't smell as well as Grimm, but it's better than a human's nose."

Kokoro smelled of watercolor paint, fresh paper, honeysuckle, and spices. She had taken on a hint of Fleurette's green, earthy smell by virtue of being around her for much of the time. I took another smell. The air inside reeked of rust and mildew. No Kokoro here.

We moved on to the next house, and the next. At the fourth building, I caught a scent of fresh milk mixed with sweat. The first smell harkened me back to my kitten days when I still nursed from my mother, a sweet, innocent time of my life full of cuddles and lick baths, tail pounces and purrs. Overlayed with these memories, I saw in my mind a picture of Holly nursing Katinka, a smile on Holly's face as she tenderly watched her infant daughter.

"This one," I said to my friends before quickly transforming to try the door.

It was locked, of course.

I shimmered back down into my less conspicuous form. "I'm going to see if there's another way in. A window, maybe?"

I scouted the entire perimeter, keeping a watchful eye out for any humans milling about. The gods must have smiled on me, for no one was present. But the windows were all too high and, as old as they were, all intact. I feared breaking one would alert the ACFers of our presence.

I returned to Jasper and Rosa. "No go on the windows."

Jasper sniffed at the junction of wall and ground. "These buildings are poorly built. This one has a dirt floor."

"Wait, it does?" I bent down to inspect what he was looking at. Sure enough, the wooden plank siding stuck directly into the ground without a floor. "I can't dig well, though. It would take me ages."

Jasper's nose twitched as he bent his long ears back. "Your feline claws are useless here. Let us pros do it."

Rosa loped over and got into position next to Jasper. "Ready?"

"Go!" Jasper exclaimed gleefully. His front legs went to work, scratching at the ground with tremendous speed. Rosa too dug her claws into the dirt, carving out a divot with each pass. I watched with appreciation as the two quickly dug out a tunnel.

Not a moment too soon, either. I heard footsteps from the other side of the building. "Quick!" I blurted, practically pushing Jasper through. Rosa was larger but managed to squeeze through with her long, thinner body. I dove into the hole, wriggling through the dirt until I popped out on the other side, just as the owner of the stomping feet turned the corner.

I hoped he didn't notice the churned-up soil next to this dwelling.

I looked around, immediately finding Holly resting on the floor with her back against some flour bags. Her eyes went wide at the sudden appearance of a rabbit, an otter, and a cat in her midst.

"What on earth ...?" she began to mutter.

CHAPTER 26

Holly looked terrible. Her short, greasy hair stuck up in spikes about her head. Her clothes, the same ones she had been wearing the last time I saw her, had dirty patches everywhere, with lactation stains on her blouse and sweat stains at her armpits. She smelled like milk, old sweat, and blood. The latter scent worried me.

Given her state, I figured it was safe to say that she indeed was *not* in cahoots with the ACF.

Her red-rimmed eyes bounced from animal to animal with increasing alarm. Something in this situation had to change, and fast. This was the moment I'd hoped wouldn't pass. If we were to help her, I wouldn't have the privilege of keeping my secret from her.

For the benefit of the greater good, I made my decision.

I approached and transformed in front of her. She flinched back at the magical change, eyes widening even more. But as soon as she recognized me, she relaxed.

"Cressida? How did you get here?"

I made a soft shushing sound. "We're here to get you out. Are you okay?"

She grimaced, and her eyes filled with unshed tears. "My leg's messed up. They took Tinka from me. I fought them when they did. All I got for my troubles was a gashed leg." She shifted to her side, showing a large, crusted bloodstain on the underside of her trouser leg. "It hurts to stand, so I've parked myself against these bags." She heaved a sigh, trying to stay stoic.

I winced. "Jasper, can you fix it?"

The rabbit nodded and hopped over. Holly stared, uncomprehending.

"This is Jasper. He's a healer," I whispered. I grasped her hand, which felt like a cold fish in mine. "Let him place his paws on you."

Holly paused, considering, before nodding her permission. Jasper placed his front paws on her bad leg. The lawyer closed her eyes and allowed a puff of breath to escape, a tiny sign of relief from the pain.

"So, they took your baby away. Why? Where is she?" I asked in soft tones.

She screwed her eyes shut at my words, allowing the gathering tears to escape down her dirty cheeks with a single sob. It was the most emotion I had seen from the taciturn woman since meeting her. "They want her for some reason. They want the witch to raise her. They only bring her to me for feedings." She let out a gasping chuckle as she gestured to her stained shirt. "Not often enough, obviously."

Why would Katinka be important to Annie? I'd have to circle back around to that thought. For now, there was another pressing matter. "And what about Kokoro? Where is she?"

"She was with me for a while. They kept her tied up, but she was at least a comfort to me after I fought to keep my baby. Then they took her away, just this morning, actually. Something about needing her for bait."

My heart stumbled over a beat. "They took her to the gate? Annie must be close to getting out."

"I have no clue. I just know I'm still here because Tinka needs my milk. Once the supplies come, I'll never see her again." Holly stifled a sob, her shoulders shuddering.

"That's not going to happen," I told her, my resolution strong. "Jasper is healing you, and we are going to break you out, get Tinka back, and go rescue Kokoro next."

"Is it just the three of you?"

I shook my head. "Fleurette and Gavin and a frost Fae are outside the wall. Grimm too."

She shut her eyes tight. "Fleurette's cottage. I tried so hard to stop them from taking us. I'm sorry for the damage."

"Hey, it's okay. Although you do have some explaining to do. We know who you are, Hollis Brothers. And Fleurette thought you might have orchestrated all of this. I'm glad to prove her wrong in this instance. But we do expect some answers."

Holly blanched. "That's even worse. Why would she think that?"

"Well, you were the missing lawyer of the trio, and so far, two out of three turned out to be on the wrong side of things. It seemed likely we'd get a three for three."

"No," she whispered, the word barely distinguishable. "It's why I left. It's why I've been on the run."

"Holly," I demanded her attention. She looked at me. "Don't fall apart on me now. Here's the deal. You saw my secret. You'll see more before this whole thing is through. In exchange, you'll tell me your story. Got it?"

Her self-pity dissolved a bit, replaced by her characteristic strength of character. "Got it."

Jasper backed away, and with a quick morphing of his body, he stood human again. He crouched to hide his genitals. "Uh, hi Holly. Nice to meet you. Your leg should be all better now."

Holly stared at the naked man. "Um, thanks?"

"Jasper and Rosa—she's the otter—are shifters. They are a

part of the prophecy too, and I'm so glad to have them on this rescue mission," I told Holly.

"And what about you? Are you a shifter too?"

"I am … but not a human shifter." I searched her eyes. If she *were* a part of the ACF machinations, she would have understood what I was.

But she only stared blankly back. "What does that mean?"

I smiled wryly. "I'm a cat. I was born a cat. I can become a human, but it's not my natural body. And … I am the only thing standing between this world and Annie Coddle."

She gave her head a small shake. "I will take your word for it."

I looked around. The room seemed to be used as food storage, judging by the flour and potato sacks I saw. "When will they bring Tinka back in for her next feeding?"

She grimaced again. "Soon, hopefully. My breasts are painfully full and I'm beginning to leak."

"Is there anyone else you know of that is being held against their will here?"

"No. There's only a handful of men here, and even less than there were before. I think this place is running on a skeleton crew. Most of them left with Kokoro this morning. But no other captives."

I nodded. "Small blessings. Okay, here's the deal. We're staying with you until they bring Tinka back. Until then, we'll hang tight. Jasper, Rosa, how do you feel about the element of surprise?"

Jasper only looked at the ground, his ginger hair flopping into his face, but he nodded. Rosa, still in otter form, let out a chirp as she turned a tight circle.

I took that as a yes.

We knew when Tinka awoke from her nap, because her hungry cries broke through the compound. It only took another ten minutes before the door jiggled. I hid behind a potato sack with Jasper. Rosa crept over to the side of the door. It opened inward, and a man came in holding the inconsolable baby.

Holly stayed in her lounging position, pretending her leg was still injured. She held out her arms to receive her daughter.

"Get her to shut up, will you?" the surly man said as he practically thrust Tinka into her mother's arms. Holly unbuttoned her shirt, wasting no time in guiding the baby to her breast.

As he straightened, Rosa, now in human form, closed the door behind him. He began to turn with dawning confusion, magnified further when he saw a naked woman standing in the way of the door.

The man only got out the start of a question before Rosa clocked him over the head with a rusty bucket she had found. The metal made a satisfying thunk against his skull. He dropped to the ground like another sack of potatoes.

Jasper and I changed into our human shapes. "Nice clobber, Rosa. You two got him?" I asked my shifter friends. Rosa beamed and nodded, flipping him over to secure his hands with some rope we had found.

I cracked open the door, shimmered again, and raced out of the building in a straight line to the entrance, leaping with grace for the hole and making it through in one fell swoop. I didn't stop running until I found Grimm, who looked anxious.

"About time!" he nearly growled at me.

I tried to catch my breath. "Stuff it for now. I found Holly, she's got her baby, and I need everyone to break her out. Where's Kyoni?"

Grimm pointed with his snout. "Up the hill. They all are."

"C'mon." I bounded in the direction he pointed, stopping in front of Fleurette with a metaphorical screech.

"Goodness, Cress. You startled me." She stood up, having been sitting near the two guards who were unconscious and wrapped in what appeared to be tree roots. Rupert perched on her shoulder, having found us again thanks to his magical homing beacon. He puffed up his feathers as he stared at me with beady eyes.

I transformed, panting slightly. "We need to take down this compound now. Holly and Tinka are with Rosa and Jasper. Kyoni, can you freeze the place once we get them out?"

"I'm on it. Best to act quick once I get started though." She rubbed her hands together in anticipation.

"Let's go." I marched down the hill, resolute, with Fleurette, Gavin, Grimm, and Kyoni behind me. We stopped at the gate.

I turned to Fleurette. "Will you pick me up and put me through the hole?"

She looked incredulous. "Why can't you just jump?"

I rolled my eyes. "Because that's what I did the first two times, and it's harder than it looks. I'd like to save what strength I have for the next step, since we are far from done. Okay?"

"Fine. Ready when you are."

I regained my true form, and Fleurette kindly picked me up, holding me out until I lined up with the hole. I pushed through and jumped down and raced back to Holly's building. The door was shut, but after I meowed once to let them know it was me, my human form opened it without issue.

"Everyone's ready out there," I told the group. "Let's get going."

Holly stood, using one hand to push herself off the ground, and the other to hold onto the still nursing Tinka. Jasper shifted back to rabbit. Rosa stayed her naked self, seemingly faster on two long legs versus four short ones.

I opened the door and ushered everyone out. Together, we ran for the entrance, an odd ensemble to behold. Halfway there, a man shouted, but we ignored him, putting on an extra burst of speed.

I reached the door and unlatched it, flinging it wide. Jasper hopped out first, incredibly fast for a small animal. I pushed Holly ahead of me before turning to look for Rosa. She was watching three men come racing after us.

But Kyoni was ready. She pushed her way through the door and raised both hands. A flurry of snow and ice flew past me, brushed against Rosa, and blanketed the men. They cried out as the flurry settled around them and grew, wind whipping and more snow falling over the compound.

Rosa pushed me out of the door to get away from the winter conditions. I couldn't blame her, given her lack of clothes. My party strode back up the hill, watching the developing storm from a safe distance. The snow flurry continued to grow, becoming a raging snowstorm that devoured the whole of the commune in its violent whiteness.

"When blizzards gorge ..." I said aloud.

Fleurette turned to me, a look of panic on her face. "*Time is due.* Cress, do you think that's what it means? And where is Kokoro?"

"She wasn't there. They took her to the gate this morning. For bait. We need to get there, and soon, but there's one last thing that needs to happen first." I turned to Holly. "I think it's time for you to explain everything, Hollis Brothers."

CHAPTER 27

H olly sighed, a resigned air pulling her face down. "It's past time," she admitted quietly, dropping her head to focus on the downy hair of her nursing daughter. Fleurette frowned but held her tongue to allow Holly to begin. "I meant to—wanted to—say something sooner, but after meeting you, I was nervous, I suppose."

"Why?" I asked.

She shook her head ruefully. "Cressida, when we first met, you had asked me how I knew about you. I did hear about you through the people you've helped, but truthfully, I'd already seen your name linked to certain files of Babcock's. I suppose I was afraid you'd want nothing to do with me if you knew my connection."

I raised my eyebrows. "It's a fair assessment, I have to say. Why don't you start from the beginning?"

She nodded. "My name *is* Hollis Brothers. My parents found it in their family tree, a great-great-aunt of sorts. I've always felt two minds about my first name. It's odd and unfeminine, and it doesn't suit me. But it also empowered me to be a strong version of myself because a masculine name can denote power, even when the bearer herself isn't actually powerful. And I was a strong-willed child. Serious. Determined. I often wondered if it was my name that made me that way."

She let out a breath as she switched Tinka to her other breast. "Anyway, I enjoyed becoming a lawyer, especially in a male-dominated world."

"I can relate," I chimed in.

Holly smiled at me. "I bet. So, I was hired by Babcock because of my skills, and soon made partner. To be clear, I had no idea that he was shady. Not in the beginning. He and I never worked cases together but split the load. And it worked. For five years, at any rate.

"And then Babcock told me that he was adding a third junior partner to the firm. I suppose I didn't care too much. Babcock seemed to have a rapport with Nic already, and he was likable enough. Very friendly."

She closed her eyes, struggling to grasp the right words. "Too friendly, I suppose. He began paying me compliments. Getting flirty with me. He was much younger than me, twelve years my junior. At first, I paid him no mind. But he didn't take my cold shoulder to heart. Constantly dropping hints. Paying attention to me. And despite myself, despite my resolve that I didn't need a man to know my self-worth, I began to feel something. I enjoyed his attention. He made me feel special.

"Still, I was professional. He was a work colleague and I made it a point never to get romantically involved with one. It was too messy. But he was persistent. Kind. My resolve was cracking.

"And, after nearly a year of his constant attention eating away at my resolve, I gave in."

Fleurette sucked in a sharp breath. I didn't quite understand her reaction.

"I felt terrible the next day and swore never again. Nic kept charming me, though, and damn me if I didn't feel like I was falling in love with him. So, I began to avoid him as much as possible.

"By then, though, I felt that something was off with the business. Babcock was becoming increasingly evasive with his answers. Certain files were off-limits to me, which should not have been the case, given our equal status. I felt like he was replacing me with Nic as his go-to person."

Holly stopped to take a breath, and to mentally fortify herself, it seemed. "Three months later, the Equinox Ball took place. We were all invited. I allowed Nic to take me. I actually wanted to look my best for him, which was ridiculous. I had never needed a man's approval before. But Nic had gotten under my skin, and I couldn't deny it any longer.

"Everything was fine for the first part of the ball. Nic was an attentive date and I found myself having a good time, despite my dress being slightly too tight and my stomach feeling off. You see, I had discovered earlier in the month that I was pregnant."

"Nic is Tinka's father," Fleurette stated.

Holly nodded miserably.

"My gods," Fleurette breathed.

I could only stare.

Holly continued, "I was planning to tell him that night. I wasn't sure how he'd react because we'd only slept together the one time. But I never got the chance. You see, I left to use the restroom, and when I came back, he was staring at a woman with a look of intensity.

"I asked him, 'Do you know her?'

"And he answered back, 'No, but I intend to.'

"And I tried to redirect him to me, but he brushed me off. It was like every sweet thing he'd said to me, every compliment, every flirty look had never happened. He was just cold to me. I left Nic and the ball once it was clear he was done with me."

"It was me. I was the woman at the ball," I realized with chagrin.

Holly nodded. "It was you."

I saw it clearly. Nic had tried to turn his magically enhanced charms on me. He had nearly succeeded. And Holly? She had just been practice.

"I couldn't believe that I had fallen for someone who could toss me aside so easily," Holly continued. "I felt used. And left with a ... condition I had never wanted. I liked my body before. I was never super skinny, but I was fit, and toned, and now, after giving birth, I have stretch marks and a flabby belly and giant boobs that leak all the time, and about ten pounds that refuse to go away." Two tears tracked down her face. "But I also have Tinka, and despite hating the way she came about, I love her fiercely, and will die for her if I need to."

She smiled ruefully. "And, as fate would have it, I've proven my devotion to my daughter time and again. I never told Nic about my pregnancy. I instead went on a sabbatical immediately after the ball. I only told Babcock that I would be gone for a number of months. After Tinka was born, I thought I owed my old partner an explanation. I visited him at his home, with Tinka. He had a guest over. I said I would be willing to come back to work if I did not have to see or interact with Nic. I'm sure he put two and two together. Katinka does share some of his features."

Now that she had said that, I *could* see a little Nic in her.

"Anyway, Babcock couldn't make any such promise. He told me to go home and think about what I was asking. I had a very uneasy feeling about it. Something about how he and the other man interacted when they thought I wasn't looking.

"A week later, I had to kill that same man because he broke into my home and tried to steal Tinka, who was only two weeks old at the time. I fled the scene, and I've been moving about ever since. I heard that both Babcock and Nic went missing, and in November I broke into my old office, finally reading the files I wasn't allowed to touch before. And I read up on you, Cressida."

"How did you find where I lived?" I asked her.

She barked out a shallow laugh. "That was pure happenstance. I traveled around, finding odd jobs through the months. And after speaking with Father Quillman and learning that you lived within a short horse ride of the area, I began moving in the same direction. I just happened to stop in the bakery for a little food and warmth when Kokoro found me. She asked if I was there to answer the ad, and I lied and said yes, not knowing about it but thinking I might get a quick job out of the deal. It was a surprise to me when you showed up. Anyway, you know the rest. And now here I am, still fighting off people trying to take Tinka for God knows what reason."

"I know the reason," I said.

She glanced at me with shiny eyes. "You do?"

"There's no easy way to say this, but ... Katinka is Annie Coddle's great-granddaughter."

Holly furrowed her brow, puzzling through what I just said. "Nic is her grandson?"

"Was. He's dead. Babcock too."

"Oh." Holly sat back, dazed by the news.

Fleurette fell to her knees in front of Holly, which startled the despondent woman. "Holly, I am sorry you've had to go through all of that. And I'm sorry for thinking you had a hand in Kokoro's disappearance. I see now that I was wrong."

Holly's mouth quirked up on one side bashfully. "I understand why you'd think that."

Fleurette nodded. "But Hecate bless us, I am so glad you found us. You see, not only was Nic Annie's grandchild, he was also my half-brother. That makes Tinka my flesh and blood niece. You're family."

"What? How?" Holly's eyes rounded and grew glassy with

tears once again.

"It's true," I added. "Fleurette's mom cheated on her husband and ran off to join the ACF, having Nic in the process. And Holly, you should not feel bad about falling for Nic's charms. Remember when we said Tinka would be a kharismorph when she got older? It doesn't always run in families, but in this case it does. Nic was a powerful kharismorph."

A light dawned in Holly's eyes as she took in my words. Her whole face brightened. "He was ... manipulating me the entire time?"

"You must be an exceptionally strong person. He did the same to me. I didn't sleep with him—" I added hastily when her face morphed into an expression of horror. "He tried to make me love him though. Same as you."

Holly glanced at Tinka, who had dozed off mid-nurse, comforted by a full belly and her mother's smell and warmth. "I often wondered if Nic had some persuasive powers. When you told me about Tinka's future magic, it only strengthened that conviction. You don't think Tinka is going to be like him, do you?"

I exchanged a glance with Fleurette. She shook her head resolutely. "Kharismorphy does have a chance to go horribly wrong," she explained with her usual gentle grace. "In Nic's case, he didn't have anybody to tell him that controlling people was inappropriate. In fact, I'd bet those around him thought it was a powerful tool and encouraged it. His mother—my mother—didn't take a heavy hand in caring for him, and the truth is she left him to live elsewhere when he was only two. Nic's upbringing didn't help him differentiate between right and wrong. Tinka's life will be different."

"How?" Holly whispered.

Fleurette smiled. "For one thing, she has you, a strong, caring mother, a mother who would never abandon her child and who will advocate for the best life possible. I know this about you. And for another, she'll have her aunt to teach her how to thoughtfully use her magic. That is, if you'll let me be in her life."

A fresh tear fell from Holly's eye. "Thank you. I've had nobody. My parents didn't enjoy my form of magic and cut ties with me once I was old enough. I have no siblings. No true friends, either."

"You've been alone for a long time," I observed, giving her hand a squeeze. "Not anymore."

Fleurette looked thoughtful amidst this new revelation. "Holly, again, I'm sorry I thought you betrayed us. But it begs the question. If you didn't tip off the ACFers to our location, who did?"

Rupert, having stayed on Fleurette's shoulder during the entire conversation, ducked his head and hopped off, flapping to gain altitude, and disappearing into the nearby trees. Fleurette hardly noticed, as used as she was to Rupert's new erratic schedule. She just enjoyed the time he was around.

I watched him go, though, and had an epiphany. Rupert was always present—albeit for short bursts of time—when bad stuff occurred. He had never bounced back after his captivity at the hands of Althea. We chalked it up to a post-traumatic disorder, but what if there was something more?

I hoped I was wrong for once.

If I wasn't, it would break Fleurette's heart.

CHAPTER 28

"Rupert? Rupert! Where are you?" I called out. Grimm and I padded through the forest in the direction he had flown. I'd made an excuse to Fleurette and the rest of the group, not wanting to upset my friend with baseless allegations. Besides, Holly needed time to rest after her ordeal before we sought the gateway.

Rupert let out a weak caw ahead of us. We rushed over to find him on the ground, head hanging low, simply waiting.

It was not what I expected, to say the least.

I approached until I was face to face with the bird. Grimm circled to his back.

"It was you, wasn't it?" I accused him.

He looked at the ground, refusing to meet my eyes. He seemed weakened. "I wish I could say it wasn't. But I can't."

In anger, I hissed. Grimm growled in frustration behind him. The Rupert of old would have squawked and fluttered at such angry noises directed at him, but this dejected corvid took no mind.

"Go ahead," he muttered. "I deserve it."

"How could you do something like this? This whole time, Rupert?"

He croaked feebly. "I didn't have a choice, Cressida! I would never willingly betray Fleurette. I love her!"

"Then *why*?"

"It was the witch."

A chill tingled along my spine. "What witch? When?"

He waved his beak back and forth. "At the coast. When I was captured. The one with the long pale hair. She looked enough like Fleurette that I first felt a kinship with her. But she placed a spell on me."

"Althea." Unkind thoughts flitted through my mind. She was the gift that kept on giving, even after death. "What spell?"

"She used my special bond with Fleurette, twisted it, and re-linked me with Annie Coddle. The old witch talks to me, tells me what to do, uses my eyes sometimes."

The shiver intensified. "Is she watching us now?"

"No, no," he assured me quickly. "I can feel when she does. It's why I stay away so much, even though it kills me to be away from Fleurette. If I feel her coming on, I get away. But her directions have become harder to ignore. I try to show her things she can't use against you, but sometimes I can't help myself!"

"It was because of you that she sent the earthquake to the shifter village, wasn't it?"

"Yes." His voice was small.

"And you stole the communication crystal."

"Yes."

"What did you do with it?"

"Annie was frustrated that she had no communication with anyone out here. She knew you had the crystal you stole from her son, so she made me steal it. I brought it to a man here. He used it to talk with her. And then Annie told them where the cottage was located. It was the worst day of my life."

"The worst day of *your* life? What about Holly? And Koko-ro?" My anger sizzled just under the surface.

He fluffed up his feathers in defense. "It could have been

worse! At least Fleurette was gone when they came. And you, I suppose. I do feel bad for the women they took. I know Kokoro makes Fleurette happy. It was at that point that I knew I needed to stay away from Lyle's, just in case Annie caught wind of it. I like Lyle."

"Shall I eat him now, love?" Grimm growled.

"I'm sorry!" Rupert yelped. "I've been trying to stay away and not show her too much when she looks through my eyes. But I *need* Fleurette."

"And why is that?" Curiosity got the best of me. I had never understood the connection between Fleurette and the damned bird.

"It was the magic she used to bond us together. That's all I know. Without her, I-I'm nothing. I can feel it in my bones."

"Well, Rupert, you piece of garbage, because of you, Fleurette is hurting. Your actions took away the love of her life and put her in danger. And because of you, Holly nearly lost her daughter to the ACFers."

Rupert let out a croaking groan as he hopped sideways away from us. "I know. I know! And Annie is about to open the gate the rest of the way as well. All things I helped with! But I'll make it right."

I flexed my claws. "You have two seconds before we both pounce on you. I've heard that crow tastes terrible, but I'm willing to try it."

He emitted a strangled caw. "I'll make it right! I swear!" He hurriedly hopped away, opened his wings, and flew off into the sky.

I sighed. "I hate being right sometimes."

Fleurette did not take the news well. The moment I told her Rupert was the traitor, she flopped onto the ground beside Holly, her tan face paling.

"I should have seen the signs," she moaned as her eyes welled with tears.

"Fleurette, what's the deal with Rupert, anyway? I never wanted to pry, but your relationship with him never made sense."

She grinned halfheartedly, despite her tears. "He was a happy accident. I was very lonely before you fell into my life, you know that?"

I nodded.

"I had hoped for a companion of sorts, although—and I'm ashamed to admit it now—I had half a mind that I wanted a romantic partner. No humans in Knobby Hill were so forthcoming, so when I found an abandoned fledgling crow in the woods during one of my walks, I had an idea. I took it home, looked up some transformation spells, and hoped that when the crow was fully grown, it would turn out to be a female."

I furrowed my brow. "You were going to turn the crow into a human?"

She chuckled. "That was the plan. I'd found some notes in one of my books about animal transfiguration. The author had not succeeded either, but had a good basis, using shifter blood to help facilitate the change. It would be a temporary change happening in a cycle, but even if the crow was a boy, I'd at least have someone besides my dad to talk to. I tweaked it a little, since I knew no shifters. I used my own blood for the spell. I did the necessary spellwork and hoped for the best."

"And what happened?" I asked, leaning forward.

"Do you mean, did I succeed in turning Rupert into a human?" Fleurette smiled anemically. "No. The spell was a dud in that regard. But I did create a strong, permanent link between us. I could speak to him, and he me. It's how I learned that Rupert was a boy. He was thus more attuned to my magic, which allowed me to place the tracking spell upon him. His life force was tied to me, however. Without being around me frequently, he failed to thrive. I felt bad for taking away his freedom like that, but he never seemed to mind."

"You created a familiar out of him," I pointed out.

She looked thoughtful. "I suppose I did, in a way. I could have called a familiar to me, but there are tight regulations in place. I'd have to register the familiar, which would draw attention to me, to the fact that I'm not just a minor witch. So, I never did. But yes, Rupert makes a fine substitution."

"Until he betrayed you."

Her face fell. "Yes. Well. I can't fully fault him, if what he says is true. I can thank my dear mother for that. She must have perverted the magic bond between us to allow Annie to use him. I'm guessing she did this before her change of heart. No matter. What's done is done. And at least now we have our 'traitor lost.'"

"I definitely don't see him coming back," I agreed, my shoulders slumping at the thought.

Fleurette mirrored my resignation but tried to perk up. "The important thing is to get to the gate before it fully opens and save Kokoro."

I took a deep breath. Fleurette's summing up of our tasks ahead did nothing to express the true enormity of our mission. My head felt like it might float off my body.

"Those two things are one and the same, if I'm not mistaken. But how can we accomplish this? What am I supposed to do?

Fleurette, I have no clue what I'm doing."

Grimm nuzzled my hand in an effort to bring me back to earth. Fleurette, as worried as she likely was for Rupert, took my other hand.

"I say this with full respect for your role," she said as she gave my hand a squeeze, "but Cress, do you ever know what you're doing?"

I barked out a laugh. "No, I suppose not. But the last time I was this clueless was when I had to face Annie for the first time. And my ancestor gave me a hint."

"Listen. I believe we have found all the components of the prophecy, did we not?"

Did we? I ran through the poem in my head, having memorized it by now. "We still haven't killed anyone," I pointed out.

"Do those poor saps down there not count?" Gavin asked.

I shook my head. "Maybe. But we didn't actively kill them; it was self-defense. Besides, do we know they're actually dead? They could be hiding together in there somewhere. But I'm not about to go and look." Kyoni's storm still swirled like a deadly ballet over the doomed compound.

I turned to Fleurette. "And your potion was ruined by the ACF."

She seemed shocked. "It was?"

"Yeah. They did a number on your workspace."

Her face fell. "Did they destroy everything? My books? My supplies?"

I tapped my lips. "No, just whatever was on your workbench. A few smashed bottles, but the rest of your supplies are untouched, and the books seemed sound."

"Thank Hecate. All's not lost, then."

"*Not lost*? Um, Fleurette, I'm not sure you heard me correctly."

She quirked her mouth to the side. "You're right. I did lose the strength potion I was working on. I have a side project going, though, and I think that one is safe."

"A side project? What is it?"

"I'm not sure I should say yet. I can't say for sure it will work, and I don't want to get anyone's hopes up. But I think I know what went wrong when I tried to spell Rupert into a human. I might have worked out the bugs, so to speak."

My eyes widened at the implication. I glanced at Grimm, who gazed at me with loving eyes. "Are you saying...?"

"I'm saying it's possible. I might have a better idea once all of this is over. However that happens."

"Hmm." I scratched my cheek in thought. "That would be amazing, Fleurette. But it still doesn't solve our potion problem now."

Kyoni approached. "Does this help?" She held out her hand, something small tucked into her fist.

"What is it?" I held out my palm, careful not to let her touch me. She dropped a tiny vial into it.

It was freezing to the touch, having come from her person, but the contents were liquid. The bottle was familiar. "Is this what I think it is?"

She huffed a chuckle. "It's the sticking potion. I have the antidote as well, but something tells me we won't need it. Do you think this potion will work for your prophecy?"

I rolled the vial about my hand, warming it in the process. A plan was beginning to form in my head.

"I think it's time to gather our crew. Gavin, where are the bounty hunters?"

He gave it some thought. "Last I checked, they were all on their way to Hokumel. I imagine they're waiting for us there."

"Can you tell them to meet us here?"

Gavin nodded, digging into his pocket for his mirror.

I turned to Rosa, who had dressed herself again. "Rosa, what about the shifters?"

She looked at Jasper—also human again, and fully clothed—who shrugged his shoulders. She responded, "We were a couple of miles behind them when you brought us here. I'm sure if they're too far away still, Kyoni could help us get them here faster."

Kyoni affirmed with a head nod. I turned my attention to the Fae. "Great. Kyoni, let's bring them here as well. And then, I'll need to get the rest of my family. It's time to gather the troops."

CHAPTER 29

I'd had a short life, in the scheme of things. The world was billions of years old. Some of the trees that surrounded us were a couple of hundred. Fleurette was thirty-two. Me? I had yet to reach my fourth birthday.

Regardless, the fate of my world rested squarely on my young, inexperienced shoulders.

Perhaps they weren't so untested after all, though. I'd faced Annie once before and gotten the better of her. I'd beaten her grandson's charms and permanently rendered her dream-invading son an empty shell of a man. And I had dismantled her gods-damned cult piece by piece.

Beating her was what I was born to do. It was my destiny.

Or maybe, it was *her* destiny to destroy me and take over this world as its new god.

Either way, I knew deep down that there would be only one person standing at the finish of this. One way or another, it would all end here.

The bounty hunters had finally reached us, and we had gathered the rest of our known allies through Kyoni's portal, as well as the shifter wolves. From there, we trekked through the forest in the direction of the worsening weather. After those few short hours, we stood in a deep, ancient forest of cedar, fir and vine maple, the view before us a swirling wall of snow. The barrier stretched up twenty feet, and blew in a heavy counterclockwise ring, the interior obstructed by the densely swelling flakes. This freezing perimeter guarded what I could only assume was a mighty treasure—the gateway to Annie's world.

As I watched this twisting tempest, contemplating all that had brought me to this point, I couldn't help but feel a tiny bit pessimistic. I had most of my allies, sure, but as to what I had to do to actually stop Annie? I was still clueless.

To make matters worse, Kyoni hit me with some bad news.

"The magic in this area has been sucked dry," she said with a shiver.

"What does that mean?" I asked, noticing Alfrothooll nod his head in agreement with his fellow Fae.

She took a fortifying breath. "I'd normally be able to control this storm. But there is no magic here. I can't create my own snow, and I can't channel the weather you see before us. I noticed my powers dimming while we were at the compound. Making the blizzard there must have drained me more than it should have. And creating that last portal wiped me out. I'm down to fumes."

I thought through what she said. "Annie's using up all of the magic?"

Kyoni nodded.

Fleurette hummed in consternation. "Mine as well. I won't be able to use my magic for fighting. More importantly, this is very bad for this world. Her overuse of magic could have disastrous consequences for us."

"What could be making her magic consumption so much worse?"

"If I had to guess, I'd say that now that the gate is more open, the prison dimension is sucking up much more of our natural magic. Annie is using a lot, judging by this storm, but even more is being wasted. She'll turn this world into a desert soon enough—magically speaking—if we can't close that gate."

"Okay, so not only will her release spell doom to our citizens, but also cause all magic to leave this realm. Permanently?"

Fleurette shrugged. "It most likely recurs naturally, but it's a slow process. The good news is that most of us don't require magic to live."

"Speak for yourself," Kyoni butted in. "I'll die without magic eventually. It's why the Queen used The Crystal Graveyard as a prison in the first place. And it's why we had to abandon some of the other dimensions we tried to colonize. Too little magic made us weak and sick. This place is fine, for now, but I guarantee you will lose some life forms if Annie keeps that gate open."

"Well, I suppose that means we need to stop goofing off out here," I muttered. "Okay, so you can't stop the storm, Kyoni. Can we just trudge through? It's only snow."

She held out a hand as if feeling the temperature. She shook her head. "Annie has put a lot of oomph behind it. It's not just snow. It's been enhanced since Alfrothooll went through it. *I* could get through it, but I think the rest of you would freeze solid if you tried."

"Well, that's just great," I grumbled. "Thanks for bringing such good news to the table, Kyoni."

"You're welcome." Either she ignored my blatant sarcasm, or it flew over her head.

I looked around me, at my gathered allies. Fleurette, Kyoni, and Alfrothooll at my right side. Gavin, Rosa, Jasper, and Holly with Katinka to my left. Mom, Dad, Lyle, and the Rambert siblings behind me. Grimm, my ever present second shadow, leaned his supportive weight into my legs.

On the outskirts, twelve wolves and six men stood guard, waiting for me to give them orders.

We still did not have our fated eye, or the fourteen Memory Keepers. Or Rupert, but that was to be expected.

If this was all I had, it would have to be enough. But there was no way I was going to let them freeze to death before we even got to the main event.

"How can we get around this, Kyoni?"

She grinned, her white teeth sparkling like snow. "You're lucky to have me around. Or, to be more precise, my little hand warmer."

"Aodh?" I frowned, perplexed.

She nodded, fumbling into her layers to grasp him. She withdrew her hand, cradling the sluggish salamander in her palm.

"What can he do?" I asked with skeptical eyes. He looked half-dead, and he was so small. I'd forgotten he existed, if I was being honest.

Behind me, a wolf growled. I turned quickly, spying a new person, old and bent, trudging toward us with the aid of a walking stick. Behind her, multiple Indigenous people followed, as well as one lone teenaged girl, with bobbed hair and round glasses.

"Stand down! They're allies!" I barked as my face broke into a huge smile at seeing Na'ah and her entourage. The wolves stepped back, allowing them to approach.

Sufia Zamani smiled at me once she was closer. "Sorry to be almost late. I told Ima I should have left a day earlier, but her sight is still recovering from prophecy-making, and she didn't see it soon enough."

"Where did you come from?" I asked with wide eyes.

Na'ah's eyes lit up, noticeable even with the wrinkles surrounding them. She spoke with a voice crackled and willowy with age, "This girl came to us out of nowhere today, and told us of great misfortune if we did not act. She is quite compelling.

I opened a portal, but it needed to be a distance away, because it would not work otherwise."

"Annie's used up the magic in the area," I told her.

She clucked her tongue. "Not a kind thing to do. If this is the future the witch has in mind for us, I want no part of it. We are here to help you, protector."

Just the thought of having the Memory Keepers on my side considerably brightened my outlook on this mission. "Thank you."

"It seems as if we are just in time. Especially since you were about to unleash the salamander. They are a wonderful ally to have, you know."

I glanced over at Aodh, who still lounged in Kyoni's palm with his eyes half closed. His frill undulated lazily in the breeze.

"I feel like I'm missing something," I said.

Kyoni laughed. "Just watch." She placed Aodh on the ground, facing the maelstrom. "Everyone, take a few steps back. On my signal, run through the storm!"

The clustered groups fell back a few steps, all eyes on the unassuming but brightly colored little creature. Aodh yawned, flashing rows of tiny teeth. For the first time, I wondered what he ate, as I hadn't seen him consume anything since he joined us.

"Nothing's happening ..." I sing-songed.

Kyoni shushed me. "Aodh, do your—"

An angry yell interrupted the Fae. We all turned in unison at the noise.

A man clad in obsidian ran toward us from around the bend in the perimeter, brandishing a crude spear. He let out another war cry as he sprinted.

Behind him, more bodies followed.

"It's an attack!" Gavin shouted.

Rosa whistled loudly. "Wolves, defend!" Her cry was answered by the pack as they charged at the aggressors with snarls and teeth bared.

The bounty hunters took up Rosa's call as well, when another group of ACFers accosted us from the other side. Within seconds, the sounds of battle filled the air around us.

Closest to us, Allen crashed into a man, knocking him backward. As he straddled the fallen individual, he yelled at us, "Go on, get out of here! There aren't that many, and we can hold them off."

I only allowed a moment's hesitation to see that yes, there were only enough ACFers to make this a fairly matched fight. I nodded at Kyoni, urging her to make something happen.

She turned her attention back to the salamander. "Aodh, you know what to do."

The salamander looked at her over his shoulder for a moment and winked. It was almost disturbing to see, coming from a nonhuman creature. He turned back, sucked in a breath, and—
WHOOSH!

A stream of fire flowed from his mouth directly at the storm. He tilted his head up, dousing the area in front of him at a height of up to six feet. The storm, disrupted from its endless cycling in a ring, shivered on the outskirts of the fire. The snow directly in front of the salamander melted and disappeared altogether, creating a hole large enough for a person to go through.

Kyoni ran over and carefully picked Aodh up as he continued to belch a conflagration. He paused for a breath.

"Go, go go!" she yelled.

I wasted no time and ran through the hole, noticing a definite chill in the air, but nowhere near freezing levels. I reached the other side with Grimm at my heels and watched as Fleurette, Gavin, Rosa, Jasper, and Alfrothooll ran through before the storm began closing in again. But Aodh did his trick again, and again, until our party was on this side of the storm safely, leaving the wolf shifters and the bounty hunters on the other side with our combined foes, the sounds of fighting greatly muffled by the barrier.

"I hope they'll be okay," I murmured.

Gavin placed a hand on my arm. "They'll be fine. Those ACF numbskulls had no training in combat. They'll be taken down quickly enough."

"My brothers and the rest of the wolves will make mincemeat out of them," Rosa cheerfully agreed.

Mollified by their sentiments, I took a moment to survey my new surroundings. The area inside the barrier was large, big enough that we needed to crest a hill before seeing anything out of the ordinary, at any rate. It also meant we might have a chance to catch our breath before being detected.

Wren huffed out a laugh as she looked around. "Quite the trick for a lizard."

"Salamander," Kyoni corrected.

"But how did he do it? I thought magic didn't work here," I said.

"It doesn't. Not for those of us who need to harness it from the environment. But his is a little different. It's just how he is. I can imagine you would have no trouble changing form here, even with the lack of magic."

"Oh. Innate magic. I understand." I said the words, but really, I didn't fully. Magic and its different forms were tricky business. Nevertheless, I was not about to question the Fae's words. "Can he keep doing that?"

Kyoni, suddenly diffident, shook her head. "Poor little guy was running out of steam at the end. I think he'll be tapped out for a while."

"Darn." There went another great source of power, at least

temporarily.

"Right. Well," I changed the subject, getting back to the business at hand. "Let's get going. I'm not sure what to expect, but be ready for anything, I suppose."

"That's not a great speech. You should have practiced beforehand," Gavin heckled with a twinkle in his eye.

I responded with a rude gesture, which only made him grin.

"Hey, there are children present," Wren complained with a teasing tone.

"Sorry. Gavin, do you want to take the lead?" I asked sardonically.

He shook his head. "Go ahead, oh fearless leader."

I knew what he was doing. I could feel my confidence flagging under the strain of the unknown, and the worry over keeping my friends and family safe. Gavin was merely ribbing me to bolster me, because he knew that a sassy Cressida was a bold and confident Cressida.

I glanced at Grimm, who also knew that I could do anything I put my mind to. His confidence in me shined like the moon in a starless night sky.

I marched resolutely forward, the sound of multiple feet crunching on the forest floor behind me. We wouldn't win any awards for quietest entrance, that was for sure.

At the crest of the hill, I stopped to inspect the scene. There, at the bottom of the hill in the exact center of a circular field, stood two metallic towers, spaced a good five feet apart. They thrummed with stolen energy, taken from Hokumel and other surrounding towns, I wagered. And between them, an odd film seemed to obstruct the view, like a gigantic soap bubble stretched between them. I peered closer. There were holes in the film, three to be exact, but these circular windows did not offer a view of the plateau behind them. Instead, they showed a darker scene, one of black rock and crystals.

It was the gate.

One of the holes was larger than the rest, near the bottom. I could see how Alfrothooll had managed to squeeze through. Even Annie's guard children could wiggle through the tight fit. But not Annie. She had more mass to her, and would need a wider hole to crawl through, thankfully.

But even as I thought this, one of the smaller holes widened almost imperceptibly, a moth-eaten texture lacing the perimeter. The barrier was collapsing, and it seemed to be happening at an accelerated rate. What Rupert had said was true: Annie planned to break out by the end of this day.

Just my luck.

The gateway may have taken up most of my attention, but further scrutiny led my eyes to a lone figure, long black hair fanned out over the ground where she slumped in front of the gate.

"Kokoro," Fleurette breathed. She lurched forward, intent on saving her love.

I barred her with my arm. "It's a trap. We need to be smart about this. I'll go with you. Slowly, though. No running."

Fleurette sighed in resignation. "Yes, mother."

"Hey, that's my line." I gave her a ghost of a smile, and then turned to address the party behind us. "Wait here. At the first sign of trouble, get out of here."

"Not happening, Cress," Fal replied, which was echoed by affirmations from various people.

I threw my hands up, admitting defeat. "Fine. Wait here, and at the first sign of trouble, come rescue us. Is that better?"

"Definitely," Rosa said. Many others nodded their heads.

My heart swelled. These people, even the ones I had just met and barely knew, were willing to risk their lives for my cause. For me.

I nudged Fleurette, and side by side, with Grimm flanking me, we carefully picked our way down through ferns and sorrel, reaching the field's edge without issue. From there, it would be just a quick run to Kokoro, who lay on the ground, flakes of snow and ice dotting her face. Before we made that last dash, I paused, using my blunted human senses to the best of my ability, but also relying on Grimm's superior faculties.

"Anything out there, Grimm?" I whispered to him.

He swiveled his ears about and gave a small half wag of his tail before looking at me. All clear.

I tugged at Fleurette's sleeve. "C'mon."

Each step toward the unmoving woman was a trial of nerves. I expected something, *anything*, to jump out and attack us. I counted to twenty steps with nothing preventing us before I began to let my guard down.

We reached Kokoro, who, thankfully, was breathing peacefully. Spelled, most likely.

I reached out. "Kokoro," I murmured.

My hand brushed her arm. She opened her dark eyes and screamed into the sky.

An arm, fleshy with sharp nails, shot out of one of the gateway holes and latched onto my arm. I tried to jerk back, but suddenly my sense of balance ceased to exist. Was I standing? Lying down like Kokoro? It no longer mattered, because my eyes rolled back in their sockets just as a consuming blackness overtook me.

CHAPTER 30

When I finally gained consciousness, I quickly grasped that I was not on the normal mortal plane.

"Awake at last, I see," a familiar voice, ancient yet timeless, said with definitive scorn.

I groaned and sat up, clutching my head, which pounded a drumming rhythm. I appeared to be sitting on nothing more than a general dark violet haze, the same shade as the surrounding environment and just as nebulous. "Where am I now?"

Annie also perched in the nothingness, her face smug as she crossed her shapeless ankles in front of her knees. She was just as terrifying as I remembered, although since our last visit, she had lost some weight, giving her an added haggardness to her fleshy countenance. Her life must have been harder these days. It gave me no small amount of satisfaction.

"You are in a nowhere space of my making, girlie. It's inside my head. I brought you here with a simple touch. It was my failsafe to make sure you didn't get the idea to place me in your pocket universe for keeps, like you did to my poor son and grandson. And I can end you here just as easily."

I frowned, dropping my hand from my head. "So why haven't you?"

She kept the self-satisfied expression plastered to her face, but for a fraction of a second, I saw it falter. It was enough to keep me hopeful. Still, Annie bragged, "I don't wish to. Not yet. Time has all but stopped in here, and I enjoy the tranquility. I'm sure, knowing you, you'll soon ruin it and then I'll get rid of you. As it is, I have an army that is about to take care of your little friends."

"You mean the motley band of your children beyond the barrier? Yeah, they weren't much of a threat."

She frowned, but just as quickly wiped it away. "Oh, no, that was just the warm-up act. I'm talking of something much bigger. Your ragtag group of friends doesn't stand a chance."

Despite my glimmer of hope, her words caused me no small amount of consternation. I stood up, brushing off my trousers, most likely a futile gesture given the fact that I was momentarily a figment of mind material. I walked to the side, finding footing easily enough despite the vagueness of the environment. I held my hands out, feeling for something. Anything.

Annie laughed, a sound that grated on me like claws on metal. "What is it that you think you are going to accomplish? My mind is a prison, kitty. And you are about to become only a memory." She raised her hands, chanting under her breath.

If I had learned anything from her son Gregor, it was that dream magic could be manipulated. Perhaps she could enjoy an eternity in my dream pocket as well. Perhaps I could dream-shield myself.

Unless, of course, this wasn't exactly a dream.

Lightning flashed through the violet haze, off in the distance. Annie's chants continued, and a building dread grew as much as an oppressive weight around me did.

I needed help.

At the thought, a lighter shade of violet appeared in front of me. I focused on the spot, and as I did, the color faded to white. A hand shot through the murk, dainty and welcoming. I grasped it and pulled.

A body followed the hand, easily pulled through the fog until the woman before me fully materialized. Her long, silky silver hair shined as she drew it out of her face with a knowing smile.

"Gilva?" I asked in disbelief.

"*Gilva?*" Annie shrieked, her chanting forgotten. The oppression lifted.

My ancestor smiled at me. "Hello, Granddaughter," she said cheerfully. She turned to Annie, changing her smile into a flat-lipped stare. "Annie. It's been a long time."

"How dare you come charging in, you lazy traitor! I'll destroy you as well, like I should have done years ago!"

I stared from Gilva to Annie, assessing, as the latter continued to hurl insults at the former. Something wasn't quite adding up. "Wait a minute. Gilva, how are you here?"

The silvery woman winked at me, ignoring the witch. "My little corner of consciousness is attached to yours, like neighbors. I heard you call out for help in your mind, and here I am."

I frowned. "But ... can you connect to other people's minds too?"

"Not like this, no. Only yours."

"Oh ho ho," I chortled as I swung my head back in Annie's direction. "*Somebody* lied to me!"

This wasn't Annie's mind at all. It was mine.

Annie screwed up her face in rage, turning a most unbecoming shade of red. "It is just desserts to trap you in your own mind like you did to my son! You meddlesome wench."

"Oh, Annie. Annie, Annie, Annie. It's not polite to lie. So, if this is *my* mind, can you really do me harm?"

Gilva cleared her throat. "The mind is a powerful thing, and she could still do damage to you. But not with me here." She placed a hand on my shoulder, closing her eyes. The air around us lit up, creating a bubble of white amidst the sullen purple.

Annie screeched, flinging her hands at us. Whatever the spell was, it bounced off the whiteness, leaving us unharmed. I smirked at her.

"If I can call to Gilva for aid, I can get rid of you. It's mind over matter, Annie baby. And I really don't like to clutter up my thoughts with garbage."

I imagined Annie disappearing from this space, taking the violet strains with her. Before me, Annie turned translucent.

"It's not over, cat!" she yelled as she faded from view. "Good luck getting out of your mind from here. I brought you in here; you can't leave on your own. And my army will finish you and your little club off in no time!" With that last shout, she winked out of existence.

The mood in my mind was much cheerier without her. A shimmering whiteness pervaded. But her last words troubled me.

"Is it true? Am I trapped in my own mind?" I asked my ancestor.

She gave me a worried smile. "It is entirely possible. Some would call it a magically induced coma. It *is* breakable, but it takes a long time for most. It is quite labor-intensive."

"I don't have time to waste! Gilva, what am I going to do?"

She placed a soothing hand on my shoulder, trying to quell the rising panic within me. "Fear not, little one. I may not be able to communicate with the outside world, but I still have a few tricks up my sleeves. Time moves much slower out there, so no need to rush back. Tell me, have you figured out the prophecy?"

"How do you know about the prophecy?"

"Because *you* know, remember? I only have consciousness when you visit me. It was a risky move, to make a new prophecy. But as long as you feel like it's paying off, it was the right thing to do."

"The only problem I see is, how do I stop her? I think I have all my allies, and a potion, and I'm fairly certain we're about to kill some people if what Annie said about an army is true. But we need to close the gate. And we need to keep Annie from emerging. And we are running out of time."

"Have you ever heard of Yggdrasil?" Gilva asked me.

I pursed my lips, shrugging with confusion.

"Yggdrasil was the name for a great tree, one that touched all the different worlds. It was said that the tree could grant or deny access to anyone wishing to cross from one realm to another. Just a thought."

I did not see how mythology would help my situation, but before I had time to ponder this, Wren unexpectedly popped into existence at my right. She looked momentarily dazed, her dark bangs mussed up and her balance off-kilter.

"Wren?" I gaped at her. "Is that really you or a figment of my imagination?"

"It's me. Where are we?" She looked around at the pervading whiteness.

"Inside my mind. What are you doing here?"

"Hmm." She quirked her mouth to the side. "I expected the inside of your mind to be a bit livelier. Woah, you're really pretty."

This last line was directed at Gilva. She smiled. "Thank you."

"Wren, this is Gilva, my ancestor," I introduced, reflecting upon the absurdity of the moment.

"Why does your ancestor live in your head?" Wren asked.

"I don't, child. I typically exist in an alternate realm, which can be accessed by my descendant's subconsciousness." She noticed the blank stare the girl began to give her. She amended, "I'm just visiting."

"Gotcha. Cress, I'm glad I found you. As soon as you passed out, Fleurette dragged you away a few feet to get you away from

Annie—that was her arm that grabbed you—and then she did something to Kokoro to get her to stop screaming. We rushed down to see what had happened, but then some freaky dead people started to emerge from the trees behind the gate, and—"

"Hang on, Wren. Dead people? There are revenants out there? What about Kokoro? Is she safe?"

She nodded quickly. "We got you and Kokoro back up away from the dead people. Revenants. I think Gavin and Fal carried you. Grimm of course is freaking out right about now. Fleurette took something out of Kokoro's throat and now she's fine. And then Fleurette told me that you were probably stuck in your mind, and we needed to get you out. I figured, if I can project myself into another dimension, why can't I project myself into someone's mind?"

"And here you are," I surmised. "Did Fleurette tell you it was okay to try it?"

Wren squirmed and refused to meet my eye, which told me the answer before she verbalized it. "Nooo, I just did it. Do you think she'll be mad at me?"

I shrugged my shoulders. "She'll be madder if this doesn't work. Let's get out of here." I turned to Gilva. "Thank you for coming to my aid. It was lovely to see you again."

Gilva hugged me, infusing me with her warmth. "I'm not certain we will see each other again."

I blinked, a sudden tug at my heart making my emotions go haywire. "Why is that?" A thought occurred to me. "Am I going to die?"

Gilva chuckled at my pessimism. "Sweet child, I can't see the future, but I doubt you'll have come this far to fail now. When you pass on the legacy, my consciousness will pass to your daughter."

"Pfft. It could still be ages before that happens."

"Nevertheless, if you win your battle over Annie, you will have no need for me again. Chin up, Cressida. And may the gods bestow their love and fortune upon you."

I wiped a stray tear away. "I'll miss you."

Her smile took on a melancholy shade. "I won't think anything of you until one of your descendants has a need for me. If they ever do. But if I did keep my sentience while by myself, I'd miss you too. Take care, Granddaughter."

I took one last look at my ancestor, memorizing her kind face, her willowy grace, her beauty. And then I turned to Wren and gripped her hand in my own. "Do your stuff, kiddo."

Wren nodded and closed her eyes. The white space vanished.

I blinked. My view was of trees against a backdrop of sky. It took my brain a second to realize I was on my back. And then the sounds of guttural moans and shouts met my ears.

I sat up, the sudden movement making my head spin. I clutched my offended skull, willing the swimming sensation to dissipate. I didn't have time for this.

"Cressida!" Fleurette gasped near me. I felt hands on my shoulders, my arms. "Are you alright?"

"Thanks to Wren, yes. Is she back?" I removed my hand, looking into not only her face, but Wren's, my mother's, my father's, and Kokoro's. "Oh good. Thanks, Wren. And I'm glad you're okay, Kokoro."

"You scared us," she replied.

"What's happening?" I asked the small group. My ears registered the sounds of chaos, but my friends blocked my view of the meadow below. I ineffectually shoved Fleurette's legs to the side to get a better look. She humored me by moving slightly.

The view confirmed what I heard. Utter madness.

Annie, the liar she was, had at least been honest about unleashing an army. And, just as Wren said, her troops were comprised of revenants. Annie had been busy, it seemed. She must have secretly been spelling countless graveyards and drawing the animated corpses to this spot for the last month. I thought I'd been on top of culling them, but clearly I had been wrong.

They came in waves from the trees, moaning and searching for warm bodies to destroy with their singular focus. Gavin led the defense, along with Kyoni, Rosa, and most of the Memory Keepers.

I stood up carefully, waiting for another bout of dizziness. It never came. I unsheathed Talon.

"Okay, Annie," I said with a voice of steel. "It's time to play."

CHAPTER 31

A swarm of undead bodies waited in the meadow below me. Some of my allies had already begun to take them down, but many more corpses took the place of the fallen. I raced down the hill, eager to join the carnage.

I had a score to settle with Annie.

Talon did its thing, lopping off limbs here and there, separating heads from desiccated necks, stabbing into the backs of soulless husks who were bent on hurting people I cared for.

Grimm weaved around bodies and attacked anything without a pulse. Gavin and Rosa fought back-to-back with pistols and daggers. Kyoni, though bereft of her weather powers, still had the chance to freeze some of the revenants solid by touching them.

I paused between dismemberments to look at the gate. The bubbles had widened even further, much to my dismay. I could see one of Annie's feet, bare with gnarled toenails, tapping a demanding rhythm on the solid stone floor in her dimension.

I made to return my attention to the task at hand, but a new movement caught my eye. A figure crouched behind Annie, seemingly unnoticed by the witch. With the lowest bubble opening further, the figure darted forward, squirming through the gateway in a bid for freedom.

A revenant groaned and made a grab for my shoulder, but Grimm took it down before I could pay it much heed. I continued watching as Annie realized what was happening and made a grab for the person. But the figure, a dusky lavender in color, shook off the grasp of the witch and crawled through the opening, setting herself completely free with a quick dusting of her dirty clothes.

Without missing a beat, she swept her deep blue hair away from her face, picked up a solid stick, and walloped the nearest revenant over the head with it.

Oh good. She was on our side.

The battle raged about me, and I jumped back into the fray, but the revenants kept coming in a solid stream. My arms grew tired, and I panted for breath. In one corner, I heard Gavin shout as one of the corpses managed to unbalance him, and he toppled over. Rosa fought valiantly above him, but I could tell her strength was flagging. My other companions suffered similar issues.

Even Grimm was pinned under a body, which snapped its teeth too close to his face. Grimm snapped back, but this undead person was wily enough to jerk its head back each time. I grabbed it from the back, trying to pry the larger body off my true love. I certainly couldn't use Talon on this one; the enchanted blade wouldn't hurt me, but it could not differentiate between friend or foe, and I might accidentally strike Grimm in the process.

I failed to free Grimm. The revenant was too heavy. Grimm slowly moved himself forward, risking a few bites to the back of his neck. But his forward momentum was dampened.

All around me, despair filled the air. We were losing.

After everything I had been through, how could this be? How could we see the finish line just feet away, only to trip and fall now?

All was lost.

Even knowing it was futile, I still fought to free Grimm, finally managing to gain enough purchase to roll the revenant off his back.

Three more joined our fight, and I was so very tired already. It was never ending.

Annie would win, after all.

Through the cacophony of the battle, the groans, the shouts, and the squelch of decayed limbs lost, a new sound filtered into my awareness. At first, it was faint, simply the caw of a crow, over and over again. But as time elapsed, the caws grew louder, thicker, layered upon one another. This was not just one crow, I realized.

I looked up at the crescendo of crowing. Darkness overtook the afternoon winter sun, blackening the sky as this ominous cloud continued to cry out in unison. All my companions froze, witnessing this new event: a flock of crows, more than I had ever seen in my life, flying high over the wall of ice and snow, making a beeline for the fight.

No, not a flock.

A *murder*.

The murder completely blotted out the light with its vastness, before diving as a single organism, with one crow alone acting as its head. The corvids may have all looked alike, but I knew, *I knew* this one was Rupert.

I'll make it right, he had told me. It sure looked like he had been true to his word.

The crows split into factions, each one targeting a revenant. They fell heavily into the corpses, stabbing with their beaks and weighing them down enough to topple the creatures. Some of the revenants were fast enough to grab at individual birds and break their bodies, but the sheer numbers of crows meant that the death toll was slight.

Within minutes, every single one of my companions had been freed from the onslaught, and Annie had apparently finally run out of revenants, for no more appeared. The crows continued to peck and gouge at the dead people, removing desiccated eyes and ripping into the brains to deactivate the magic. I joined their mission, finishing off the remaining moving corpses with Grimm, Gavin, Rosa, and Kyoni by my side.

With the last of the revenants dispatched, the murder of crows, minus a handful of departed members, rose into the air again, crying out with lusty abandon. All except Rupert, who bashfully fluttered to Fleurette and landed on her shoulder. She petted his blue-black feathers as she surveyed the scene.

A murder dark to turn the tide. It did, indeed.

Annie screeched her rage from the gateway as she witnessed the literal dismemberment of her army. I glanced her way with a smug look, only to have the blood drain from my face.

The tattered holes had gotten wider, to the point that I could see most of Annie's body now. The gateway was nearly fully open.

"Artali!" I heard Alfrothooll call out. I followed his gaze to the new Fae who had escaped through the gate. She still clutched her branch over on the far side of the meadow, closer to the gate. Alfrothooll would have to wade through the dead bodies to reach her.

"Stay put, you two!" I called out. They obeyed me reluctantly.

I stepped over dried-out limbs to reach Fleurette's side, on the outskirts of the meadow. She had a hand wrapped around Kokoro's waist, with Rupert rubbing his head against her hair. Together, we stood directly in front of the gate.

Annie saw me and cackled. "You think you've won, don't you?" She mocked. "You were too late to find me, silly cat. The barrier is nearly gone, and you won't be able to do a thing to prevent *this.*" She stepped a fleshy foot out of the gate, planting it on my world's soil. Only a tatter of the barrier at her waist prevented her from snaking out the rest of her body.

My blood boiled. Despite her bravado, I knew there was a way to end this, to save my world. But how?

Sufia ran toward me, a look of panic on her face. "It's time! You have to stop her! I've seen what happens."

"What? What happens?" I demanded.

Her eyes took on a faraway look for a brief interval. "The potion!"

My eyes widened. "Fleurette—do you have it?"

She nodded, reaching into her pants pocket and withdrawing the tiny vial Kyoni had given her. She carefully unstoppered it and passed it to Rupert, who grasped it with his beak. "Fly this to her."

Rupert bobbed his head with a muffled caw and leapt into the air, flying toward Annie. The gateway's tattered remains of the barrier fizzled into nothingness as he flew straight and true. Annie began to move herself forward, freed from her prison at last.

She was half out of the gateway, one foot on each plane, when Rupert reached her. He dove to fling the vial at Annie, flying straight for her face.

In a move quicker than I thought her capable of, Annie darted out a hand and plucked Rupert from the air.

"Rupert!" Fleurette cried.

Rupert let out an angry squawk but held onto the bottle. Annie grinned with corrupted delight at the crow in her hands. Her nails dug into his feathers. He fell silent, but with one last fling of his head, he doused Annie's arm with the contents of the vial.

Annie laughed as she dropped Rupert to the ground. I watched in horror as he plummeted like a black rock, bouncing slightly as he hit the earth. He feebly tried to flap a wing, but he remained on his back.

"Is that the best you can do?" Annie roared.

Fleurette's sobs broke me. I may not have been the biggest fan of the bird, but he meant everything to Fleurette. And to see him on the ground, clearly ailing, made me see red.

"You bitch!" I seethed, drawing Annie's attention back to me. "You just sealed your fate."

"Oh, what are you going to do about it?" she replied with a sneer. "I'll stomp the life out of this … this … traitor."

Her countenance of gleeful disdain morphed into confusion as soon as her words left her mouth. Her upper body rocked upward a couple of times, but her feet stayed where they had been planted the moment Rupert had reached her—one here, the other still in the prison realm.

"What's this?" she said to herself as she continued to try to move her back foot forward.

My heart lifted. The potion had worked, and just in time, too.

Fleurette realized the same thing and rushed forward. She stopped in front of Annie, just out of reach, and spat at her. Annie flinched, shielding her face from the spit.

"I hope you rot, wherever you are going," Fleurette seethed. She bent down and carefully scooped Rupert up, being careful to stay out of reach. With Rupert in her clutches, Fleurette walked back to our group.

Sufia tapped me on the shoulder. "Nice work. But the potion won't last forever. It's time."

"What do I do?"

She shrugged. "I don't know. I just see two outcomes. Either there's a big tree where Annie is now, or there's an open gateway with Annie fully on this side. I figure the tree is the better option."

My ancestor's mythology lesson flitted through my mind. "A

tree to span the different dimensions. I think I know what to do."

I turned away from Annie, who was busy spewing hateful words at anyone who would listen while she flailed to keep her balance. "Listen up, everyone! I need you all to form a circle around the gateway. And hold hands!"

My allies jumped into action, spreading out, finding people to join, connecting into a wide circle. Fleurette carefully tucked Rupert—who was still unmoving—into the front of her blouse, and then linked hands with me on the left. Grimm raised up on his hind legs when I bent down to grasp his front paw. Wren took hold of his other side, helping to stabilize his balance.

I glanced at the forming circle. The Memory Keepers took up the bulk of the far side, along with Artali. On Fleurette's left I saw Kokoro, Mom, Dad, Holly with Tinka tucked in one arm, and Sufia, who tenderly held little Tinka's hand. To Wren's right were Fal, Gavin, Rosa, Jasper, Alfrothooll, and Kyoni, who I gathered was waiting until the last possible moment to link hands, lest she give someone a mild case of frostbite.

All my allies were present and accounted for. Annie had finally gathered her wits about her and had gone silent, mumbling the beginnings of a spell under her breath to break herself free.

"It's now or never, folks!" I yelled. "You're going to have to trust me. Ready? Here we go."

With one last look to make sure Kyoni had completed the circle, I shimmered.

CHAPTER 32

I had rarely shimmered before with others in tow. Once with Lucky, once with Kitty the fox, and once again with Nic. I suppose I also took Gregory Elkins into my pocket with me, but that was in a dream, so perhaps it didn't count. Jasper and my father were the first time I had transitioned with two people in tow. Regardless, I had never before shimmered while connected with so many individuals.

My last anxious notion I thought up before I attempted this was, *what if I can't transform?* After all, Annie had sucked this area dry of magic, to the point that Fleurette, the strongest witch I knew, could not use her magic, and even Kyoni with her seemingly bottomless well came up momentarily dry.

But my worry was unfounded. At the thought of changing, I did what came naturally and lost my physical body.

My change caused a chain reaction down the line of connected hands and paws, each person blinking out and becoming amorphous within a split second of each other. Within three seconds, all that remained of us was a shimmering band of energy that surrounded Annie and the gate.

The ring of trust was complete.

As I lost my corporeal body, my awareness expanded, along with the allies. My vision spread out, as if I looked out of many eyes. In a way, the thirty-four of us *were* united and shared. I took a moment to sink into this new state of being, and then I took stock. I could feel each emotion as my companions registered their new state: some excitement, curiosity, and more than a little fear. It was understandable. With so many people on board, the reactions were bound to be akin to an emotional tossed salad.

Each personality was a new flavor for me to explore. The magic users among the group, while powerless in the vacuum Annie had created, still teemed with magical potential. My power was innate; it did not need an outside source to work, and best of all, it seemed to be enough to reawaken the dormant magic in the others.

All of this I discovered within the first second of the complete change. I had already reached my usual maximum time before I had to complete the shift, but melding so many bodies together must have helped me stabilize this form. Still, time was of the essence in more ways than one.

The words of the prophecy ticked through my consciousness as I analyzed each new facet, using their unique skills to shape a new magic. My energy form allowed me to borrow powers from others, as I had in the past, but this ... this was a lot to handle.

A sunshiny presence tickled my consciousness, followed by a shyer nudge from a twilight manifestation. Alfrothooll and Artali, I realized. I recalled what the yellow Fae was capable of, remembering when he used Wren's power for his own use. I had often wondered why he and his other half were included in the prophecy, and now I knew why. I tapped into their magic first, feeling a heady rush of power at my proverbial fingertips. With their magic on board, I could now manipulate the powers of everyone else in my shimmer. I swiftly got to work.

First thing was first: I had to stop the gateway from taking my world's magic. I was shocked by how low in reserves some of the people were. If this continued, there was no telling if our magic could recuperate.

And my plan was simple. I created a bubble around the towers and the gate—and Annie, of course—made of Na'ah and Kyoni's portal magic. While their magic differed in subtle ways, the mechanism was the same, and I formed it carefully to envelop the gateway in a pocket universe, similar to my interdimensional pocket in scope if not in size. I made sure not to connect this bubble of universe to any sort of time. It would, in effect, place the contents in stasis. Simply put, time would not pass. Annie, unkillable as she was, would be frozen, not asleep. She would not think, or breathe, or age. She would simply *be*, so long as she stayed in this pocket. Given the circumstances, I thought I was being rather generous to her.

Annie let out one last horrified scream as I formed the bubble around her. With glee, I took one last look at the witch who had hounded me and my ancestors in one way or another as I removed time from her ultimate prison cell. Her small beady eyes bugged out comically, and she made one last desperate lunge forward in an attempt to unstick herself. She actually *did* move forward slightly, but I was just quick enough to seal the bubble, forever locking her in place in a clumsy lurch.

It was just desserts for her.

Satisfied with my pocket universe, I used Kyoni's cold magic to place an icy film over the stasis chamber, obscuring vision of the contents from the rest of us.

Now, it was time for the trickier magic.

The prophecy had called for forging a tree, and Sufia had seen one in her visions, so it looked like I was making a tree. I cracked my proverbial fingers. No problem.

Fleurette's plant magic left a strong green and earthy taste to the meld. Holly's was potent as well, but with a bit of destructive tang. I pulled from Holly's magic to dismantle much of the nearby plant life, rebuilding it into something completely new. Fleurette's stronger botanical powers allowed me to morph my creation into a scale larger than anything Holly could accomplish.

I didn't stop at scooping up plants to use, either. I could feel a residual of magic left over in the dead bodies of the former revenants. In the spirit of "waste not, want not," I gathered up all the corpses, using Rosa's shifter essence to transform their elements into something compatible with botanical life. It infused the very cells of my tree-to-be with potent magic.

This tree would have to last an eternity if it was to keep Annie contained. I sensed the calming blue energies of two healers, Fal and Jasper. I infused their healing magic into every fiber of my new creation, ensuring it would heal from any injury, no matter the cause or severity, and all but guaranteeing its immortality.

In addition, I placed some safeguards. Fireproof bark, thanks to Aodh. Invulnerability to cold with Kyoni's energy. And to make sure no one would ever accidentally stumble upon it, I added two last things. A near-invisibility using Wren's projectionism; anyone not actively aware of the tree would simply not see it. And if they *did* get too close, I borrowed a little of Tinka's kharismorphy to give the tree the ability to project a sudden perception of fear or anger to scare off the unsuspecting individual.

This was a massive project, and I would have grown exhausted if not for the sustaining magic of the rest of my cohorts. Even the subtle presence of the mundies urged me on, knowing what was at stake if I failed now. My mother especially radiated a hefty dose of love, more than I believe she had ever shown me before, proof that a mother's love really could brace the heart.

And Grimm. His small amount of innate magic may have been a drop in the ocean compared to some of the other allies, but his love and support outshone them all. He cheered me on the loudest, despite the silence of our shared existence. I had never felt closer with my soul mate than I did in this moment.

At last, my architecture of the tree was complete. All I needed was one last bit of magic to seal it in place. I broke the bond between Fleurette and Rupert, knowing that their shared magic would soon come to an end regardless. Rupert's time away from Fleurette had greatly weakened him, and I now knew that he had flown to Annie with the knowledge that he probably wouldn't have gotten away from her. It was the perfect last ingredient, either despite or because of the sacrifice it would entail.

I willed the shimmer to stop, staying away from my pocket. I gained my body back, noting that I was still human, and I still held the hand of Fleurette and the paw of Grimm. The whole circle de-shimmered, and the occupants collapsed to the meadow floor, exhausted. I followed suit, consumed with a crushing fatigue.

Fleurette propped herself up on her elbows, staring upward. "Oh, Cressida," she breathed with wonder. "It's magnificent."

I followed her gaze. Our collapsed circle now surrounded the base of a mighty specimen. The trunk was easily ten feet in diameter and rose into the air fifteen feet before separating out into artfully sweeping branches. At first glance, I thought I had created an oak tree, one that looked to already be a few hundred years old, but upon further inspection, I realized that the leaves varied from branch to branch: oak, maple, ash, and dogwood to name a few.

I had imbued a riot of colors into the tree as well, somehow. The trunk's bark swirled upward in hues of brown, red, orange, and violet. The leaves shone with the usual green, but with veins of every color imaginable. And they shimmered in the waning afternoon light, as if mica chips were embedded. Perhaps it was an homage to the way the tree had been born from my shimmery energy state.

"It's so *pretty*," Wren declared emphatically.

"More importantly, it's here, and Annie's not," I stated with a smile.

It was over. We'd won.

Sufia cleared her throat and spoke as if reading my mind. "Um, it's over for now."

I did not need this negativity in my life. Not right now. "What are you saying?" My words had a bit more bite than was polite.

The teen looked nervous but spoke up. "I saw a warning. Annie *will* escape if the magic of the tree is not refreshed with each generation of your family."

"I suppose it's good to know these things ahead of time," I grumbled. "How? How is that accomplished?"

Sufia's eyes widened as a vision struck her. She sat motionless for a few seconds, and then she smiled, her eyes focusing on me.

"I saw a young woman, tall, with black hair. She approached the tree, her hand bleeding. She placed her hand on the bark and the tree glowed. It was a good vision."

"Who was she?" I asked.

Sufia shrugged. "No clue. But if I had to guess, I'd say she was a descendant of your line."

I blinked at Sufia, shocked, and then looked at Grimm, who wagged his tail as he stared back at me with his sunflower eyes.

CHAPTER 33

The battle may have been over, but it was not a happy ending for all involved.

Fleurette gave a start as if remembering something important that had been momentarily lost in her mind. She pulled out the crow from her blouse and gave a gasp of dismay.

I leaned over to view Rupert, although I already knew the outcome. Still, in a show for my distressed friend, I called both Fal and Jasper over as Fleurette cradled the lifeless body in her hands.

Jasper shook his head with an air of despondency. "I wish I could," he said. "My magic only works on mammals, though. Believe me, I've tried before."

Fal laid a hand on Fleurette's shoulder as she dropped her head. "He's gone, Fleurette. There's nothing I can do."

She nodded while hiding her face in a cascade of hair. Her shoulders shook.

Kokoro hugged her side to offer support. I placed a hand on Fleurette's arm, above where Rupert lay. She looked at me, her eyes already red and puffy from tears.

"He knew the risk when he agreed to deliver the potion," I soothed. "And in the end, his sacrifice saved us. It saved our world. And the magic of your bond strengthened the tree. He was not lost in vain, Fleurette."

Fresh tears streamed down her cheeks. "I know," she acknowledged with a quavering voice. "But he was all I had for so long. I can't believe he's gone."

My own eyes prickled. "He was all you had once upon a time. Now you have a whole family. He embraced your happiness with the new people who came into your lives. He'll always be in your heart."

She lurched forward, grabbing me in a one-armed hug as she audibly sobbed. I threw my arms around her. Kokoro and Fal hugged her from behind, as did Wren and Lyle as they joined from behind me. Together, we hugged out the worst of the grief, allowing our family witch the time needed to unstopper her emotions and show her vulnerability before she once again donned the strength and resilience we knew her to normally possess.

When she was ready, we buried Rupert at the base of the tree, his earthly body designated to become nutrients as it decomposed in the soft earth. For his bravery and sacrifice, he would forever be connected with the magical tree.

We milled about for a bit afterward, many of us still in shock and disbelief that the terror had passed. Some individuals caught up with each other, and others simply sat and watched the tree's unearthly leaves flutter in the breeze.

And then there was Alfrothooll and Artali. They had been kept separated ever since Artali had escaped from the gateway and we formed the tree. But once Annie was sealed away, they ran for each other like dehydrated people to a river.

"Artali!" Alfrothooll screamed as he ran, opening his yellow arms wide.

"Alfrothooll!" Artali shouted back, her voice husky as she mimicked his actions.

They collided into each other in an almost violent manner, hugging each other fiercely. My heart gladdened at the sight of two people, clearly in love, reuniting. But the hug continued, and grew tighter, until ...

"Did you see that?" Wren gasped.

Indeed, I did. The two Fae hugged so hard that, with a momentary flash of light, their bodies merged.

Kyoni laughed and walked toward this new, singular person. "Manisol, there you are. You are much more palatable when you are whole."

The new Fae, Manisol, was of indeterminate gender. They were now a dusky rose color with hair of gold and violet that fell to their shoulders. Their golden eyes twinkled. "Thank you for that, Kyoni. You know how uncomfortable it is for us to be separated."

"Only because you complain about it ceaselessly." Kyoni smirked.

Manisol turned to me. "Ah, Cressida. Thank you for making it possible to reunite us. We are most appreciative."

"Uh, my pleasure." The line from the prophecy, *two halves, once whole, now torn apart,* now took on a much more literal meaning.

Kyoni eyed the Fae seriously. "I know only half of you was there, but do you recall the Queen's pardon?"

Manisol nodded. "Yes, we recall. And we will be on our best behavior, we promise."

"Good. I'm taking us back home as soon as my magic stores fill enough. In the meantime, Cressida, what's the plan?"

"Um ..." Truthfully, I had never been able to see past either being killed or defeating Annie. This was a whole new world, full of possibilities.

"You are all invited to our sacred house," Na'ah answered for me. "I believe we have much to discuss, and I think we can all agree it would be more comfortable. And warm. It is a small walk, but if these old bones can do it, so can you."

She winked at me.

Our walk to the Memory Keeper's sacred house was brisk, as Na'ah promised, but satisfying. It was the walk of victors, of the knowledge that our world would be left untouched by the hands of Annie. It lifted my spirits considerably to discover the ring of snow was gone, the only remnant left of the magical weather being a pile of slush on the ground, like a giant's salt circle. We strode through the pile in high spirits.

The bounty hunters and wolf shifters waited just outside the vanished perimeter. We'd had no casualties on our side, but the wolves had not taken to the attack kindly, and the bodies of fallen ACFers littered the forest floor. I found I didn't have it in me to feel badly for this. Neither did the rest of my group.

Gavin took charge and thanked the six men for a job well done, promising them a bonus for the grisly work, and sending them on their way. Rosa told the wolves to go home, and, surprisingly, her brothers listened to her without animosity. Na'ah tsked at the mess, but told us since it happened on sacred land, her people would dispose of the bodies and cleanse the land in their way, and to not worry about the carnage. I agreed easily enough.

The sacred house was the same plank house as the one the Memory Keepers had taken me to previously. It was just as grand on the outside as it was on the inside, with brightly colored patterns painted on the front, an adorned gable, and a perfect circular entryway. Evening had descended with a gloomy atmosphere, but welcoming lights could be seen from within the entryway, beckoning us.

At the entrance to the lodge, Kyoni hesitated. I motioned for the bulk of our party to go in, but stayed outside myself, along with Grimm, Fleurette, Wren, Fal, and Manisol. Sufia began to go inside but stopped, loitering on the outskirts of our smaller group.

The frost Fae smiled at me. "I'd like to stay, but my work here is done. I can already feel my magic returning. I think it's time to take Manisol home."

"Are you sure you won't stay a bit longer?" I asked.

She shook her head. "Thank you, but no. We will recover faster in Elphame, and I have duties to my Queen." She stared at Fal. "You, young man, also have a duty to uphold with her."

Fal shrugged with downcast eyes. "I know."

Kyoni scrutinized him. "When will you be joining us?"

Fal straightened, a resolve steeling his back. "After the summer. I promise."

"I'm coming too," Sufia piped up.

We all turned to stare at her. She ducked her head at the sudden attention. "Fal must go to the Fae world for a year, correct?"

Fleurette nodded slowly. "Yes, that's true. How did you know?"

Sufia pointed to her glasses, although I'm sure they were a metaphor for her gifted sight. "There's something important there. For me. And there's a connection ... between us," she finished shyly with a glance at Fal. She shook her head briskly. "I don't know the details. I can just tell I'm supposed to go. If it's alright with you, that is." She once again sought out Fal.

He gaped for a moment before answering, "Uh, sure. I don't mind. It will be nice to have another human around."

And that was that. I bit the inside of my cheek to keep from grinning like an idiot, sure that fate would bring these two together, even if Abigail hadn't seen it yet.

Kyoni clapped her hands together, bringing the focus back to her. "Excellent! Fal, random girl, I will be back to collect you after the summer. Be well."

She turned away and opened a portal in front of her, perhaps a bit slower than usual, but her magic worked all the same. She turned back to me.

"I'm not a hugger, for obvious reasons. But I wish you well, Cressida. Thanks for alleviating some of my boredom for the past couple of days."

I chuckled. "I'm not much of a hugger myself. Thank you for your help. I can safely say I wouldn't have done it without you. Or Aodh, for that matter."

At his mention, Kyoni brought the salamander out. He was wide awake this time, and he appeared to be grinning.

"Goodbye, Aodh," I told him.

He let out a small gruff chirp in response and ran his tongue over the surface of his eyeball before Kyoni tucked him away.

"Goodbye, Cressida. Thank you for your kind treatment of us," Manisol said in their silky voice.

"So long, Manisol. Don't get into trouble again. I won't be there to bail you out," I replied with a cheeky grin.

The two Fae stepped through the portal, which filmed over and shattered to the ground, the ice slowly melting into the bare earth as if it had never existed.

After a lengthy discussion within the sacred house, our party further split ways. Na'ah's magic had also recovered after a period, and she thoughtfully opened portals for those of us who had a long distance to travel. Rosa and Jasper were returned to Cedrus, but not without first vowing to aid us further. I had recounted for the group how Fleurette's home had been damaged, and Rosa swore up and down that the shifters could help rebuild.

Fleurette was touched. "You've already done so much for us."

Rosa smacked her lips. "And you not only rerooted one of our grandmother cedars, but you also saved the lives of two of our villagers. It's the least we can do to help."

Fleurette hugged the otter shifter. "Thank you."

Rosa and Jasper stepped through Na'ah's portal with waves and smiles, only turning their backs to walk into the village when the portal began to shrink.

"And now, for you," Na'ah said, a hint of exhaustion weighing down the old woman's words.

"We would be most grateful," Fleurette spoke with some hesitancy, "but if you don't mind, I'd like to do one last thing with the tree before I go home. I'd like for Cressida and Wren to come with me. The rest of you can return to Knobby Hill. We won't be far behind."

"I'd like to stay just a day or two longer, if that is okay with you," Sufia added, speaking to Na'ah and the rest of the council.

"Very well." The elderly Memory Keeper opened a new portal, one that showed a view of Lyle's pasture. She gestured to my family. "Off you go, my friends."

Fal, Lyle, my parents, Kokoro, Gavin, and Holly with Tinka

gratefully stepped through, eager to rest after our shared ordeal. Grimm, of course, stayed behind.

Once everyone had been situated, we thanked the Memory Keepers for their hospitality and left, hiking back to the tree. It was a faster walk, now that there were only four of us.

Fleurette paused at the edge of the meadow, deep in thought.

"So, are you going to tell us why we're out here?" I asked, noting the increased chill in the air now that the sun had sunk well below the tree line.

Fleurette created a floating ball of light before answering. "I wanted to give the tree one last line of defense from interlopers. Your hand, please."

I placed my hand on top of hers. She turned the palm up and nicked the tip of my finger with a concealed pin.

"Ah, what are you doing?" I yelped as she squeezed my finger until a drop of blood welled out.

She had the gall to shush me before she muttered a few words under her breath. The blood drop splashed to the ground. She let go of my hand.

I held the offended digit to my chest. "It's not nice to stab people, Flo."

"Always so dramatic. Look." She pointed to the ground where my blood had fallen. A small shoot poked out of the ground, growing bigger as we watched.

"What is it?" I asked.

"*Rubus ursinus*. Blackberry. Albeit with a magical twist." She curled her mouth to the side, apparently pleased with herself. "I'll need to come back to monitor its growth and pump more power into it, but when I'm done, this will be a nice thick hedge of vines. Impenetrable by anyone but you or bearers of your bloodline, that is."

"You can do that?" I gasped.

Her wry grin grew. "It worked for Sleeping Beauty, so I figured, why not for this?"

CHAPTER 34

Wren transported us back to Lyle's after Fleurette finished pumping her blackberry barrier full of as much magic as she could. As soon as we materialized, we were showered with affection from friends and family members upon return. Fal took his little sister under his wing, guiding her up to Lyle's room with his blessing, since traveling with other people always wore her out.

Gavin bade us a good night and left to stay at the guild dormitory, where he still had a room for reserve. It had come in handy since Holly had taken over the apartment he was supposed to share with Kokoro.

And speaking of Holly, she held back from the general gaiety of the end of day, clutching Tinka to her with a fierce protectiveness. I couldn't blame her, given that she had almost lost her daughter.

I nudged Fleurette to draw her attention to the solitary woman before I took matters into my hands. I approached, using a margin of caution as if Holly were about to turn into a ferocious panther. "Are you alright?"

She nodded, her expression guarded. Then she sighed, her shoulders dropping. "I'm exhausted, filthy, I've just come back from being kidnapped, I nearly never saw Tinka again, my boobs hurt, and I just learned that not only was Tinka's dad the grandson of Annie Coddle, but he was also a very powerful kharis-morph, so now I can add worry over Tinka's future to the list."

I waited for the end of her anxious speech before adding to the conversation. "I know, it's a lot. I've been in your shoes. Not the boob thing, but the kidnapping thing, the exhausted, filthy thing …"

"What Cressida means is that she understands," Fleurette cut in. "We do not believe you have anything to worry about, because Tinka will have a solid upbringing, unlike her father. We won't let her use her powers the way he did."

Holly's eyes shone with forming tears. "You still want us around?"

"Of course we do. Why wouldn't we?" I asked with genuine curiosity.

She scrubbed at her eyes, as if trying to blot away any signs of tears. "I lied to you, for one."

"You came clean in the end," I pointed out.

"I'm not loveable."

"Who says?" I asked.

"I do. My parents didn't like my magic, so they stopped en-couraging me. They wanted me to be a mundy, so I went to law school to use my brain instead. They still weren't impressed. Nic liked me until something better came along. I have no friends, and no family, which was evident by the fact that I've been homeless for the last few months. I had no one to turn to." She finally broke down into sobs, which made my eyes prickle with sympathy.

By this time, Kokoro had joined our little corner and heard the last of Holly's words. She too looked exhausted by her ordeal but living with her abusive husband had conditioned her to hardship. "You might not have had friends and family before," she said softly, placing a hand on the crying woman's arm, "but that does not mean you must resign yourself to that life. I was a prisoner in my own home for ten years. I only had a maid to talk to before I came here. My marriage was loveless and cruel. And now, I have a woman I care very much for. I have friends, more than I ever had before. They risked their lives to get not only me back, but you too. Does that not count for something?"

"It's true," Fleurette stated. "I misjudged you, I admit. I had built up an image in my head of who Hollis Brothers was, but you aren't that person. You're Holly."

Holly spat out a watery laugh. "I was never called that before. But I think I'll keep the nickname. A fresh start."

"It suits you," I interjected.

"You're also my only niece's mother, which accounts for a lot." Fleurette glanced at me, and then Kokoro. "I think I speak for everyone here when I say that I'd like you to stay in town, and to be a part of our weird and slightly dysfunctional family. Please don't travel anymore. Your hiding days are behind you."

"Yes. Please don't go," I added.

Kokoro nodded with enthusiasm.

Holly remained skeptical. "Really?"

"Really."

"But where will I stay?"

Kokoro took a deep breath. "Stay at the apartment. If Fleurette is willing, I could stay with her."

Fleurette's eyes rounded. "You will?"

Kokoro looked abashed. "I mean, if that is too much trouble, I can still share with Holly—"

"No," Fleurette cut her off with that one emphatic word. "You misunderstood. I would love for you to live with me. I only thought you'd think we were moving too fast if I asked."

"We *are* moving too fast," Kokoro cheerfully agreed. "And I do not care."

"I don't either," Fleurette replied before swooping in for a hug and kiss. Holly and I exchanged amused glances.

When the lovebirds parted, Holly said, "Very well. I accept. I'm not sure what I'll do with myself, but it will be nice to have people around that I can trust and rely on. Now," she wiped her eyes one last time, the old, resolved Holly coming back, "I need to get this little one cleaned up and to bed. Myself too, for that matter."

"Thank you for being a part of this, Holly," I told her.

Her eyes welled up again, but she shook her head fiercely. "This isn't like me. I don't cry. So, I must be more tired than I thought. Have a good night. I'll stop by tomorrow."

I only smiled as she let herself out the door.

The next couple of days were a blur. The day after the prophecy was fulfilled, Rosa showed up with no less than ten shifters, including her dad Leander and her two brothers, and began construction on Fleurette's house. They refused to let Fleurette work on it, or even approach the property, much to my amusement. Kokoro had a quick conversation with Leander out of earshot of her exasperated girlfriend. I caught a head nod from the leader, but the conversation itself was too low to hear, even for my sensitive ears.

That same day Fleurette told me she put in a request for an official meeting with GOGS, and we were both surprised when, two days later, we were invited to join the members for our requested audience.

This time, it was not just Fleurette and me who showed up. We also had Lyle, Fal, Wren, both of my parents, Grimm, and

Towakh and Leander as official representatives of their respective groups.

When the ten of us entered the chamber, Head Grossman's face turned ruddy. "This is not allowed!" he fumed.

"Take a seat, Lester. This meeting is not about you," I said to him.

He puffed up even more. "My name is not Lester, it's Dale. And I am the head of this council, so I am in charge. There are outsiders with you. You must leave."

I eyed him with my blue, steely gaze. It was a look I reserved for individuals who annoyed me beyond great lengths, and it somehow never failed to make the recipient squirm. Grossman was no different. In my calmest voice, I told him, "You're a head, all right, but the kind of head you are is not polite to speak of in public. I just busted my butt to save your sorry ass from the whims of Annie. And, in case it wasn't clear, you wouldn't have your little club if not for me and my family line. So kindly shut up."

A voice in the back piped up, "For Odin's sake, Dale, sit down and let the woman speak!"

The red tinge of his face turned a shade of purple. I half expected him to collapse from apoplexy. But after a beat, he relented, taking his seat with a scowl that would put a toddler to shame.

"Thank you, kind stranger," I called out. "Folks, I am here to tell you that as Glivver's descendant, I am deeply disappointed in the direction this society has taken."

"We have run it this way for five hundred years!" Grossman yelled out, unable to help himself.

I stared at him again. "And that is something to be proud of? An archaic running of operations for an archaic society? Listen. I have had conversations with my ancestor Glivver—yes, it's true.

And I can tell you that she would not be pleased to have a club such as this with her name attached to it."

A few people muttered amongst themselves. Grossman simply stared as if steam would start to pour from his ears.

"First of all, why did you think it was important to keep this society from the cats you were sworn to protect? Don't you think if we had been made aware, we could have made better choices? We could have been better protected, perhaps. Instead of a guardianship, which infers that we are weak and need tending, perhaps what we needed all along was a partnership."

Heavier rumblings from the audience. It was clear that my words were either meeting interested ears, or dissident ones.

"I am here to tell you plainly: I no longer want your services. I just deciphered an entire prophecy on my own, with the help of some loyal supporters, that is. Annie Coddle is no longer a threat to our world, so long as my line continues."

"Then, you do need our protection!" Grossman sounded smug.

I shook my head. "No. Where were you, Dale, when I was whisked to Faeland? Or when I was fighting revenants? You were snug in your little den, I'm sure. What I *need* is people like Fleurette, like Fal and Wren and my father, people who respect me as a person—or a cat—and wish to work alongside me, not keep me back. Because your method has proven not to work. My mother and I are the last two surviving cats. There should be more of us still alive! But you took away your protection and left them to the wolves. And they didn't even know it."

I took a pause to breathe, getting to the heart of the matter. "If you had even bothered to come to the battle, to show your support, your *protection*, you would have seen that Annie has been locked away in a magical tree, a tree that spans dimensions. So long as that tree remains, our world is safe. And so, people of

GOGS, I am here to tell you that I am forming a new society, one that I am a part of, as will be my daughter, and her daughter when the time comes. One in which the members work as a team. And the goal is simple: don't protect me or my descendants. Look out for each other. And above all, protect the tree.

"And this is open to anyone who proves they are capable and trustworthy. No more inherited positions. People can leave if they wish. And most importantly, our society will work closely with both the Memory Keepers and the shifters. We also have honorary Fae members."

Three camps to claim, split from the whole echoed in my mind. I smiled.

"May I present some of the first members of The Allied Protectors," I proclaimed with a swoop of my arm.

Wren piped up, "Cressida, you forgot 'of the Tree.'"

I pursed my lips. That's because I'm not sold on that part."

"But we are protecting the tree. Not just anything. It's the most important part."

"Fine. May I present to you, The Allied Protectors of the Tree. Subject to change."

Fleurette stepped forward, waving an arm as if parting through the increased noise level from the society members. "Good people. My father and I have been a part of GOGS for a very long time. My mother's family line dates back to the time of Glivver. And I fully support the words of Cressida Curtain. I see that GOGS has done a disservice to her kind, as well-intentioned as we are. As of this moment, I withdraw my membership from GOGS to join The Protectors and the future."

Lyle stepped up even with his daughter. "I too withdraw my membership to align myself with The Protectors."

"Of the Tree," Wren loudly whispered. I smirked.

Fleurette added, "I know you mean well, but GOGS is a relic.

We are entering a new era, one in which Annie poses no threat where she is at. I would like to offer anyone who would like to join us a spot in The Protectors, to continue keeping our world safe."

At the end of her last sentence, there was a pause in activity. I scanned the crowd, wondering if these people would rather stick with a dinosaur. I'd be disappointed if they did.

But Melokuhle stood up. "I would like to be a Protector," he declared.

"Sit down!" Grossman ordered. Melokuhle ignored him.

Lawrence the lawyer stood up. "I will join your cause."

"And me," piped up Dora Willoby, the secretary.

Grossman's face once again took on that unhealthy shade of scarlet as more people stood up. He yelled for order but was largely ignored.

Within minutes, all but a handful of people had decided to move on to greener pastures. I looked Grossman in the eye. "Thank you everyone. This meeting is adjourned."

The shifters finished renovations on Fleurette's cottage three days after the dismissal of GOGS from our lives. One of the shifters must have had magical prowess to speed up the process, but none of them fessed up to it. I suspected it was Victor, the large man who had kept the ceiling from collapsing when rescuing my father after the earthquake.

It was just as well that the cottage was ready to be lived in again. Lyle's house was larger than the cottage, but he was already housing my parents while they built their home, and with Fal, Wren, and Fleurette needing beds as well, plus somewhere for

Grimm and me to rest, the poor house was bursting at the seams. As it was, Fleurette spent most of her nights at Kokoro's, even though the apartment was also quite full now that Holly had permanently moved in.

Naturally, when Leander invited Fleurette to inspect the shifters' handiwork, the entire household jumped at the chance to see it. I stood in the yard with Grimm, Fleurette, Kokoro, Fal, and Wren, taking in the completion of our little home.

Despite the swiftness of the renovation, the work was impeccable. The wall was whole, the debris cleared away. Some of the plants still suffered from being partially burned or uprooted, but Fleurette could fix them in a jiffy. Even part of the roof looked brand new ...

"Is that a second story?" Fleurette asked. She gaped at her cottage, not quite comprehending the change.

Indeed, the roof now boasted two dormers with small windows over the bedrooms, one facing the side of the house and the other pointing toward the road. It gave the cottage a lopsided charm.

Leander smiled widely. "I thought you might notice that. You had a decent attic space up there that was going to waste. Kokoro asked if it was possible to add a second floor, and sure enough, it was. I only had to bump out a little there to add some light. It's not a huge space, so don't get too excited."

"How can I not be excited?" Fleurette exclaimed. She beamed at her girlfriend. "This was your doing?"

Kokoro gave Fleurette a smile of her own. "I thought you could use a bigger space for your workshop. One with better light too."

Fleurette bounced on the balls of her feet. "Well, come on, then! I need to see the space."

The hallway now housed a narrow set of stairs leading up to

the attic, which turned out to be a small but charming room with plenty of natural light from the windows.

"I can put my workbench here," Fleurette pointed excitedly, "and look, there's enough space for a couch over here. This can double as a guest space."

"What about Fal?" I asked. He'd had an outbuilding transformed into a bedroom for his use. Perhaps he'd like to be a part of the actual cottage, though.

"Oh. Yes, I got carried away." Fleurette turned to the teen with some reluctance. "Fal, would you like to make this your bedroom?"

He chuckled at her almost crestfallen appearance. "I like my little outbuilding bedroom," he assured her. "I'd rather keep the privacy it offers. You should use this as your workroom. It's what Kokoro intended."

She gripped him in a surprise hug. "You sweet boy," she whispered. He hugged her back.

She straightened. "Welcome home, everyone." She turned to Leander. "I can't tell you what this means to me. This cottage has a history of being added on to. This second floor is just the latest, and it will always be near and dear to me."

"We'll eventually turn this little home into a mansion, eh?" Leander teased. "It was my pleasure. We look forward to many years of working alongside you. Cedrus is in your debt."

"And you're in mine," Fleurette replied without skipping a beat. She paused, considering. "Actually, I'd like to ask one more favor."

Leander leaned forward. "Oh? Name it."

"Do you think I could collect a blood sample from one of your sons?"

I grimaced at the odd request. "What on earth for?" I asked her.

She waved a hand in my direction, a clear dismissal of my question. Her attention stayed riveted on the shifter prince.

He rubbed his chin. "It is their decision, but I don't see a reason they would say no. Somewhere along the way, your group has made an impression upon their young minds. They seem to finally be growing up and acting responsibly, much to Rosa's relief."

Fleurette appeared to be delighted. She brushed her hands together with sudden determination. "Well then. I'd better get my tools together. In the meantime, who wants to help me move stuff?"

Everyone groaned.

CHAPTER 35

"Happy Birthday, darling!" Fleurette trilled at me on her way to the kitchen.

We'd been moved back into the cottage for a week, happy to have our space back. Kokoro had also officially made the move, although she was still sound asleep in Fleurette's bedroom. I supposed it was her bedroom now, too.

It had been a week of new normal all the way around. The late February weather was perfect—no snow—and not a single bad event had taken place. I'd forgotten what life felt like when one wasn't expecting the world to crumble about their feet at any moment. I had to keep reminding myself that there was no other shoe to drop. Although that pessimistic side of my brain kept nudging me with the fact that if I didn't have a child at some point, Annie would come back in a heartbeat. It was a fly in the ointment of my life, for sure.

Fleurette's jubilant greeting came at me in the middle of a grooming session, one leg sticking straight up in the air. Grimm and I were still using the love seat in the sitting room; a new couch for the upstairs had not yet materialized. I stared at her, frozen in this awkward position as she sauntered past to make tea. It was still dark enough that her human eyes needed a light on in the kitchen. She was much too chipper for being up so early.

Grimm yawned beside me. "What was that about?"

I placed my leg down with a sigh, my grooming concentration broken. "She was wishing me a happy birthday."

He nosed my side. "It's your birthday?"

"Yes. Cut it out," I snapped.

"Why didn't you say something earlier?"

I stood and stretched, bending my spine into a perfect arch before sitting next to his head. "Because birthdays are pointless."

"Who says?"

"I do. I'm four years old. Or I'm in my mid-twenties, depending on who asks and which body I'm in."

Grimm let out a small sneeze. "That doesn't make them pointless. It makes you unique."

I flattened an ear. "Alright, smart aleck, if you have all the answers, what will make this birthday any different from the other three I've had?"

"You beat Annie two weeks ago. I'd say it's the first birthday in which you didn't have to live in utter fear of her return."

"Hm. Good point." I jumped down. "Come on. Let's go see why Fleurette is in such a good mood."

As Grimm slid off the love seat, I shimmered and took on my human form, giving this larger body one last stretch before rubbing Grimm's head in affection and heading into the kitchen. Fleurette had just put the kettle on the apple-green stove and was rummaging in her tea cupboard for a morning blend.

"Why are you up so early?" I demanded.

She turned to me, her cheerfulness not at all sullied by my words. "Why are you so sullen this morning?" she shot back. "The sun is rising, it's going to be a beautiful day, and I've had a major breakthrough. And all on your birthday! Now, which tea would you like?"

I scowled, refusing to let go of my sullen mood. "I don't care." The words left my mouth before I had thoroughly thought them through. "The peach one."

She grinned. "There, see? That wasn't so hard. Peachy black it is."

Fleurette measured the tea out into the strainer and placed it in the small teapot, humming softly. After a moment, she asked me in a conversational tone, "Aren't you going to ask me what my breakthrough is?"

"What? Oh. What was your breakthrough?"

She lifted the kettle from the stove and poured the hot water into the pot before answering. "This spell I'm working on. It's very old and the original creator admitted that he never got it to work. But I've been perusing the literature anyway, and I do believe I figured out where he went wrong." She paused, trying not to grin. "It was my mother's notes about the enhanced werewolves. Remember?"

I nodded. Althea had found a way to create a "super werewolf," one that could transform sooner than the full moon by a few days. It was not necessarily a discovery that would win a peace prize, so I still had no idea what Fleurette was talking about.

She was too keyed up to notice my confusion, however. "I obviously don't want to create a werewolf, but the mechanism of the transformation is the ticket, and that's what has eluded so many. I've been gathering the necessary ingredients for the past two weeks."

I thought back to her odd request of Leander. Ty had been kind enough to lend her two vials of blood, one in his human form and one as a wolf. "Shifter blood?"

She smiled with a nod. "Incredibly important. I think having both forms is key to helping the transformation."

"Fleurette, you still haven't told me what the spell actually is. What transformation?"

"Hold onto that thought, Cress. Anyway, I've been working

on gathering all of the ingredients, but then I got stuck on one of them, and I thought I'd have to scrap the whole thing."

"What was it?" Despite myself, I was becoming invested.

"Two drops of pwca blood."

"What's a *pooka*?"

"A pwca is a Fae creature that can transform into a variety of shapes, including rabbit, horse, and dog."

Dog. "Is this for Grimm?"

Fleurette tried to keep her face straight, but her twinkling eyes gave away her excitement. "Well, I didn't want to get your hopes up. After all, no one has been successful yet. And without pwca blood, I won't be either."

"Oh." My own excitement deflated.

"But as I said, I got stymied on the pwca blood. They don't live here, naturally, although they've been spotted on occasion in the Pretanic Isles. Clearly, though, I was not about to travel halfway around the globe in search of a rare Fae that may or may not even be living here."

"Clearly. So, that's it? No transformation spell for Grimm?"

Her smile cracked wider. She was actually enjoying stringing me along. "It was looking that way, I'll admit. I stayed up half the night poring over journals and books looking for a workaround. About two hours ago I stumbled downstairs to make myself a pick-me-up tonic. I needed one of the bottles from my collection on the wall over there. And to my surprise, I found an assortment of little bottles that were the same size and shape as mine, labeled, but not by me. Someone had shoved them to the back, and I never got a good look at them."

My eyes widened. The first time I had met with Annie, I'd been trapped in what appeared to be her storage room, filled to the gills with bottles of bodily items she had gleaned from the many deceased Fae brought to her prison world over the years. I had stuffed a handful of said bottles, sight unseen, into my vest pocket after using multiple more as missiles to defeat the guards that had trapped myself and my companion within the room. After returning home, I'd simply emptied my pockets and placed them haphazardly on Fleurette's shelf that contained similar bottles without telling her. I never gave them a second thought after that.

Fleurette pulled a small green bottle out of her skirt pocket. "I think this is Hecate's way of saying she approves of your union," she said as she held the bottle out for me to read.

The label, written in Annie's scrawl, clearly said "PWCA BLOOD."

I held a hand over my mouth, at a loss for words.

"After this little discovery, I immediately got to work upstairs, testing the efficacy of the blood. And ... Cressida, I think it's going to work. The magic feels positive and right to me, and the spellwork came together like a dream."

"Then what are we waiting for?" I practically yelled. I bent down to ruffle Grimm's ears with my bounding excitement.

Fleurette doused it like a wet blanket. "Hang on. It's not ready yet."

"But you just said—"

"I said the magic was happy. I didn't say it was complete."

I flattened my lips in disappointment. "Oh."

"Cress, don't do that. I'm entirely confident it will work. But the potion needs time to fully coalesce. And I think it's important to explain the rules to you."

"Rules?"

She patted my shoulder and turned to pour the tea. "You of all people should know that magic, like everything else, must follow certain rules. This potion is no different." She added a splash of cream to my mug and handed it to me.

I inhaled the scent of black tea, the aroma sweetened by the essence of peaches. "Okay, you're right. What are the rules for this spell?"

Fleurette took a small sip of her tea before answering. "First of all, the time. You know that normally, werewolves can only transform during the three nights when the moon is fullest? Well, this spell is very similar to the magic that created werewolves."

An alarming thought crossed my mind. "Wait, are you saying that Grimm will become a man during the full moon? That's going to put a huge damper on our business."

"I had the same concern," Fleurette responded with a chuckle. "But no. The spell is essentially the opposite of that. It's not a man turning into an animal-like monster during the full moon, it's a dog turning into a man. And so, the spell is set up to be functional during the new moon."

"So, Grimm will be a human for three days during the new moon every month?"

She hesitated. "Not exactly, no. I'm sorry, Cress, but the best I could do was three days during the new moon that happens before the equinoxes and solstices."

I did some quick mental calculations. "He'll be human for three days every three months?"

Fleurette nodded, her face chagrined.

I beamed. "That's amazing!"

Fleurette blinked in confusion. "It is? I figured you'd be upset. Three days four times a year is not very much time. I tried to make it more, but the magic was finicky and stretched as thin as it would get without breaking."

"Fleurette, you forget. I love Grimm just for who he is, and I can talk with him any time I want. To have him in his human form at all is a wonder. Twelve days a year is a gift."

She heaved out a breath. "I'm so glad you see it that way."

My nervous energy was back in full force. "Well, when can we get started?"

"I checked the calendar. The next new moon starts on the second of March. The Spring Equinox occurs on March twentieth this year, so this upcoming one is the ticket."

"March second? So soon!" That was only three days away.

Fleurette did not look entirely pleased, however. "There's a small problem, though. The potion needs five more full days after today to be fully ready."

I counted on my fingers. "That would mean it won't be ready until the last day of the new moon."

"Exactly. You would only get one night with human Grimm this time around. Otherwise, we could wait until the Summer Solstice ..."

"No," I decided after a quick mull-over. "I'd rather have a short amount of time sooner than wait three more months to meet his human form. You know me; I'm impatient."

Fleurette laughed. "Yes, I do. I had a feeling that would be your answer. Very well. March fourth is what we will aim for. Provided Grimm is willing, of course."

I gazed at Grimm, who rested his head against my thigh. "Considering he'd do anything for me, I think I know what his answer will be. But I'll ask him." I beamed at my friend. "I can't wait. And Fleurette? Best birthday present ever."

She chuckled. "I thought you might say that."

CHAPTER 36

Word spread quickly through our little circle about the upcoming transformation of Grimm. A general air of excited anticipation infiltrated the group, and it was all anyone could talk about when I was in human form.

I should have been ecstatic—and I was—but the more people who chattered to me about Grimm's transformation, the more my excitement was tempered by less fortunate emotions. Worry, doubt, and feelings of inadequacy plagued me any time someone brought up the subject. As a result, I began to limit my human time in order to avoid ongoing conversations.

Grimm, the intelligent dog that he was, caught on quickly.

"Do you not want me to take the potion, love?" he asked me the day before the scheduled spell was to happen.

We lounged together on the loveseat. I had been nervously grooming my stomach, working the same spot over and over with my tongue. I was sure I'd removed a small patch of fur in that spot. I had to tell myself to stop licking. Grimm's question helped me break the pattern.

"I do. I really do. But I can't help but feel ... nervous, I suppose."

"About what?"

The emotions swirled within me. I'd been wrapped up in them for the last few days, intimately connected with them, and yet putting them into words was difficult. Still, this was important. I did my best to pick my feelings apart and diagnose them.

"What if ... you change shape and there's no attraction?" There. That was the brunt of the issues plaguing me.

"You mean, what if I'm ugly as a man?" There was no insult lacing his words, just simple curiosity.

"No—I mean, I guess that's a possibility. But even if you're attractive, what if I don't feel it? Or what if you don't desire me once you're a man?"

"Cress. Love. I don't find you attractive *now*. You're a cat. Or a human. Neither form does a thing for me. But I'm not worried about that."

"Why not?"

He licked the side of my head. "Because of what I feel for you. It's *you*, not your physical body, that my soul longs for."

I flexed the claws of one paw to work out some energy. "But here's the thing. If you are my true love, you're my ticket to having a child and continuing the legacy. Which means we'll have to do certain acts."

"Mating?"

"Yes. Which would be a hell of a lot easier if there's attraction."

He blew out a breath through his nose before nuzzling it into my fur. "Let's just play it by ear, okay? Maybe, and I shudder to consider this possibility, but maybe I won't be the person for you. And if that's the case, we'll figure something else out."

My mind flashed to Gavin's conversation with me, telling me he could be a backup for Grimm. It still didn't feel right.

"But we won't know until tomorrow, and in the meantime, just know that I love you, and whatever happens, happens," Grimm concluded.

I let out a breathy purr, feeling some of my nervous energy dispel. "Thanks, buddy. That's actually helpful."

"I'm here for you, Cress. I always will be, no matter what."

The next day dawned bright and clear, a perfect March morning. We'd still had no more snow since Annie's end, and our little corner of the world decided to get a move on with spring. I was a fan of this decision, personally.

Wren and Fal were beyond excited for the day. They both couldn't wait to meet human Grimm, and expressed how difficult it would be for them to concentrate in school. But Fleurette refused to let them stay home.

"You've already missed too much school this winter as it is," she told them. "And Fal, with your graduation coming up, it's extra important not to miss any more."

They reluctantly left to attend their classes, but not without extracting a promise from me that they could be there to watch the transformation.

Fal and Wren were not the only ones wanting to view the transformation. Kokoro asked in her delicate way if she could be present, and even my parents requested to be there. "This is a monumental event in our daughter's life," they argued. "We'd like to show our support."

In the end, Grimm's transformation would be witnessed by no less than seven people. Fleurette decided that with so many bodies in one place, she would move the operation to Lyle's barn.

She made a move toward the back door of the kitchen. "I'll just send a quick message with—" She stopped in her tracks, her face falling as she remembered she no longer had Rupert with which to send messages.

"You miss him, don't you?" I asked, laying a hand on her arm.

She nodded, her eyes welling up.

"Why don't you find a new crow to place a spell on?"

Fleurette shook her head with conviction. "I won't put another creature through that. Besides, I don't *need* that anymore. My life has changed so much since Rupert came along. I have a home full of family. But it's still hard, not having him. I just forget on occasion."

I could understand that.

She shrugged her shoulders, briskly wiping under her eyes to remove the tears. "I guess I'll have to get used to messaging my dad the old way." She pulled out her message mirror.

I'd spent the morning oscillating between excitement and fear. Grimm was cool as a cucumber, convinced that everything would work out. I'm sure my highs and lows were driving him bonkers. But it was closing in on noon, and I still did not know when the spell would be ready. I was beginning to get antsy.

"When are we meeting at the barn?" I asked, trying to sound nonchalant.

Fleurette saw through me. "Ready to do this, are we? Well, unfortunately, it will need a little more time. I've decided the potion will be ready by eight."

"P.m.?" I groaned. "That's later than I thought."

Fleurette's face was chagrined. "I know. I'm sorry. That will give you until dawn. It's not much, but you'll have more time in three months."

"I'll take what I can get," I agreed, trying not to be sullen.

The rest of the day was torture. But, at last, the moment had come.

"Are you nervous?" I asked Grimm as we walked over to Lyle's. I was soaking up the last few minutes of Grimm in his normal body. I was also trying to dispel my nervous energy by running in bursts down the country road.

He trotted along, his shaggy tail waving merrily behind him. "Nah, I trust Fleurette. I'm excited, honestly."

"Me too. But just remember, if you don't like how I look through human eyes, just say so."

"I imagine if I don't like how you look through human eyes, there's something wrong with my human eyes."

"Smart aleck. Just … let me down easy, okay?"

"You worry too much. But yes, Cress. We will know soon enough if you're my type. And vice versa."

We arrived at the barn, where Fleurette had been setting up the potion and subsequent spell for the last hour, with Fal's help as her apprentice. My parents were already there, it being a very short walk for them. Wren and Kokoro had walked over with us.

Mom joined me as a cat for a moment. "Now, Cressida, if this doesn't work, we will figure something out. You still have time to find your *true* true love."

"Freya's feet, Mom. Grimm is right here. You don't have to be insulting."

She lowered her ears for a beat. "I only meant, if he can't turn into a human, you'll need to find one. Perhaps he was needed to break the curse, and now that it's been removed, you are free to fall in love with a man."

I hissed, letting her feel the brunt of my displeasure at this statement. She backed off, knowing I wouldn't listen to any more of her pearls of wisdom.

Truthfully, though, I'd had the same thoughts. They did not make me feel good when they entered my brain. What if she was right?

No, I mentally chided myself. *Ignore your mother's occasional toxicity.* It was sound advice.

"Ah, Grimm, come here, please," Fleurette instructed. Grimm pranced forward, his tail an exuberant flag.

She looked at me, still small and furry, and gave me one of her lovely, calming smiles. "You too, Cress. In human form, please."

I shimmered and approached, my nerves jangling every fiber of my body. On the outside, I tried to remain unruffled. "What's up?"

"It's time to start. Now, I understand if you're not ready, or if Grimm chooses not to do this. We can always try again at the next appropriate new moon."

I met eyes with Grimm. He was ready, I could tell. There was no hesitation in the bond, no fear. Only acceptance. Excitement. Anticipation.

"Let's do it," I told my friend with as much resolution as I could muster.

"Good. Please stand over there. We'll get started with the potion first."

I walked to where she had directed, a good ten feet back from Grimm. He faced me, wagging his tail in slow, graceful arcs. My heart soared with love for this beast who was willing to change his very shape to fit with me better, at least part of the time.

"Ready, Grimm?" Fleurette asked, and he gave a short bark in reply. She placed a saucer down between us. The contents looked to be no more than off-color water, but I knew better. "Drink this."

Grimm followed the simple command, his large pink tongue scooping up the liquid into his mouth in greedy slurps. I doubted it tasted good, considering the fact that Grimm kept pulling his lips back between bouts of licks, but he never gave up and powered through the potion, even going so far as to lick the saucer clean. When he finished, he sat and let out a small burp in my direction.

"Fal," Fleurette whispered to get the teen's attention. He jumped forward and started a low chant with Fleurette over Grimm, who groaned and settled down onto his haunches, lowering his head to rest on his front legs.

Fleurette held a bundle of herbs over Grimm and Fal lit the tip with a well-placed match. The bundle burned quickly, the ashes falling upon the dog's black fur. Fleurette and Fal increased the rhythm of their chanting.

A subtle white glow formed around Grimm, growing in intensity as the witches' voices grew louder. The white turned to yellow, and then softened into a deep green. Grimm stayed still under the glow. I wondered if he was asleep, or simply couldn't feel anything.

The chanting continued, growing in speed and loudness, until the green dulled into a soothing blue. With this final color change, both witches ceased speaking. The sudden quiet in the room amplified the tense atmosphere, but Fleurette's spell wasn't finished. She poured an unknown liquid upon Grimm's head from a small bottle by her side. It fizzled upon contact with the blue glow, and the barn filled with the smell of ozone. Steam rose from Grimm's form, enveloping him completely and diminishing the blue aura until he was wrapped up in a cocoon of fog.

Nothing happened for a beat. I suppressed the overwhelming urge to ask if it had worked, hoping it had but scared it didn't. But I knew that a break in Fleurette's concentration could be disastrous.

I counted to ten in my head before she made one last movement, a sweeping of her arms from over Grimm's body and out to the sides. The draft from the motion disturbed the foggy cocoon, and tendrils began to lift and disperse. Fleurette inspected the decaying fog with a discerning eye, her brow furrowed in concentration.

I stopped breathing.

She must have liked what she saw, because she straightened and locked eyes with me, her frown morphing into an intense look of satisfaction.

I took a gulping breath, my heart pounding.

"Did it work?" I barely whispered.

She nodded.

CHAPTER 37

Both Fal and Fleurette took a step back from the dissipating cloud, allowing a better visual of the scene. As the fog rolled away, I set eyes on Grimm for the first time since his encapsulation.

My hand flew to my mouth reflexively.

There was no dog that lay on his haunches within the disappearing fog cover. Instead, I saw a naked human resting on his elbows and knees, his body tucked into a tight crouch, his head hung between his arms, his face hiding behind a swath of black hair.

"Grimm?" I squeaked.

He moved then, rising up onto his hands, his head raising up slowly until I could see his face.

My other hand flew up to join the first at my mouth.

His eyes were still closed, but I could see enough to make my heart patter. The hair on his head was a perfect match to his canine form: black and shaggy. It was chin-length, framing his face to perfection. Fierce black eyebrows, a large, aquiline nose, and a square jaw with a smattering of stubble made up the rest of his face.

He opened his eyes then. From where I stood, they were darker than his regular sunflower yellow, more of a gold color. Like a homing beacon, they locked on me. His gaze was intense, fierce.

He made to stand, a bit awkwardly considering he was new to this body. Still, he managed, and now stood vertically, his eyes never leaving mine.

"Woof," Fleurette uttered appreciatively as my mom ran over with a towel in her hand. She quickly wrapped it around his naked midsection, careful not to touch him too much. He ignored her, and Fleurette's opinion.

Kokoro must have nudged Fleurette over the comment, because my friend said, "What? Just because I have no desire to purchase a work of art, doesn't mean I can't appreciate its craftsmanship."

And he *was* a work of art. Tall, much taller than anyone else in the room. He was thoroughly muscled but still slim, with a tapered waist. That much I could discern from the periphery, because through it all, I never broke contact from his golden eyes. Everything else stayed in the background, where it belonged.

I slowly dropped my hands from my mouth, finally exposing the whole of my face to him. His gaze grew more intense, and he stepped toward me. His brows dipped slightly for a moment. And then they smoothed out as he opened his mouth, those beautiful lips forming their first word.

"Cressida."

His voice was as deep and growly as I knew it would be, and that single word caressed my ears and sent a welcome jangle through my stomach. I heaved out a breath. His feet moved quicker, bringing him directly in front of me.

We stared at each other, learning the other's face all over again. I had to look a good foot and a half above my head to meet his gaze. His face broke out into a smile as he moved his hand to caress my face.

I placed a hand of my own on his arm, marveling at the feel of him. His skin was slightly darker than mine, a deep olive complexion that contrasted nicely with my lighter shade.

The brush of his fingers on my cheek made my pulse skitter.

He bent down, bringing his face closer to mine. On instinct, I leaned toward him.

"My god," he breathed. "You're gorgeous."

I let out a tiny chuckle. "So are you."

He dipped down the rest of the way, wrapping his solid arms around my backside and scooping me toward him. His lips met mine with reverence.

My gods. I thought my first kiss with Gavin had been exhilarating, but now I realized just how unimportant it actually was. This was the real deal. Grimm's soft touch against my lips lit a fire deep inside of me, one that traveled through every nerve and made me come alive like I never had before. I opened myself to this fiery passion, kissing him back first with the same veneration, and then with heightened intensity as we learned the shape of our mouths and how we fit together perfectly.

Everything else fell away—the room, the other people, my fears. Grimm and I were meant for each other. This was what I had been waiting for. This was my everything.

Grimm deepened the kiss, lifting me up off the ground as he straightened his back. I wrapped my arms around his neck. Nothing else mattered in this world.

Finally, we broke apart, panting slightly as he kept our faces within nose-touch. Grimm bent to deposit me back on the ground. His golden eyes stared intently.

"Marry me," he growled.

It took a moment for my brain to process the words. "What?"

"Marry me."

"You want to marry me?"

He nodded.

My heart soared with the wings of love and updrafts of happiness. "Yes."

Grimm smiled, a rather toothy grin that showed off canines that were longer and pointier than most men's. "Tonight."

"Tonight?" I clarified dubiously.

He nodded again.

"Grimm, weddings usually take some forethought and planning—"

"Cressida," he cut me off. "We were meant for each other. I have a limited time before I change back. I'd like to make the most of it."

"Grimm. We don't *have* to get married to ... you know." I blushed despite myself.

He chuckled. "Oh, I know. But you once told me you'd like to get married, and this is me trying to prove that I deserve you. I want the world to know that you are marking me as your forever mate, and I you. You want to get married, and I'd like to make that happen for you. Tonight. Because I love you and I don't want to waste another minute."

"Very well. Tonight." I felt giddy.

Grimm tucked my hand into his much larger one. "Excellent. How does it work?"

"Oh." I frowned. "We'll need someone to marry us. Usually an ordained religious leader."

"Do we know of one?"

A thought crossed through my mind, making me light up with a smile. "You know what? I might know just the guy."

He smiled again with a playful growl before swooping in for another passionate kiss.

We broke apart only when the voice of Wren cut through our shared bliss. "Can I look yet?"

Grimm set me back down and turned part way. I peered around him, remembering for the first time since seeing human

Grimm that other people in the room existed. The first thing I saw was my mom covering Wren's eyes with her hands. Fal was beet red and turned halfway from us, studying the barn rafters with much interest. Kokoro and Fleurette had their arms entwined over each other's waists, leaning into each other lovingly. Fleurette's knowing smirk spoke volumes.

My dad cleared his throat. "Uh ... son, the first lesson as a human is to keep it covered in public settings."

I frowned in incomprehension at his words until I glanced down. Grimm's towel had come undone and was lying in a heap at his feet.

"Oops," I said as I bent down to grab the towel. I secured it around his waist, my face as heated a surface as the sun. "First order of business is to find you some clothes," I said to Grimm. He just smiled with a twinkle in his eye. I straightened and addressed the group, "Sorry about that. It's safe to look now, Wren."

Wren frowned and tapped her foot, displaying a perturbance that only a young teen could pull off. She turned to my mother. "I'm not a little kid. I know about body parts."

"For the love of Pete, Wren," Fal muttered with an eye roll.

"There's knowing about it and there's seeing more than you need to see at your age. Let's keep you innocent for a bit longer, duckling," Mom said with a shoulder pat. Wren just sighed.

"Well, what's the word?" Fleurette asked.

I beamed at my friends and family. "We're getting married!"

"Tonight," Grimm added, snaking a hand around my side to pull me against him.

"Tonight?" Fleurette rubbed her chin. "There's a lot to do, plus we'd need to find someone—"

"Don't worry about that," I said, the excitement of the moment carrying away all my previous doubts. "I know someone who owes me a favor."

"Well, then, we'd better get going," Fleurette said with determination.

Fleurette sent out a few messages as we figured out the ride situation. In the end, I took the wagon along with Fleurette, Wren, and Kokoro, and Lyle drove Grimm, my parents, and Fal in his old MC. He said he'd pick up Holly and Katinka along the way.

"Why can't I ride with Grimm?" I asked with petulance as I climbed up into my old seat. It felt good to be back here, I wasn't going to lie. I saw a return to bounty hunting in my immediate future.

"It's traditional for the bride and groom to have some separation right before the wedding," Fleurette explained as she joined me up front. Our other passengers had already climbed into the back.

"Phooey on tradition." I scowled. "A cat and a dog are about to get married, both while masquerading as humans. What part of this oddball scenario screams traditional to you?"

Fleurette patted my hand. "Just go with it. It's what Grimm wanted, as soon as he heard the rules of weddings. He's got a soft spot for rules. Who knew?"

"Oh, I did. He only bucks them for my sake."

Forty-five minutes later, we rolled past the same small cemetery in which I had destroyed a bunch of revenants. I thought back, how long ago was it? Exactly a month, I surmised. It amazed me how much had changed since then.

The church was dark, but from the road I saw a faint light through the windows of the small house on the outskirts of the parish.

Excellent.

Swiftly, I knocked on its door. "Father? Are you awake?"

After a minute, the door opened. Father Quillman poked his head out to survey us. "Oh, Miss Curtain. Is that you?"

"It's me, Father. Do you remember how you said you owed me a favor?"

He opened the door wider, but still did not invite us in. He wore a nightshirt. "I do recall that, yes, my dear."

I looked at my small party and took a breath. "Well, I thought I'd call in the favor."

"Now?"

"Yes. I'd like to use your services to get married."

"Now?" he repeated.

"Yes, as soon as possible."

"It's 9:30 at night, Miss Curtain. This is highly unusual."

"I apologize for the lateness of the time, but it really is important." I turned my blue eyes on him in a pleading manner. "Please?"

The priest sighed. "Very well. Where is the groom?"

"He's en route. We have a couple of guests on their way as well, plus I need to get ready." I glanced down at my usual linen shirt, vest, and trousers.

Quillman nodded. "As will I. It would not do to officiate a wedding in my nightshirt." He gave me a wry smile. "Ladies, you are welcome to use my humble home for preparation. It will be an honor to marry you, Miss Curtain."

"Thank you, Father," I replied with much esteem. "You have no idea how much this means to me."

"I'm quite certain I do not. But I will take your word for it." He moved aside, allowing us entrance.

As he shut the door behind us, he asked, "Is your dog not with you?"

My brain faltered. "My dog?"

"Yes, the large shaggy one. What was his name? Shadow?"

It was for the best that he did not remember Grimm's name. "Yes, that's right. I left him at home."

Did I feel guilty for lying to a man devoted to his God? Yes, I did. But not enough to *not* do it. Besides, I was used to lying to protect my true self.

Now I would have to lie on behalf of Grimm's identity as well, it would seem.

The things I did for love.

CHAPTER 38

I had no idea how we pulled it off, but the wedding was ready to go after just half an hour.

Mom showed up shortly after Quillman had opened his home to us and surprised me with a simple but elegant white silk gown, one she had held onto from her own wedding.

"It was in the trunk in the abandoned barn," she told me with a wistful smile. "I had your father collect the trunk for me in October after we came out of hiding. He had to pick through some rubble, but he dragged it out and brought it home with us." She smoothed out a wrinkle in the fabric. "It's a bit stained, and it might not fit you perfectly, but I hope it will work."

I had once accused my mother of being a heartless cat for the way she left her husband. It was simple acts like ferreting away her wedding dress for no other purpose than a memento of happier times that now reminded me that she was just as sentimental as the rest of us lovestruck fools.

I hugged her. "It's perfect. Thank you."

Wren studied us. "I can help with the stains. And the fit. And can I do your hair?"

I laughed. "Of course. You sure you're up for it?"

She gave me a sassy look befitting a thirteen-year-old. "I do my own hair all the time."

Her idea of doing her hair usually meant a hasty ponytail, but

I was past caring. I'd get married in a burlap sack at this point.

While I changed, Fleurette left the parish house with Kokoro. When they returned, she handed me a bouquet of pale pink rhododendrons, red flowering currants, and purple irises, interspersed with leafy fern fronds. I gaped at the bouquet before I looked at her.

"I'm fairly certain it's much too early in the season for you to find these," I accused her, noticing the dark circles under her eyes that hadn't been there before her departure.

She grinned despite her exhaustion. "I might have pumped a bit of magic into the plants I found to speed their growth. Consider it my wedding gift."

"I'm considering *Grimm* to be my wedding gift, but I'll take this too," I said, trying not to allow tears to form in my eyes. "Thank you. I love you, friend."

Tears *did* well in her eyes. "I love you too, Cress."

Wren worked her magic to project the illusion of the removal of water stains from my dress, plus she tucked in the sides a bit for a better fit. Then she finished my hair, a simple style of two braids that she made into a crown around my head, with wisps hanging at the front. It was elegant for all its simplicity. Before I could properly thank her, though, she jumped up and ran for the door.

"I need to do one last thing, and then we can get started," she said. "Stay here. I'll send Roger to get you."

Ten minutes later, my father showed up. "It's time."

I nervously took his arm as we walked the road toward the church, the rest of my friends and family walking in front of us to take their seats before we showed. Dad slowed his stride slightly, giving them a bigger lead.

"You know," he said in his mild voice, "a year ago, I didn't even know I had a daughter. But here you are, and you are so much more witty, accomplished, and beautiful than I could ever imagine I could help create. I suppose I can thank your mother for that."

"Oh, Dad."

"And now I get to walk my only daughter down the aisle to give her away. I just want you to know what an honor this is for me, Cressida. I'm so proud of you."

"Oh, Dad," I said again with more feeling. I could see that I would not be going into this event with dry eyes. His words made sure of that.

All too soon we stood in front of the doors to the church. My heart kicked up the tempo.

"Are you ready?" Dad asked.

I didn't pause. "Ready."

Together, we pushed the doors open and strode in. My pulse skipped as I took in the sight of the interior. Small dogwoods in full blossom lined the outsides of the pews, and birds of every color flitted through the trees. White candles lined the pews on every surface, casting an unearthly glow about the room. The only other source of light were tiny wisps that danced in the air, shimmering and twinkling in their erratic pattern.

Upon my entrance, the birds burst into song. I thought at first it was the normal chirping of their feathered kind, but I was wrong. Within a couple of bars, the birds' voices coalesced together into a melodic harmony. They whistled this beautiful tune as we walked down the aisle toward my intended.

It was no surprise to see that only the first two rows of pews were filled with people. Most of them I expected: Lyle, Fleurette, Kokoro, Mom, and the Ramberts took up the front row. Holly gave me a little wave from her seat in the next row back. I was rather shocked to see Abigail Zamani and her family sitting next to her. Abigail winked at me with her blind eyes.

I also hadn't expected to see Gavin in a fine suit or Rosa sitting next to him. Her cheeky grin cheered me on silently.

And Grimm. He stood straight and proud with Father Quillman at the front, waiting for me. His black hair had been smoothed back to the best of its shaggy ability. He wore clothes that actually fit, which made me highly suspicious, given that the last time I had seen him, he'd been stuffed into Lyle's old clothes. His entire ankles had shown below those pants.

As I got closer, I saw that not only was he dressed to kill, but it was a tuxedo. Where on earth had that come from?

Grimm only had eyes for me as I walked down the aisle. He smiled, a look of love and devotion crossing his face that matched the emotions I felt through the bond. I returned those feelings, my own smile firmly planted on my face.

I gave my dad a quick hug as we reached the end of the aisle. He returned it and sat down in the front pew next to my mom, who was decidedly and unconventionally teary-eyed. Fleurette stood briefly to take the bouquet from my hands before she sat back down.

I gave my attention back to my groom. "Where did the tux come from?" I asked in low tones.

He took my hands in his. "Wren."

Ah. It was not a real tux, only his other clothes disguised. She must have been responsible for the ethereal decorations and the birds as well.

Quillman cleared his throat. "Shall I proceed?"

"By all means," Grimm answered with a squeeze of my hands.

Louder, the priest began. "Dearly beloved, we are gathered here tonight to witness the joining of this man and this woman in matrimony. This is a bond not to be taken lightly, as it is done in the sight of God—and all gods—but should be entered with love, respect, and joy in your hearts.

"As it is well past my bedtime, I will proceed to the vows, if there are no objections."

I stifled a chuckle. "We're ready."

Quillman turned to me. "Do you, Cressida Curtain, take this man to be your wedded husband, with love and regard, through hardships and triumphs, and in illness or health, for as long as you both shall live?"

I peered into the golden gaze of my true love. "I do."

"And do you ..." Quillman trailed off and then looked embarrassed. "Dear me. I don't know your name, sir."

"It's Grimm," my groom answered succinctly.

The priest shuffled on his feet. "Very good. What is your first name?"

My eyes widened. We had not discussed this prior. Of course, the priest would assume that Grimm was his last name.

But Grimm did not skip a beat. "Oh. Um ... Alec."

Satisfied, the priest began his vows, "Do you, Alec Grimm ..."

I cocked my head slightly, mouthing at him with a puzzled frown, "Alec?"

He only grinned back at me and said, "I do," at the appropriate time.

"And now, the rings?" Father Quillman asked.

"Here, Father!" Holly strode forward, one arm wrapped around her sleeping daughter, the other fisted tight. She deposited something into the priest's hand before regaining her seat.

Quillman held two rings, each seemingly created from twisted wood, but thin and dainty. They gleamed with a magical polish. My heart thundered as Grimm plucked the smaller one from the man's palm and reverently slid it onto my finger. My hand shook as I repeated the act for Grimm.

Father Quillman beamed. "May no man tear asunder what love has created this night. By the powers of God and the universe in all its glory, I pronounce you married. You may kiss the bride."

Grimm leaned down as I tilted my face up. We met in the middle for a kiss that hopefully was chaste enough for the setting. Claps and cheers erupted in front of us as we sealed our union.

Above the adulation from our audience as we turned to face them, Father Quillman proclaimed, "May I introduce to you Alec Grimm and Cressida Grimm!"

"Well ... how about Cressida Curtain-Grimm?" I said loud enough for Grimm to hear.

"I wouldn't have it any other way," he responded.

We moved as one down the small step to be level with our friends and family. They swarmed us with their love and well wishes, filling me completely with gratitude.

I hugged my mother, who openly cried tears of happiness. "You did it, Cressida. You defeated our enemy, *and* you found your true love. I'm so proud of you."

I squeezed my eyes shut, happy to hear those words she often held back. "Thanks, Mom."

Wren wormed her way into my arms next. "Did you like the birds and the trees?"

I looked around. The church was once more a normal church, no blooming dogwoods, no singing exotic birds or ethereal twinkling motes in the air. "It was gorgeous. You are quite the artist," I told her as I gazed with wonder into her face. This girl had come so far from the surly and scary child I'd met a year and a half ago.

Fal approached from the other side, his gangly height the only one who could be considered competition with Grimm's, although he was still outmatched. "Congratulations," he said shyly. I pulled him in for a hug.

"Thank you for everything you do for us," I whispered. He hugged me harder before letting me go.

Abigail and Sufia approached us next, wide smiles on both of their faces. Haris quietly brought up the rear.

I clasped Abigail's warm, dry hands. "How are you here?"

She had a knowing smile on her face. "What, you don't think I saw that this would happen?"

I cocked my head back. "You knew?"

"Well ..." she seesawed a hand back and forth. "Not initially. But once you successfully completed the prophecy, it started coming together. I hope you don't mind we crashed your wedding."

"Mind? Not at all! It's good to see you again. Thank you for your help."

Abigail patted my hand before letting me go. "It was my pleasure. You really know how to work a prophecy, girl. And I see you got that new organization off the ground too. Sufia here will be a great addition."

"Oh yeah, the new organization you mentioned to me," I recalled her saying something about it, what felt like a lifetime ago. "We are happy to have you be a member, Sufia."

"Thank you," she said so quietly that I almost didn't hear her. She nodded her greeting and walked over to where Fal stood.

"Listen. Fal and Sufia will be fine in Faeland. Her love life is still unknown to me, but I'd rather have it that way. Regardless, I think those two will be a part of each other's lives in some way." Abigail's face softened as she turned her head in the direction of her daughter. "It will all work out."

"I have no doubt," I agreed. Grimm placed a hand on my shoulder, the warmth seeping through the thin dress into my skin.

Abigail sized him up with her blank stare. "Who knew a dog would be so good looking?" she said with a wink before moving away.

Holly approached next, Katinka awake and fussy. I knew instinctively that she wasn't a hugger, like me. Still, I gave her an affectionate pat on the arm.

"Thanks for saving us with the rings," I said, twisting the new object upon my finger.

"It was nothing. Thanks for inviting me to your impromptu wedding."

"Of course. You're part of the family now, in case we hadn't mentioned that before." I grinned.

She returned it with a smile of her own. "Yeah, you might have said it once or twice. Listen, I'll need to get this sprout to bed soon. She's going through a growth spurt and her moods are off the chart."

I nodded in understanding. "I don't think anyone is staying much longer. Lyle can give you a ride again."

"Your baby is precious," Grimm added as Holly turned to walk away. She shot him a glance, a serene smile gracing her face as her answer.

At the doors, Gavin and Rosa talked in low tones. When we approached, they broke apart slightly. Gavin seemed nervous in Grimm's presence. He looked up at the taller man and held out his hand.

"Grimm, it is very nice to meet you," he said.

Grimm remained stone-faced for a moment before cracking into a sardonic grin and shaking his hand. "Gavin. Looks like the best man won."

"Oh, please!" I interjected, whacking Grimm on the arm. I might as well have hit a wall.

His only reaction was to crush me into his side with a look that lit something deep inside of me.

Gavin grinned, though. "Looks like." He turned serious. "Cressida. I'm honored to call you my friend. And I'm happy to have been practice for you. Grimm, she's all yours."

Despite the fact that I wasn't a hugger, Gavin's blessing motivated me to throw my arms around him. "Thank you, Gavin. It looks like you've already moved on, anyway." I threw a wink at Rosa over his shoulder. She winked back.

He clutched me to his chest and whispered, "You might be onto something," before releasing me and pushing me toward Grimm. He then held out his arm to Rosa. "Shall we?"

She gripped his arm. "Let's. See you around, Cressida. Don't be a stranger."

"With this group? Never." I looped my arm around Grimm's waist and headed for Fleurette and Kokoro, who chatted with Lyle.

Fleurette beamed at me and engulfed me in a hug, her fluffy hair swallowing my shoulders in the breeze. "Don't worry about anything," she told me. "I'll help Father Quillman clean up and get everyone home. You have a very short window for your honeymoon with your husband and should make the most of it."

Husband. That was a word I would have to get used to. "Thank you for everything. Will you all fit in Lyle's MC?"

"Don't you worry about us," Lyle interjected. "We'll be just fine. Grimm, I'm glad to see you are as fine a human specimen as you are a dog. Genetics are a hell of a thing."

"Thanks, Doc," Grimm said, amusement filling me through our shared bond. He turned to me. "Let's get out of here."

CHAPTER 39

W e drove Humbert to a secluded road about twenty minutes away from the church and took the time to unhitch him. Then, in the back of my old wooden wagon, we laid out the mattress, got under the blankets, and explored a new way of bonding.

Grimm may have been a giant of a man, but he was gentle and thoughtful with his actions. He removed each article of his clothing before tending to mine, and each move was worshipful. We took our time exploring our bodies, learning about ourselves and each other in deeper, more carnal ways. Each touch was thrilling, each kiss deep and purposeful. When our bodies finally connected, there was no fear, only devotion and a growing euphoria that broke over both of us in a wave of magical elation. Everything we did was with love and respect, just as our vows had promised.

After three bouts of blissful lovemaking, Grimm and I lay in each other's arms, naked, sweaty, and content. Despite the new soreness that permeated me in places I'd never felt before, I could not keep the smile from my face. Our time was nearly over, as my watch told me it was now 3:30 in the morning, and Fleurette had seemed to think the spell would retract around 4:00 a.m. As such, we simply soaked up as much of our time as we could.

Grimm drew lazy loops on my bare stomach. "Penny for your

thoughts."

I blew out a small laugh. "Honestly? I never expected this."

"What? Did you think I'd be a terrible lover?" His voice was growly, but I knew he was jesting.

"I didn't think we'd ever be lovers, period. Even when Fleurette told me what she was aiming for, I thought deep down that it wouldn't work. That I didn't deserve happiness as substantial as this."

His voice grew serious. "Your actions alone literally saved this world from a gruesome fate. If anything, you deserve all the happiness from it by default. I just consider myself a lucky dog for being able to supply you with a fraction of the happiness you deserve."

My heart swelled. "Your contribution is more than a fraction, I'd say, given how we just spent the last few hours."

"My work is done, then," he said as his arm squeezed me against his bare chest. "Now that you've saved the world and have had me in mind, body, and spirit, what's the next plan?"

I toyed with the hairs on his chest while I formulated my response. A small slash of them were white, just like the tiny blaze of white in his dog form. "I miss bounty hunting. I think I'd like to get back to it as soon as possible. Have Fleurette reinstate my membership with the guild."

"Good plan. I support that decision. I've missed it as well."

"Of course, we'll be taking time off for about three days every three months, give or take. You'd be useless to me in this form on the job."

He gasped with fake outrage. "I'm quite sure you found me very useful these last few hours."

I giggled, a rather foreign expression to me. "You know what I mean, smart aleck." A thought occurred to me. "Oh. Is *that* why you chose that name?"

Grimm chuckled. "You've called me that a few times lately. Other than 'Lyle' and 'Gavin' and 'Fal,' I didn't have much experience with male human names. So, I figured 'Alec' was a safe bet."

"Alec Grimm. It's nice. You did well. It sure threw me for a loop, though. And as long as I don't have to refer to you as such very often, it's fine with me."

He hummed in his throat as I snuggled into his side. We soaked in the comfort of our bodies touching, a pleasant silence overtaking us.

"So, bounty hunting again," he said, breaking the silence. "That will be nice."

"Mm-hm. I figure it will keep us occupied on the days you aren't human. I'll need to stop for a bit, take a vacation, if I become pregnant, obviously."

I felt him tense beneath me. "I hadn't thought of that. Are you sure we can even have a child together?"

"I'm not sure of anything," I replied honestly. "It took Mom a number of years to get pregnant with me, so I wouldn't expect anything less, especially given the reduced amount of time we'll have as humans together. I'm not worried, though. We're still young. If it takes a while, so be it. I'll enjoy the practice in the meantime."

"Mm, so will I," he said with another squeeze and a kiss. His handsome face was drawn with worry, however. "But *should* we have a ... offspring together? It wouldn't be an abomination, would it?"

I drew my head back. "Is this what worries you?"

"I'm a dog. You're a cat. What would our progeny be?"

"That may be true, but it's not how the magic works. Both partners are human at conception, so my egg and your sperm are human. If—when—I'm able to become pregnant, the first time

I transform back to my true self, the impending baby would also be transformed into feline DNA. And since I wouldn't be able to become human during that time, I'd give birth to a kitten, which would eventually be able to shapeshift into a human. She won't be part dog, part cat. Your genetics are human now, and they'll be transcribed to feline along with mine when the time is right."

"If you say so," he said.

"I do say so. It's been this way for five hundred years. Nothing will change."

"Even if your spouse is normally a dog?"

"Even then. The gods have smiled upon our union so far; I don't see how that will change."

"I love you, Cress."

I moved my head up to see his eyes. They glimmered in the low light of the lamp, the gold more pronounced around his pupil. "Where did that come from?"

"My heart. It beats for you like it did for no other. But I was spurred into saying it this time by your headstrong optimism."

"You know I've always been stubborn. I lost sight of some of my optimism when I was cursed, but it's back with a vengeance now." I heaved out a contented sigh. "It's strange. When I was younger, I thought love was this big, all-encompassing emotion. And it is—don't get me wrong, but it's also the small, day-to-day interactions. It's curling myself up to sleep by your head. It's hunting for prey in the woods with you. It's even play-bopping you on the nose while you sneeze at me. Love can be pocket-sized, or it can fill a universe. Perhaps if I'd realized that sooner, I could have broken my curse quicker."

"Hindsight, love. We got there, no matter what. And that's all that matters."

"And now that I know the shape of my love, I'll never stop saying it to you. I love you, too."

"I only regret that soon I'll not be able to physically vocalize my love for you. The change will be upon me soon."

"I know." I sighed. "I wish we had more time together. Like this. But we'll have more days and nights at our disposal soon enough."

"In the meantime, take my ring. I doubt I'll have a pocket like you do when I transform." He dragged the wooden ring off his finger reluctantly.

"Good idea. Alas, I do believe you'll be more like the garden variety of shifter." I took it from his fingers, giving the digits a caress as I trailed away.

He kissed the side of my head with a sigh. "Do you think we'll ever get tired of this?"

"Definitely not. Look at my parents. It's a perk of finding one's soulmate. And the best part is, I don't have to hide who I am from you."

"That's nice. I can't imagine-*gack*!" Grimm moved away from me, the loud noise in my ear startling me and making my heart race. I sat up and gave him some space as he curled in on himself.

"Grimm? Grimm!" I cried out.

He shook his head without looking at me. Slowly, he rolled over until he stood on his hands and knees, panting heavily. After a moment, his body gave off a slight shimmer, which did not entirely hide him, but gave his surface a glassy appearance.

I watched as his features shifted and morphed, and his coloration darkened. Within seconds, the shimmer dissipated, and Grimm was once again a dog.

I sighed with a small amount of disappointment and transformed in order to continue our conversation. "Are you okay?"

Grimm stood and shook his body. "I feel fine. Changing shapes is not my favorite thing in the world, though."

I rubbed my head along his jawline. "It's nice to see you this way again, even if I'll miss the other Grimm."

He lay down again, nuzzling my ear with his nose. "This feels much more like me. I'm glad I won't be changing all too often, as much as I enjoyed myself."

"And how do you feel about me now?" I asked, my curiosity getting the better of me.

He regarded me with his yellow eyes. "It's strange. I still love you, of course, but in the old way. I want to be with you always. Before, when I was only a dog, I never gave any thought to what you looked like in either form. But as a man, you are the single most beautiful thing I've ever seen. And now, back as a dog, I don't see the attraction anymore."

"Same. You're my Grimm, and you'll always be my Grimm, but as a dog there's no attraction for me."

He licked me between my ears. "I'm glad we are on the same page. I'm sure I'll want nothing more than to kiss you senseless and hold you in my arms when I'm human again."

"And I can't wait for that." I snuggled into the crook of his neck.

He yawned. "It's very late. What say we get some sleep?"

"Fine by me. And then let's get the ball rolling with the guild first thing. I can't wait to get back to work." A thought struck me. "I'll need to remember I'm naked when I change. This is the first time I've not worn clothes since the first time I transformed."

"I'll remind you, if I remember myself. Clothes are very much still a nonissue for me."

"Thanks for that."

I let out a contented sigh and closed my eyes, my memories stuck on replay of the last few hours. Wedded bliss had found me, and I couldn't be happier.

"Oh, what was it you were about to say before you transformed back?" I asked.

He took a deep breath. "I think I was going to say something about how I can't imagine trying to hide oneself in a marriage. It must be exhausting, and I'm happy you won't feel the need to do so. Something like that."

I let out a breathy purr. "Thanks, partner. I couldn't ask for a better husband."

"I'm glad to have marked you as my own, Cress." He let out a subtle groan. "Hey, the light is still on. Can you turn it off?"

I opened my eyes again. The lamp was up by the hatch, which was opened just a bit in case I needed to exit the wagon in cat form. Turning off the lamp required the use of my hands, however.

"I forgot. Hang on."

I stood up and stretched my spine. I shimmered.

At least, I *tried* to shimmer.

Nothing happened. I was still a cat.

Puzzled, I tried again.

Nothing.

I sat back down, my mind racing. I looked over at Grimm, my partner, my husband, my everything, and it clicked.

Oh.

It would appear I'd be taking that vacation sooner than I thought.

ACKNOWLEDGEMENTS

And with that, a chapter of my life closes.

The Familiar's Legacy has been a part of my everyday thoughts for much longer than it has been a tangible series. It's hard for me to believe that the story in its entirety has actually been transferred from my brain into print. After all, just two years ago I still did not have the gumption to publish my debut novel, let alone three more after it.

But I'm so glad I did. Now, Cressida and Grimm are out of my head and into the world at large, hopefully entertaining my readers. This has been a wonderful experience for me, and now I can't imagine *not* sharing these characters that have become so dear to me.

Many people have also become dear to me in the process of writing and publishing this series. The people I have hired to polish this book and others are so very cherished. Tina S.Beier, I'm so happy I found you and chose you to be my editor! If you thought the end of this series would be the end of our working relationship, I have news for you. I'm looking forward to many more books with you! Angelee van Allman, I'm honored to call you a friend and love the work you put into making my covers amazing, as well as your beta-reading skills. Many thanks to Cynthia Ley for your proofreading, and to Nanci Remington for making sure my formatting doesn't mess things up too badly before the book hits the ground.

Beyond my professional people, I am grateful to have a community of friends and family backing me up. Rachel, you believed in me since day one, and that means the world to me! Who knew reading a random manuscript your friend wrote would turn into this? You did. And Jennica, thanks for being an ear anytime I need one, and for always proudly announcing that I'm an author in social settings. You always know what I need.

For my husband Matt: thank you for always supporting my dreams. Without you, I don't think I would have gotten very far. For my girls who I wish will one day read my books, I hope you also know you can chase your own dreams, whatever they may be. Thanks to my parents and Matt's parents for being incredibly supportive throughout this journey. And Aunt Carolyn, thanks for being proud of me!

I also want to thank David G. Lewis, PhD, for helping me with naming certain characters. The Memory Keepers in my story are based on the Indigenous people of North America, and in this specific book, the people Cressida meets are a fictitious version of the Confederated Tribes of Grand Ronde. I wanted to bestow these characters with names they would have had if not for the settlers removing their way of life, but tribal names are special and not shared. Dr. Lewis pointed me toward the Chinuk Wawa Dictionary for name ideas. His help was incredibly invaluable to me, as I wanted to be respectful toward the idea of the Memory Keepers.

Special appreciation to NIWA (Northwest Independent Writers Association) for building such an excellent community for indie authors. And to all of my readers, I truly owe it all to you. Wonderful messages from the likes of Eileen and Jennie, or in-person gushing from readers like Susie or Brigitte go a long, long way toward making me feel like I'm on the right path. Your support, big or small, makes this endeavor completely worth it! From the bottom of my heart, thank you.

So, what's next? If you've fallen in love with this particular world, I have a feeling I'll be revisiting it someday in the future. In the meantime, follow me on social media to keep up to date with what I'm up to. *The Familiar's Legacy* may be finished, but I am definitely not!

ABOUT THE AUTHOR

R. Lindsay Carter wanted to be a zookeeper when she was a girl. Now, she is content to stick with her small menagerie at home, which includes her supportive husband and her two daughters. When she isn't in the throes of writing, you can find R. Lindsay creating art, reading, gardening, ignoring household chores, and otherwise lounging about, usually with her lap taken up by her dog and/or one of her three cats. Born and raised in the Pacific Northwest, R. Lindsay happily lives in Oregon.

BOOKS BY R. LINDSAY CARTER

The Familiar's Legacy:
Unfamiliar Territory
Relative Truths
Chasing Tails
Curtain Call

CONNECT

Follow R. Lindsay Carter for all the latest news!

Social Media:

https://www.rlindsaycarter.com

https://www.facebook.com/rlindsaycarter

https://www.instagram.com/author_rlindsaycarter

https://www.tiktok.com/@author_rlindsaycarter

Newsletter:

https://www.rlindsaycarter.com/newsletter/